The Forgotten Little War

Translated by Richard Torrington

www.guid-publications.com
2015

That Forgotten Little War

©2015, Guid Publicaciones
Bruc, 107, 5-2
08009 Barcelona
España

Email: guid@guid-publications.com

Design: Estudio Hache

ISBN:
978-84-943842-9-5 paperback
978-84-943916-4-4 ebook

www.guid-publications.com

Acknowledgements

Apart from interviews with Argentine veterans of every armed service and different military ranks, this novel required reading more or less fifty works on the 1982 South Atlantic war, by both English and Argentine authors, with astute analyses, dubious reasoning, shocking lies or blood-curdling anecdotes. But it was from "A Soldier's Song", by Ken Lukowiac, an ex-member of the Parachute Regiment, that I took scenes, moments and mostly a way of looking at life that I used to create my character Big Bad Wolfe.

Graciela Speranza and Fernando Cittadini wrote "Partes de guerra" ("War Dispatches"), the most understated, profound and powerful journalistic report I have ever read about this particular war. Some very young and brave Argentine officers cited in this text became the raw material for my own Lieutenant Félix Martiniau, although "The Three Musketeers" looking after this character: conscripts Palacios, Sonrisal and Corporal Lata, are distant echoes of my own military service in the Argentine Army, in 1974. The surname Cittadini appeared out of nowhere as another important character in my novel, a fact I assume today to be a tribute to "Partes de guerra".

My friend Mario Faust gave me many pages based on his own years living in Israel as a psychiatrist. They are so vivid that he can't read the fourth chapter of my novel without feeling robbed of his soul, like an Indian who has allowed a tourist to photograph him. The Tupamaro political leader, writer, and Director of Culture of Montevideo, Mauricio Rosencof, with 13 years incarcerated by the Uruguayan Army at the bottom of a well, without having met him, added more ingredients, and these form the substance from which I created my doctor Mario Rosenfeld. "Above all, Courage", by Max Arthur, is another text that provided me with the atmosphere aboard the Hospital Ship Uganda, and the character Nurse Jackie.

To the now Brigadier Gerardo Isaac I owe one unforgettable hour that he spent telling me of his part in the air attack against the British aircraft-carrier HMS Invincible, Isaac being one of the four survivors. It was 2001 and my story, originally written in English, for Flight Journal, an American air war magazine, contained also –as suggested by the editor– a sidebar interview with the engineer Kaiser Kress, designer of the carrier fighter Grumman F-14 "Tomcat". Not long after the 1982 war, Kress had been briefly contacted by the UK Ministry of Defence to remedy flaws in the anti-airplane defences of the British carriers, and he came up with some ideas that –as he told me– were not accepted. Asked by me about the Argentine air attack against the HMS Invincible, officially a complete failure according to the British Government, Kress said to me he thought that in 1982 the ship had taken a beating.

Flight Journal meant to run the story in its April 2002 issue, to coincide with the 20th anniversary of the war, but at the very last moment decided not to publish it. So I remade the piece into a Spanish short story free of any journalistic intentions, and then in 2008 I enclosed it in the larger, purely fictional story of journalist Gustavo Enríquez. Finally, in 2009, the product was again repackaged as a chapter of this novel. Nothing is lost, everything is transformed.

Eduardo Elortuondo volunteers in his free time to help the psychological, physical and social problems of other VGMs (Veteranos de Guerra de Malvinas, ex-conscripts who fought in the South Atlantic war) like him, and he gave me a lot of scenes and stories illuminating what it is to be a veteran in today's Argentina.

As for the rest of the many other characters, they didn't come out of the blue, but as I can't even confirm their *"Appellation d'origine",* I'll take Flaubert's easy way out, *"Madame Bovary, c'est moi".* I am all the mentioned and unmentioned characters and this, I repeat, is a novel, so its actors are not obligated to imitate anybody who may have acted or persist in doing so in this other narrative we call reality. They just try to appear alive.

Professor Adriana Muñoz meticulously corrected the original in Spanish. My friend, photographer, journalist and weapons expert, Roberto Pera, detected more than one flaw in the original, and not only technical but also literary. Richard Torrington, who translated the novel into English, diagnosed a number of mistakes in dates, names and circumstances, and gave the product a lot of "street language" and a youthful élan. Tommy Buch, a chemist and engineer who helped develop the materials of Argentina's nuclear power plants fuel assemblies, saved me from a "faux pas" regarding Israel's geography. The late and lamented economist and editor Waldemar Sarli did the same job in relation to Uruguay's recent history.

Doctor Eloísa Klasse and her brother Álvaro gave me, without their knowledge, not only part of their endearing personalities as raw material for two of my characters, but also the necessary strength to make this piece of work progress into an unpublished short story collection.

After a reunion for the class of 1966, from the Southern District British School in the Atlantic beach resort of Cariló, 2009, these short stories, like a thermonuclear reaction, fused into a novel. Doctor Betina Panick, to whom I owe too many things, put me in contact with the keen-scented Scottish businesswoman Gillian Pollock, who is now my publisher.

The basic analysis of the causes, happenings and fortunes of this war I have taken from my own life as an Argentine, including my military service. But I owe a lot to Bernardo Verbitsky, journalist and writer, most specifically from his book "La última batalla de la Tercera Guerra Mundial" ("The Last Battle of the Third World War"), published a couple of years after the conflict. His opinions, alas, still appear irrefutable.

V

Preface

This is a story about the Malvinas-Falklands war, not a history book. Not taking into account the research and interviews before and during its creation, the characters and occurrences much of my own invention coexist (as they would) with people that were actually there, in flesh and blood, when it all happened. In the end, it's nothing war novelists haven't done before me, including Homer, Tolstoy, Pérez Reverte and other smugglers of their own demons into the larger and more real hell of human conflict.

The list of fictional characters includes an assortment of British and Argentines, males and females, soldiers, NCOs and officers crafted out of sheer dream-stuff. One also must consider an interpolated Argentine rescue helicopter that met the same fate of a very real one on 9th May 1982, although half an hour later. Add an Israeli psychiatrist and former Uruguayan guerrilla leader and his ex-wife, chimeras created by the fusion of very different people I've met in the real world. Throw in shrinks, lawyers, journalists and a lethal MI6 spy with a heart of gold, a resolutely non-existent London pub, a similarly ontologically challenged English rock band, and there you are: fantasy embroidered upon a fabric of facts. Facts, it has to be said, still under debate. I only hope that my workmanship will put the uninformed reader at odds in discerning the fictional from the real, while enjoying a good read. But I insist: all in all, this book is not scholarly stuff. It's just plain invention, different in spirit and means from the type of fiction concocted by historians.

It is also different in intention: I wrote it to put an end to my own pain concerning the war. This seems to be a contradiction in terms, as writing novels can be a pain in itself. Ana María Shua, Argentina's minimalistic narrative genius, thinks short-story writers go about life with a smile on their faces, while novelists look like like they suffer from haemorrhoids. Well, she puts it in a more refined way, but she is bloody right: excluding the research, giving birth to a narratively complex baby like this may take thousands of hours if you have to deal with the kind of characters that afflict my stories.

They are a convoluted, anarchic bunch of bastards, for starters. They keep sabotaging any fictional plans I may try to trap them into, elbowing me aside, taking the wheel and after a wild ride through the unexpected, usually slamming the action into a wall of impossibility or stupidity. Then they calmly get out of the car, let me fix it as best as I can and and get it going again. Which may take months.

Repeat this process umpteen times, end up in despair, and one night an unexpected ending lands on my head like a piano falling out of a fifth floor, and suddenly everything makes sense. Then spend a lot of time reworking the piece so it will look engineered by somebody who really knew what he wanted, polish the rough edges to make it as seamless, streamlined and readable as possible, and there you are. As a production process, I rate it as pretty inefficient, but it rarely fails to give the reader a jolt or two, because I experienced the same during the writing.

To be frank, I didn't even know this thing was a novel. I became obsessed with writing independent, unrelated short stories about the war after its twentieth anniversary, in 2002, with this conflict (this hell) as their only shared theme, and because I just had to write them. Some of these were dispatched in one sitting, but others, usually the longest and structured as *"nouvelles"* or short-novels, put up a strong resistance before surrendering the end.

As these narratives piled up, I didn't really know what to do with them. You see, the marketing geniuses in the Spanish language publishing industry decreed, three decades ago, that short stories (a genre that has nourished us since our hunter-gatherer times) were commercially dead. I simply aspired to provide a response: "The dead that you kill, are all in good health" ("Los muertos que vos matáis, gozan de buena salud"), an excerpt from "The Suspicious Truth" ("La verdad sospechosa"), by the Mexican Juan Ruiz de Alarcón, 1630. Then, come 2009, all this stuff suddenly achieved a critical mass, and bang, chain-reacted into a novel: the fusion ended my confusion. That's why you could call this an emergent novel, and explains its curious puzzle-like structure.

As a writer, you only undertake such slavery for money or at least fame (if you are in the literary milieu, which I'm not, being just a science journalist). Otherwise, you only go through this because otherwise you'll explode. That's my case.

Call it bad conscience: if war is hell, I hated this particular one like no other, but nevertheless the primogenial Argentine in me feels like a rat for having missed it. But there was also fun in the writing of this novel too: the kind you get when you stand up to the Devil, stare him right in the eye, and tell him to fuck himself.

Read and you'll understand.

Daniel E. Arias, 2011

War shatters stories.

Peace sometimes puts them back together, as and when it can.

Memory weaves its plot with whatever remains.

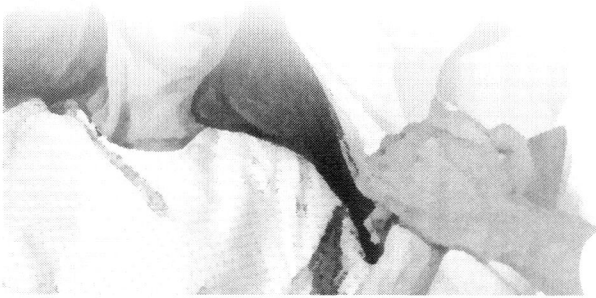

I Used to Make her Laugh

Just before the end, they let me see her.

The Jamaican internist, who directs intensive care at St. Bartholomew's on Saturdays, felt sorry for me and allowed me a few hours at her side, although it wasn't visiting time. She was unconscious for almost all of this time, so I just sat there on the stool they'd provided, stroking her forehead now and then, watching her breathe and remembering things from the old days, stuff I prefer to forget, from the time before we knew each other.

She was nothing more than skin and bone: the cancer had hollowed her out from inside in a couple of months. However, despite this and the tangle of tubes and cables that went into and out of her body, her face continued to be, in its own way, that of a strong young woman.

Outside, sleet was falling. It was already dark and the noise of the traffic on Holborn Viaduct was a constant hum. London was preparing itself for yet another soaking wet autumn night.

They were about to ask me to leave, when she opened her eyes suddenly. Stuffed full of morphine, she didn't focus on me at once.

'Gabriel. How long have you been here?'

'Just a few minutes,' I lied.

'They let you out?'

'My lawyer persuaded them to give me permission,' I lied again.

She looked at me from far away, and if she didn't believe me she didn't say so or lead me to think so. She is so reservedly English. And so beautiful.

She made an effort to speak and I had to lean over her to hear better.

'Gabriel, I don't know if we'll ever see each other again.'

I didn't say anything. She smelt faintly of medicines and of the Kenzo perfume that I'd somehow managed to get delivered to her the previous week.

'I've only a few things to say to you: that I have never loved another man as much as I have loved you, that you're sure to get along without me, because I know you've been through worse, and I wish that I'd met you before.' She smiled, without vigour, but also without sadness. 'Thanks to you, I learned to laugh again. No man has ever made me laugh so much. And I must beg you to forgive me, for lying to you.'

'We will see each other again,' I lied once more, 'and you can tell me what you lied to me about.'

She made a slight gesture, which she sometimes did whenever she blushed. But she no longer had enough colour to blush.

2

'I never told you about my illness. I mean, it was in remission, I never thought it would come back. And, well, I was worried it would frighten you.'

The Jamaican internist came back and regarded me from the other end of the ward with eyes that were beginning to show annoyance because I was breaking our pact: two hours, and out. But he looked quickly away when he saw the expression on my face.

'It wouldn't have frightened me, girl,' I lied for the fourth time, 'they were only three years, but they were…there's nothing at all to regret. For the record, I wasn't entirely sincere with you, either.'

She smiled, a tired smile. Her eyes wanted to close. Unconsciousness was rapidly returning. One second more with me, please. One second.

'Yes, you were sincere. Sometimes too sincere. You always were,' she sighed, beginning to let herself go. She closed her eyes.

'No, not always. I only told you the things you would have found out about anyway: about the cocaine, my problems with the police. But I never told you about the war.'

Bingo. She opened her eyes suddenly.

She regarded me with enormous curiosity, completely forgetting that she was supposed to die. I love it when she looks at me with such intensity. 'Death, that hath suck'd the honey of thy breath, hath no power yet upon thy beauty,' I murmured.

'I didn't understand what you just said, Gabriel,' she said, her voice just a whisper.

'I said yes, that I was actually in the war. That's why I was so screwed up when you found me, and why you had so much trouble in straightening me out.'

'It wasn't so much trouble. And I didn't straighten you out much. So... were you in Iraq?'

'Cold, very cold.'

'I don't remember any other wars we were involved in. Iraq in '91, after the one in Kosovo - I've already forgotten when that was. Then Afghanistan, and Iraq once more, which Blair led us into...'

'I warned you not to vote for him.'

'I don't think I'll make the same mistake again,' she laughed slowly. I laughed too.

'And the Falklands?' I asked her, just as her laughter was beginning to become something else.

There was a pause.

'You were in the Falklands war? But, baby, that was a long time ago. I was just a girl.'

'And I was a boy. I was just 19 years old'.

She took in this new notion with astonishment.

'Her Majesty's army prefers young flesh doesn't it? I should know all about that...'

I know exactly who she was reminded of just then, because I had watched him die cursing me. Then she was back in the here and now.

'But how come they let you fight in the Falklands? With your nationality?'

I didn't answer her immediately. Then she began to see the light, but was still unable to believe it.

'What do you mean, Gabriel? Weren't you an Argentine then?'

4

With an effort, she managed to lift her head up. She was now totally awake and attentive, concentrating on me one last time with the full power of her eyes and her mind. My girl.

'*Argentino hasta la muerte, y nacido en Buenos Aires, no me importan los desaires con que me trate la suerte,*'[1] I recited in Spanish, which she pretty much understood. 'And I didn't fight for Her Majesty,'

I paused for dramatic effect, which made her smile.

'I fought against Her,' I finished the sentence.

She looked at me, doubtfully, for a few seconds. Then she understood all at once that I was serious. And she laughed. With her typical laugh. A stunningly beautiful laugh. In that ward, full of cardiac monitor screens and people in coma.

That's how I remember her.

---

1 An Argentine until I die, born in Buenos Aires, I don't care how badly Lady Luck treats me

Chapter Two

A Man with a Mission

I spoke to God on 8 June 1982, at 14.10, when the Argies appeared like a bolt of lightning and smashed us to pieces at Bluff Cove. If I'm alive to speak to you today it's because, I believe, that those few seconds when time stood still – during which I haven't a clue what we said to each other – somehow gave me immunity while all around me on the beach, the machines, the soldiers and other transient things, flew through the air, caught fire or disintegrated.

No, please, it's not that I became immortal, or eternal or anything like that. It's much more complex. Let me try to set things in order. That was more than thirty years ago, just as the afternoon was drawing to a close. In three winks, the Argentine air force appeared and disappeared, leaving us with two ships in flames and a balance that would end in nearly a hundred corpses, starting with an even greater haul of burns victims and amputees (my figures, not the official ones): England's darkest day in that almost forgotten little war.

That afternoon I spoke to God but, again, please forget any clichés about listening in raptures to a white-bearded gentleman, or getting instructions from a burning bush. The word "speak" isn't really exact either. Neither is the word "God". But what happened, happened; and from that day on, people treat me differently - and there's no adequate word to describe this change either. The funny thing is that I'm still an atheist in spite of everything, perhaps more so than ever. I'm saying this to discourage you: I'm not the usual pious fool or New Age idiot – excuse me for being frank, mate – that your programme is looking for. No, I've never seen it, we don't get Argentine TV over here and, to be honest, I hardly ever watch telly.

Did I sell my story to another broadcaster? Don't make me laugh! I don't want to be rude… but look, pal, this particular story has no commercial value. I very rarely tell it, to avoid being taken for a nutter or an imbecile. But if I do tell it to you, I'll do it for free and in the knowledge that it will probably be of no use to you whatsoever. I can guarantee though, given that you've taken the trouble to cross the Atlantic just to hear it, that I'll give it to you without leaving anything out, and I'll tell everything exactly as it happened. As far as words will allow, at least.

Can I introduce myself first, you say? So they know what a supposedly enlightened being like me is doing with his life today? You're going to be disappointed, pal. I'm the electrician, solo guitarist and manager of The Rascals, a covers band that's been doing the Midlands club circuit for years. I wouldn't say we're that bad. We sound, well, we sound more or less alright. When the music scene is slow I get by doing sound and lighting for rock programmes on the local cable TV stations. And that's about it.

No, I've no idea, I don't know what you mean, people don't think of me as being special. I reckon they've been telling you lies or exaggerating. Oy! Jonesy! Is there anything special about me? You see, the barman says no, and Welsh barmen never lie. Yes, Jonesy, of course I'll have an IPA on the house, but only if you'll let me get in a few pints for the Argentine gentlemen.

Well, what's got into Jonesy? He's offering to get you and your cameraman a drink. Can you believe that in this shitehole of a village they call him a tightwad? And he's our best brewer, apart from being the only one. Try this nectar, sir, a full-bodied ale, medium dark, with a malty taste but a complex aroma, over 7 degrees of alcohol, reinforced with a double helping of hops, almost like resin it's so bitter. They made it like that so that it would last without fermenting out in the heat of India before the days of fridges, so that our Tommy in Bombay or Lahore wouldn't have to go without his bitter.

It seems like your cameraman likes it. Yes, Jonesy, give him another one and put it on my slate. Ah, I see you're making a face like the Cheshire cat...too bitter for you, Mr. Journalist? Yes, but you'd like another one? Excellent! Mind if I join you? This is one of the few creations that, in my opinion, justify the existence of the defunct British Empire. The one we went to defend back in 1982, when this thing happened to me.

II

'Are we recording already? Why didn't you tell me? Where do I begin exactly? Let's see…can you put up with a long story? Sorry if I go into too much detail and lack originality: there's not a damn thing in my previous life story that's at all noteworthy.

Well, then, I grew up in Shepherd's Bush, which was then still a working-class area of London. My old man drove a double-decker, a proud red bus two stories high, as as tall as a transatlantic liner to my childish eyes. He was a Labour man, of course.

My old dear was a librarian in the Transport and General Workers' Union's rather considerable library. She made me read a lot: Kipling, Shakespeare, Engels, Baudelaire, Ginsberg, Trotsky… they had everything there. My adolescence began just in time for me to enjoy one last deep drink from the terminal glories of our welfare state and pop culture.

It was a very special time: socialism was inevitable and while we were waiting for it to appear onstage, we at least had a new Beatles LP every two years, each one a miniature revolution. Yes, LPs; those big, black, round things. But my adolescence ended more or less at the time that John Lennon told us that the dream was over, just before some idiot – as if to prove him right – put a bullet through him. Then Maggie Thatcher over here and that clown Ronald Reagan in the United States came to power, and the entire world went down the pan.

When our dreams were dead, all that was left were nightmares. My nightmares didn't take long to appear. At school I used to sing those old McCartney songs that still defy extinction. Yep, and I used to accompany myself on a Fender Strat, a great guitar if ever there was one, and still is. My dad had to work very hard to buy that for me. I've still got it. No, no chance of that, sir. Listening to me provoked disgust and deep misery. I had the musical ear of a bombardier and as for fingering skills, well, someone once had the guts to tell me that I played with ten thumbs.

You say you miss the Beatles as well? The fact that you've even heard of them is much to your credit, sir, despite your age and your South American origins, and that, without doubt, entitles you to another IPA. And another one for the cameraman, of course. And one for me. Take care of it, Jonesy!

For these gentlemen, yes sir!

Yes, I know, I'm drifting. As I get older it happens more and more. I'm less quarrelsome, but grumpier. And my mind loses track of things.

Quarrelsome – that was me right from the start. Very quarrelsome. Look, I was sixteen when the Greater London Council put my old man out into the street, and I was seventeen when my mum walked out on him too, because her man, unemployed all of a sudden after twenty-odd years of loyal service, was drinking too much.

As things got worse at home, I started getting into trouble with the police: I left school and got into sniffing, trafficking and gaining a reputation as a nasty piece of work. As my surname's Wolfe and I am, as you can see for yourself, on the large side, I immediately earned the nickname Big Bad Wolfe. And as usually happens when you get some sort of reputation, you have to defend it and you end up becoming a slave to it. Perhaps I even had to hurt a few competitors, during an exchange of opinions about the limits of our respective turfs.

Anyway, in order to avoid things getting out of hand, when I came out of my second stay in borstal, and on the advice of the judge at the juvenile court, I joined 2 Para, the 2nd Battalion of The Parachute Regiment where "I could exorcise my demons and become of some use to society" as that shyster of a judge said. And I took the advice and went first to Colchester, then to Brize Norton, and finally to Aldershot. My folks were absolutely against it, of course. There were already at loggerheads by then, but I gave them one last reason for seeing eye-to-eye.

As soon as I finished my basic training, which is brutal and destroys nearly everybody, but which I enjoyed rather a lot, I was sent to make some Irish people extremely unhappy in Ulster, at the beginning of the eighties. This was during the Troubles, in which the Paras lost fifty-odd blokes all told. I spent a year there and I did and saw things that I'd rather not talk about. At night I used to ask myself how a good, educated lad like me, with socialist parents who were proud of being working class, could be living that sort of life, and even whether pushing coke in Shepherd's Bush was more ethical. But I never doubted for a moment what I wanted to be: a soldier, and nothing else. A soldier wherever there was lots of war and lots of chaos. And it didn't bother me if I was a soldier in the service of the worst kinds of arseholes.

The fact is that after doing a lot of reading and thinking, I'd come to my own conclusion that to soldier for Leo-

11

nid Brezhnev – who's Brezhnev? Does the Soviet Union ring a bell? Let's just say a Russian, then – was as immoral as obeying that old bitch Thatcher or Gerry Adams from Sinn Fein. For me, life was about fighting, fighting and being transformed into a wild beast, inspired and happy, something that I'd discovered in the streets and borstals and if they were willing to pay me for such ecstasy, instead of putting me in prison, then everything else could go to the devil. And if that's your philosophy in life, then your place in the world is with the Paras, the boys with the maroon berets. As Field Marshal Montgomery said about us in 1942: "They are, in fact, men apart – every man an Emperor." And it's well known that emperors have a psychopathic streak.

Then my old man got seriously ill. A stroke. He didn't last long. I blamed myself for a while but, anyway…my mother also blamed herself, although probably a bit more, because she also took up drinking and then, although a lifelong atheist, she joined up with some nutty evangelist sect. Anyhow, that's how she and I started to lose contact, each of us with our own particular obsession with the heavens above. In my case, as a paratrooper, I liked being up there, but only temporarily and during this lifetime.

And I swear that being up there in the heavens is worth it. I found that out during my first real jump from a Hercules over Weston-on-the-Green. I realised that free-falling was much better than what the French call "la petite mort". Who needs women when you've got airplanes? Then, as part of advanced training, I jumped from every conceivable means of air transport and from every imaginable height, out of the skies of half the planet, over the poles, the prairies, the jungles, the swamps, the deserts and the mountain ranges, all paid for by Her Majesty.

There's something sacred or even erotic about flying towards Mother Earth, and penetrating her atmosphere like a sperm plunging into an ovule. In that hypnosis, it didn't bother me so much that I never got any letters from Blighty. Never. Not until I received notification that my mother had been officially admitted to hospital with Alzheimer's, all paid for by the National Health Service, and a year later – while I was training in arctic conditions, in Norway - another letter informed me that she had died a peaceful and delirious death there. Without my having visited her.

I honoured my mother's memory with a free fall from a very great height over the Spitzbergen glaciers, during the course of which, after weighing things up as I hurtled down, I finally decided that yes, I would open the parachute. But I did it much later than my mates, who all saw me plunge downwards like a cannonball, lost sight of me in the golden mists that shrouded the fiords and gave me up as dead. The white silk opened with an explosion at the last possible second and I landed elegantly on the tips of my toes. That got me a severe reprimand and added to my reputation for being a nutcase.

They weren't really happy times, but they weren't unhappy, either.

Then, suddenly, in May 1982, I found myself aboard the Norland, a ferry requisitioned by the Government, sailing full steam ahead towards those islands that you still call the Malvinas and we call the Falklands.

Everything I could say about the days leading up to my affair has already been narrated by others like my old friend Ken, who we used to call Luke, and much better than I could ever tell it. I'm talking about the night we landed at San Carlos.

I can't begin to describe how frightened we were. If your lot had wanted to, you could have turned it into another Omaha Beach. That was in Normandy, France, in 1944. "Normandía" in Spanish, not Norman Díaz. Get it? No? I'll explain it later... The thing is that from the frozen top of Fanning Head, which overlooks the entrance to the estuary, your lot fired a few mortars, our frigates responded with their 4½ inch guns and the summit of that knoll was lit up like a volcano all through the night. And that's all that happened.

The idea was to quickly capture the heights that ring the great stretch of water known as San Carlos and thereby stop you lot from doing so, so you couldn't kill us at will from up there. So, without wasting a minute, still soaking from wading from the landing craft to the beach and loaded up like mules, the officers made us yomp all night over peat bogs and fast-flowing freezing streams to the Sussex Mountains and then climb another five miles in the black and cold darkness before dawn. And we didn't stop till we got to the top, which looks out onto the western reaches of the firth.

Once there, in spite of exhaustion, instead of letting us slip peacefully into a coma, they ordered us to dig trenches. We dug in, and spent the following days and nights waiting for your lot to come once and for all and drive us out of our little pits, or for our helicopters to turn up and to smoke your lot out of their foxholes.

But nothing like that happened. The Argentine army didn't lift a finger. And with so much aerial bombardment of the beach head, out Chinook helicopters were still aboard the Atlantic Conveyor, a container ship prudently anchored far from the coast. Which was a waste of time, because on 25 May an Argentine missile sent the Atlantic Conveyor to the bottom of the eponymous ocean, along with helicopters, tents, general cargo and a whole bunch of blokes, including the captain.

San Carlos was, up till then, a windblown, half-deserted firth with an abandoned refrigeration plant, a ramshackle dock, a few houses and shacks and a stable population of perhaps five inhabitants. But when we disembarked there, on 21 May, we transformed the place into an active, teeming port, as well as a breaker's yard for planes and a place for Argy flyers to rehearse the many ways of dying for Argentina.

I saw beautiful little Mirages dive amidst orange-tinted rivers of anti-aircraft fire and suddenly lose control and Splat! bury themselves in the sea, and at such speeds that you could see a trail of splashes a mile long from the point of impact, caused by the cascade of little pieces of airplane. I saw desperate, ancient A4s twisting their way through the low hills, followed by a zig-zagging ball of flame with a blue trail behind, probably one of our Rapier missiles, and suddenly the Argy would explode like a bottle of gas, boom!

And I never saw a single parachute open. They told me about one, but I didn't see it.

Whenever they could, however, the Argies inflicted disasters on us. I saw the first one on the very day I arrived. As I'm so big and we were so short of helicopters, four of us, the brawniest, had to carry various sets of very heavy communications equipment on our backs to the place where 45 Commando was dug in, on the west side of the Sussex Mountains. That's the side overlooking Falkland Sound, a wide stretch of water running north to south that separates the main islands of the archipelago.

We were cold and frightened: we weren't in the mood to appreciate the austere beauty of Falkland bloody Sound. It was a hard and empty landscape, although you could learn to love it, because it seems to either hate you or ignore you.'

Three of our own minuscule frigates were at sea, disturbing the peace. Everything is so big out there, though, that these minor human matters pale into insignificance. Two of the frigates were criss-crossing the black water in silence, maybe on the lookout for Argy submarines, but the third one was busy firing off four gun salvoes, boom, boom, boom, boom, pause, and then the same again, on about a 170 degree angle, meaning above our terrified heads. They were shooting at some faraway, unfortunate Argy target, a long way behind us and out of our sight. I found out later that it was the landing strip at Goose Green, where there were Argentine planes.

In places that vast, things seem to happen more slowly. The roar of the guns came in concave waves, distorted by the wind, and then the echo, three or four seconds after the muzzle flash. The shells, as they passed overhead, made a noise like ripping velvet, rooaaca! And you could clearly make them out as they flew, streamlined and malignant. The Argies wouldn't have had a clue where so much grief was coming from, I thought, and they must surely be very interested in finding out.

16

Suddenly, I felt it very clearly: that is exactly what had just happened. Not very far from there, two Argies were hiding and watching us, and they had just reported the frigates' position to their base. I was convinced of this. That's right, at least two. Where the fuck were they? I searched the shores in vain with my binoculars. That peninsula, maybe? They must be over there, well hidden, the little dago bastards. I could feel them there, very clearly. Over there, but invisible. I've always had the ability to detect people hidden away, spying on me, aiming a gun at me or grassing me up, and I think in Northern Ireland that saved my skin at least once and maybe twice. It happens to a lot of us soldiers. The ones who live to tell the tale, at least.

And there I was, at around 14.00 on 21 May, with bad forebodings, and not knowing how or who to tell them to. Out of pure frustration I got into an argument with some twat of a chef from the Royal Bloody Marines so that he'd at least give us some hot tea and a few bars of chocolate for carrying all their gear like a bunch of coolies. The gentleman refused and I was just beginning to question his ancestry out loud when a solitary airplane spouted from the gauzy rains hanging over the south of the channel, and practically skimming the water, charged straight at the frigates: an old, ugly, mud and moss coloured Argy A4.

I don't believe that the pilot even saw the pair of portable missiles that we fired from the top of the hill and which chased him with their usual Blowpipe apathy. Those missiles were never worth shit. He, on the other hand, went past literally right beneath our feet like a lightning bolt, ignoring us, heading without flinching right into the anti-aircraft fire that

17

turned the water white in front of him, because the three astounded boats were already throwing all they had at him.

To collide with one of those spouts in a little plane like that would be like slamming into a column on a concrete bridge. But I swear that that doomed bastard went straight on as if nothing was happening, through a maze of artillery blasts, unconcerned by his imminent death. And it was then that these odd things started happening to me.

Because, all of a sudden, I saw myself very clearly up there, sat in that 1950s tin can with wings, a plane so old it hasn't even got radar. I can see myself falling horizontally inside a radiant funnel of British anti-aircraft fire whilst shouting a prayer in Spanish to a Roman Catholic god, my finger poised ready on the bomb release mechanism. I'm bursting with fear, courage, adrenaline and pleasure, after the way of all great warriors, and my name is Carballo, I don't know how I know, but I know. Typical Argentine name, Carballo, isn't it?

The woman in the photo next to the collimator is my wife; how strange, to have a wife…The other woman stuck on the opposite side is the Virgin of Luján. And I'd never ever seen a virgin before – wives and religion have never been my strong point – and I've no idea whatsoever what Luján is. A place, probably. You're from there? Well, what a coincidence.

I can see with exquisite lucidity how the frigate fills the windscreen, a gigantic wall of grey steel into which I am about to crash. I can even clearly distinguish the rivets on the hull, each and every one of them. The ship's waterline is framed in the collimator, between the two women, who seem to be winking at me: now's the time, boy, fire now and that fucking pirate ship is fucked. Uncommon vocabulary for a virgin –

Madonna's influence, no doubt. I press lightly on the bomb release mechanism, click, I drop the bomb from 300 metres, and pull desperately on the joystick upwards and to the left, to avoid the ship's funnel.

Yes, that's right. I was that Argy pilot for a second or two, maybe three. A slim, good-looking lad with a black moustache and a face like an Arab prince, which was seen a few hours later on the covers of newspapers the world over, recently landed and still sitting in the cockpit, giving the thumbs up for the photographer with a ferocious smile; victory, night time's coming, gringos: beware! And to think that was my handiwork! It wasn't a hallucination, please try to understand. It was something else. As if it were real. I mean, look, I never pray. And if I did, it wouldn't be in Spanish, a language I don't speak. And I'm not used to thinking in metres, either. I really was some other bloke, that bloke, Carballo. And that was just a taste of things to come.

But, like I said, all of this happened so quickly, it was almost over before it had begun, and all of a sudden I'm back in my old skin and looking out through my own eyes, and I see that damned Argentine whatever the fuck his name is, racing across the ship, between the funnel and the mast with the plane's wings tipped up almost vertical, incredibly, and just enough space each side not to touch. Behind the plane, a green-coloured, thousand-pound bomb is flying in, Made in Britain, which, maybe in honour of the ship's name – HMS Ardent – is just about to turn it into an inferno.

Oh, my good God, the white flash on the poop, steel plates and heavy objects that fly spinning slowly into the heights, the explosion of the hangar deck that reaches us a bit later but nearly blows us out of our boots, despite the distance. Two things dawned on me at that point: that we might lose this war, and me, my mind.

About 45 minutes later, the sun had sunk very low and the Ardent, stoked by the incessant wind, was spewing out plumes of smoke parallel with the water, which made it look like a volcano emerging from the sea. Carballo, you bastard, I was thinking, meanwhile. How did you get into my head, such a private place? Was that a real experience? A load of small silhouettes with red suits capered on the ship's decks, trying to put the fires out. It didn't look like it was going too well.

Now, from the frigate, I felt the terror of someone trapped in a dark place, full of toxic smoke and about to be flooded. My brain was clearly raving, it seemed to be acting like an antenna, picking up other brains, and now it had tuned into this bloke. This time the reception wasn't as good, as if unfocused, but it was, however, very convincing. There was no name attached to this one. But still it kept coming from the ship, in waves, and the one who was dying was a fellow countryman, an Englishman. Killed by me.

Stop this nonsense, I thought to myself, trying not to perceive identity, age, sensations, prayers or memories. The last thing I need is to get on intimate terms with a corpse, whether imaginary or imminent, I thought. I pulled out the worn-out paperback edition of The Hitchhiker's Guide to the Galaxy, which had been with me since Northern Ireland and I could recite word for word, opened it any old where and sat down to read, but the wind almost tore the pages out and my head continued to be securely cohabited by someone else who, although he was on the way out, was making it very clear that he was another being and wished to continue being so. His mind latched on to mine in the same way that you would grab hold of a bush hanging over a precipice.

"Let yourself go, damn you," I said, probably out loud, and the blokes around me all stopped in their tracks for a second and stared at me: He's talking to himself again, for fuck's sake. There's a history of schizophrenia in my family – an uncle on my dad's side and before that, a great-grandfather. I'd read quite a lot about that illness, and I was always frightened of it. I tried to forget about it, to concentrate instead on Douglas Adam's zany prose, when in the space between two seconds I clearly felt a plunk: the ugly sod on the ship had died. Now I'm screwed, I'm the next Wolfe in line to go mad and start seeing and hearing things, I thought. And I also thought: Death is so strange...

It was my first time. My first death, I mean. To be more exact, the first time that I lived the death of another person. As an experience, it is so untranslatable that even today, many deaths later, I still lack the words to describe it. At that moment I could only express myself by retching - I vomited so much and so uncontrollably that finally, half an hour later, the only thing coming out of my throat was pure gastric juice. The Marines and my own muckers looked away and nobody said a word to me. You know, us Brits are so polite, we're capable of letting someone die before we'd bother him. But I must have looked terrible because a sergeant medic finally reached for a Dramamine, angrily, and told me to swallow it. Great for the hallucinations, I thought rather bitterly, but I gulped it down anyway: orders are orders. And maybe it even worked.

The weather in those islands is very changeable. In the meantime, a bank of grey and black clouds had appeared on the opposite shore and obliterated the view of the hills on West Falkland: we could see only the foot of the mountain range. My vomiting began to subside, but then came back again. Something was coming. Damn. Then, wham! We hear an explosion. We all look in that direction and I swear that through a very small V-shaped hole in the hills, capped with clouds and flanked by two slopes, and not big enough for a bloody wheelbarrow, three Mirage Daggers appear, thin and deadly looking. They make a beeline for the burning frigate, ignoring the other two as if they weren't there. Something bad has just happened to those pilots. I believe one of their comrades has been brought down on the other side of the hills – this is another inexplicable perception - and that the three survivors are hell-bent on vengeance.

Everything happens so fast. The Ardent, bravely holding her ground, is spurting out energy and material like a supernova at the three planes, which zoom down in staggered formation firing their guns, surround the ship in spouts of spray and plumes of smoke, discharge their bombs, fly over the masts and disappear suddenly towards the north, before turning once more westwards. The whole thing happened in the blink of an eye. One of the escaping attackers zigzags at the last moment and manages to evade a twisting missile shot from the burning vessel, which is still in there fighting God knows how, despite a bomb that has gone through its prow like a battering ram a little over the waterline, but failed to explode. Another must have hit the bridge, and has definitely exploded, because that part of the ship is a mass of flames. Bad, very bad.

The ship is going round in crazy circles now. You can see her out there, rudderless. The red puppets that were running around the bridge disappear in the thickening smoke. The Royal Marines, who are watching through their binoculars in silence, inwardly curse that they've no boats to help evacuate the survivors. But I perceive that even if they did, they wouldn't be too happy to lend a hand. The Ardent is now a lost cause....

I recover, little by little. It's now been a while since I picked up the terror of the bloke trapped in a dark, flooded chamber. Luckily for me, the bastard has died at last, for God's sake, and can't bother me any more. I'm sure he died. I clearly felt the moment. It was the strangeness and inexplicableness of the fact, not the fact itself that made me vomit. It was that, the otherness of the fact of his death, not that he should have died. And it wasn't my sense of guilt, either, because I'm not troubled much by guilt, and I took that British life quite fairly, in a couple of deranged seconds in which he was my enemy and I was a damned Argy and that was why I killed him, for fuck's sake. Or isn't that what we both do for money, irrespective of the currency we're paid in?

But then I cut short this self-serving argument and prick up my ears, because something else is about to happen. Is there no end to this? And who am I going to tell that there'll be another attack, if I can't say where or when it's going to happen? I'm cursed, just like Cassandra. What shall I do? Who do I warn about what? My only answer, despite the Dramamine and everything, is to keep vomiting up nothing. My stomach muscles are all tied up in knots, so are my throat muscles. It's really painful, I can tell you.

Forty minutes have gone by and my retching has calmed down, but my prediction has yet to be fulfilled. The Marines concentrate on digging their trenches. I feel weak, I must be dehydrated. The frigate, which everybody now avoids looking at, seems to have regained control of the helm and for some time has been heading off towards the north at half-speed, seeking salvation somewhere or other. It already looks smaller to us. And I've still got tears in my eyes. It seems the ship, by sheer guts, might yet save herself after all.

But, no, damn it. Suddenly, my premonition turns out to be right: the third attack also comes flying out from the eastern hills. Sadistic Argy cunts, rubbing it in on the wounded. Three more A4s cross the strait and can be clearly picked out despite the distance because they lack camouflage, three cream-coloured points in the sky: it looks like the Argentine navy have turned up for the party.

Bad news for us: those lads know more about maritime matters than their air force colleagues. They go for all three ships, not just the damaged one, zigzagging after them like a pack of wolves after scattered deer, and they are dropping plenty of winged bombs that make the ships disappear amid enormous explosions of water. Then they go away.

This time, I manage to shut myself off in a way as strange and inexplicable as the way I was, let's say, opened up. Drawing a veil over my spirit, however, seems to depend somehow on my own will and on some mysterious mental process. In this way, by concentrating hard, I can remain blissfully unaware of the results. I can feel the fourth attack coming, but I'm not there to see it: the radio tells us four Paras to get back to our lines. Incredibly, it won't be until the following day, 22 May, that The Ardent allows herself to sink, officially with 23 dead, our sergeant informed us later. I counted more, but I refrained from commenting.

On 21 May, my final view of the ship was almost nocturnal, with the setting sun flooding in horizontal yellow streams beneath the purple-tinted clouds. She was burning far off in the distance, with a red, tenacious beauty in the dark solitude of the channel.

On the night march back I got to thinking to myself that if, as it seemed, I was losing my mind, then I should do it quietly. I don't want my mates to think that I'm pretending to have a schizophrenic breakdown just to get out of what's in store for us, the surely bitter ground fighting that we'll have to face within a few days. If there's a mental asylum awaiting me in Blighty anyway, I prefer to get there as a nutty hero than as someone chucked out of the battalion for cowardice.

Byt when we get back to the camp, I feel that I can't keep pretending anymore. I refuse to eat, even though I'm empty from so much vomiting of bodies and souls, I'm so exhausted from terror and other people's agonies that I go straight to my trench, throw myself down beneath the rain with no cover whatsoever and fall into a deep slumber surely troubled by nightmares, because the next day they tell me I was screaming all night.

Well, that's how it all started. But, luckily, that's where it also seemed to end. For several days I didn't experience any more visions, hallucinations, channellings, or whatever you want to call them.

Until 26 May, when we were held up in the Sussex Mountains, shivering beneath the rain, mostly without tents or sleeping bags, which had sunk along with the helicopters on that other unlucky ship, the Atlantic Conveyor. We patrolled, fearful of bumping into Argy patrols or of shooting at each other in the darkness, we drank gallons of boiling-hot tea to warm us up and, instead of TV, we would watch, as if from a balcony, the sporadic but spectacular aerial attacks against our ships a thousand feet below us in what the BBC baptised "Bomb Alley".

The Argies died like suicidal flies. Whenever one of them flew roaring past us, wings almost cutting the grass, we threw everything we had at it. I swear to God, there were enough of my fellow-countrymen on the hillsides to fill a city and enough ships in the channel to pave the water. And we were all so well-armed and dug in that, during the air raids, our bullets and rockets formed outlines of gothic arches over the firth, cathedrals of fire through which not even a bloody seagull could have got through unscathed.

Somehow or other, I managed to do the same, not with aerial intrusions, but with intrusions from other minds. I was learning to switch off, to cocoon myself and still carry on being me. Recovering myself. And while I was struggling to maintain my fragile uniqueness, the Argentines were very generously dying all around, in the sea and in the sky. Meanwhile, though, they were also hitting us hard and totting up sunken and damaged ships. I know the Admiralty even thought about cancelling the operation during winter and trying again maybe the following spring, for fuck's sake, but Maggie went ballistic at the mere mention of it.

I'll never understand why you lot didn't make a coordinated all-out attack, by land and air. Political considerations, I suppose.

The truth is I don't think you even really tried to win. We were very lucky.

III

Yes, sorry, I was drifting off the subject again, it can't be helped. What you're really interested in is the moment of Revelation, aren't you? The Beyond, and all that jazz.

Let's start with the most modest beginnings. I had a reputation, ever since Northern Ireland days, for winning my bets. On 23 May there was another frigate, the HMS Antelope. It could be seen far off in the distance, patrolling the entrance to San Carlos Water, providing air cover to several landing craft. It was beautiful, brand new, a real gem. We couldn't take our binoculars off it. I had bet that in the next attack the Argies would trash it and half the squad bet in favour of the frigate, although you could say that they were really betting against me. Have I already told you that my mates couldn't stand the sight of me by now?

On that day the Argentine aircraft attacked the Antelope with all their fury (one even smashed itself up on the mast), but hours later the ship managed to limp somehow or other into Ajax Bay, a natural fortress ringed by mountains and the best defended site in San Carlos. My mates celebrated until midnight the fact that they'd cleaned me out: I wasn't, like I said, a very popular bloke. Apart from always beating them at nearly everything, I was too big, too silent and I read too much.

But during that discreet, spiteful party thrown in my honour, I suddenly got my own back: one of the bombs that had lodged in the Antelope's hull without exploding suddenly went off by surprise, at midnight when two experts were trying to disarm it. For hours afterwards the ship vomited enormous spurts of flame, which were reflected in the water. Then there was a second explosion, she broke in two and the two halves of the red-hot hull sank slowly the next day amid hisses of steam. I followed the whole process very closely. To my relief, I had no odd sensations at any time. I was the only occupant of my head. It felt like my own again.

I was also the owner of a lot of other blokes' wages. When the Antelope finally went down, lock, stock and barrel, I took off my helmet. It was passed around in silence, without comment, and the lads filled it up with fivers and tenners, with some black looks that were well worth seeing. When the helmet came back round to me, I'd skinned them for a few hundred quid. So, the good news was that I wasn't schizoid, or perhaps only a little bit, and that I was temporarily rich, although I was also hated a bit more than before.

Since I was a lad it's always seemed natural for other people to resent me, it's never something I've lost any sleep over. That night, therefore, I should have slept very well. But I didn't. While the dawn struggled to appear through the sleet, I couldn't sleep a wink, gripped by a kind of hyper-awareness.

I ought to stress that metaphysics, although I'd read quite a bit of continental, British and Eastern philosophy since I was a boy, has never attracted me. It's just not my cup of tea. But throughout that dark early morning I pondered (and I apologise for such a hackneyed cliché) about the Meaning of Life. Not of my own existence, which I had in some ways already given up as a lost cause, and from which I no longer expected very much. And I didn't ask myself about the meaning of that especially idiotic little war, even more idiotic, if it's possible than that in Northern Ireland.

I knew that while there were blokes like me around, there would always be wars, and there are a lot of blokes like me in this world. Especially if you take into account the ones who think that they are different. But the incredible phenomenon of being, of existing in this world without having asked for it, of disappearing from it one day equally arbitrarily, either due to a bullet or a heart attack, didn't seem to me to embody more intelligence than the day-to-day life of the dumbos and psychopaths who surrounded me and who were, at the end of the day, very much like me. Is this life? Is this all there is? I asked myself.

I was awake for a long while, while the snow got worse and worse. Alone, and more lucid than ever before.

What I want to say is that at that moment I believe that I put in an order for Knowledge.

And that my order, I found out later, was despatched.

Talking of orders, I notice that Jonesy is looking a bit worried because our juice is running low. Cheers, Jonesy, three more pints of IPA.

IV

What happened next was that, when it became obvious that no-one was going to transport us by air, dry and comfortable, our officers drove us like cattle from the Sussex Mountains to the isthmus where Goose Green and Darwin are located. Let's get this straight – we marched without our own personal backpack stuff, and weighed down with only ammo and gear. That's officers for you. Right bastards!

So, what's wrong with that, if a soldier's life is all about marching, I hear you ask? Have you any idea what the ground is like on the Falklands? The Falklands are just like one big flabby paving slab beneath the rain. Jelly-like peat all around. I don't think that I ever had dry socks in the entire campaign, or rather as long as it lasted for me, and I lasted a bit longer than my feet. On the dry land, however, the local grassland grows in grey, hairy clumps and underneath they are as hard as stone. One false step, especially if you've got nearly a hundred pounds of gear and ammo on your back, and you twist your ankle. That happened to quite a few blokes.

Between peat bogs, river beds, pastures and rocky ground, nobody can cover more than a thousand yards an hour on foot. And there are no paths, just sheep tracks. And there's so much sheep shite on the ground that the river water, no matter how much you boil it or how many chlorine tablets you chuck in, gives you the shits big time. Your asshole's like an open tap.

We yomped thirty miles beneath the rain, snow and sleet and always that damn wind and then more rain, driving into us. Every other minute someone would break off hurriedly from the file, and get as far away as possible before whipping his trousers down. This happened time and time again.

We could never get warm, despite all our efforts. Thousands of loose sheep and the odd cow watched uninterestedly as we crossed ravines and gullies, soaking wet and dumb with fatigue. Half way through the march, the swift-moving permanent cloud cover suddenly lifted. The wind dropped and there was the blackest, coldest, most beautiful starry night ever seen arching above us and our suffering. The next morning, once more in the drizzle, as we neared the north end of the isthmus, we could already hear shots and artillery fire. With hardly a rest, we went into battle when evening fell.

I recall the combat itself as a sort of desultory disaster.

That's always the way it is. We're British paratroopers, the best soldiers in the world, unstoppable, we always take the fight to the enemy - on this occasion to gain a few empty square miles: sparse pasture land, some hillocks, and a few collections of houses, enclosures, docks and shacks that don't even deserve to be called villages, but which pass for towns in the Falklands. And that's your lot. This non-place cost hundreds of lives. My memories of what went on there are fragmentary; in general I try not to recall them. Do you really want me to speak about all that? For fuck's sake...well, will you have another beer with me, in that case?

Cheers. Right, then. Darwin and Goose Green are on a pretty narrow isthmus, with that horrible stormy sea on both sides. It's just about in the centre of East Falkland, the one you call Soledad. If you want to take Port Stanley, or Puerto Argentino as you lot still insist on calling it today, if your aim is to get there, sing God Save the Queen, raise the Union Jack, drink a toast with a pint of Guinness, declare that the war is won and leave these god-forsaken islands for somewhere decent where the sun shines, then Goose Green is the place to avoid, know what I mean?

Let me try and draw it out for you, right here on the bar. You see? Goose Green is miles away from Port Stanley, and in a completely different direction, according to the paths and the bearings. But Mrs. Thatcher, who's just getting over a serious internal political crisis, is in urgent need of some Argentine bodies to show to the British newspapers. These might come at a better price in Goose Green than in Port Stanley.

Our Government and chiefs of staff maintain that sixteen of us copped it there, which is a joke. My personal version? At the time, I did everything within my power not to find out. I had shut everything off, as I told you. You can't allow those who give up the ghost during a battle to carry on chatting inside your skull, not unless you want to get on the death roll yourself.

As for the number of dead on the Argy side, that was a long list alright. Just think of the numbers. There were six hundred of us and over a thousand Argentine soldiers waiting for us on the isthmus, all dug in ready to protect a muddy airfield, almost inoperable for their Pucará aircraft. When we finally got there, to their forward positions, the Argentine soldiers, all conscripts, hardly any pros, were half mad or sick with hunger, cold and diarrhoea. They'd been left there forgotten by their officers for two months, with the same thin and soaking clothing they'd turned up in, waiting for us in strung out positions completely open to the elements and with no-one even hardly bothering to take them food or drinking water. Add a couple of weeks of our aerial and naval bombardment on top of that and, as the man says, they were finished before they'd even fired the first shot.

One Argy second lieutenant (Gómez Centurión, or some such name; one who put up too much resistance and nearly drove us mad) confessed much later that in that long vigil each of his soldiers had lost an average of nearly a stone.

Some conscripts had even died of cold and hunger while they were waiting. They died a few miles from the Argentine supply positions. You didn't know that? Well, you don't have to believe me. We were fighting against a pack of wretches.

What happened next wasn't that unexpected as far as I was concerned, because I know full well how unpredictable human beings are. It was a surprise for my mates, though. Some of these wretches surrendered immediately but others, instead of holding up their hands, giving themselves up and probably receiving more humane treatment than they'd got from their own chiefs, motivated by the example of some idealistic beardless second lieutenant or other, fought like scorpions. What followed became, for us, one of those days when you have to go conquering trench after trench, one after another, and at a very high cost. It was like that non-stop for a day and a half, bloody awful for both sides.

"Non-stop" is wishful thinking, though. I lost count of the number of times that your lot held us up on low or exposed ground. We were unprotected, whilst every one of your damn fellow-countrymen was stuck down deep in a hole, brimming with enthusiasm and ammunition. Before the surrender I only saw your lot *post mortem*, roasted in their trenches by white phosphorus grenades. When we finally got there, the burning and destroyed bodies all belonged to conscripts and NCOs. The officers were evidently away fighting another war.

Obviously, we felt no compassion. That never happens. Before being barbecued, these geezers had pinned us to the floor, and machine-gunned the fuck out of us. Even when it was raining, rain that often lashed in horizontally due to the wind, you couldn't lift your nose out of the mud without getting your head blown off by a sniper's bullet. And every time that one of our sections got held up for one reason or other, you can bet that some miserable well-hidden little Argentine cunt was giving the coordinates to the mortar sections in the rearguard, and then suddenly one of our blokes would lose a leg, or a leg would lose a bloke.

Right towards the very end, when we had them damned Argies surrounded and penned in without a hope with their backs to the sea, when we were calmly coming down at last to take the airfield and get the kettle on, the few nutters who were still alive there, who'd been blitzed for weeks and weeks by our frigates, Harriers and finally our field artillery, suddenly came back to life and welcomed us with their remaining workable anti-aircraft guns. They caught us by surprise and blew the shite out of us again. And there we are, just for a change, without a single hole to hide in – and we'd already won the battle! Why didn't anyone tell those bleeding Argentines that they'd lost? They even fired at us with the rocket launchers from the Pucarás that were scattered all over the airstrip, burnt and broken. Those madmen had also hooked up a missile launcher to a tractor belonging to the Falkland Island Company and were firing off one round after another with this aero-agricultural mutant, without the slightest chance of hitting jack shit. The dago bastards, I'd never been so scared in my life. Nobody had ever fired so many different things at me. We were all shit-scared. But we are paratroopers, and we keep it simple; we always attack, and when we are frightened, you don't want to be there when we do. We're unstoppable. *Utrinque paratus*. That's our motto in Latin. Look it up in the dictionary.

But if you ask what my main occupation was during the 36 hours that the battle of Goose Green lasted, I must confess that it consisted in lying as flat as a pancake in assorted freezing puddles or buried in grey, butter-like peat, reciting a Tibetan mantra as the tracer bullets flew haphazardly overhead from one side to the other like supersonic embers. And suddenly the diminishing whistle of a falling mortar would be added to this background and then boom! You couldn't tell who they were, but people were dying all around, and they died screaming.

And it was strange, because sometimes you'd hear some bloke screaming in English in front of you, where you supposed he should be dying and screaming in Spanish, and vice versa. That's how confusing it is to fight without defined battle lines, and with visibility down to nearly zero due to the rain. At dawn on the second day, when the dancing was nearly done, the peat itself, ignited by the phosphorus grenades, burnt in great patches, despite the downpour. Fat, lazy clouds of smoke and steam rose above the fires. It was a nonsensical, vaguely infernal sight.

I've only got three definite memories of when we scaled Darwin Hill. In one, out in open ground and under fire, I'm holding a soldier down onto the grass with all my weight, and he's fighting for all he's worth. He's a British soldier, he owes me money, but he's got absolutely no intention of paying me. Half a yard away a captain, also British, lies face down, calmly amputating the soldier's leg, smashed by a mortar from who knows where, it certainly doesn't matter now.

And it's raining bullets, and the occasional explosions nearby keep splashing mud onto the injured man, and the captain swears and cleans the wound once more, then starts cutting and digging again, but now and then tells some stupid joke or other to cheer us up, and I'm sincerely laughing my head off, because he's great at telling jokes. The operation is carried out with a little Swiss Army penknife, those red ones; you know the ones I mean.

The second memory is etched on my body: I spent so much time lying down, motionless and freezing, with wet socks and soaking boots stuck in the swampy ground, that I ended up losing three toes from my left foot. Much later, back on the Uganda, our hospital ship, when the whole show was nearly over, they decided that my toes were too black – from freezing or from trench foot – and that they had to go. But in Darwin, paradoxically, that same spongy peat saved me from having the rest of my poor old body amputated.

And that's my third memory from the battle and the next stage in my transformation, the step leading into the matter for which you've come to see me.

We're already on Darwin Hill, alright? At great cost, we've finally conquered the summit. It's getting light and we can see the seaside farmhouse and its dock 150 feet down below us. I've managed to hold on to my by now almost ex-pertly-closed mind, and I'm the only occupant of my triumphant individuality. A few miles away, through the mist, we can make out the outline of the slightly bigger village that is Goose Green proper, where the main body of enemy troops are dug in, and where we're not going to leave a plank or a corrugated iron sheet standing. Because now it's time to give back to those bleeding Argies each and every serving they've given us, and we couldn't give a shite if in the process we also exterminate all of the 140 or so fucking seaweed-heads that we've come here to save from General Galtieri's evil South American tyranny.

We've got very clear orders in that respect.

So, we're setting up a GPMG, a machine-gun that's pretty difficult to lug around, getting ready to fire it, when another mortar grenade falls about a yard away from me and, due to the velocity of its descent, explodes about three or four feet beneath the peat. A geyser of mud throws me up in the air and heaves me a long way away, covered in mud and soaking wet, leaving me stone deaf for 48 hours. If I'd been on rocky ground, where things go poom! rather than plop! it would have been a different story. I'd have been blown into fourteen pieces, or maybe fifteen. My two trench mates, however, are reasonably intact. Decidedly dead, though.

That plop! noise was something that was pretty common during the campaign and probably saved a lot of lives, both British and Argentine. So I don't consider that I was already immune at that moment. That was something that really happened later on.

But I do believe that this was the second step in my transformation into that other thing that I am today. It opened up my head, inexorably. The experience somehow programmed me for what was going to come next. Of course, that all seems clear to me today, but it didn't at the time. Because after having escaped by a hair's breadth like that, I remained in a, let me say, odd state. I don't think that I can describe it very well, sir. It's like… like I seem to be acting in a film that I'm not too convinced by. It's bad, really bad. Terribly made. Even worse even than Hollywood.

Conclusion: Shell shock, which is what they've been calling the matter since WWI? No, this thing is much more subtle. Let me try to explain better. The world loses its emotional consistency, it becomes, let's say, an empty sham. Do you understand? Unimportant. Things just simply happen, but they don't mean anything. You do understand me? No, I suppose that you don't really...I don't blame you. How long did it last for, you ask? Ha-bloody-ha. Thirty years have gone by, and it's still going on.

I'll come to that later.

Towards night-time on 28 May, the pastures and mud banks surrounding Goose Green were already chock full of unburied bodies, hundreds of them, lying here and there in the snow. And those bodies, which don't rot because of the cold, are luckily by now nearly all Argentines, youngsters, for the most part. With the surprised faces of children, if they had any expression on their faces at all - or if they still had faces.

The higher-ranking officers we captured never left the rearguard, which is the healthiest place to be. When they surrendered they were well-fed, they had impeccable warm, dry clothing and their boots were brightly polished. "They've no idea what gunpowder smells like", said the late, lamented Jorge Luis Borges shortly afterwards, much to his fellow-countrymen's outrage, and whose stories I've read and re-read over the years in search of an answer to the question that concerns us, and which I'm coming to, so I'll have to ask you to be patient for a little while longer.

Have you ever read *The Secret Miracle* or *The Writing of the God* in particular? No? That's odd, you being an Argentine. Your colleagues and compatriots are always quoting

Borges. He wrote the best prose of the twentieth century in any language. And I suspect that the two stories I've mentioned hold some of the keys to my affair.

When your lot finally surrendered, I noticed that my rifle was now useless from having fired so much, and that my trenching spade was bent from smashing in the head of some poor sod who – I'm almost certain today – was only trying to surrender. I will only say in my defence that we had gone two days without sleep and had amphetamines coming out of our ears. That's why I don't really know if I was at the battle of Goose Green or if the battle merely took place around me. I know that I watched my body fighting at Goose Green. And bodies make decisions that are not always ethical.

Or logical. In combat your body becomes so tremendously alive that you lose all awareness of being alive, of being you. If you're in the Paras, you're not there just for the very good money but rather for these short, lethal episodes. This drunken binge, however, has a poisonous hangover that will last you for the rest of your days.

For example, after having killed so many little Argentines, at first we were laughing about it, ha-ha-ha. After all this, we were still alive, for fuck's sake, and the dead bodies were theirs. How can you not laugh about that? Then the company perverts start up with all those revengeful acts that accompany almost all wars. For example, someone sticks a fag into the mouth of an Argy corpse, someone else lights it and two others lift the corpse under the armpits, they make it stand up, one on either side and they open its eyes so that they can pose for a fifth idiot, who's taking the photograph of the group who are holding up this amiable and dead Argentine, who we're sharing a laugh and a cigarette with.

Inevitably, someone else searches amongst this photogenic but rather silent gentleman's scorched clothing and, also inevitably, finds some family photos, and you can bet there's a girlfriend or a wife, or some kids smiling contentedly at you because you've just killed Daddy. So then we pass the pictures around and everyone gets a lump in the throat, because even though we nearly all come from shitbag families, who is there that doesn't love his own shitbag family, which looks just like the one in the photo, just a little bit?

But you can also bet that in fifteen seconds one of the frightened psychopaths that we've become will comment out loud that that Argentine lady in particular, mother of the kids, looks like she likes it up the jacksy. Then everyone competes to see who can make the most disgusting comments. And everyone is in stitches about how damn witty we are.

Ken Lukowiac, who we all called Luke, told all this in writing, and a lot better than I'm doing. But there's more.

In a war, one enters into absolute states of consciousness, in which good and evil lack any sense at all. I watched a mate of mine, for no reason at all, blow one of your lot's brains out with a pistol. I'm talking about an Argy who had not only surrendered a long while before, but was already a prisoner, beaten, kicked, disarmed and harmless, happy to have survived and even having had his boots taken away (the Argentine boots, made of leather, were incomparably better than the pressed-cardboard rubbish that Her Majesty provided for us, and which cost me three toes).

I don't know why my mate did that, but ten minutes later, the same bloke was trying hard to save, with compress bandages and, I think, without success, another Argy who had lost an arm and was bleeding to death.

40

Don't try to understand it, my young man. War is a powerful drug, and the fact is that those of us who've consumed too much of it, either in time or intensity, are fucked up for the rest of our lives.

Take those hallucinogenic creepers and herbs that they call "plants of knowledge" in the books. As a rule, they never kill anybody, in fact they have the opposite effect – they cure. But war really does kill – it kills those that get killed and those who don't, because it gives access to too much knowledge, more than bearable, about what the universe is and one's place in it. One can put up with the idea that the world is bad - that happens to all of us. What's different, and unbearable, is understanding that evil and goodness don't exist.

As happened on your side, some of my old mates committed suicide many years after the goings on in the Falklands. I know of at least three who live with almost untreatable depression – they're walking around pickled in alcohol or cocaine just waiting to die as soon as possible. The others manage to live normally, but with an effort. You see them and have a few drinks at the club bar and everything seems normal. They're like cars with the bodywork intact and well painted on the outside, but rusted and rotted on the inside.

They never talk about themselves, because an Englishman would never do that and, moreover, because there's not much left of "themselves" to talk about. After the war, the family lives of at least half of them, if you want an objective indication, have been disastrous. A lot of blokes' wives have left them, couldn't stand them any longer. Most of them have retired by now and live out an uneasy peace, searching, or not, for the meaning of the passing days, although there's probably one or two who are now at war in Afghanistan, full of medals, probably even happier, more ferocious, invulnerable, focussed, addicted, and more immune to death than ever.

On the other hand, I know that on your side the extreme sadness and post-war suicide was made worse by society's contempt and abandonment of its war veterans, which is inconceivable here in dear old Blighty. The Argentine soldiers were killed first by the indifference of their generals, then by their political parties and, at the end of the day, I reckon by nearly all their compatriots. There's something wrong with your society. In the decades that followed, I made friends with a few of your veterans, at first on the Internet but then in person. And we always understand each other, even though I don't speak a word of Spanish and they don't speak English. At least one of them became a friend of mine. An NCO; a simple bloke, lots of medals. After two decades of suffering unemployment and boozing his life away, they gave him a job as a policeman. But by then not even this bloke's kids were on speaking terms with him. The solitude and poverty in which he died, the general disdain, I'll never understand that. I'll tell you about it some other day. Well, one day my friend hanged himself from a beam. I cried my eyes out when I found out.

As far as I'm concerned, I don't reckon I behaved any better or worse than my mates. The fact is that after that mortar burst on the top of Darwin Hill, I felt a long way from everything and tried to join in with every idiotic ritual they came up with, like that thing with the photos. I had to show that I was normal, if you'll pardon the contradiction.

But even if I played up my darker side, I don't think that I convinced anybody. I'd always been a bit like that, a bit withdrawn, ever since Northern Ireland. I was always the bloke who observed all the rules and the codes, but at the same time always had my nose in a book, never got drunk, didn't have a girlfriend or a dog, or any friends, or feel the need for any friends. Blokes like me, no matter how well they do their job, are never trusted or welcome. When faced with people like us, true loners, other people feel like they're being judged or, worse still, they feel that they're being understood.

Well, anyway, they couldn't stand me for some reason or other. Who could blame them?

My last mission on Goose Green was to run around the isthmus supervising the collection of Argentine bodies, their identification, whenever possible, and their burial. The ones who put the bodies into plastic bags and loaded them onto a captured Unimog were Argentine prisoners. They often broke down when they came across a body they recognised, of a mate who they thought was alive or who'd somehow escaped.

A mechanical digger made a gigantic rectangular hole in the grey peat, a long way from the village, and we were filling it up for days. Hard work, that was.

Then we covered over the pit. I felt no emotion whatsoever.

V

You would have thought that we'd done enough by now for the glory of our non-existent British Empire, and it was time to take us to somewhere nice and quiet (which turned out to be Bluff Cove) to clear up our cases of trench foot, and to lick our many other wounds. I mean to get us ready for the next massacre, like maybe capturing the heights around Port Stanley.

But as we're Paras, and as they were thinking of making us walk to Bluff Cove, we commandeered the only Chinook helicopter that Britain had during the whole bloody war and obliged the pilot almost at gunpoint to take us where we wanted to go: Fitzroy, a farmhouse next to Bluff. With 60 of us crammed on board, the enormous apparatus just about managed to take off and take us, panting and hanging in the sky by pure turbine power, to that far-off farmhouse. Here's a funny thing: our artillery observers took us for Argies, given that we were an unauthorized flight, and were on the point of ordering our destruction as soon as we landed.

Bluff Cove is a bay protected by high cliffs, with a few pebbly beaches and an island in the middle. It's a bit sheltered from the constant torments of the wind. Because of that, and the deep water and the relative lack of waves, the place is considered to be as good an anchorage as any in the islands. There's a little-used dock there, Port Pleasant. Those who were fed up with Northern Ireland and the bloody Falklands and were dreaming of a posting to Belize, looked at the scene and thought: "Well, there's no palm trees, or native girls with no togs on, but at least we'll be getting a bit of beach life at last."

I was unaware of this. I was unaware of everything around me. It was still like being in a cloud. The much-feared apparition of a Pucará, which never happened, or getting blown apart by our own artillery, which nearly happened, wouldn't have bothered me either way. Since that mortar burst I'd hardly said another word. Apart from Ken, who was a bit of a silent type himself, my mates tended to ignore me more and more. I probably had an odd look on my face.

With the blessing of the owners of Fitzroy, and with a collective sigh of relief, we all piled into a gigantic corrugated iron shearing shack. If it'd had windows, it would've had a five-star view of the sea.

The manufacturer's mark on the corrugated iron sheeting, I remember, said *Gurmendi. Industria Argentina.* Nearly everything there that was manufactured, like for example the wool-packing machines, or the shovels, shears and other tools and even the rolls of barbed wire, all told the same story: *Forja, Industria Argentina,* or *Acindar, Industria Argentina.*

I remember thinking that those very same kelpers on whose behalf we were killing Argies were, in economic terms, so Argentine themselves that all they needed was to speak Spanish and start dancing the tango as well. The truth is that a lot of them did anyway, having studied in the schools and universities at Cordoba, and a lot of them had relatives on the continent. I also recall that, apart from the smell of lanoline and sheep's piss that seeped into our clothes and flesh, that enormous, freezing shack seemed like the Club Med to us. In the Falklands, anywhere out of the wind is the Club Med.

We were unlucky, however, that Her Majesty's army, and I mean the regular troops, mind you, had still not fired a shot in anger during the whole campaign. So, some modern-day Wellington had decided that the best place to disembark the Scots Guards, the Welsh Guards and the Gurkhas from their LSLs wasn't on the faraway beachhead at San Carlos Water, but right here, at our private farming spa, relatively near to Stanley, where the first skirmishes were already taking place in the town's most outlying surrounding hills. I mean, you couldn't expect the regular army to miss out on the victory parade, even though they'd done absolutely jack shit up till then, could you?

The Guards had to disembark – as we'd already had to – in LCU launches, just like in the old WWII days. As regards the Welsh, well, they took ages and ages to do it because they didn't want to land too far from their destination and have to yomp some miles to it. And they weren't bothered in the slightest about the Argentine air force. I mean, they were nearly all dead by now, weren't they? And, I mean, who's going to go out flying on a horrible day like today?

But then, suddenly, the storm opened up in isolated downpours, one over here, another one over there, and it's now where my story begins to get a bit theological, Mr. Journalist. I suddenly get the feeling that we've been spotted. It's like a lightning bolt in my brain. There are two Argentines – up until a moment ago there were three, one has just died – and they are invisible, about five miles away, I know exactly in what direction, and they have just relayed the details of the landing by radio. I know, but just for a change, I don't know how or why I know, and I cannot talk. My mouth cannot pronounce a single word. But, instead of getting desperate, I take it with all the calmness of a lunatic and carry on going about my business. As if it was unimportant.

When, an hour later, the first three A4 Skyhawks appear in the suddenly clear skies, they are flying close to ground, gaucho- style, and they approach from the south east, an unexpected direction. I watch unsurprised as they come in amidst a barrage of rifle fire, because they have flown in almost tearing the helmets off the terrified Scots Guards already on the beach, whom they ignored and probably didn't even see. What they did see, right in front of them and a bit to starboard, were the fat, delicious LSLs. They flew over them, deafeningly, made U-turn licking their chops and then dived down towards them. I mean towards us, I mean towards me, poor little me. Because we were on the beach situated behind the ships, in the perfectly straight line that represents the bomb corridor.

And I'm stuck there like an idiot, on that imaginary line. And all because that morning I'd decided to make a major effort to get out of the shack, although not out of my silence, for a while. Trying to re-establish contact with the world, as if the world was worth it.

In that instant I was concentrated on listening to the conversation of seven recently-landed Welsh Guards. They were trying without success to set up a Rapier missile launcher. Something had gone wrong with the electronics. I remember that the blokes still had their trousers wet through, were suffering from the cold and were swearing blind about the damned anti-aircraft gear and the bastard that made it.

The thing is, and here's when things begin to get extraordinary, is that I can pick up on every detail, because my mind is going through an explosive expansion process, just like when the Ardent was sinking. But this time...

My sense of self had disappeared, or something like that. In a full out-of-body experience, I looked at the bay from above, about a thousand feet above. I saw the beach clogged with lorries and people, oil drums, artillery ammunition, the anti-aircraft battery yet to function, some Gurkhas with oriental faces comically trying to play a game of football in a field of tussocks, a couple of Scorpion light tanks with their engines turned off, that launch just about to reach the dock and the two round LSLs, Sir Galahad and Sir Tristan, tranquillity itself in the middle of the bay, with their cranes bobbing up and down as they lifted crates of anti-tank ammunition and then slowly lowered them onto the launches. In the background, there was an old frigate far from the coast, watching over the sea reaches with its radar, thinking there's nothing over here and there's nothing over there, either. A lovely scene; almost a picture postcard of a military picnic. Nobody worried about anything in particular.

I saw my miniscule self, amid the group of Welsh Guards. I saw myself watching without interest that lightning-quick appearance of two more A4s from the same sector, that also turned180 degrees on descent and start on a second bomb run towards the Galahad – behind which is where we find ourselves. It was interesting to see how the five aircraft staggered themselves over the same line to all hit the same ship, but then the last two, seeing that the Galahad was going to be getting plenty, turned off slightly to make their delivery to the Tristan.

The Welsh looked on in absolute horror. They were inexperienced troops, they couldn't believe what they were seeing. One thing was certain: they stopped talking. This moment of disbelief lasted about ten seconds. Then the man on the Rapier pressed the trigger a few times, knowing that all was in vain. Obviously, it didn't work. No rocket fired off. He smiled at us shyly and somewhat guiltily.

But I couldn't smile back, or even speak, for other reasons.

Firstly, I repeat, because the scene was a very beautiful one, and because more even more extraordinary things began taking place within my head, for which I had, in that instant, no words to describe. Many years later, however, I did begin to find some, although they describe things only clumsily and tangentially.

What I can tell you, by using pretty inadequate computer-age metaphors, is that Something stuck a cable into my cranium and another into my navel, and then got inside me and started downloading files lickety-split from some all-powerful server somewhere in some far-off corner of the universe. But before that, it reprogrammed the hard disc of my soul, or something like that. And then subsequently it started to fill the disc up with indescribable contents.

If a human consciousness is equal to a computer screen, then I can only say that the screen representing my mind displayed only junk, extremely fleeting glimpses of complex characters and images, faces and shadows, flames and fragments of what must have been enormous, but highly-compressed files, stellar quantities of new information that were being recorded at extraordinary velocity on my brain, and that my brain had no hope of understanding.

In a similarly inexplicable way, I can also tell you that while this was happening, I understood that this new download of information would give me a new view of things, although I mightn't be able to read it at the time. When those files were to be run, they'd be opened automatically, without needing my permission, like a virus activated by a time-delay mechanism or a password. I think that something like that has been happening in my subsequent life. I also reckon that if my health holds out, there are still lots of surprises waiting hidden in my head.

What was least important, within my new expanded consciousness, was the view that I had from up above of the entire scenario of Bluff Cove, where the first three aircraft were heading towards us, already closing in on their target. The thing is that there was now a new element, nine 500 lb. PRBs, in restrained flight towards the Sir Galahad. They had little parachutes on the back that acted as brakes, in order to give the pilots time to escape the explosions.

It was obvious that not all of these bombs could miss their target.

In this panoramic vision I was able, if I tried, to perceive time as if it stood still, like a freeze frame shot in a film.

The thing was that I'd suddenly discovered a new mode of eternity. After thinking about it for many years, I've managed to describe the matter in a somewhat Euclidean way. Look: just as there are an infinite number of points between any two points on a straight line, I understood that between any two points on the line of time, although they appear to be immediately consecutive, there is an infinity of intermediate moments, a micro eternity, which is not a whit less than macro eternity.

Parmenides of Elea would have loved my reasoning process, but he was a mere theoretician, whereas I really know what I'm talking about. That's where I live, inserted between moments that are inserted between more moments, so to speak. And I can also add that micro eternity is more complete than macro eternity, because the second law of thermodynamics, which dictates the before and the after, means that for the rest of you the arrow of time only flies in one direction, forwards. But for me it can also fly backwards, and at the same time inwards on itself because, like I said, there are no indivisible minimum units, there are no atoms of time. Whilst what was about to happen to me lasted from that day onwards, I was able to perceive time's triple infinity and travel along it forwards, backwards and inwards, to scrutinize it in all its detail.

In effect, I think that I was experiencing time in the same way that God does, from outside the arrow of time. At the same time I knew with all certainty that God does not exist, and that it's probably just a name that we give to time.

Now, more than twenty years after these events, a part of my mind is still held prisoner in those few seconds of eternity, analysing them to the millionth degree and even smaller fractions, which are in reality infinite, like any fraction of the infinite itself must be, and I still keep on finding interesting new details, like what happens to you when you watch a film that you love for the umpteenth time. For example, while I'm talking to you, with that other part of my dual mindset, I can read the inscriptions written in chalk on one of the six bombs that fly towards the fat Sir Galahad. They belong to the second group; two A4s that are following the first three.

The letters in chalk say: "Up yours, Brit".

I detect – but not in a visual way – a conscripted soldier from Buenos Aires, who can speak a few languages, and is vaguely left-wing. He's fainted and starting to go into shock. A few hours ago, as the advanced observer alongside a civilian Argentine radio ham, he sent through the details of the landing. They were under the orders of a first lieutenant, a sadistic bastard, a coward and an ignoramus. They've lived for many days in misery, hungry and cold, hiding away day and night from our special forces, who've been looking for them since the day before yesterday. The officer is already dead, the civilian died a few minutes after and now the soldier is beginning to die. The ELINT surveillance detected the radio signals at the same time as I did, they recognised the code used by the Argy Centre for Information and Control, they managed to triangulate the position of the antenna and they bombarded it with 81mm mortars.

The aforementioned bomb, meanwhile, is travelling through the air, bearing its obscene message in defiance of Britain, because that little Argentine patrol signalled details of the landing at Port Pleasant. The soldier and the civilian did it, despite their officer's determined opposition, terrified as he was that he'd be blown to smithereens. There's another story here that's worth telling, but I'll leave it for another day. No, don't ask me anything, but I know everything about that boy. His name, his age, his character. I could even tell you his story minute by minute, from the moment that I first perceived him in a corner of my mind, watching us through binoculars before sending us all to our doom. He's a good person, although he makes out that he's not. We'll be friends one day, or something like that.

I could also talk to you for hours about the girlfriend of another lad, a Welsh Guard called Howard, although that's not his real name. Howard's not just a great lad, he also looks it. He's a private, and he's cleaning an interior stairway, with a bucket and swab, down amidships on the Galahad, where one of his mates got sea-sick and threw up. They're making him clean it up like he was a sailor because the relations between the Galahad's crew and the soldiers have been getting worse. Howard is frightened because he's just heard the screech of tearing metal when the first bombs hit the ship.

A few seconds later, the bombs, triggered by the delayed fuses, will explode. The entire bay will be shaken, the water will be shaken, the Galahad and the Tristan and the entire world will be shaken. The lad who I've called Howard will get up, splattered with blood, leave the bucket and swab and start running up the stairs, searching for the light.

He'll never get there. Three seconds later, that boy will be knocked over by a wall of flame caused by the fuel and the munitions stored on the ship catching fire. It's like getting caught right in the middle of a burst of flame from a giant blowtorch. He's going to get burnt, indescribably badly. The thick, heavy Antarctic clothing he's wearing will burn and turn into ashes almost immediately.

Twelve seconds later, as this boy's consciousness becomes obscured by pain and the loss of body fluids, the Galahad will become a ball of flame. Someone will rescue him, still alive, but he'll die on the hospital ship Uganda on the way back, not far from the bed I'm occupying. I'll watch him die, cursing an injured Argentine in the bed in front of him.

Howard's girlfriend, a very young and lovely girl from Southampton, will cry her eyes out for months on end, completely shattered, but finally she'll start to see that electrician from Liverpool again, the one she was having an affair with when this thing happened. She wasn't a bad girl, just confused, at that time, and maybe she still is, but from where I perceive her, I reckon that's she's met too many sad men and as a result she'll fall ill.. The electrician, unlike Howard, wasn't really worth it. I still couldn't tell you how this story ends.

What I can tell you, at the end of the day, is that in few those seconds I underwent a sort of internal Big Bang and I took charge, without wanting to, meaning to or understanding how, of a piece of the universe in which I am now the equivalent of God. And from that time on I roam around this micro universe, probably in the same useless way that God roams around our macro universe: like Him, I'm a witness, pure and inexplicable, navigating through a sort of internet of consciousnesses and perceptions, wherein He neither judges nor intervenes, and Whose capacity for observation is infinite, as infinite as His impotence, and Whose observation, however, is subject to some important external limits.

I have managed to measure the limits of my God-Being in units of your time, or rather the time that you and I live in and share, the here and now where I matter very little. In that objective time, not the here and now but the there and then, for want of a better name, my moment of omniscience lasts for fifteen seconds. Fifteen eternal seconds, in which I live for ever.

My omniscience also has physical limits; although they are very diffused and far off. They take in all the places in the world that have been passed through by those 1,233 people who shared during those fifteen seconds – and still share with me, for at least as long as my consciousness endures – the Argentine Air Force's attack on Bluff Cove.

Why do I say "for at least as long as my consciousness endures"? Because all of those characters live for fifteen seconds inside of me, including those who died in that brief lapse of time or immediately afterwards, or who have gone on to die for unconnected reasons during the slow passage of time since then. I am, Mr. Journalist, and I don't know why, not a man, but a multitude. I am full of the life of those others. I'm like a storeroom for souls. I'm the God of those souls – they are in my care.

I don't know what will happen to them, to my flock, when I die. Because I'll undoubtedly die. Will the dead inside of me die once more? Or will we all continue to live, they and I, inside of a consciousness even greater than mine and which in turn is thinking about me, bestowing being on me, like in a set of Russian dolls, those dolls inside of dolls inside of other dolls? Is there, as the defunct Borges asked, another God behind God?

It's odd to be God, even the second-rate version, and not to have the answer to that question. If there is nothing behind me, then life and the universe, and I in particular, are all a big failure. If, however, that thing about the Russian dolls really is true, Mr. Journalist, then Death does not exist. That is my unconfirmed suspicion. And that wouldn't be bad news, would it? If things are as I suspect they are, one lives eternally within ever greater and more powerful consciousnesses. But I have never found one, so I can't say whether this is true or not. I simply just can't say. You can't found a religion on just this, in the same way I'm not made of the right stuff for a god or a prophet.

Within its defined range, my Bluff Cove omniscience is also not limited by what is human, but rather by what is living and a little bit more. Not only do I know what happens to the people spread out around the bay, I also know about every-thing else that's in it and that surrounds me.

Wherever there is Being (and I feel that even the rocks have some sort of numb sensation of rockiness), I enter and read it, just like someone opens a web page or a page in an instruction manual, and I can describe to you everything that I find. But here my limit – like I warned you at the beginning – is language itself. There are no human words that com-municate the being of stones or of the wind or those Falkland clouds, so changeable and wandering, so full of chiaroscuro and drama. But believe me that in their own way, they con-sist, they think.

In my view of Bluff Cove there are many minds, millions of them, that are no less human but rather more understand-able than the minds of clouds or stones: the air is full of sea-gulls, skuas, Antarctic pigeons, the odd black-chested buz-zard eagle, a lot of the local caracaras that the islanders call Johnny Rooks, loads of red-breasted mergansers, and a kind of giant petrel that shares the Argentine Air Force's penchant for flying close to the water. Everything is alive, the sea, the water and the rocks are teeming with conger eel, pollock, mussels, giant mussels, jelly fish, crabs, cockles, green sea-weed and brown seaweed. I can also detect each unicellular alga, each marine bacterium, I know what they feel.

What I can definitely tell you is that this huge concert of animal, vegetable and geological minds hardly knows we are there. In True Reality, as I always suspected, human beings don't even amount to a footnote. Our "to be or not to be" is irrelevant.

At any moment I can lose the notion of the seconds or of the centuries. Time is like an enormous wave, immobile, perplexing, in which I advance or retreat without noticing, free of any notion of before or after. I go backwards and detect a large shoal of pollock under the water, very busy being totally unaware of us humans. I touch each one of those tiny minds and can feel them breathing in the water. I sense their terror of the cormorants that plunge and zigzag after them like torpedoes.

Those little minds, and the rather larger minds of the cormorants, are all going to die when the last Argentine pilot of the first wave drops his bombs on the Galahad, which is already holed but which has yet to explode. When it finally does two seconds later, the Galahad will go in a flash, in a burst of vaporised diesel flame, because it's loaded with fuel and explosives. It'll burn like a match; it will go off like a firework. The Tristan, still intact, expectantly awaits its destiny. There are bombs hanging statically in the air, on a course for the ship. Howard, the girl from Southampton's fiancée, is getting ready to burn as if he'd plunged into a volcano.

The Galahad's third attacker has overshot his target; the bombs sail over the ship and land in different places. Two explode in the water and the shock wave will destroy the swim bladder and/or backbone of all the fish within a radius of hundreds of yards. The pollock are literally turned into mincemeat. Their thousands of little minds disappear all at once, like street lights turned off by a power cut. The cormorants' minds will also disappear, but in a more complex fashion. Don't ask me for details, I don't understand them myself.

The third bomb will bounce on the water like a stone skimmed by a boy, it will leap in my direction from a distance of only a about a hundred yards at a speed of more than four hundred knots and will end up running aground on the steep shingle beach, over which it will race uphill like a runaway express train, in a flurry of pebbles, until it stops intact right in the middle of the group of Welsh guards that I was listening to. It interrupts them almost like one of those boring drunkards at a party that butt in uninvited on someone else's conversation.

All of this is almost instantaneous, lasting just the wink of an eye in your time.

We don't manage to scream, because we are experiencing a very major cognitive overload, although mine is worse: the Sir Galahad is now in full eruption, the Tristan starts to explode and both begin a multidirectional ejection of live ammunition. And there we are, surrounding a smoking Argentine 500 lb. bomb, with the fuse activated, surely on the point of blowing up, watching it respectfully and in silence, as if the artefact were a sick relative.

Then the bomb explodes.

I see again, for the millionth time, again impartially, as the Welsh are turned into gases and fragments and ions, as their souls are rubbed out in a kind of hissing or crackling of electrified silk, and I take charge of them, I ingest them, I swallow them, and they are now me.

Then I disappear. In that instant and for a short lapse of time I cannot locate my self, at least not accurately, in my concentrated form. My concentrated self disappears mysteriously, perhaps rubbed out too. But my expanded self, dispersed, a conglomerate, continues to exist and to absorb minds.

The thing is that in my expanded self, I continue to be Bluff Cove, Port Pleasant and everything that is in it, as well as time itself, limited and divisible, but innumerable: God.

Then I manage to locate myself, my accurate, human, limited version. I condense or reappear in this self-thing, who knows how or why, but at about sixty yards or more from the explosion, and without clothes or hair or boots – all that has been torn off me – but unharmed, except for some painful, but inexplicably minor, burns.

In an equally inexplicable way, I was absent for a few seconds, perhaps a minute, from the Inventory of Reality. And I am not surprised: I take everything in my stride, my nudity, my still being alive, my being there, my knowing that I am Protected. I am born again. But I don't know why I'm protected, for what reason, or by whom, or until when. And I still don't know today.

As far as everything else is concerned, nobody pays me the slightest attention. The bomb, as well as obliterating the men that I was talking to, has injured and mutilated dozens of other soldiers and NCOs, who squirm in a 180-yard radius like lizards and vipers cut with a spade. On the Galahad, meanwhile, they are being cooked alive.

There are Nepalese soldiers who run like cartoon characters from one side to the other like they were still playing football, only now their hair and clothes are on fire. Just then the diesel fuel from the Rapier anti-aircraft battery's electrical plant begins to explode. The live ammunition inside the crates that still swing from the Galahad's cranes keeps on going off like fireworks and killing people unawares hundreds of yards away. The water is full of burning petrol and desperate, waving arms. What a picture!

Two hundred yards away, my mate Ken, who was unashamedly having a shite right in the middle of the beach, stands up shocked but intact. As what he sees is too much for him, he takes refuge in the little things: he carefully wipes his bum with a page from his Danish porno mag, then pulls up his trousers, walks a fair way away from his defecations and sits down again on the pebbles, incredulous. Then he opens his magazine again and loses himself in the contemplation of a sex scene that is more gynaecological than erotic.

But the gigantic massacre that is happening right in front of him on the coast and in the sea distracts him at times. He is saddened by what he sees, both around him and in his magazine. Both failures of Humanity.

His mind, which is capable of looking at things from different angles, asks itself what is more pornographic, whether it's his new magazine or the scene of carnage and chaos that surrounds him. He will write about this scene, like I told you, in that memorable book that will make him briefly famous. Poor old Ken.

The Argentine aircraft have been gone for quite a while when some medics find me wandering naked along the beach. They try in vain to make me speak, then hand me over to a military doctor who also tries to get me to talk, also in vain.

The following day they evacuate me by helicopter to the Uganda, classified as a minor burns victim, but gravely catatonic. A case of serial shell shock, miraculously saved twice in a row. Nobody understands how I managed it the second time and there's really nothing to understand, but nobody could give a shite anyway because the Galahad's fate has meant that services on the floating hospital are stretched to the limit. As there's very little that the doctors can do for my poor crazy little head, they go to the other extreme: they look at my feet, making very English "hem-hem" noises. Then they chop off all the toes they don't like the look of, which is quite a few.

Although it's not what the first doctors who treated me on the ship had in mind, the amputation provides an entirely different second group of doctors back in Blighty with the perfect excuse to give me an honourable discharge, but without having to pay me a juicy lifetime's pension for total incapacity. In fact, they pay me a pittance. My madness is left out of the reports and my incapacity is therefore partial and I'm leaving supposedly by my own will, and that's what they make me sign. And I can't be bothered to argue and to prove to them that I really am nuts. And why not? Because I'm nuts, of course.

So, they make sure that nobody states on paper that they're chucking me out of the Regiment for nuttiness. That might mean that I - or some relative of mine, if I had any – might take the MOD to court one day and thereafter to the cleaners. That's what the MOD's lawyers think anyway. Just in case, the quacks remove from their reports any references that state I'm a bit catatonic and that before that I was as sane as the next man, depending on how you look at it, and that I turned to stone during the war. None of that. In reality, they know, and I know, that I can be missing three toes from one foot and still be a good Para, but not if I'm missing language from inside my head.

Like I said, I'm too busy wandering around absorbed in the contemplation of Time. The doctors seem like ethereal marionettes, manipulated by invisible strings. I'm not the slightest bit interested even when they amputate my toes. I don't really understand the terms of my discharge until much later, although I had signed what I had to sign. Why should I want to carry on being a Para anyway, now that I am thousands of people?

When I was admitted to a civilian psychiatric hospital it took me months to overcome the hypnotic fascination of that bay where I continue to be God, and a full year resigning myself to understanding - or pretending, rather, - that I'm only a tiny insignificant man. It took me many more months before I would condescend even to talk to mere mortals, like I'm talking with you today.

And it's still an effort today, believe me, because my attention is always wandering over to the Other Side, to Bluff Cove and its enclosed eternities. Over the years, I've managed to double up my mind and function on both sides without it being noticeable, nothing more. Let's just say that you are talking to my representative. I'm on the other side.

Yes, Jonesy, I think that the gentleman urgently needs another IPA. No, not for the cameraman, better leave him alone, poor lad. He already can't keep the camera straight, or even his head. I'll tell you something else, Jonesy, I bet you a tenner that the entire second half of this interview comes out badly. I bet that the image is shaky and out of focus and won't be fit for broadcasting. What a shame.

Tell me something, Jonesy, and stop laughing for a moment, you bastard. This IPA must be about 13 degrees proof. Aren't you making your bloody beers too strong?

VI

That's right, eight hours have gone by and now that you've finally woken up you're furious, and quite rightly so - but nobody forced you and your cameraman to keep drinking. Yes, I know, several months of work on this project have gone down the plughole, I understand. Your bosses will probably dock it off your travel expenses.

They'll give you the sack, you say? Wait, try and vomit into the sink, at least, while I hold your head up. That's better.

Right then, if you're listening, you'll understand that I refuse, in my own sweet way, to be transformed into a guru. I can't stand those gurus, with their bloody Rolls-Royces and their churches fit for idiots. I prefer to carry on being the person I am, and for that reason certain things have to remain a secret, but it mustn't seem like I'm trying to keep things that way. Do you know what I mean?

You don't know what I mean, I can tell. Look, if I told the occasional journalist that knocks on my door to bugger off, that would only attract more of them, and they'd be buzzing around my door like flies. They'd ruin my life, like they did to Diego Maradona or Princess Diana. That's the way you work. I prefer to make your colleagues leave in confusion, ashamed and unwilling to talk about what really happened to them. That's the only way that I can carry on being a relatively unknown person.

I see that you're feeling a bit better. There's nothing like a good spew after a good piss-up, that's what I always say. And now Jonesy will make you a nice coffee, that's if there is any nice coffee in the whole damn British Isles. No, there isn't any – that was a joke. Drink this poison, there's a good lad. Here, have a couple of Aspirins.

Normally, at this stage of the hangover, after they've emptied their stomachs, intestines and bladders, some of your colleagues and predecessors also give vent to their indignation and disbelief: they become sceptical, even downright bolshy, and they ask for proof that I'm not just another lunatic. After all, wasn't I shut up in the loony bin until after 1984? And haven't I been admitted several times since then?

Well, I don't feel obliged to prove anything, but let's see…how come you've crossed the Atlantic to investigate my story? Because you've probably heard the rumours about this old guitarist who's been touched by Grace, but who, God only knows why, wastes his time with a bunch of other old farts, none of whom can play a note. Together they form an insignificant band that plays trivial songs in obscure places. But, now and again, this guitarist performs miracles.

For want of a better word.

Well, there is some truth in those rumours. Beyond the fact that music has healed people ever since music and people have existed, the only importance of my actions is this: in my band, we're all broken-down army, prison or asylum fodder. If I hadn't got them together and made them play, they'd all be dead from overdoses by now, or killed in some idiotic fight. Or they'd have killed others and been locked up for life in the clink or the nuthouse.

Alright, you can call me an Enlightened Being, A Man With a Mission if you want. I've already confessed to you that my "enlightenment", condensed into fifteen seconds and fixed on a place like Bluff Cove at the back end of beyond, is rather modest. Well, then, don't be surprised if my mission is, too. I am the repository of a few souls that died on 8 June 1982, and of others that are still alive and somehow related to that time and that place. And, at the end of the day, I look after the lads in my band.

If I'm to carry out my mission, it has to be pretty low key. And that's where the trouble starts. In the same way that it's hard to maintain a coherent conversation with you now, because I could just as easily become the seagull that floats over the eternal fires of the HMS Sir Galahad, I also find it hard sometimes, when I'm onstage, to play deliberately badly.

When I was young I couldn't play anything but badly, and worse than badly, but now I sometimes find it almost impossible. It happens now and then. We're playing a concert, on a Wednesday night in some shithole or other and I forget myself. And I play all that which has flooded and gushed through my head since 14.10 on 8 June 1982.

And then my mates put down their instruments, bewildered, and the cripples throw away their crutches and the potential suicides start to smile, and the public goes mad, or starts crying, or smashes the place up and the next day there are a lot of undesirable journalists of all types appearing. From Rolling Stone, or from the big newspapers. Or from nutty TV stations, like yours. It's bloody awful.

No, nobody gave me My Mission and I prefer to consider it as "my mission", in inverted commas and with small case letters, just to show the doubts that it arouses in me. Did you know that the Universe is a pretty cold and amoral place? There can be no missions in it because there are no chiefs in it. There are no ethics, there are no prizes or punishments, there's no heaven and no hell in it. There's not even that Buddhist thing about reincarnating as a prince, or at least as a cheerful spud-basher, if you've been good in the previous life and helped out your neighbours, instead of running around setting fire to nurseries, in which case you come back as a cockroach.

You can forget all that pious shit. The Universe is much more complex and inhuman and confused, it's not a moral machine for soul promotion. To be good, or to be a complete monster, are only human options, they are not options imposed by the Deep Structure of Reality. One chooses to be one thing or the other to paint a veneer of sense onto human life, but there is nothing as inhuman, mysterious, lacking in meaning or as incomprehensible as life itself. Do you understand? The Universe couldn't give a shite about us, do you get me?

No, you don't get me. Do you think the bloke needs a bit more of your coffee, Jonesy?

Look, seeing as how your cameraman is fast asleep and can't record us, and just so as you don't feel that you've made the trip for nothing and given that, despite your tender years, you're a gentleman and a fan of the old Beatles, and that you've turned up here with a great sadness hidden in your soul, me and Jonesy will give you a little recital,

66

something completely private. Yes, that's right, maybe one day Jonesy will tell you his life story. Mine is nothing in comparison. Have you got your Fender handy, Jonesy? Shall we play "While my Guitar Gently Weeps"? I reckon that this here gentleman might like to hear two guitars howling with sorrow.

And when the years have gone by, and these two old farts have died from cirrhosis, just as we deserve, and when you, my young man, are as experienced and foolish as we are today, I can assure you that the music you're about to hear, in this unknown, empty little Cotswold pub, will keep on playing in your head.

It will play for ever.

It will keep playing long after you are dead.

It is the music of Time.

But whilst you're still alive, it will make you want to cry and be a good bloke.

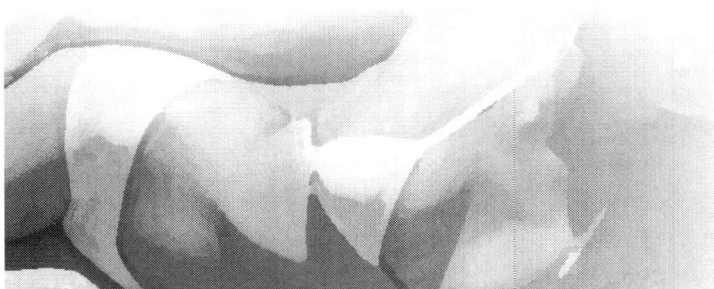

Chapter Three

Hysterical Argentine Girls

On the afternoon that they killed him, Private Ibáñez opened a letter of support that had recently arrived from the continent. It was one among thousands. Brought from the continent by the Hercules aircraft that managed to evade the British blockade, these missives landed addressed to anonymous recipients, to be distributed in heaps and haphazardly amongst the soldiers serving in Las Malvinas[1]. Ibáñez slit open the envelope, opened it, read it and was shocked.

'I can't believe those bitches back in Argentina are so hysterical,' he shouted at First-Lieutenant Calligari as the Huey was warming its turbine and the dual rotor blades accelerated their chop-chop-chop sound as they cut the air into thick slices.

Ibáñez held the letter over to the pilot's position and showed the officer the photo of a more than acceptable twenty-year-old brunette in a bikini. "To the soldier fighting for the

---

[1] In Argentina, the name for the Falkland Islands is Las Malvinas.

Fatherland in Las Malvinas: Please, kill lots of Englishmen. My measurements are 95-60-93, and my telephone number is 7914404, in Vicente López. When you get back, you can phone me and find out whether I'm telling the truth" was written in biro over the photo.

'Hysterical. A serious case,' shouted Ibáñez.

'I don't agree,' answered Calligari, as he opened the throttle and the RPMs of the turbine increased into a piercing whine. Then he added, knowledgeable and resigned. 'My wife, now that's hysterical for you. Spends all day carping and she's always in a strop. This little darling looks pretty hot, though. If I were you, soldier, I'd give her a call. Guaranteed leg-over.'

'That's right. If we ever get back,' Sergeant Ibrahim, who acted as co-pilot and navigator, seemed to be thinking. He looked with little interest at the photo his chief offered him and turned around to hand it back to Ibáñez, who looked at it again for a second and said nothing. It was unusual for Ibrahim to speak, but lately he always made himself understood.

Private Ibáñez thought that such a display of useless femininity would spell exactly the opposite of an easy shag or, at least, a good one. But it was useless to explain the clinical meaning of the word hysteria to these two barrack-room animals. It would be easier to describe an ice floe to a Tuareg, in Sanskrit.

There were other pressing reasons for Ibáñez to keep quiet. In spite of the earphones and the intercom, the cockpit of a Huey helicopter on the point of take off is a noisy place; the pre-flight checklists are lengthy, complex and require full attention. And if you are about to go far out to sea on the Choiseul Sound, bound on a rescue mission under the very noses of the British fleet, then you haven't really got the headspace to swap opinions about the female condition.

Aside from such cultural chit-chat, though, the three men understood each other. Ibáñez was aware that danger faced together creates ties as strong as autogenous welded seams.

And these ties were involuntary, at least as far as he was concerned.

II

At the age of 28, Mario Carlos Ibáñez was quite old for a soldier. He had done his military service at last in 1981, postponed for many years, firstly due to an extended stay overseas and then due to his dazzling student career. As soon as he got back from England in 1978, he had enrolled in Psychology and finished his degree in only three years, while working at the same time – an achievement usually requiring five years of full-time study.

In order to "regularize his military situation", which his national ID card confirmed as legally postponed due to his studies, the newly-graduated Ibáñez, in common with all Argentine conscripts (the so-called *colimbas*[2]) with or without education, washed dishes, swept out barrack rooms, painted walls, did guard duty, swore allegiance to the flag, saluted his superiors and listened to them spouting pure drivel. He watched them thieve and embezzle and commit other crimes with impunity; he paraded, marched, jumped, ran, did squat thrusts in the mud for hours and days, ran some more, learned

2 So-called *colimbas* because they run, clean and sweep. (*Corren, Limpian y Barren*).

to steal clothes and food, to humiliate himself and eat refuse, and was immeasurably bored by the sheep of Class 62, who were ten years his junior. And this went on and on until finally, after 15 interminable months, when he was just getting used to barrack-room nothingness, in the same way that prisoners adapt to prison, one fine day they gave him back his civvies, the street, his life and the use of his disconcerted personage.

But just like many other soldiers who had just finished military service, in April 1982, a week after leaving the Army, they called him to the colours again to go and fight in the islands, recently conquered by Argentina.

Ibáñez could have saved himself the trouble, as his father was an anaesthetist. However, he refused to pretend to suffer from a grave illness, and declined to turn up at the barracks a month later, walking with the unsteady gait of a convalescent, hypotensive and pale from Amlodipine consumption, on a date and in a state which would have made it impossible for the military doctors to send him south, and would have made it much more likely that they'd leave him painting doors or cleaning toilets for the troops in some garrison on the continent.

On the contrary, Ibáñez plucked up courage and went the day after he was called, whilst his parents and his girlfriend Ana despaired of him and called him a fool. He turned up and fell in with the rest of the fools, feeling, of course, like a fool, knowing that he was one, but unable to avoid being one.

A month later, he didn't regret having done it. But, at times, he tormented himself trying to discover the wherefore of that decision. A young psychologist still needs to believe that he knows himself.

So, that was why he found himself, as a machine gunner, rescuer and improvised medic on a helicopter that was just beginning to take off and defy the wind. The strong gusts immediately began to rock and pummel the machine, like a swollen river buffets a car, as he checked and made safe the *MAG* machine gun. Or held on to it for dear life, more like.

III

Ibáñez was a graduate with a Humanities degree from the University of Buenos Aires which, in the eyes of the Argentine Army, not only disqualified him for the rank of second lieutenant in the reserve, which a degree in Medicine would have guaranteed him, but also made him suspicious of being a subversive or, at the very least, a faggot.

Due both to his university education and to his age, the graduate treated his soldier peers, who were all younger than him, as if he were a distant but concerned uncle. Meanwhile, the NCOs and officers didn't really know how to deal with an older soldier who was also a specialist on lunatics, and had therefore put him on a helicopter as soon as he arrived on the island, just to get him off their hands.

Private Ibáñez was happy to be got off their hands. Quite simply, he detested the Military. The son of Spanish republican immigrants, he had lost his first girlfriend, Helena, when he was just seventeen. That had been eleven years before, in 1971, when Helena had had to make a hurried exit from Argentina and head to Uruguay, sought by the police of the military dictatorship of the day. The inexperienced pair of adolescent militants was unable to surmount the separation. Months after her flight, by now already signed up as a student at the *Universidad de la República* in Montevideo, Helena met one of the leaders of the *Frente de Liberación Nacional Tupamaros*[3] the greatest and most successful urban guerrilla moment in the history of South America. And that was that. She wrote him a letter.

Ibáñez's sadness lasted for many years.

In 1976, when he was already 23 and under a new military dictatorship that was even worse than the previous one, he himself had to leave Argentina just in case, in order to avoid ending up like one of his cousins, disappeared and probably murdered by the Argentine Navy. These were the kinds of things that had shaped the story of Ibáñez's life.

Until his arrival in the Falklands, the graduate had always thought that the Argentine Army was made up exclusively of institutionalized numbskulls, out-and-out military coup proponents and a not inconsiderable number of psychopaths. During 1981, an extended stay at the Army Cavalry School, an aristocratic army barracks in the Campo de Mayo, had confirmed that undoubtedly jaundiced view.

But the Falklands had changed a lot of things, such as his view of the notoriously bad-tempered Staff-Sergeant Ibrahim (alias *El Turco*). In the day-to-day life of the barracks, he had been one of the many minor nightmares afflicting the troop: the classic depressive so common among the Argentine NCO class, the sort of character that could not function when sober, and became sadistic and hit the soldiers when drunk.

There was something about Ibáñez, though, perhaps his age or his attitude, which made it impossible for Ibrahim

3 *FNL-T.* The Tupamaros National Liberation Front.

to pick on him, and he therefore had to look for other victims. For his part, Ibáñez never imagined that he would one day owe his life to such a complete bastard.

But, regretfully, this had been the case for about a week or so. During the air strikes on 1 May against the BAM Malvinas[4], Ibrahim had suddenly thrown himself on top of Ibáñez, covering him with his gigantic, soft, bear-like body. As he struggled to get out from under that lump of flesh and Antarctic clothing, Ibáñez heard for the first time the shrapnel from the 147 anti-personnel bomblets of a cluster bomb.

He didn't hear the dozens of explosions that occurred around him: they were too loud to be experienced as anything other than pain in the eardrums. He merely sensed the flashes, although he certainly heard how the steel balls struck and pierced the iron sheeting of the hangars or strafed the soldiers' tents, which were erected right next to the runway.

By the time he'd managed to get out from underneath Ibrahim, there was a scattering of dead bodies all around.

IV

A confused Ibrahim couldn't really say why he had done that; leaping on top of Private Ibánez, some ponce with a degree who seemed to look down on everything as if from another planet. Nor did he really ask himself. The truth is that he hadn't known he had the guts to do something like that; he'd surprised himself. Pleasantly surprised. Since the invasion of the Falklands he felt better than he'd felt for the last 30 years or so.

---

4 *Base Aérea Militar Malvinas*, the Argentine military air base in the Falklands.

Firstly, they'd put him back to doing his old job. He was co-piloting one of the Huey helicopters at the BAM Malvinas, which occupied the old Port Stanley aerodrome on the Freycinet peninsula. The place was about fifteen kilometres away from the nearest drink, which was behind the bar of the equally inaccessible Upland Goose Hotel, in Puerto Argentino (previously Port Stanley). The Goose accepted Argentine pesos, but charged a bomb and was therefore only frequented by officers.

Moreover, there had already been an air force second lieutenant – almost a god – who had ejected from an A4 fighter and who Ibrahim himself had pulled out of the water in heavy seas, while in danger of plunging, helicopter and all, into the waves.

And now he had just saved a university graduate. His subordinate, and a graduate in some sort of nonsense to do with loonies, but definitely a creature from a higher sphere than his own. Now, how about that…

Finally, Ibrahim surprised himself by thinking seriously about giving up the booze for good. Or even of leaving his wife. Or perhaps both at the same time. Although that would mean having an IFS on his record, the much-feared Irregular Family Situation rating, which means that your colleagues stop talking to you and you can forget about ever getting promoted again. Mad ideas, brought on by these islands where everything was turned upside down, but nevertheless seemed somehow better.

You were better.

And some blokes, who'd enjoyed a much better life than yours, owed you their lives.

This time they were going to rescue a civilian Argentine fishing boat, the Narwhal or something like that, strafed, bombed and sunk by some Harriers, Calligari had told him as they were strapping themselves in. The shipwrecked crew, it seems, had managed to radio an SOS.

An enormous Puma helicopter had left half an hour before them, much bigger than the Huey, with room for about fifteen or twenty survivors, at a squeeze. Typical orders from the generals there in Puerto Argentino; go out and die.

Almost as expected, they had just lost radio and radar contact with the Puma. Ibrahim didn't keep the details in his head, it was just another search and rescue mission to him. They were nearly all like that, with no guarantee of returning, but this one seemed a bit worse. He was thinking about that little brunette tart in the bikini, and feeling anguished. What would happen if he asked Private Ibáñez for the letter? And if he, Ibrahim, then called her when he got back?

Would she be too young for him?

Too high-class, perhaps too good-looking?

Was it ever too late to change?

V

While Ibrahim was torturing himself by his side, Calligari was grappling with his own demons as he flew. Overweight and prematurely aged, he was already over 35 and he had never had a single noteworthy attribute, aside from his bad luck and his good appetite.

His appetite had made him fat before time and his bad luck meant he was still stuck in the rank of first lieutenant at an age when his old military school peers were now captains or majors. And on top of this general misfortune, his resentment only seemed to fuel his appetite.

But now, in the islands, he had discovered unlimited courage. Courage more voracious than even hunger itself, which had appeared from nowhere and now controlled him almost absurdly. He was the helicopter pilot who was always available to rescue pilots from the sea. He now hungered for danger.

And always available to go out meant just that: always. It didn't matter if those shot down were Argentines or British, or that the radar operator at the Puerto Argentino Centre for Information and Control suddenly plotted a new patrol of three Harrier jets arriving at 400 knots from radial 48, and shouted that they had to turn around or get blown to hell, for fuck's sake.

In cases like that, Calligari would become the nutter who disobeyed, the one who never turned around. He'd fly glued to the surface of the water, burying himself in the valleys formed between the waves, to evade the Harriers' Blue Fox radars…and he'd carry on. His commanding officers didn't know whether to put him in the cooler or give him a medal: they hoped the British would help them avoid making the decision. Half in jest, half in admiration, a few of his colleagues started calling him "Mission Impossible".

His previous nickname had been "Meat with Eyes".

And you had to have eyes in the back of your head in this job. By 9 May, the British had already attacked rescue missions several times. The British couldn't give a damn if their targets were flying criss-cross over the sea, in the rec-

77

ognised shipwreck survivor search pattern. They were quite clear about that: shuuum! Missile, then ba-boom! And off to find another one. One less chopper for the Argies!

There was nothing personal in it. Given the impossibility of ground transport in those impracticable islands, the first country to run out of helicopters would have to surrender through hunger and a lack of ammunition. It was just business.

But, notwithstanding all that, if a plane went down, Calligari would dash to his helicopter, here I go! Unable to stop himself, hating the very lack of courage that might enable him to resist such courage. And his damned courage would drag Ibrahim and Ibáñez along in his wake, with their own similar internal screeches and doubts, and they would climb aboard without a word.

As Calligari's eyes and hands went through the motions of verifying the route, checking speed, position, exhaust gas temperature, liquid levels, the altimeter, the pitch, wind direction, drift and other vital statistics of machine and navigation, the officer tried to wipe from his mind the image of that splendid female who had written to Private Ibáñez, and whose poisonous bitch beauty caused him such pain. Was he really going to fall in love just on sight and with such a slut? What an idiot! Was he really going that mad?

Suddenly, he felt jealous of Ibáñez, the conscript he was carrying behind him. Young, slender, vain, undoubtedly brave, with that bloody university degree, a bachelor, with no bosses to answer to, the owner of his own life…

But hang on, Calligari, said Calligari to himself. We must be getting near the sinking zone. There were oil slicks and, here and there, and signs of floating debris.

VI

Now the Huey was flying obstinately on its search-square pattern while it struggled against the wind. Each time that it completed one transect and turned 180 degrees, the wind attacked its flank, first on starboard then on port. It was hard even to fly in that avalanche of air. Below, the southern waves rolled monotonously, like an immense chain of mountain peaks.

It seemed about to rain, just like it always seemed about to when it wasn't raining, and about to get dark, although it also always seemed about to get dark in the islands, with their background aquarium lighting. On the horizon, beyond the shadow that suggested Soledad Island to starboard, the sea's emptiness was perfect, inhuman. Silence reigned aboard the helicopter.

Silence is fundamental to search and rescue operations. One needs all one's attention focused on the visual plane in order to discern a tiny shipwreck survivor in an orange dinghy, in the midst of that vast watery waste, where the only signs of life are the low-gliding acrobatics of a few large, serene and ferocious albatrosses.

But the sea, apart from some debris that floated here and there, was impassively empty. The Narwhal had evaporated. The survivors had evaporated. Lieutenant Fiorito's Puma, which had been in the zone only half an hour before, had also evaporated. Things were not looking good.

Calligari fought down the temptation to use his radio and report the situation, and thereafter be ordered to return. With the British Fleet presumably near, that would have been

like striking a match in a dark and empty dance hall and saying: Here I am!

There were further reasons for maintaining silence,
even regarding internal communications. The headphones
can sometimes act as antennae, and translate the radio-fre-
quency pulse of a fire control radar illuminating you into a tell-
tale zung-zung-zung. Then you know you're screwed, and
you have to search desperately for the missile's luminous
nose as it approaches from one side or another, in the hope
of dodging it like a bullfighter. Olé!

A faint hope, of course. A Huey helicopter is about as
agile as a grand piano. It's not made for bullfighting. That
zung-zung-zung heard so far out there at sea really means
"Bye-bye, Argy!"

But you want to hear it anyway, said Calligari to himself,
because if you're going to die, you've a right to know about
it beforehand. And to beat yourself over the head for having
never had a female like that brunette from Vicente López.

VII

The Narwhal, it was subsequently found out, after the
avalanche of lies that were published on both sides, was carrying fishery workers, who had nothing whatsoever to do with
the war. The ship had been commandeered by the Argentine
Navy, with the crew included, and placed under the command of a first lieutenant in order to spy on the British Task
Force. The latter did not, it seems, take kindly to the idea of
being spied on.

The Harriers had seen her with their radars. They approached once more that fucking fishing boat that we've al-

ready kicked out once, and what the hell is she doing here again right next to the zone where we've got our aircraft carriers and our ships under repair? Makes me feel like blowing her out of the water. Ask for instructions, Peter. At 09.30 GMT, Admiral Woodward answered back from HMS Invincible: "Sink her."

Hours later, after a thorough strafing, with one dead and dozens injured on board, as well as an unexploded bomb incrusted in its destroyed side, the Narwhal somehow continued afloat. She was listing badly; the sea was flooding in through the side and surging over the deck.

At sunset the enormous British Sea King helicopters appeared, and the lads from the SAS scaled down on ropes like black gorillas, herded the crew with their rifle butts and winched the sailors off flying through the air, in bunches of three, with their hands tied, hanging over the sea and kicking in terror in their harnesses. In the helicopters they were heaped together with kicks and blows into a corner, and made to sit with their heads down and their hands behind their necks. And anyone who dared to look at his captors got a smack in the gob for his trouble.

Everyone aboard the Sea Kings seemed pretty angry, including the pilots. They're all spies, all this lot. We should have let them sink with the boat. The lads down there are risking their necks on a pile of junk that could sink at any minute. Yes, you're right, but Woodward's orders were different. Board the ship and capture the crew. The Admiral's playing the Good Samaritan, is he? Leave it out; we all know what he's like: he's a submariner. Those blokes neither give nor expect any mercy. Yes, but have you seen that bloke Brinks?

The spy? That's right, SIS or something like that. It makes me nervous just seeing his fat arse over there. Well, Brinks wants the Argies to interrogate them, he said so, I heard him. Listen, if any of those frightened idiots have any valuable information, I'll kiss my own arse. And yours, while I'm about it. Steady there, that's it, we've got the last three! And now what? We get our lads back when they've finished their job and we're out of here.

It seems that their task was to search and empty every corner of the boat that hadn't yet sunk and Bingo! they found the Argentine Naval Officer's code book. So they took it. Then they mined the ship with delayed fuse bombs, abandoned her to her fate, sent the correct SOS according to the codes and left in their immense flying machines. Then the boat exploded, boom, ba-booom, and it sank, slooorp, pluuff. Someone was bound to come.

And someone did. Firstly, along came a Puma, which appeared clearly on the radar screens of the Class 42 destroyer, HMS Coventry. Shall we hit it, Captain? Fssshh, out flies a Sea Dart missile and a minute later and thirty kilometres away, the Puma disappears all at once from the screen. In that dark operations room, lit only by screens and dials, the people slapped each other on the backs and, on the orders of Captain Hart-Dyke, served themselves coffee with a splash of rum.

And twenty minutes later, as night was falling over the empty sea, the alarm bells rang again on the Coventry because, inexplicably, another dot appeared on the radar screens. It appeared and disappeared. They must be flying very low; the idiots think that we can't see them. Are these damn Argies mad, or what?

In silence, full of forebodings, Ibáñez, Ibrahim and Calligari were about to arrive on the scene in their old Huey.

VIII

Private Ibáñez glanced at the photo of the brunette from Vicente Lopez every now and then, God knows why. He thought that he'd put it safely away in his pocket. Yes, he had. Then why had he taken it out again?

The photo was trying to tell him something. A woman so beautiful, yet so crazy. How resentful, how evil she was. To write such a letter to some poor unknown and, probably, doomed young man. The letters that arrived in the Falklands came, 99% of the time, from primary school kids: they bore an overdose of patriotic tenderness and stupidity that could thaw even the most sceptical pacifist sentiment, Ibáñez's included.

But that bitch's letter...Kill lots of Englishmen! My measurements. My telephone number. How sadistic, to offer herself like that to someone who doesn't know if he's going to get his leg over ever again. One of the ten thousand fools condemned to act as targets for the British, in that second wave of massacre of Argentine youth perpetrated by the Military Junta, known as the Falklands War.

Tired of himself, but stubborn, the graduate Ibáñez, ever the psychologist, tried, as always, to counter the tedium and the fear of that search by examining his motives for turning up at that party. When one has his head stuck in the lion's mouth, one begins to think with stunning clarity. There's no time to lie to oneself, because time is running out. And this time, his reasons for coming became suddenly quite clear to him. He saw at last that he was no different from Ibrahim or Calligari, or from any of the other nameless blokes who discover, bit by bit, the drug of courage. In its purest and most powerful form.

What had Ibáñez been doing on the day Ibrahim leapt on him and crushed him to the floor, protecting him with his body? Shooting at the Harrier that was flying overhead, about to drop an enormous one-ton cluster bomb!

A psychologist from Buenos Aires, weighing 62 kilos, standing straight and shooting it out toe-to-toe with such a monster, unprotected and armed only with his ridiculous *FAL* rifle, while dozens of professional soldiers, for kilometres around, are flinging themselves to the ground in desperation. In that instant, Ibáñez's life mattered not a jot to him, if he could only bring down that fucking airplane, the English bastard in it and the whole shebang.

When Ibáñez and Ibrahim were finally able to stand up, it was still going on all around them. Amongst the many bodies writhing with pain, giving off smoke and spouts of blood from their burnt and broken clothing and screaming for their mothers, there were still some little unexploded bomblets. These would explode later, when their fins were touched by medics and rescuers.

Immune to the horror that surrounded them, Ibáñez and Ibrahim smiled at each other, equals at last, each one saying to the other with a mere look that the other was a brave, and if they ever had to die together, then it would be worth it just for the company.

But what on earth was he thinking of? Was Ibañez the graduate's head now so full of drivel? How many of Ibáñez's own militant comrades had that obedient human ruin Ibrahim shot, following orders, during the period 1976-1979? Isn't that what had made him an alcoholic? Or even more of an alcoholic, at least?

Ibáñez had survived those years as a political refugee in England, a country he loved deeply. Busking on the London Tube, playing Argentine music, had enabled him to eat once a day, which was all he needed. With all of his British culture, he had fitted in very well with those circumspect but very humorous people. When two years passed without anyone kicking in the front door of his parents' house in Buenos Aires, he became convinced that they were no longer searching for him, or that maybe they hadn't been looking too hard in the first place.

He began to think about returning home, but couldn't make up his mind. He loved England, including its women, its pubs, its music and literature, but he couldn't stand living away from his own country. It was during this confusing time that his first girlfriend (years without a word from Helena – she was alive!) rang him unexpectedly in London. From Uruguay. She said that she had to see him, it was urgent. And he didn't ask her or himself any questions. He used up his savings and came back. To her.

He spent a month with Helena in Montevideo, until it became clear that it was useless: too much time had gone by. She had another life, an almost impossible life, and there was no place for him in it. Her husband, the Tupamaro guerrilla chief, had been a prisoner since 1973. He was still alive, but stuck – and this was no metaphor – in the bottom of a cistern in the Paso de los Toros barracks, subjected to regular torture sessions and refusing to die. It took Ibáñez a month to realise that he could never compete with this absent god. And although she, devastated by her solitude, took refuge in her first boyfriend so that she could sleep free of nightmares, the thing tore him apart.

So, Ibáñez plucked up his courage and like someone who amputates his own arm, said goodbye to Helena, crossed the Rio de la Plata and went back to his true homeland. And after that he got his degree in three years.

That return was the beginning of a series of foolhardy, useless acts of bravery that had more than likely put him in the firing line of a British missile. But each act had had its own reward.

The troubled return to Argentina had given him back his own language, the twisted humour of Buenos Aires dwellers, the Sunday afternoon dinner-table family conversations, the bars in which he had first fallen in love.

After anguishing that he was nothing compared to that hero in the cistern, facing up to combat, when he could have deserted, had given him a bitter calmness.

Standing up to a fighter jet armed only with a rifle had brought him another major reward: the moment when, alongside Ibrahim, they had watched together, with savage joy, the flaming descent of that same Harrier into the water many kilometres away. They had hugged and danced like kids.

From the smoking, radar-equipped 20mm and 35mm anti-aircraft batteries that surrounded the landing strip could be heard the faint, faraway cries of Viva la Patria! For a few moments they almost drowned out the screams of the burned and wounded in the tents and hangars all around them.

What did all these dead matter, if Ibáñez had contributed, albeit symbolically, to bringing down that plane? What did it matter that Ibáñez couldn't give a shite about those treeless, useless islands, surely uglier than anything else on earth?

What did it matter if he and thousands of young Argentines like him had been sent to die there by a Military Junta whose ineptitude was matched only by its immorality, capable of inventing that war in order to distract the population and avoid paying for six years of continuous atrocities, State terrorism, thievery, spiralling debts and of the conscientious and comprehensive destruction of the basis of what had once been the most progressive, educated and equitative society in South America?

And, yet, there was Ibáñez, the fool, happy, risking his skin for these fucking islands, shouting "Long live the Fatherland!" and celebrating the death of some Englishman who might possibly have applauded him on the Tube five years before. There he was, exchanging hugs and compliments with the same bunch of military scumbags he had utterly detested a month ago. Scumbags who now considered him one of their own for that very brainless act of standing up, armed only with a *FAL*, to a jet fighter that zoomed in spitting death. Scumbags whom – worse still – he was beginning to love desperately.

Whilst the Huey, moving sideways like a grenadier's horse, was fighting with its turbine to stop the wind from plunging it into the sea, and Calligari kept the helicopter as low to the surface as possible to try and remain hidden, Ibáñez reviewed bitterly the triumphant growth of his own incoherence, the destruction and fall of an entire system of ideas and values for which, years ago, he had been prepared to die.

He did not regret this destruction. He felt intensely alive.

He heard a faraway zung-zung-zung in his headphones and he remembered a custom poem that someone had published in La Prensa in 1969, after the Americans had landed on the moon for the first time. "Today, every man is happier or braver", said the verse, which summed it all up.

What did it matter if it'd been the Americans who'd got to the moon first? A single man's bravery illuminates Humanity as a whole. And for that reason, an enemy's bravery illuminates you. It makes you happier, and braver. How true!

Calligari and Ibrahim exchanged glances, seemingly alarmed. Had they seen something? The Huey made a sharp turn, tilted on its flank, turned its nose towards Puerto Argentino, on bearing 238, accelerated its turbine and began to make zigzagging evasive manoeuvres, although nothing could yet be seen outside.

Private Ibáñez, terrified, had grabbed hold of the mounting of the MAG machine gun with both hands to avoid falling into the void. He saw the photo of that adorable, hysterical Argentine chick fluttering away triumphantly until it was lost in the wind, and in the sea.

Despite the urge to throw up, his thoughts had accelerated to an incredible speed. He thought about his current lacklustre girlfriend, Ana, whom he loved very much, but not in that searing way that, he now understood, was life's only justification.

He thought about Helena, whom he had loved in that way, and who he would probably keep on loving for ever.

Ibáñez imagined the impossible: getting back safely to Puerto Argentino, surviving the war, returning to Buenos Aires, crossing the Rio de la Plata, kicking that other bloke out of Helena's heart, and winning her back. Winning her back through sheer courage because he, Ibáñez, was now also a brave.

In a few seconds, he imagined an entire life with her. He slept for thousands of nights at her side. They had children together and he watched them grow.

Those were the things that Private Ibáñez thought about on the afternoon that they killed him.

Chapter Four

The Tale of the Ancient Mariner

Today I met a man who has been living in hell since 1982. It is a real hell, a steel cave full of torrential fires and smoke, and sinners burning like howling torches that totter and twist and fall in the darkness.

That hell existed on earth for a few minutes in the war operations room of a destroyer that was bombed and then sank. A commonplace episode, occurring in a minor war.

But since then, in the form of a flashback, that episode has happened again and again at least three, and sometimes four, times a week inside the mind of my new patient, Mr. Bernstein. And it will probably continue to do so until his death.

As more than twenty years have gone by since the Falklands War, I surmise that this exhausted man has gone down to hell at least 7,600 times. How many more descents await him?

Not many, I believe. According to his Israeli clinical history – the previous one was lost or never arrived from England – Mr. Bernstein has made at least one suicide attempt here involving drugs, and another physically traumatic one, all in May, nearly coinciding with subsequent anniversaries of that event. A rather impressive *curriculum mortis* for an internment that has now lasted on and off for two years, and in which he has spent more time inside hospital than outside.

Each episode left him all played out and when he entered intensive care, and there was little hope for him. My intuition tells me that the thing inside him that saved his life back in 1982 has twice saved him again. But I don't know what it is. Will I have time to find out?

And, above all, will finding out serve any purpose?

The Abrabanel is a large psychiatric hospital in what is to him a strange country, making it full of unlikely characters. But even here, Bernstein is an outsider. He shouldn't be here among us, and by that I don't mean only in Israel but the world, or this world, at least. He did not die, but he already belongs too much to death.

I begin this course of therapy with little hope. I've lost more than one patient with severe post-traumatic stress, chronic and compounded by endogenous depression. With its old wars this country - my new country - produces quite a lot of them.

But Bernstein's illness is an imported product. He is, too. Affable, extraordinarily circumspect, the man is not at all Israeli, despite his good command of Hebrew. He is totally British. Grey-haired, fragile and intelligent, he has surely seen too many psychiatrists fail in his case to place much belief in our art.

Well, perhaps in that we are alike.

Even so, when we met today, he made an effort to pretend that he was slightly interested in me, even though his heart was discreetly somewhere else. Bearing in mind the darkness in which he dwells, this pretending is rather more than courteousness. It is pure goodness. If he can, Bernstein will try to kill himself without hurting my professional pride.

He is a decidedly good person. He deserves another life. Or any life.

I shouldn't be here, either. And now I am talking about Israel, not the wide world. I have a very Jewish surname and profession, as well as Israeli citizenship, which I easily obtained some years ago, as did Bernstein.

I am, however, utterly Uruguayan. The wonder is that it has taken me several years inside this nuthouse to really understand this. And when I say nuthouse, I'm not referring to this hospital or Israel in particular. I'm referring to the entire, incomprehensible Middle East and its codes of behaviour. What am I doing here?

Now, in the silence of my Kfar Saba apartment, while I listen to the gurgling plumbing from an upstairs apartment and the faraway murmur of a TV, I spend too much time thinking about that ice-cream parlour in Maldonado that I was fond of frequenting at night. Overfond, probably.

Except for an enforced exile that lasted far too long, I lived continuously in that provincial city after I graduated in 1968, and I used to go to that ice cream parlour nearly every night. It was always open, even in winter and when it was raining.

I still hadn't met Helena, who was several years my junior. I got my baptism of fire in the small and ruinous psychiatric wing of the local hospital. I was so young and foolish, however, that not only was I going to cure schizophrenia, I was also going to cure injustice. I got my baptism of fire on that front, too. The furious "Tupamara Spring" had begun in Uruguay, and we were part of that spring.

Three blocks away from here, near the new Kfar Saba train station, there was also an ice cream parlour that I used to visit at night, both in honour of my old Uruguayan customs and to get out of the house a bit. But it was blown up five months ago by a fifteen-year-old Palestinian girl. She blew herself up with an explosives belt hidden under her jacket. She had left Kalkilia, the nearby enigmatic and overcrowded Palestinian town that I can see from my balcony. She took a taxi to Tel Aviv and was driving down our Weizman Avenue when she saw the ice cream parlour and must have thought that it was a very rewarding target, and less complicated. She told the driver to wait and entered. She managed to kill quite a few youngsters no older than herself.

She also killed my night life.

Nowadays, except for a sexual "service" every Monday night with Maia, the head nurse in another department and owner of a lovely pair of Ukrainian knockers – and nothing else – I don't go out. I drink iced tea here, in the living room, to get through the heat of another dreadful, dusty Hamsin night, and I re-read some books that were important to me in their time to see if they'll become important again, and I note down the significant events of the day in a Word file.

I named the file "The Logbook". Is this Bernstein's influence? Do I identify so strongly with our naval patient? Undoubtedly. Joking aside, I do wonder what strange course of events has led Simon Bernstein, ex-weapons officer on the destroyer HMS Coventry, to this country, to his current situation, to my consulting room.

All that we know about him is contained in his clinical records. He emigrated from England (how absurd - nobody emigrates to Israel from England!). He worked for three years at Tadirán, an arms manufacturer closely linked to the Ministry of Defence. Apparently he was very good at his job: he designed anti-aircraft systems for ships, it seems. And he must have been earning a lot of money.

A few days ago, the company doctor at Tadirán — Schlutzky, whom I know and who owes me few favours — confessed to me by telephone and with some hesitation (everything is top secret in that company) how Bernstein had managed to lose his position. He had suffered two successive panic attacks.

Even though the Shin Bet observes and vets the technical and management employees in the defence sector, in search of weaknesses and oddities, it seems that my new patient managed to keep his hidden for several years. Until he suffered his first, irrepressible attack during work hours, that is.

After removing him from his office babbling nonsense for a second time, the security people spoke to their bosses. Shin Bet got involved and, between them all, they decided to kick him out. They gave him a very generous severance package, they reminded him of everything that could happen to him if he ever spoke about his work there and they fired him. That's it, as far as Schlutzky's story goes.

Then, don Simón, obviously fearing worse to come, beat a path to our door here at the Abrabanel, on his own initiative. He got off a bus, and asked to be admitted to the Psychiatric Emergency unit, where he was listened to by my Israeli colleagues, all of whom have a very Yankee and neurochemical background. He told them he'd probably kill himself if he stayed at home. He told them about the flashbacks.

He also told them that he was vegetarian, as if this were tremendously significant. That was indeed noted down in the clinical history, but insufficient importance was paid to this fact. That, I believe, was to have grave consequences.

The Ancient Mariner was admitted immediately and to bring him out of his hell, they pumped him full of Fluoxetine, Paroxetine and every new selective seretonin re-uptake inhibitor approved by the FDA. That, alongside art therapy and music therapy. The veteran took his Prozac, he painted seascapes (actually quite good ones, in fact) and he listened to Beethoven. All in a very disciplined way.

Months went by, without result. The extreme nightmares continued.

Then, as a Plan B, my colleagues began adding Lithium Carbonate, then Beta blockers, then atypical antipsychotics. I don't know if the fires in Bernstein's private hell got any better, but they certainly didn't get any colder.

After a year spent in hospital, calm and desperate, he somehow managed to gain access to the medicine cabinet. And he started stealing, little by little, enough Digitaline tablets to give King Kong cardiac arrest.

And he took them all together.

That happened, I was able to confirm with a little checking, on the same day that a great barbecue had been organised in honour of the director of our department, who was leaving. The entire first floor of the hospital was suffused with the smell of meat, burnt on the outside and raw on the inside, just in the way mandated by the regional lack of gastronomical culture. Nobody noticed this fact. It's not noted in his record.

Bernstein was transferred to the nearest general hospital, already in coma, where he suffered a bradycardia that appeared to give him no way back.

But as the days went by, his hesitant heartbeat - now it's beating, now it's not – refused to stop altogether. And, finally, the intensive care people realised that the man intent on dying possessed a heart intent on living. And they watched him wake up and, with genuine British embarrassment, beg forgiveness for any trouble caused.

So they took out the tubes, the probe, the electrodes and the pacemaker and they sent him back to the Abrabanel. All yours, gentlemen!

Where the Russian doctors, of whom there are many since the days of Gorbachev, were waiting for him, licking their lips, among them my boss. The Russians here can be divided into the following, in my opinion: those who faked their Jewish credentials to enter the country, those who bought a degree to enter the profession, and those who did both. They are little more than a torture mafia escaped from *Glasnost,* that threatened to limit their sadistic practices.

So, the Russians got hold of Bernstein by the ear, tied him to a bed and gave him electric shocks until the cows came home. This practice is so common here that the patients themselves, when they feel that their Windows is about to crash, come and ask for *jashmal* (electricity), and calmly queue up in front of the ward where it's administered (under anaesthesia).

It is like a routine for them, a kind of mental and emotional reset of little importance. The treatment changed the Ancient Mariner's hell a little bit, at least. Daily electricity instead of nightly fires. And when they'd given him twelve sessions with no response whatsoever they put him – and this was criticised for being an outmoded approach – into an insulin coma. The new director, a cowardly sort, approved it although he pulled a few faces

But as soon as Bernstein (who was quite used to living in a coma) woke up, he went back to his old ways. Two months later, with his symptoms "clearly in remission", as my Russian boss wrote without blushing (may Yahweh and Allah confound her!), he managed to get into the laundry without being noticed, where there is an unbarred window.

I must mention at this point that don Simón knows the hospital better than any of us. His organised engineer's brain possesses an exact map of its spaces and its time-tables. He knows at what time such-and-such a nurse turns off the machine and goes to smoke a forbidden cigarette in the patio, or gives his wife a call from his cell phone, leaving an unbarred window, for example, unguarded in the laundry. A window we were all, except the maintenance staff, unaware of.

There were four floors from the window in question to the pavement. And ancient mariners, even if they have a dead albatross around their necks to atone for existential guilt, like Coleridge's...cannot fly.

After a few more days in the Bat Yam Hospital Traumatology Department, Bernstein woke up wracked with pain, and with heaps of screws and titanium plates holding together various broken bits of skeleton and perforating his skin.

In spite of the pain and disappointment, however, he did not seem any less embarrassed, less intent on dying or less polite than before.

Always the best boy in class, my future patient complied religiously with the physical exercise and Kinesiology routines laid down by the physios. Bit by bit, they started to take out the most conspicuous lumps of iron. He walks almost normally now, although with a residual limp. I suppose that he wants to make a fresh attempt and feels that a certain degree of mobility is needed to guarantee success.

They have heightened the security measures for him. He's a tough nut to crack.

They hate him here, although they don't say so, from the director down to some nurses. He's the living testimony of institutional failure and the proof of organisational shortcomings, which are really very few, but nonetheless real.

I think this man makes them uncomfortable for another reason. In this urgent and brutal country, his politeness is not easily understood or tolerated. The Russian has already had him tied to the bed a couple of times and left him there for days, staked out under video surveillance. She did it supposedly for his own good, but really it was a demonstration of authority. Suck on this, you English bastard. And think twice next time before you answer my diatribes with your polite ironies.

When the psychiatric tribes at the Abrabanel had run through the catalogue of therapies and out of patience, they threw me the case. The Uruguayan émigré who speaks awful

Hebrew, the one with the Freudian formation – or psychodynamic, as they say here - the idiot who, instead of shouting at the patients, sits down and talks to them as if they had something to say. They probably said: put all the Martians in together.

It's been like that ever since I got here. I get all the discarded patients, the ones who resist therapy, the ones no-one else wants.

The first thing that I did, after the preliminary interview, was change his bedroom. It's true that on the second floor, where he is now, he's more at risk from falling, but he's also further away from the dining room. And therefore from the kitchen, with its periodic whiffs of incinerated meat.

Whiffs that surely induce memories of people getting roasted aboard a destroyer in flames.

I mentioned this to him and to my colleagues, to justify the move. My colleagues smiled with comprehension. I suppose they think that you have to give nutters a bit of leeway (referring to me, not my patient). Bernstein, however, listened but hardly smiled. Yesterday I noticed that I had passed some sort of admissions test with him.

This is routine. My Israeli patients almost always examine me first. At least half of the nutters here, and this is interesting, think they are Jehovah, or perhaps his Messiah. This is a common regional symptom of various delirious pathologies. And Jehovah always puts those who believe in him sternly to the test. Just think of the sacrifice of Isaac, if you don't believe me.

In Uruguay, an agnostic but patriotic country, some of my mental patients thought they were Artigas which, as any

Uruguayan knows, gives them a lot more points than Jehovah on the megalomania scale. But the loonies there examined me less.

During yesterday's administrative meeting, one of the internees, a blond lad, about 22 years old, very handsome and vain, stopped and showed us the palm of his hand with the fingers pointing up, as if to say stop.

"Now have you noticed? Have you finally noticed?" he boasted.

I coughed a little and asked him what it was that we were supposed to have noticed.

He looked at his palm, mystified, but what he saw there made him smile.

"There it is! Can you see it? A luminous number One. That means that I am The One."

"One more idiot who thinks he's the Messiah," a man of about forty in a grey overall whispered to me, winking his eye. "Listen, numbskull," he stopped, addressing the young blond man. "If you're the Messiah, then what the hell does that make me?"

It's like that here most days.

I must admit that I'd like to have another Artigas or at least an Obdulio Varela or an Alfredo Zitarrosa, to place in the minor pantheon. Madmen and gods from my own country. Oh, how I miss them.

Being in charge of so many tired Jehovas and their not less worn-out vicars doesn't really bother me. I don't cure them, obviously, but sometimes, if they are good people, we become friends.

And in a place like this, it's nice to have a few.

■ II ■

It's been three weeks now that don Simón has been in my care. I think I've managed to get him to like me. And that is due, I've discovered, to the fact that he thinks I'm vaguely Argentine.

I explained to him, with a map and by other means, that Argentina and Uruguay are two different countries, with divergent histories and traditions. I told him that in the nineteenth century they even fought out brutal wars. That the *Porteños*, which is what the Argentines were called in those days, even laid siege to Montevideo. I told him that Uruguay exists as such because it broke away from Argentina, and quite rightly, too.

But there's a part of Bernstein, irrational but operative, that continues to think that I'm an Argy of sorts. Of whom he has killed, according to him, his fair share. And some in a most vile way, it seems. He offers no details.

It was a mistake to try and make him see his mistake. Today I am trying not to oppose his belief in my immanent Argentine-ness. The man finds, I believe, certain solace in this. If he killed so many Argies, and I'm an Argy, making friends with me might be a way of expiating old wartime sins. The ones he continues not to talk about.

The slightly absurd relief that my pseudo-Argentineanness gives him can also be expressed in measurable terms. i've managed – after a few arguments with my Russian boss – to eliminate those unnecessary anti-delusional drugs with which they used to keep him psychologically flattened, so he wouldn't be a nuisance.

Nobody doubts that Bernstein will one day get his way and kill himself. "History is on his side," as we used to say. But does that give us the right to turn him into a vegetable? Not in my book. The Russian prefers him to kill himself doped up, so that nobody can recriminate her for anything. My position is that if our mariner is going to live a few more months or a few more years, then he should at least do it awake.

That's the way it is. I give Mr. Bernstein some benzodiazepines, which at this stage of the game are like water to him. I give them more to tranquilize the Russian than to tranquilize him.

My real activity with the Ancient Mariner is limited to long daily chats. We stroll together along the central street where I usually park. It's surrounded by pavilions and low buildings, some in use but others abandoned and in ruins.

Although we don't talk about very much, as we wander we are mysteriously tuned in to each other and thus manage to avoid diverse interferences. Bernstein, from the other patients cadging cigarettes (he smokes two or three Dunhills a day); myself, from the ironic half-smiles of some colleague or other. I don't even see them anymore, although I do see the approving wink of the Argentine odontologist.

We only have a therapy session if it's raining. Because if we stay quietly in my room, I feel that a part of Bernstein's mind gets up, heads for the door and tiptoes out.

Heading for the South Atlantic?

That's where the secrets are. That's where the key is that would release him from hell.

That's what I tell myself. Got to study this.

▬▬▬▬▬▬ III ▬▬▬▬▬▬

I've been searching for that key for two months.

I always leave Bernstein's session until last, he is my final patient of the day.

That usually means that I'm tired, I know. And my old custom of leaving the hospital at six o'clock in the afternoon has gone west. This isn't too important - there's no-one waiting for me at home, except on Mondays.

My wager is that at some point we'll go beyond the level of amiable but insubstantial chit-chat and enter into what happened, what happened to him. And when that happens, I won't have to cut short – due to the arrival of another patient – a critical, illuminating moment.

That illuminating moment, however, seems a long way off.

I am very patient. But English people have had many centuries of cultural practice in avoiding intimacy. I religiously respect his reticence. But I wait in vain.

What happened, in objective terms, I have investigated for myself anyway, on the Internet. I've even bought a load of books on the subject, which I read by the shelf full. All hells interest me, due to my profession and because I lived in one myself. But this one, Bernstein's private hell, especially attracts my attention.

That hell was formally inaugurated on 25 May 1982. On that day he was serving in the operations room of the HMS Coventry, a destroyer sailing in formation with the frigate HMS Broadsword.

Apparently, the British Class 42 destroyers are fast, agile ships, with a displacement of 4,100 tons. They have terrific long-distance anti-aircraft capability, thanks to their Sea Dart missile system, which can knock out a plane 50 kilometres away. They are the sailing equivalent of a sniper.

The Class 22 frigates, however, are smaller but equally fast ships. They defend the "penalty area": they prevent aerial attacks close in. For that purpose they use a different system, the Sea Wolf, which functions more like a bodyguard with a sawn-off shotgun. The Sea Wolf fires short-range missiles that, according to the manufacturer, are capable of stopping in flight not just a plane, but also another missile and even a cannon shell.

The manufacturer, as far as I know, is neither interned nor medicated.

This duo, the sniper and the bodyguard, turned out to be rather less invincible than Britain expected. It's well-known that the Argentines destroyed several of these ships in their air raids, albeit it at a dreadful cost.

As a Uruguayan militant, I paid little attention to the Falklands War at the time. Not because I wasn't interested in all things Argentine, but rather because when that war broke out I was spending my eighth year in prison, in a subterranean cell measuring one metre-sixty in diameter – it was really an old, dry cistern – in the Paso de los Toros military barracks, due to my militancy in the MLN-T. I spent nearly eleven years in that cistern.

In 1982, in spite of my being an old lag from the 1975 vintage, the officer gentlemen still tortured me whenever they could with *jashmal*, although without anaesthesia. Other times they used crueller methods. And they didn't do it to get information out of me, which they knew I wasn't going to give them, but just to get even with me for my silence, or to break the monotony, or to earn their corn, I suppose. I mention this to explain how I was rather distracted that year, as I was in the ones before it and the ones after. Furthermore, what happened in the far-off outside world filtered down only in tiny droplets into my fourteen-metre deep hole, where no sunlight, not to mention newspapers or radio waves, ever penetrated.

Now that I'm not a Uruguayan, a guerrilla or a prisoner, I'm becoming Israel's most expert psychiatrist on the South Atlantic War. And the only one, because all of that business matters here very little. Here they've been living for more than half a century with an even dirtier and more detestable war, with an even gloomier prognosis, where little fifteen-year-old girls explode to kill twelve- or thirteen-year-olds.

Anyway, enough of that. Let me continue with the tale of what I suppose happened to Bernstein. I still don't know. But I'm beginning to understand how and why.

IV

From almost the very beginning of the conflict, the Argentine Air Force bore a grudge against the destroyer HMS Coventry, and with good reason.

The records show that, on 3 May, one of the Coventry's helicopters participated in the attack on the Alférez Sobral, a tug belonging to the Argentine Navy that was searching for the crew of an Argentine bomber shot down the day before. After being hit by two missiles, the Sobral managed to stay afloat, turned into a pontoon, full of dead and wounded. It miraculously managed to crawl into port, days after everyone had given it up for lost.

On 9 May, the Coventry was up to its old tricks again and, with successive missile strikes, shot down a couple of Argentine helicopters that were also on a rescue mission over Choiseul Sound, a large stretch of water to the east of Gran Malvina, or East Falkland as the gringos call it. Lieutenants Fioritto, Calligari and all aboard were lost whilst searching for the crew of a fishing vessel, the Narwhal, already sunk by the British for spying. Nothing more is known about the rescuers' fate.

Two weeks passed and on 21 May, during the landings at San Carlos, Admiral Woodward decided to deploy the Coventry-Broadsword formation as a "missile trap" between the landing zone and the mainland. A good spot: this was the only route available to many of the attacking Argentine planes, and they could be made to pay a heavy toll there.

Hidden between the mountainous islets to the northwest of San Carlos, the British duo's radars directed the intercepting Harriers against the incoming Argentine fighter-bombers. They also did some turkey shooting of their own at the planes coming back, already shot to pieces, from their encounters with the bulk of the British fleet. With their fuel tanks riddled with bullet holes, the Argentine survivors had to reduce their fuel consumption at any price, which meant leaving sea level, where they were practically invisible to radar, and seeking an altitude of 18,000 feet or more.

During these desperate ascents they were located by HMS Coventry's radar, and, a minute after being acquired on the screen, the Argentine pilot would be transformed into light and heat above the sea, without even having noticed that death was winging in from behind at twice the speed of sound.

Between 23 and 24 May, according to the British Admiral Sandy Woodward, the Coventry-Broadsword team downed five Argentine fighter-bombers. The Argentine Air force denies these claims, but was furious anyway. On 25 May, a day of patriotic significance, they went out looking for revenge.

I've gone over subsequent events with a fine-toothed comb: there are hidden clues here. The Coventry-Broadsword formation had been spotted some twelve miles northeast of Pebble Island (Isla Borbón for the Argentines). With just a two-minute interval, two squadrons of decrepit A4 fighters took off, intent on giving the Brits their breakfast, dinner and tea.

Typically, technical problems forced two planes, one from each squadron, to return to the mainland: both machines really belonged in a museum. The remainder carried on ahead. Following the usual Argentine strategy, at about 160 kilometres from the Falklands the fighters descended until their bellies almost touched the sea, which in autumn and in those latitudes is a lonely, violent place to be.

The first squadron, known as Vulcano, didn't realise they had a Sea Harrier interception patrol on their tails. In other words, that they were fucked.

The British pilots were getting ready to shoot them down like partridges when they suddenly turned around and left the zone, under the instructions of Captain Coward of HMS Broadsword, who obviously didn't live up to his surname. The gringo wouldn't risk shooting down a Harrier by mistake, and rather chose to brave the attackers into a showdown using his Sea Wolf missiles instead. He believed the manufacturer: he trusted in them.

Unaware of their good luck, the Vulcano squadron (a certain Captain Carballo and one Lieutenant Rinke) continued flying full tilt at sea level and headed straight for the Broadsword, whose captain had so kindly just saved their lives. The Broadsword was sailing in line behind the destroyer.

Some British lieutenant on the frigate, convinced of his own immortality, took two unforgettable photos from the ship's deck.

He took them while his comrades were shooting at the Argentines with the ship's main guns, the anti-aircraft battery and also with rifles and pistols, or were throwing themselves face down on deck, because something was going seriously wrong. Both photos show two very small planes flying close together, wings tilted and just metres above the dark sea. They are charging between high cone-shaped spouts and columns of spray caused by fire from the anti-aircraft guns. Pebble Island stands out behind the planes, tall and grey.

The photo explains why the aforesaid Carballo and Rinke are alive today: the Broadsword's confused Sea Wolf radar couldn't distinguish between the weak echoes of the planes and the stronger ones generated by the rocky island situated fifteen miles behind.

Suddenly, the computer picked up the attacking pair, but interpreted it as a single object (the pilots were flying that close together). The missile launcher turned and aimed at them. One of the pilots, Carballo, according to the record-ings, was shouting "*Viva la Patria!*" knowing he was about to die.

When it was just about to grant him martyrdom, the Sea Wolf perceived that it was really two targets and not one and, due to the conflicting information, took offence and, demon-strating typical computer system perversity, locked down. As the British looked on in horror, it switched to "Off", cancelled the attack and ordered its missile launcher to retract.

All this happened in four or five seconds. Of the six 250 kilogram bombs that Carballo and Rinke dropped on the Broadsword, only one hit the target: it fell short, bounced up-wards, penetrated the hull and, in its upwards flight, turned the helicopter parked in the hangar into aero-naval purée. It then sailed out through the hangar roof and fell harmlessly into the sea.

That was the third miracle of the day, and the last. The Broadsword was now dead in the water, with no engines and several incipient blazes aboard, albeit with its weapons systems intact. That was the beginning of a longer series of magical or tragic coincidences, depending how one looks at it.

The second Argentine squadron, Zeus, (First Lieutenant Velasco and Second Lieutenant Barrionuevo), had treacher-ously hidden behind the giant rock of Pebble Island, instead of attacking frontally. The blow could now fall from anywhere.

Suddenly, Velasco and Barrionuevo leapt over the is-land at 900 kilometres an hour, raced down the slope close to the ground and sped towards the ships on a suicidal bomb run, a straight line of ten kilometres (or 45 seconds) during which time everything that could be fired at the planes was fired, including the rifles, machine guns and pistols that were handed out even to the cooks and stewards aboard both ships. Everything. And this time the Broadsword finally managed lock its Sea Wolf fire control radar on the new attacking duo. This was the moment when the hell in which Bernstein is still trapped was ordained.

In previous days, the captain of HMS Coventry, David Hart-Dyke, with his predilection for killing Argentine rescuers, had proved himself to be a heartless bastard. On that 25 May, he proved two more things: that he was also a brave and an idiot.

Instead of letting his bodyguard ship, the Broadsword, do the job she was made for, Hart-Dyke ordered one of the Sea Darts to be fired at the advancing planes. But the Sea Darts, a sniper's weapon, are no good over short distances and the planes easily evaded the missile. So Hart-Dyke ordered the Coventry to accelerate brusquely towards the attackers, as if to run them over with the bows, before suddenly turning his ship, as agile as a launch, in a shower of spray. And he left the Coventry interposed between the Argentine planes and the damaged frigate, to protect her.

It makes you want to sing *Rule, Britannia*! Brave, but stupid.

Because, instead of protecting the Broadsword from the planes, Hart-Dyke was protecting the planes from the Broadsword. If the frigate had fired at that moment, her missiles would probably have blown the Coventry to hell and back. The destroyer was standing full-square in its firing line.

Almost colliding with the Coventry, the pilots Velasco and Barrionuevo emptied their 30mm machine guns into it, dropped their bombs, and flew over the ships in a blur, just managing to clear the antennae and escaped, turning and zigzagging close to the waves. Three bombs, Velasco's, penetrated the ship.

The following is a quote by Admiral Sandy Woodward, Task Force Commander, whose memoirs I purchased.[1]

"(The bombs) went into David Hart-Dyke's ship and they all exploded, one of them in the computer room. Nineteen men were killed instantly.

David remembers not the impact, just the heat, and then he blacked out from the blast. Coming to, still in his Ops Room chair, he found himself in total darkness, in a room full of acrid choking smoke. Then he became conscious of light, flickering light, and to his horror he realized it was people burning, their clothes on fire, like screaming candles.

'I thought,' he once told me, trembling again at the memory, 'that I had died and this was, literally, Hell.'"

And there we have Bernstein's hell, described as such on the printed page.

So literal, so real.

■■■■■■■■■ V ■■■■■■■

The rescue helicopters came from the faraway landing beaches. They performed amazing feats in picking up the survivors. The aerial photos taken at the time show the Coventry as a sort of forest fire in the middle of the sea: only the antennae are visible. They are just sticking out over a cloud of smoke that bellows out at water level, swept by the Patagonian wind. And all on a beautiful sunny afternoon.

---

1 One Hundred Days. Admiral Sandy Woodward with Patrick Robinson.

The Coventry is an oven that's roasting human flesh. And Bernstein is inside there.

Seeing the photos and imagining the stench, you can understand why he's a vegetarian.

In just 25 minutes HMS Coventry went up like a tinder box, listed, capsized, exposed her belly to the seagulls and went under.

If you've had any experience helping survivors of fires on that scale (which I have) you'll know that inhaling just a little smoke can kill, either straight away or days later, from chemical pneumonitis. Many British must have died during or after that sinking.

Woodward, who is not medicated either, declares there were nineteen deaths out of a crew of 270 men. I reckon the Admiral is lying through his teeth: the British must be covering up an absolute slaughter-house. Twenty years later, I have to extricate Bernstein from this hell, before he becomes its umpteenth victim.

VI

Three months and a week with Bernstein have gone by. The more I delve into that war, the more my patient's initial courteous scepticism towards me and my profession evolves into relative appreciation.

For me, at least.

I surprised him today by showing him a splendid aerial photo of his old ship, which I got from the Internet. As we studied it, I said, without thinking:

'I think it's a beautiful ship. One of the prettiest I've ever seen. A work of art.'

'That's what I thought when I boarded her for the first time, back in '77, on her maiden voyage,' he answered, also without thinking, with the photo in his hands. His eyes were watering slightly.

I had never seen him so moved. Bingo.

There was a moment's silence. I always converse with Bernstein in English, and I realised that for an Englishman a ship is feminine. So, he really did say: "I boarded her". The HMS Coventry was a pretty girl. Ships are women.

Just then I made a second inspired comment.

'I read the other day that Velasco, the Argentine pilot that sank the Coventry, said something similar. He called her "majestic". I don't know if he used that exact same word, that's just the word that occurs to me. That raked bow has such grace, strength, elegance. It makes me think of the statue on the Daru staircase at the Louvre; The Winged Victory of Samothrace. It's...' I searched for the right words. 'It's just…very pretty,' I added, rather lamely.

Bernstein smiled with tired irony.

'It seems that we now share an old flame, doctor.'

As I correct these notes, the significance of that comment becomes apparent. It was the origin of my next move.

Helena.

VII

Seven months with Bernstein have now passed, and one since the "restructuring" of the Abrabanel began. That's the euphemism the Ministry of Health uses for its drastic service cutbacks. The old recipe: close down consultancies, get rid of staff, farm chronic patients out to other hospitals – where they're not wanted, either – and reduce costs in hospitalisation and medicines.

The plague of neo-conservative economists, the same treacherous technocracy that destroyed public industry, healthcare and education in Uruguay and Argentina, first with the Military in government and then without them, has now struck here. It's eating away at this country, which was founded by socialists and where growth and prosperity were based on fairness. The results, it seems, will be similar.

The neocons got in here because of distraction. They govern as a result of the eternal war waged since the days of Begin against all Palestinians. A war we continue, and will continue, to wage.

We spend so much money on occupying other people's lands with our own religious lunatics, we spend so much on those fanatics to save them from being, understandably, eaten alive by the Palestinians, that military expenditure ends up cannibalising the State. Then it's bye-bye free schools and hospitals, bye-bye high salaries, bye-bye full employment, and bye-bye Israel. But because of the atrocious Palestinian bombing campaign, nobody notices that the country is being stolen from the people.

The clergy now unashamedly calls the shots here. A clergy that sits religiously scratching its bollocks in the rearguard and dispatches our little adolescent soldiers to serve in the occupied territories. Meanwhile, our civilians get killed by little Palestinian girls who blow themselves up on buses, or in our cinemas, ice cream parlours, and cafeterias, in revenge for being evicted from their villages by the army.

Here in Israel they are stealing everything from the people, and the thieves are Jews, but your average working man isn't interested: he's too busy hating the Palestinians. In his idiotic opinion, he thinks that the time of the fat cows won't return until his Palestinian neighbour is given the only land he deserves - somewhere to bury him. That's why he voted, and continues to vote, for Sharon, who's not exactly a lean cow himself. They see it all so clearly.

A barbarous and fanatical culture, outwardly expansionist and inwardly exploitative, is emerging from the innards of the just and cultured country I thought I was escaping to, when I could no longer stand my own country of origin.

A month ago, I had some argy-bargy with six or seven of these oafs. They were dressed (it was 41 degrees in the shade!) in long, black frock coats, as if this were the eighteenth century, and we were in the mediaeval ghetto of Linz. I was in a square in Jerusalem, quietly reading Idea Vilariño under the shade of the trees. They came up and asked me to sign some sort of petition. I declined without reading it - quite courteously, I thought.

Their leader harangued me. I squared up to them – I was up for some trouble – and asked them if they were the Polish Jihad. They looked at me in astonishment. One, the oldest, spat at me. I insulted him. Then another, younger one, pushed me. Another even dared to slap me in the face. I immediately put him down with a knee in the goolies. The rest all jumped on top of me. I was giving and taking just like in the good old days, but at the end of the day, they were younger and there were more of them. I was saved by the police.

We are becoming just like our enemies.

I now feel like I did in Uruguay, when they released me back in 1985: bewildered and futureless. All of a sudden, I was walking around like a man lost, like an exile in another country, which was a pale caricature of my own. And I couldn't recognise anybody, not even my old left-wing comrades. My brave companions of yesteryear had become so absorbed into the system during my time in the shade that even the word "expropriation" now frightened them.

But to return to the current situation: they can't throw me out of work – yet – because I have a long-term contract, and a signed document here is still worth something. But I'm under no illusions. In the long term, in Israel just like everywhere else, the chain breaks at its weakest, or its most foreign, link. With my Tarzan-style Hebrew I'm still just another immigrant in the eyes of the *sabras*, in a country where, for the first time in history, there is high unemployment and immigrants are surplus to requirements.

The Abrabanel is also surplus. It has one well-maintained building, endowed with the supreme honour of air conditioning, but the rest of the structure is obsolete and going to ruin. The hospital, however, still houses the last Holocaust survivors, forty-odd elderly people with differing degrees of serious mental problems, all exacerbated, in general, by Alzheimer's. And that makes it, for the time being, a national symbol and therefore safe from the bulldozers.

But the country's main motorway has just extended a tentacle this way. There's now a slip road just half a block from the hospital, which is a mere stone's throw away from the sea. Meaning that the value of this place has gone up... Can you imagine the sharks already dreaming of knocking the hospital down and building a shopping mall?

That's what a rather sad Tubby Mielnik told me, the last time we chatted.

======= VIII =======

Mielnik doesn't want me to leave.

He's a colleague from New York, quite a bit younger than me (he's about 48). He's very religious – meaning right-wing – but only on the inside: no goatee beard, no side-locks, no phylacteries up the sleeves or astrakhan hats. Free of any visual affiliation to the Polish *Jihad,* Mielnik patrols the hospital in a shirt and tie, smart trousers and moccasins, just like me. Meaning, in stark contrast with the rest of our colleagues - a bunch of *schleppers* who wear ragged Bermudas, flip-flops and T-shirts in clashing colours. They look like their mothers have dressed them.

People here don't dress, they just throw their clothes on. Mielnik and I have very different takes on life, but if we dress with a certain decorum at work, it's out of respect for the older patients and for those of European origin, who are the majority. And in spite of spending almost their entire lives in a country where clothing is little more than a uniform (I'm a soldier, I'm orthodox, I'm a colonist), these crusty old Ashkenazim are comforted by the fact that the doctor appears to be, well, a proper doctor.

Wearing a tie is similar to not shouting at them, which we don't do either. And that is what sets our professional approach apart.

Both Mielnik and I know that courtesy works.

IX

Eight months with Bernstein. Will we complete an entire year? I foresee that they'll medically stabilize him, so they can discharge him without feeling guilty. That way he'll no longer be a burden on the State. And he'll kill himself in peace, somewhere else.

It's strange how I think so much about him and so little about myself. It's not that I'm not important. I'm not bothered about losing this job, even though I've done it very conscientiously for ten years and it's enabled me to belong to a profession. And to a country.

I've lost much more important things in my life than this job. The thing is, I don't want to leave Mr. Simon high and dry.

I could almost say that we were friends, but for his part it's the kind of English friendship that, as Borges says, begins by excluding confidence and very soon omits even dialogue.

Clinically speaking, we are pretty much where we started. The striking thing is how well we get on. I'm in no hurry to see therapeutic progress. Faced with the economic crisis, I concentrate on living with what I have. And lately, the only real things in my life are my conversations with this chap.

Maia and I don't meet any more. She's not at all religious, but she's very right-wing, like many local working-class people. That was never a problem, but three weeks ago I rather stupidly turned on the TV when we were having breakfast. Some of our Apache helicopter gunships were on the news, firing at something in the streets of Gaza.

Maia said they should throw napalm instead and burn the lot down, and an argument ensued that neither of us could, or wanted to, stop. The end of a strictly sexual relationship, with no ties, but that even so lasted for two years. I suppose we'll both regret it. We got on well together, albeit in between the sheets and from the waist down.

I've managed to get Bernstein a weekly four-hour exeat every Monday, although he must be accompanied. As the man is alone in this country, I provide the company, in my newly acquired free time. So every Monday, after six o'clock, we wander though the markets and cafes of Jaffa, just a few minutes' bus ride away.

We inhale the scent of the Mediterranean amidst old walls, stairways, squares and walkways, all built of stone. At the end of the streets you can see the port. Small and ancient, Jaffa unconsciously resembles Colonia del Sacramento, but this Israeli town smells like…well, I swear it smells female. And the stone is an adorable golden limestone, instead of our harsh grey Uruguayan granite. There's a park, from the heights of which we get an aerial panorama of the tourist liners and the other ships resting peacefully at their moorings, which sometimes inspires Bernstein to explain some principles of naval design to me.

We wander, exchanging monosyllables, through the local flea market, the Shuk Hapishpeshim, surrounded by old furniture and bric-à-brac, engulfed in a gesticulating mob that buys and sells absolutely everything and negotiates by shouting. Another street – I don't remember the name – has stalls with mountains of water melons, pyramids of apples and hills of rosy grapefruits. Or tables shimmering with recently-caught fish.

We avoid the occasional shish-kebab stand (and thus the smell of burnt meat). And, lost in a tide of tourists, hardly speaking, we immerse ourselves in the tranquil stridency of this ancient site.

Now that I no longer have a girlfriend, I sometimes find myself telling Bernstein things about my previous women in some half-empty bar, the sort one chooses because it doesn't look like an appealing target for a suicide bomber.

I've spoken to him several times about Helena. I don't suppose I can avoid it. It's been years since I talked to anybody about her. Not even to myself. Helena has been silenced inside me for years, smothered by my work. And outside of work, by a procession of circumstantial Maias, a range of Israeli females with whom there was always sex of a practical rather than a passionate nature.

When I decided to leave Helena, in 1987, I did it by making one of my typical Pharaonic decrees, those drastic decisions that have been the key, and the bane, of my life. And of the lives of those who've shared mine.

I decreed that Helena should become my lover back in 1971, when she was my youngest student – not quite seventeen – in the Humanities Department at the Universidad de la República. I was a junior lecturer and she was just some Argentine chick, informally registered as an occasional student. It didn't bother me too much that she was just passing through or that she had an Argentine boyfriend who, it seems, was rather affected by my sudden interference in their relationship. At that time I was ten years older than those two little fools and, between work and my clandestine militancy, I used to sleep just three or four hours a day, waking each day without knowing whether I'd be alive at the end of it. Alongside my serious, dedicated comrades, I dictated who was to live or die with impartiality. I reckon I destroyed that charming little couple in the same way one runs over a toad in one's car, hardly even noticing.

And I squashed that couple for good, because in 1972, after a short absence in which she fell out with her family, she came back to Uruguay to look for me. I didn't take her seriously at first. But she quite quickly became a solid and responsible member of the leading cadre, and she rose rapidly in my column. And when, due to her pure persistence, something akin to love began to grow between us, I decreed she would be Uruguayan for all time.

With supreme selfishness, I invited her to the party just before the imminent coup d'etat, when Bordaberry, the Military's puppet, overthrew Pacheco, the head of what was a mere police state. That's right; I made her a Tupamaro chief at the height of our military and political debacle, when comrades were falling at a rate of dozens a week, prisoners, dead, or both. Welcome to the Titanic, young lady. And Helena climbed aboard anyway, fully aware it was sinking. And it wasn't just out of political commitment, which nobody of my age can nowadays convey to anybody under forty. It was also for love.

After the defeat, in 1973, we were by now living in hiding, disguised as traditional smallholders, on a tiny plot of rented land in Rio Grande do Sul, when my third decree made her my wife, complete with legal documents and everything. And in 1975, when I thought that they were no longer looking for me and that the *MLN-T* had been wiped out and swept away seemingly for ever, my name came up in someone's notebook. Someone who had fallen captive very late on. And so I fell as well.

121

There, in my Brazilian isolation, I had no idea what was coming. If I had, I would have fled, or resisted. They were Uruguayan police, plain-clothes, operating under the aegis of the Brazilian dictatorship. They drew up in three cars, burst into my field by surprise and dragged me, with blows and kicks, bleeding and shocked, off the old tractor we'd strived so hard to buy. And thus began my own descent into the inferno. Luckily, Helena was away that week in Buenos Aires, visiting her family, trying to patch things up. That was what saved her.

And saved me. A neighbour warned her and she escaped immediately to Paris, knowing they'd surely go after her in Buenos Aires. She wasn't wrong. I don't know if I'd be alive today if it wasn't for the campaign she organised on my behalf from Europe, between 1975 and 1979, at embassies, international organisations, Lutheran churches...she didn't leave a stone unturned. Eventually, the military had to acknowledge my existence and I was no longer a disappeared person, who could be rubbed out at zero cost. I found all this out later.

It's not surprising, therefore, that in 1987, a year and a half after returning from my own private hell and now a free man, that I should make my fourth Pharaonic decree: to forget her for all eternity, for reasons I won't go into for the moment. I erected a pyramid on top of her and I left. Bye-bye. But now it seems that the pyramid is starting to tremble, and cracks have started to appear.

The mummy is still alive. The Pharaoh's wife rises from the dead beneath the stones.

I've been dreaming about her constantly for over a month. Sometimes I feel the imperious need to talk to someone about her.

I could try to explain this old problem to my colleague Mielnik, who is, above all, a cautious and respectful person. But my political prejudices won't let me.

I've seen the wives of the religious Jews here. They're subjected to such Martian concepts, they're so orderly, strict and cautious that it makes me wonder what poor Mielnik could possibly know about real women. How can I explain my imperfectly-stifled love for a girl who at the age of eighteen left her family and her homeland and became a *Tupamara* at the height of our extermination, when the average life expectancy of our cadres was just two or three months?

But I'm saying that being unable to talk with Mielnik is my problem, not his. He's so perceptive he can see through fog.

A week and a half ago I entered the hospital, my face green. It was half past eight in the morning. I went straight to the bathroom, hardly saying hello. Mielnik watched me, concerned.

I'd just spent an hour and a half stuck in the morning "pkak", a word they give to our rush-hour traffic bottlenecks. It means "stopper" in Hebrew. From Sunday to Saturday, from half past seven to eleven in the morning, the inevitable pkak blocks all traffic along the country's north to south axis. More than fifteen kilometres of pkak. The country's main motorway, turned into a car park. And the July sun up above, hammering ferociously down.

I'd heard on the radio of my Subaru, a car I bought precisely because its dual radiator system is overheating-proof, that a pizza restaurant had been blown up in Tel Aviv. Eighteen dead, the radio said. Without counting the injured, who would die over the coming week, or the Palestinian kid who'd blown himself up, I thought.

So I turned it off, and put some music on instead.

In spite of the car's air conditioning, however, I was feeling dreadful when I got to the hospital.

I came out of the toilet cubicle at last. I was cleaning my face in the sink, checking that there were no vomit stains on my tie, when I saw Mielnik in the mirror. He'd come in to see what was wrong with me. He looked at me, without speaking.

"It's this pizzeria thing in Tel Aviv, Meilnik. Haven't you heard?" I said. I believe I still had tears in my eyes.

Mielnik sighed, with biblical bitterness, before fixing me with a serious look.

'Yes, Mario. They told me when I arrived. But one shouldn't get overly distressed,' he said, in his American English. He knows how bad my Hebrew is.

'But I can't stand these things anymore!' I suddenly exploded. 'I can't stand these answers. For fuck's sake, I can't stand you and I can't stand this country! I hate this damned heroic death cult, both theirs and ours. It's all shit, a gigantic pile of shit, Mielnik! And I'm not saying that because I'm a saint. Because, believe me, in my past life I kidnapped policemen and bumped off torturers. But I never, believe me, never ever planted a bomb. I never killed an innocent, never killed anyone by chance!'

Mielnik thought carefully about my words, surprised. He suddenly knew more about me than the rest of the country put together. Then he prepared his answer:

'I didn't know you'd done these things, Rosenfeld. And I grieve for your soul. But what you don't know is that there's a Plan behind all of this. At least here."

'A political plan?'

'A Divine Plan,' he explained, his patience wearing thin. 'For each one of our dead, my rabbi says that a hundred miracles occur. A few years ago, Hamas killed one of our congregation, Schlomo Hojman, a good lad. So we did a survey amongst us and it was true: we counted exactly a hundred miracles, all occurring within the following 24 hours. Not one less. But those miracles pass unnoticed in the daily chaos, and nobody draws the strands together, because only God can see them, only God moves them and understands them. A lady who is dying from cancer is suddenly cured, inexplicably. And a soldier on leave from the Tzavá turns up in Kathmandu, when he was given up for lost in the mountains. Or some inconsolable widow falls in love once more. A hundred miracles, Mario. For every murdered Jew. I don't pretend to understand why, but the balance is favourable.'

Marvellous, isn't it? That meant we could expect at least 1,800 miracles that day. I didn't know what the hell to answer, I was too shocked. Mielnik is a good psychiatrist, not only because of his decency and politeness, but due to his thorough training and his fine, totally scientific mind. Or that's what I thought.

'I see that you don't believe me, Mario,' he observed rather disappointingly. 'You're an atheist. You don't believe in these things.'

'I do what I can, Mielnik. I like to keep an open mind, but not so open that my brains fall out.'

He laughed. He'd enjoyed this answer, which I'd stolen from Carl Sagan. But then he became serious again.

'The thing is that you're not from here. You can tell a mile off that you're not from here. I'm telling you because I appreciate you. And I appreciate you because you're a good doctor, one of the best here, and a good person to boot. But you're not from here. I know; you're going to say that I'm not, either, because I was born in New York."

'Well, that's almost a suburb of Tel Aviv.'

'But I am from here,' he said, ignoring my quip, 'and I do believe in these things. And that's why I'm going to stay here. The Palestinians also believe in their Allah and their mullahs and that's why they'll stay, too. At the end of the day, it'll be just us and them, each with their own weapons and their own faith, just like in biblical times. The others are fallen leaves in the wind, here today, gone tomorrow. A shame. But they are failed Jews, people of the Diaspora, rootless. You're just passing through, Mario.'

Tubby Mielnik patted me delicately on the shoulder and left, leaving me alone in front of a mirror that seemed to confirm his opinion. Fallen leaves.

That's the other reason why I'm not going to talk to Mielnik about Helena. Without having told him too much, Tubby already knows too much about me and, moreover, his appraisals are too close for comfort. A fallen leaf...I'm not in the mood to be analysed.

So, the only victim within reach who will listen while I vomit and purge myself of this internal Hellenistic disorder is, therefore, Mr. Simon. The good thing about Bernstein is that he gives me his complete attention and makes no comments, until I finally get embarrassed at laying bare my internal disasters to one so circumspect, change the subject and opt instead for ritually insulting Sharon and the damned colonists.

I'm rather surprised, and a bit frightened, by my verbal incontinence. Am I getting old? So quickly?

Like today, for example, I was having a coffee with Bernstein, (aromatic Turkish coffee – so strong you could almost chew it) in a little bar that overlooks the sea, when our attention was drawn to a twenty-year-old brunette.

She passed hurriedly in front of our table, in a soldier's uniform, with glorious tits and ass, wearing a blue beret that couldn't quite contain the torrent of black locks that cascaded down her back. She disappeared in the crowd, anxious to get somewhere or meet up with someone – a lover no doubt – with her M4 carbine slung over her shoulder, muzzle downwards.

That's when I got over my embarrassment and spoke about Helena, because she used to look like that soldier, although even better. I talked and talked. About a girl who – despite myself, I came over all epic-lyrical – was like the Winged Victory of Samothrace, like a warship.

I swear I said that, *oy vey iz mir*! The things an old lecher is capable of saying on a Monday evening, when he's left without a Maia or the like! Luckily, I managed to shut up. There's a way back from everywhere except from ridiculousness.

Bernstein merely smiled a little, with a touch of melancholy but with no irony whatsoever.

X

Ten months since the relationship with Bernstein began. I thought they were discharging him, but it seems they're discharging me instead.

The letter that arrived at my house last week from the Ministry of Health states that from next month the Hospital no longer needs my services, that it's grateful, blah, blah, blah.

I'm not the only one. Incredibly, for the first time in history, doctors from the Abrabanel are forming small, comical picket lines that – I swear – are trying hard to pass unnoticed with their tiny protest placards in front of the hospital gates, rather than making themselves seen and heard.

They are eminent professionals and they seem uncomfortable in the role of protesting proletarians to which they've been driven.

They splutter to the TV or radio station that comes to interview them, not really knowing what to say. Really, they are ashamed at what's happening to them. So am I. So much so that I, who've never missed a protest since I was a youngster, watch everything from outside, as if it were a film, unable to join in with anything.

Something like that happened to me in Uruguay when I came out of prison. To me, the great militant, my country's public life seemed so remote, like an old, mediocre silent film.

This new attack of passivity still troubles me, though. Some of those who hand out fliers at the entrance are permanent ward staff: their jobs are safe and they know it. They are acting in solidarity with those, like me, who depended on a contract and have had to pack their bags. They are fighting my fight. Why aren't I there with them?

I don't know. It is unimportant. I am unimportant.

What lies in wait for my un-sacked colleagues? Either a progressive decline in working conditions, or they'll end up like us.

And what's in store for those of us who've been sacked? We're mostly all immigrants who speak primitive Hebrew. With that linguistic handicap it's obvious we can't rely on a private practice to save us.

Within a year or two, my sacked colleagues' destiny, when they've got over their depression and the severance pay is running out, will be in the ranks of the medical neo-proletariat, that Yankee invention.

They'll work for fourteen hours a day for appalling salaries in the myriad pseudo-psychiatric private clinics that are springing up everywhere, like mushrooms, around the previously magnificent fallen tree of Israeli public healthcare. On their rare days off, these veterans will do ambulance shift-work to make ends meet, fighting for crumbs with the newly-arrived youngsters.

They'll scheme and stab each other in the back to get a "flexible" position, meaning one with an unregulated timetable, in aesthetic and cosmetic medicine chains that resemble shopping centres. They'll bid farewell forever to their expertise in mental health and carry out medical check-ups and do shifts at the sports club swimming pool.

They'll do laser hair removal for the pure-blooded Mediterranean *sabras*, dark women who've always been fat, and will be fat, but who no longer want to be hairy.

The truth is that there's very little future ahead. The important things are all behind them, or us, rather. They've made us old.

The only thing left will be to remember for the rest of our lives that we were once respected psychiatrists in the top institution in the country. One day we'll throw all our course and congress-attendance certificates in the bin. And we'll go on a binge lasting two days. Or several binges. Or we'll get an ulcer. Or a divorce. Or all of that, and a tumour.

Aagh...I've been through this before.

Oh, no, not more of the same old shit, please!

My severance pay is quite high. It equates to about 100,000 US dollars. At today's exchange rate, I could buy – or so my friend Waldemar tells me by e-mail – a two-bedroom apartment in Montevideo, well situated in Pocitos or even close to the Rodó Park, which would serve both as a dwelling and a private consultancy.

And what was left of the cash would be enough to live on for a year, while I begin to find my feet again in the depressed Uruguayan labour market.

If I have to live in a psychiatric ambulance, doing night shifts like a new boy, I'd rather it were in Montevideo than in Tel Aviv. At least, between emergencies, I could eat a *chivito*[2] in La Pasiva, or share a *maté*[3] with the driver. And we could grumble together that Peñarol have let too many players go to Spain, and that there are no good ones left.

Other friends, who never left, send me e-mails saying things have been so destroyed for the last twenty years that the situation can't get any worse. It might, I tell myself, but at least I'll be surrounded by my own people. And, who knows, things might even get a bit better, if the *Frente*[4] wins the elec-

---

2 The typical Uruguayan sirloin steak sandwich.

3 Also typical: an invigorating herbal infusion made from *yerba maté* sipped from a gourd.

4 *Frente Amplio*: The Broad Front, a left-wing coalition.

tions. I don't believe it will, but who knows? I couldn't give a fuck, of course, but who knows? Who knows?

This place, however, once marvellous, is on its way out.

I also spoke to Helena, my ex-wife, by telephone.

I'm coming back to the old country, I told her.

She wasn't surprised. Nothing surprises her.

I don't even know if she was moved or not. She's got another life now. She lives with some other bloke. A better one than me, I'm sure.

The other thing is that I don't know how to break the news to Bernstein, either. I believe that's the only thing bothering me. The rest is relief - tiredness and relief.

And a tremendous sense of grief. I've really come to love this place.

XI

Eleven months now since I met my final patient.

I'm chatting more and more to Helena on the phone. I think I've lost control of things and that she has too, because she still hasn't told me to stop calling. My telephone bill is getting a bit steep.

The bloke she lives with seems to raise no objections about my intrusions, which began cautiously once a week but are now daily. He's either very wise, or a perfect idiot. I couldn't care either way.

Helena and I have also begun to correspond by e-mail. Now that I've got so much time on my hands, I write her very long mails.

I get laconic answers. Short but precise.

I'm astonished by the emotions that come up when I see I've got an e-mail from Helena. The trepidation with which I open it, the fear of seeing the words: "Don't write to me any more".

That could happen at any time. It will happen.

But it hasn't happened.

Yet.

I keep visiting Bernstein, in my capacity as surrogate relative. I pop round to see him every Monday and we go for a wander. On foot now, because I sold my Subaru for whatever I could get for it. My flat in Kfar Saba is also up for sale. As soon as it's sold, I'll take the money and run.

The doctors at Abrabanel who survived the first wave of lay-offs now treat me with a friendliness they previously concealed. Part of this new-found goodness is shown by the fact they haven't altered Bernstein's therapy. He is now formally in Mielnik's care. Tubby pretends to check the medication and signs the papers, but he really leaves things to me.

This is one fiction on top of another. There's not much left to do or undo. The Ancient Mariner isn't really in anybody's care, except God our Father's, if he exists. He's still in his nautical hell, which he revisits two or three nights a week in flashback.

From what I can see, the albatross is his survivor's guilt, permanently hung around his neck. I swear I won't leave Israel without having cut that string, however I have to do it. Although if the cut I have in mind goes wrong, it will be Bernstein's throat that ends up slit.

You have to take risks sometimes. I always liked taking risks.

I feel almost young again.
This is madness.

━━━━━━━ XII ━━━━━━━

They've given me my severance pay, which I've paid into the First Republic Bank of New York, which has branches here and in Montevideo.

This meant I could pay cash, without recourse to my credit card, for a business-class ticket and an expensive hotel for Helena. She told the bloke who lives with her (alright, her husband) that she was going to a congress. The dickhead believed it. In her field, childhood traumas, Helena is known all over South America. With her duties as a deputy and her many congresses, there are years in which she's travelling more than she's at home. And it so happens that there's a paediatric conference taking place at that hotel, although not important enough to attract contributors from South America.

In this underhand way, I'm bringing Helena over here to clear up more old stuff than she suspects or believes possible. Down in the bilges, I can feel my old demons roaring. All of them.

Helena.

━━━━━━━ XIII ━━━━━━━

Helena still loves me. She came for that reason, and to tell me that. She still loves me – in the same way that she probably still hates me – but she's very much in love with the other bloke, her current husband, so there's nothing I can do. She came to tell me that, too.

I already broke up one of her relationships, back in 1971. I know I paid for that later, and in spades. And I know that when it comes to her new husband, a pretty decent bloke by all accounts, I haven't got a hope in hell.

And I've got no chance because the truth is I was never very good to her before and I don't think I'm a better person now than I was in 1987, when I left her.

She doesn't believe I'm any better, either.

And she's right.

A reencounter of this kind between two people, whose relationship has been so dreadful and even despicable, can really only be a magical parenthesis. That's why I put Helena up at a sumptuous hotel, disconnected from its surroundings.

I really wanted this to be like a film, with little to do either with my current life or hers, or with our previous life as a couple, or with most people's day to day reality. I wanted to give us back, even if just for a moment, our golden age, if we ever had one. An age that, if it existed, wasn't just our youth *per se*, but the time before we'd fucked up our lives through ignorance, fear, pride, egoism and cruelty.

After fifteen years of not seeing or talking to each other, she got off the plane and the illusory but overwhelming happiness of the first 48 hours of the reencounter occurred. Then we started to calm down, our feet on the ground, and recovered a sense of perspective that, although not bitter, was at least realistic, without hopes or recriminations.

We'd already said all that could be said about the fuck-ups we'd made - an area in which I win hands down. And she'd forgiven as far as a woman can forgive (which is not usually very much).

Even so, I let a few hours go by.

We got dressed. After a silent breakfast and a Dominican cigar that I smoked alone on the balcony of our suite (she told me she gave up smoking years ago), I then talked to Helena about Bernstein. Rather, I dared to talk to her about him. I told her what influence this man had had in her life. And why I wanted them to meet, and what for.

Her face became graver as I explained my story and gave her the dates and the details.

Then she asked me to leave: she wanted to be alone. That was something Helena always used to do years back, when we were a couple, when she needed to cry or gather her wits.

I left, feeling like a rat.

XIV

And, in effect, I am a rat. But a rather wise one.

For a day and a half Helena gave no signs of life. I had to struggle not to call her at her hotel. I left the ball in her court. I spent the entire day by a phone that refused to ring, trying to read online newspapers, listening to music and doing crossword puzzles in English.

After what seemed an eternity to me, and what for her was probably very sombre deliberation, she called. I snatched up the phone. With a rather neutral voice, she told me that she was willing to meet Bernstein.

Bingo.

It was a Saturday, and Bernstein's exeat was only valid for Mondays. I didn't want to ask to meet her beforehand, on

135

Sunday. If she hadn't proposed it, then she really didn't want to. And I'm too proud to hear the word "no".

I organised the meeting for Monday and got ready to spend the longest Sunday in history. With the woman I've loved the most, and still love, just a few kilometres away, but inaccessible.

I tried to imagine how both of them were feeling, both now alerted to what was going to happen. I could almost feel Helena's vague curiosity and absolute, visceral hatred. And Simon's probably more sceptical curiosity.

At last, something strange is happening, my friend would be saying to himself. At last something of unforesee-able outcome.

Woman's hatred and ferocity is much worse than Man's. Here, for example, the worst bombings – although statisti-cally fewer – are carried out by Palestinian women, not men. The subject of feminine ferocity is universal.

My friend Waldemar Sarli, economist and doyen of Uru-guayan journalism, told me that in his thirty years as a news-paper editor he'd verified that men commit 98% of murders. But that in the remaining 2%, committed by women, there's typically not enough left of the victim for an autopsy.

Helena is already a mystery unto herself. You never know what she's thinking. She doesn't know herself, half the time. It is impossible to hate or to love a complete stranger. In that sense, Helena can't hate Bernstein very much. He is, after all, a stranger. War, however, is based on hatred be-tween strangers.

And Bernstein the stranger owes an important death to Helena the stranger.

Everything I know about the few hours in which these two people spoke privately together is indirect.

I merely introduced them and left. It was insufferably hot. The Mediterranean shone like steel and smelt like oil. I left them alone at the table of a bar on the seafront, where there is a long wooden walkway and great canvas awnings. They were watching each other guardedly as they thought, paralyzed by shyness, about what to say, in what terms, in which language. I must add that Helena's English is no great shakes and she doesn't speak Hebrew. She's not Jewish and she couldn't care if I was or not. Judaism is just not an issue for her.

So, not only am I unaware of what they spoke about, I don't know what language they used. But speak they did. They spoke for hours.

I didn't expect Helena to recount the whole conversation to me, but I never imagined either that she would leave Israel without telling me a single thing. Not a word. Zilch.

I always get it wrong with my ex-wife.

Like I got it wrong back in 1985, after I finally got my freedom back. I always suspected that Helena had fallen in love with another, or others, during my nearly eleven years at the bottom of the pit. But she hadn't. My mistake. She had fallen back in love – but for just a month – with her first boyfriend, an Argentine like her. That had been six years before, in 1979. The same absolutely loyal lad, who'd got the big heave-ho when she met me.

A surprise: it wasn't "another" in general. It was "The Other". First love resuscitated is extremely powerful. It's something against which I, and no mere husband, prisoner or otherwise, has any defence. A first love is something too powerful; it has the strength of being born perfect. Second loves are never born so perfect. One has already done and suffered unforgivable things. One mistrusts, negotiates, breaks off, acts stupidly. A second love lacks absolutes, it is too real.

Helena turned again to that adolescent love when there was still more than half of my time in prison remaining. But nobody was to know that. And, as things were, amongst them my health, it was possible that I'd die in prison, like so many others did. And Helena could no longer cope with her role of faithful widow at the age of 25, with her husband buried. Buried, but alive.

Helena eventually got her degree. After a quiet celebration party with her faculty companions she remained alone in the apartment washing the dirty plates and glasses and, on an impulse, called her old boyfriend in Buenos Aires, who was also called Mario like me, although his surname was Ibáñez.

The Ibáñez family told her that young Mario had gone to England. As nobody gave out delicate information over the phone in those days, they hinted that Mario had had to go rather suddenly. They refused to give her his London telephone number.

His parents probably remembered the terrible time that the flighty young Helena had put their son through.

Helena, however, drove the London directory enquiries mad with her bad English until, after a few days, she'd got a dozen possible numbers. The ninth corresponded to Mario. My rival. My victim.

And Helena spoke to him. And asked for forgiveness for everything. And the bloke not only forgave her instantly, incredibly enough, he blew all his hard-earned cash, even though he was just a street busker, and got the first plane back to Uruguay. Furthermore, he took the risk that the Uruguayan police, who collaborated with their Argentine counterparts, would recognise him and kidnap him. He took the chance and came.

I understand my little namesake, only too well. He saw things more clearly than I did.

And Helena went back to that lad because she could no longer stand her life. But she quickly saw the error she'd made. She thought a ghost from the past was less dangerous, as a rival, than another man like, say, someone from work, someone with less of a black history and more chance of building a relationship with. Which was exactly what she wanted to avoid.

So when Helena discovered that the lad was too good, and she was reliving the past too much, she threw him out, or at least that's what she told me and I believe her. Probably wracked with guilt about him, and about me, too. Poor Helena. She must have been driven to distraction.

I've nothing to forgive her for, I told myself when she told me about it, much later. That was 1985, I was free, and we were trying to rebuild our relationship. Nothing to forgive her for, for fuck's sake.

But then a whole load of crap started happening between us and in 1987 I couldn't stand her anymore and I left. And I still don't forgive her, even today. Or I don't forgive myself.

Poor sod, that Ibáñez.

Because three or four years after that rather brief reencounter, in which Helena left him for me, for the second time in his life, he got killed in the Falklands. Fuck knows how he ended up there. Instead of going back into exile in England, the idiot returned to his country, got his university degree then straightaway got called up for military service, just in time not to miss the party.

When he got killed in the islands he would have been about 28.

And all that happened whilst I, completely oblivious, was making pencil marks on the walls of my cistern, counting the days I'd been in there, like a prisoner in the cartoons. Marks that told me how many days remained before Helena's next bi-monthly visit. She was the only visitor. My parents couldn't come. They were never allowed to visit me and they died during my captivity.

I'm not the only prisoner to have suffered that kind of thing.

In 1985, my instinct was shouting out loud that I was mad to think that Helena and I could try to pick up our marriage as if nothing had happened.

Because it wasn't 1979 anymore, but 1985, and my new-found freedom didn't thrill me. They were talking about elections in Uruguay and my old fellow soldiers, after hanging up their arms and joining legal parties, were getting ready to contest the ballot. But what they did or didn't do mattered little or not at all. I didn't understand it myself. Had I wasted eleven years of my life just to become so indifferent, so apolitical?

The democracy that followed on from the dictatorship wasn't particularly inspiring. I couldn't get any work in the public hospitals, already run down and administered by scum from the private sector who only wanted to empty and close them. All this despite having been hospital ward chief back in Maldonado, and practicals supervisor at the Universidad de la República. Private practice, and a consultancy, no longer interested me. The patients noticed this and left.

I was a broken man when I came out of that hole in Paso de los Toros. Broken, although I wouldn't admit it. In clinical terms, I managed to avoid depression during my captivity because, down there, otherwise it would have killed me. But I did get depressed with knobs on when I came out. It didn't kill me, but it destroyed nearly everything that I called my life and my world.

In more political terms, I felt like a Martian in the new world of 1985. I didn't belong. The Right advanced, triumphantly, the world over. Residual Uruguayan politics couldn't have seemed more idiotic, the *Blancos* and the *Colorados* were the same shit as always, but worse. Even Helena, at that time a Frente candidate for congress, could no longer hide her irritation with the inert lump that I had become.

And for which she had paid too high a price.

There were fights, arguments, reproaches, and bitterness. We had to separate. This was apparently by mutual agreement, but both Helena and I knew that really I could never forgive her fling with that lad. I threw a spanner in the works.

Shortly afterwards I also left the country. The *Colorados* had won the elections, with "Godfather" Sanguinetti as president, a direct collaborator with the 1973 military coup and accomplice to the ten years of brutal repression that followed. I'd almost say a necessary participant in my ten years of agony in a dried-out cistern. And the bloke was now governing as if nothing had happened. A great democrat, canonized by the ballot box.

If I couldn't forgive Helena, who hadn't betrayed me, how was I going to forgive my bastard compatriots, who had really had, and knowingly?

That was when I talked to the Jewish Agency. 'I've never been a Zionist, but I am Jewish,' I told them. 'And my mother was Jewish, as well.' They smiled, understandingly. That's not a trivial matter.

They carried out a discreet check and I obviously didn't seem too bad, bearing in mind the state of the market. The thing is that Jews in Uruguay make up hardly 1% of the national population and those of my generation were more likely to study *Das Kapital* than the *Talmud*, which meant they couldn't be too choosy.

All things considered, including my academic credentials, they offered me a job and a new country, in Israel. And I can't say that they didn't deliver.

But I don't want to talk about myself or my failures.

I really want to talk about Bernstein. About my only triumph.

XV

Helena came back from that interview very upset, hating me in silence. She insisted on getting a taxi and going back to her hotel, alone.

Bernstein, whom I accompanied in another taxi to the Abrabanel, looked exhausted. He had a split lip, a black eye and his shirt collar was torn and blood-stained.

Whatever had happened, it had been tough.

After her meeting with Bernstein, Helena lost no time in going back to Uruguay. She left on Thursday. She brought her flight forward by two days, even though that meant stopovers, transfers, and irritating complications. She didn't want to be in the same country as Bernstein or myself. Full stop.

I took Bernstein to my apartment in Kfar Saba first, to clean him up a bit and get him a new shirt. He didn't say a word, and I couldn't bring myself to ask him anything. Mielnik raised his eyebrows a bit when he saw Bernstein arrive back two hours late, in different clothes, with a stitched lip and sticking-plaster on his forehead. But he made me sign the Ancient Mariner's entrance chit without writing or making the least comment himself. A gentleman.

Helena phoned me from the airport on Thursday, fifteen minutes before leaving. Don't call or write to her ever again. Full stop.

The following Monday, with understandable anxiety and curiosity, I went around to the Abrabanel to sign Bernstein out for our evening walk. The doctor on duty, some big, blond, new character whom I'd never seen before, allowed me to sign the chit as "family member or companion", made a phone call and told me to wait in the hall.

But instead of Bernstein, it was Mielnik who appeared again. He gave me a confused look and said:

'Your patient prefers to stay inside today, Mario. He apologises. He won't say anything more than that.'

It was as if they'd smacked me on the head with a stick. The entire world was turning its back on Doctor Rosenfeld.

The following week, I went back again, a prey to anxiety. Once more, Bernstein refused to come out. Mielnik, understanding, uncomfortable, took something out of his pocket.

'Your Ancient Mariner sends you this,' he said.

Without daring to open the envelope, I looked at Mielnik in alarm.

'He's absolutely fine. He hasn't had an episode. To be honest,' here Mielnik smiled, disconcerted, 'I've never seen him so well. And it's not just me who says so. Even that useless Russian says so, and you know how she hates him. Lately, Bernstein chuckles to himself, without noticing. Have you ever heard him laugh? No, nor have I. He's got a pleasant laugh. He's even joked with me a couple of times. And there's more: he suddenly asked me for Internet access so he could look up yacht builders and I don't know what else. He's even started designing yachts.'

I scratched my head.

'I don't understand anything, Mielnik.'

'Nor do I, Rosenfeld. But that's normal isn't it? It's his job to be a madman and ours to be psychiatrists.'

'Did he say anything else?'

'Only that he'd like to think a bit more about what happened, that's what he told me to...' Mielnik seemed uncomfortable again. 'Well, what he told me to tell you, which means nothing to me. Are you alright? You also look upset these days...sort of rather sad? Listen, I've got to run, I've got 35 nutters waiting for me. And you can read your letter in peace. But I'll tell you something else: you were right to hit that old idiot a bit. I often feel like it, too, the damned English snob.'

XVI

Dear Mario Rosenfeld (MD, PhD).

I should have written this letter to you some time ago. If your colleague, Dr. Mielnik, raises no objections, I'll hand it over to you personally the next time we meet, perhaps for the last time. That might be at Ben Gurion airport, on the day you return to your country. Am I right in thinking that day is not far away? Your colleagues inform me that you've already sold your apartment.

I'll miss your company, as I'll miss a very dear friend who'll remain in my heart for the rest of my life. A life I owe to you, and for which I am eternally in your debt.

In the meantime, please don't be offended by my refusal to continue with our Monday afternoon meetings. The good news is that they are probably no longer necessary. Important things have happened and I still need time to think about them.

Perhaps you've been successful, Doctor. The important thing is that I'm better. I say this with caution. You know me well, but I feel that I know what I'm saying. If I'm proved right, I will lack both the words and the time to thank you.

In the three weeks that have passed since my encounter with your ex-wife, Doctor Helena Estévez, I had had only four recurrences, or flashbacks, as you call them.

As an engineer, I cannot help thinking in statistical rather than psychoanalytic terms, but I know that you'll understand me. According to my calculations, it seems that I'm going from fifteen to five episodes per month, or somewhere in that region. It remains to be seen whether this can be maintained over time or is a mere fluctuation.

HMS Coventry seems to be finally sinking in my psyche. Although it may never settle deep down in the mud, I may at least finally remove myself from the list of its victims.

They attribute my "discreet but indubitable improvement" here to a change in medication ordered by Dr. Mielnik. I have no wish to contradict them, but you, your ex-wife, Dr. Mielnik and I all know that this is not the case.

To put it clearly, your ex-wife managed to break and release certain things fixed inside my head. This, as you know, happened in a quite literal fashion.

The greatest release occurred as we were walking together along the beach, some time after Dr. Estévez had shown me some photographs, letters and poems pertaining to that young Argentine man, Private Mario Ibáñez, who I, as chief weapons officer, responsible for the Sea Wolf missiles aboard the Class 42 destroyer HMS Coventry, killed in the Falkland Islands.

Ibáñez was not an entirely unfamiliar name to me. I know the names and surnames of almost all the Argentines to whose death I contributed, by pressing a button and waiting until a luminous dot disappeared from the radar screen. Obviously, it is a wholly different matter when you are shown the actual face, entirely commonplace, of a bearded, skinny youth and then told: You killed this one.

We walked along in silence, bitterly calm, each one preoccupied with their separate thoughts. We'd already talked too much, there seemed to be nothing more to add and, as you know, certain linguistic barriers existed between us. To make matters worse, I am not known for my fluid conversation.

But then Dr. Estévez began to cry. When I tried to offer her my handkerchief, she let out a stifled groan and then split my lip with a blow and smashed my glasses with another.

I can vouch for the efficiency of whoever taught her self-defence in her political militant days. She certainly packs a punch. She continued to hit me for a while and, I believe, tried to strangle me at one point. If she did not finish the job, it was only because she suddenly changed her mind. Due to the heat, the walkway was deserted and there was no-one around to help me.

I made no effort to defend myself, but you shouldn't draw psychoanalytic conclusions from this, as is your wont. I was almost unconscious. I would have defended myself if possible, but this woman's first two punches had nearly knocked me out. The last time that anybody hit me that hard was at secondary school, during a lamentable incident with a rather anti-Semitic classmate who had drunk too much.

After pardoning my life, Helena helped me to get up. As I was bleeding profusely from the nose and mouth and it would've been embarrassing for you to see me like that, she told me to wait there on a bench, by the beach, while she went to buy some sticking plaster and hydrogen peroxide at a chemist's in the nearby shopping centre.

As I could do little else, I agreed. I stayed where I was, staunching the flow of blood from my top lip with my handkerchief. I thought of nothing in particular. I believe I was in shock. Luckily, the heat had made the entire city take refuge in air-conditioned places. Our little, absurd, open-air incident had passed unnoticed.

147

Helena came back in silence. I think that was the moment when I noticed quite how beautiful your ex-wife is.

After cleaning me up somewhat, she sat down at my side, offered me a cigarette and asked me what she called "the million dollar question".

Nobody has asked me this before, myself included, and it struck me as very original.

"Did you hate your captain very much?"

XVII

Bingo! As you are fond of saying.

God, how much I hated, and still hate, that heartless bastard.

I'm sure that Hart-Dyke is not troubled by ghosts. I'm not talking about the people we killed in a fair fight - the crew of the Sobral, for example. They were on a rescue mission, and shouldn't have opened fire on our helicopter, which was only monitoring them. They brought it on themselves.

I must admit that during the first moments of the war, on 3 May 1982, when we attacked the Sobral, things had not yet got so heated between Great Britain and Argentina, and David Hart-Dyke was not yet the person he would later become.

On that day he hesitated and delayed the order to return fire. And once the Sobral had been disabled, Hart-Dyke gave the order to cease fire immediately. We could have finished the job and sank them, but we refrained from doing so. We let them live.

Less than a week later, however, we brought down, one after the other, those two Argentine search and rescue helicopters that were clearly – due to their flight pattern – also looking for survivors.

I can only say in my captain's defence that at that stage of the game there were already piles of corpses on each side. Your side – excuse me, Doctor, but you are aware of my pathological tendency to consider you almost Argentine – had lost the Belgrano, with nearly 400 deaths and we had lost the Sheffield, the Coventry's sister ship, with a number of burns victims aboard that we will never own up to.

The idea that "anything goes" was already gaining ground on both sides.

With the first helicopter, Hart-Dyke had to give me the order twice. I would like to say I was on the point of insubordination, but that wouldn't be true. It was a brief vacillation, a few seconds of delay. Three, perhaps. When the man looked at me furiously, I lowered my head and pressed the button. The missile fired off and a minute later three Argentine rescuers were dead. End of story.

With the following helicopter, the one with Private Mario Ibáñez aboard, I did not hesitate. We had to take out all helicopters, to restrict the Argentines' movement around the swampy, road-less islands. All helicopters; Hart-Dyke made that clear. These were orders directly from Whitehall.

I know you'll understand this. You're a doctor, and I'm sure you've saved many lives. But you were also a soldier, back in your native Uruguay, for a cause I don't understand and will therefore refrain from judging. You've led me to believe that, as a soldier, you've taken lives in combat. This, however, does not seem to represent a major problem in your existence.

149

Furthermore, I would've liked to explain to Doctor Helena Estévez that my 22 years of post-stress trauma, that albatross hung "Coleridge style" around my neck, like the Ancient Mariner, as you described it, are due precisely to having killed her first love, Private Mario Ibáñez.

But nothing would be further from the truth. She has also been a soldier, and has killed. She wouldn't have believed me, either.

The naked truth is that during the Falklands War I could have blown up a hundred lads like that young soldier with my missiles every day before breakfast, without losing my appetite. My self-hatred has a rather more inglorious origin: the captain.

Your ex-wife fired a shot in the dark that hit the target, right in the bull's eye. Is she some sort of psychic, a clairvoyant? What is she? How did she know? She must know Jewish people and their paranoias very well - perhaps because she was married to you. God, how I've hated Captain Hart-Dyke. That brief three-second hesitation of mine, before complying with his order to destroy the first helicopter, on 9 May, was later punished in a much crueler way.

The word crueler is perhaps excessive.

The truth is that it's not really appropriate.

Hart-Dyke called me to his private quarters, in order, I must admit, to avoid adding to my humiliation. There he threatened me with a court martial if I ever hesitated to follow orders in a battle situation again. He also shouted that I could forget about promotion as long as he was in command of the Coventry.

I would be lying if I said he called me "a dirty Jew". Hart-Dyke is no fool, and has no death wish. Furthermore, I don't even believe today that he's an out-and-out anti-Semite. Perhaps he's not an anti-Semite at all, all things considered. In those days, as you know, one of the Admiralty heavyweights was a certain Lewin, which meant that overt displays of anti-Semitism in the Royal Navy were frowned upon. But I suspect – without any proof – that, at heart, Hart-Dyke had little sympathy for Jews. I know for a fact that we could never get on together, and that our mutual antipathy arose the moment we met.

Perhaps Hart-Dyke resembled too closely two or three upper-class twits of my acquaintance who were indeed openly anti-Semitic. The sort of people you inevitably meet in English high society. Children from good families, who made my schooldays a misery. I'm talking about regrettable scenes, of which I spare you the details: beatings in the showers, that kind of thing.

That night, after the scene with Hart-Dyke, I was so furious I could hardly sleep. I could forget about promotion as long as he was in command, were his words...

Sixteen days later, when my missile missed its mark, I made sure that bastard would lose command for ever - and lose the damned ship as well. It's regrettable that this action caused the deaths of so many of my companions, in such a dreadful and, for me, unforgivable manner.

You are, Doctor, an excellent psychiatrist but you know little of either anti-aircraft engineering or the Sea Dart missile system. It is ineffective at short distances, as you were able to find out but, even so, I can assure you that it was difficult to fail. My most experienced colleagues still ask themselves why I only fired one missile.

With a combination of two missiles, fired with a three-second interval, our two attackers would have least been put off their aim by having to zigzag at sea level to avoid the staggered salvo. And firing manually would've been enough to achieve this.

Your ex-wife, although she also knows nothing of anti-aircraft systems, made me understand everything with just one simple question.

Frankly, I don't think she put the question in order to cure me. In truth, I believe she was condemning me to death, or perhaps giving me an option. The option is this: either I stop detracting from the world's joy with my depression and guilt, or I kill myself quickly and promptly, and have done with it all.

But the truth is that, after duly considering the matter during the lonely week when I declined to see you, I came to the modest conclusion that I've already paid off that dreadful moral debt to my shipmates. Here in Israel, as in England before, psychiatric hospitals have been my prisons. Some of your colleagues, Doctor, have been my worst tormentors and the nightmares and flashbacks my torture. On top of all that, I have even been nearly strangled (!).

I believe that I have now expiated my sins.

I can calmly accept that I might continue to suffer the same kind of recurrent episodes, those damned flashbacks. It's even possible that I might need them, in small doses, as part of my new-found equilibrium. I think it would be folly to try and live without guilt. But I swear I'll live with less guilt than before. Much less.

Because it's not an albatross that this ancient mariner has hanging around his neck, Doctor Rosenfeld, but a whole bunch of ratings. I'll continue to see them often, stumbling in their burning clothes, in the darkness, swallowing smoke and scorching their lungs. It's impossible to turn the page and forget them forever.

But if there is an afterlife, they'll have seen me purging my errors for over twenty years, and they might perhaps have forgiven me. The fact is I'm no longer in any hurry to be reunited with them. In this way I can even think of forgiving myself, and face the fact that there's still a world out there, with seas and beautiful ships. And even beautiful women, like Doctor Estévez.

These things no longer depend on you, someone who has taken such grave risks on my behalf, but on your colleague, Doctor Mielnik. I believe, however, that as the months go by, Mielnik, who is an intelligent and reasonable man, will gradually let me go. At some point he'll discharge me and I'll become a free man once more.

I've always been well paid, both here and in England. I have amassed considerable savings, Doctor. I won't deny that I'm thinking of buying a boat, a yacht. Or, better still, of designing one and having it built for me. Perhaps I shall choose to spend the rest of my time at sea. As you know, most Britons have salt water in their veins.

Would it be too much to ask you to write to me here at the Abrabanel from Uruguay? Although we may never see each other again, please let's keep in touch. I'd like to witness how you rebuild your own life, and to encourage you on that difficult path.

Perhaps I'll send you greetings by e-mail from time to time to demonstrate that I'm still in the land of the living – all because you dared to go beyond the call of duty, and triumphed.

I'm one of your success stories (and your ex-wife's). I am eternally in your debt. My future life won't be easy, but then neither will yours. Nobody's life is, I suppose.

Yours sincerely,

Simon Bernstein.

XVIII

This letter represents my last contact with Bernstein. On the day I finally left for Madrid (and thereafter for Montevideo), he didn't come to say goodbye. I excused him on the grounds that perhaps Mielnik hadn't given him permission.

But it was still a disappointment. Damned gringo.

I've often thought about writing to him. I could easily find out the whereabouts of my Ancient Mariner, with an albatross around his neck. He would surely have left me his e-mail address. Mielnik would tell me. I should write, but I never do.

I prefer to imagine him on his yacht, navigating alone through grey, desolate seas. Living out his life.

Chapter Five

That Hole in the Soul
(For Roald Dahl, the master)

This had never happened to Martiniau the lawyer before. A man stands full-square in front of him, arms akimbo, and calmly says:

'Now, you listen to me: You are a complete and utter bastard."

Martiniau, who has a 9mm. FM semi-automatic in the car glove box, is flabbergasted. Perhaps he hasn't heard properly. He's been a bit deaf since 1982, and he has a permanent buzzing in one ear.

Furthermore, the man who's just insulted him has threatening, ape-like arms that stand brazenly out from his overalls. These arms are stained with oil up to the elbows. Up to a few seconds ago, they were hidden from view, doing mysterious things to the engine of the lawyer's car, that had stopped for no apparent reason, but which has now started again God knows why and is purring like the day it left the factory. The hands on the ends of those forearms are a monument to grime, calluses, size, skill and strength. They discourage argument.

Also, all this is happening far from any human witness, on Santa Cruz provincial Highway 43, which crosses the plains of ash and gravel and connects Los Antiguos, at the foot of the Andes, with the roads leading to the faraway Atlantic.

From Las Heras and Pico Truncado towards the east, enormous lorries carrying equipment to and from the oil fields can sometimes be seen, slowly wending their way across the plains, grouped together like galleons. But Martiniau's car stopped more to the west, on some higher plateau beyond Las Heras. This is the back of beyond, where nothing is moving except for the immense flocks of clouds shepherded along by the wind.

Félix Martiniau Otheguy, the lawyer, has too many surnames to be any good at the plebeian art of motor mechanics, so he spent six or seven hours in perfect solitude waiting for some help to turn up. Disciplined, indifferent to the cold, he allowed himself to smoke two cigarettes during that time.

The lorry appeared in the distance at about four o'clock in the afternoon. It took about fifteen minutes to reach him, finally arrived, and halted with a screech of brakes. The lorry driver got out and gave a sort of grunt in reply in reply to Martiniau's courteous welcome. With an unlit cigarette butt in his mouth and a slightly superior demeanour, he listened to a summary of the situation. He grunted again, began to investigate underneath the bonnet and forgot all about the lawyer.

After performing his "get up and walk!" routine with the Ford Focus in just three minutes, the lorry driver suddenly blinks and studies Martiniau's face closely with rapt attention. He shrugs his shoulders, seems not to believe his eyes, then looks at Martiniau again, this time very closely, as if inspecting him on parade. He nods – again to himself – before insulting him in the aforementioned manner (without passion, as if he felt obligated to), then ignores Martiniau once more and directs his attention to the engine, which he listens to for a while, meditatively. Then he gives a sign of approbation and carefully closes the bonnet, despite the wind's resistance. He turns towards his own patiently waiting, battered Chevrolet lorry. He was so sure he'd fix the car quickly, he hadn't even turned his engine off.

He climbs into the cab, puts it in first and lets out the clutch, but before resuming his own life he realises that Martiniau has not understood a thing. Of course, he thinks, that asshole was as deaf as a post. He winds down the window to give him another clue:

'Puerto Argentino. That was about thirty fucking years ago. Amazing how time flies, isn't it? You haven't changed at all, though. Bye-bye, Lieutenant. And go and fuck yourself.'

II

Stupefied, Martiniau, who hasn't been a lieutenant for a long time, watches the lorry get further away as it heads towards the mountains. Finally, it becomes a just a point in the vast, flat landscape.

Absorbed, he gets in his car and heads off in the opposite direction, towards the coast.

He drives for about forty minutes along endless straight stretches through a grey nothingness, where anything that stands more than a yard above ground, be it a hirsute pepper tree or a sculptured guanaco, becomes a land mark for miles around. And the lawyer proceeds to methodically trawl through his memory banks, searching drawer by drawer to identify that unknown lorry driver who believes that Martiniau is still what he used to be. In another lifetime. A long time ago.

Martiniau never got past the rank of lieutenant.

In 1982, a few months after the surrender of Port Stanley, the man rejected decorations and promotion to first lieutenant and asked without fuss to be let out of the army. For personal reasons, which he didn't explain to anybody.

This, in an aristocratic family, with three generations of moustachioed generals framed and hanging from the walls of the family mansion, meant painful scenes, harsh separations and self-denials difficult to describe.

Félix Martiniau Otheguy had to be born again, to a new life. A grey, arid, common, civilian life. He did it alone, in a little dark one-roomed flat in the Once district, which he kept very tidy. He only realised later, in 1987, when he began to see the other shore, that his actions had constituted, in effect, a rebirth.

That was the year he finally obtained his law qualifications, and the moment he realised that he was already thirty-odd years old and that in the previous five, between his job as a legal pen-pusher and his evening classes, he hadn't had a single day's holiday. He also realised that total immersion in a large legal firm was really an almost military way of belonging to a greater organism, of being just another cell and avoiding the solitude an individual feels. But then, precisely to experience more of that solitude, he resigned from the firm, despite the fact that his qualifications, his background and his unyielding scrupulousness guaranteed him a job as head of the administrative litigations department.

His old army friends had, more or less, stopped speaking to him, but he didn't miss them much. Whilst quietly celebrating his degree, with two or three friends from the faculty, new blokes, bearded and different, whom he continued to think of as "civilians" and who for that reason made him slightly suspicious, he thought it would be silly not to call his family and tell them the good news. Or to call his mother, at least. It remained just a thought, however.

The following years, both good and bad, went flying past.

In 1991 he suddenly found himself married to Alejandra, a fascinating colleague with a Jewish surname, with slanted eyes that were sometimes like a geisha's and sometimes like a samurai's. She had ochre-coloured curls and skin like sumptuous slow cream. Divorced, with two strange kids (or two stranger's kids), she was a woman with more facets and fires than a diamond, and about as tough. She was also a business whiz, and a whiz in the business of living: she opened up whole new universes for him.

When he came out of the Registry Office he never even dreamed of calling his mother, to avoid exacerbating the sense of shame he knew the discreetly anti-Semitic Martiniau family would be feeling. A shame that he, in spite of such happiness and trepidation, somehow, in his heart of hearts, remorsefully shared.

In 2000 he found himself divorced at last from that hypnosis, and returned to the solitude that had cost him so much to buy, and which he now preferred to defend. He had gone to live far away, in Comodoro Rivadavia, Chubut, and, after his own fashion, he continued to act as an adoptive and adopted father to those children of another man, the strange ones, now doubly strange in adolescence. He loved them as if they were his own, but he saw them only on the odd weekend when he went up to Buenos Aires, and if they had nothing better to do.

A discreet womaniser, Felix Martiniau hadn't fallen in love again. For that you need to fall out of love with the previous woman, and that still hadn't happened.

Tenacious and focused, as always, he grew quite wealthy in the up-and-coming town of Comodoro Rivadavia, representing the foreign oil companies that appropriated the Argentine sub-soil during Carlos Menem's rule. He lost money, but felt a little better, in spite of his scorn for union chieftains, when he crossed to the other side and represented the workers.

He did it well: he was acquainted with all the incorruptible judges, knew too much about the others and maintained strong links with the independent local press, solely represented by Gustavo Enríquez and his small, but well respected, newspaper. It was a pretty frightening business. His work called for him to travel regularly to the gas fields at Pico Truncado and the oilfields at Cañadón Seco, places half lost in the cold Sahara of the steppes, where perpetual industrial unrest is the order of the day.

He was often threatened, usually anonymously. As a precaution, and given that as an ex-soldier he had a lifelong firearms licence, he used to take his old *FM* along with him. A pretty mediocre pistol, but it was the last remaining souvenir from his past life, and had also saved it one night on Mount Tumbledown, back in 1982.

At the age of fifty-odd, Martiniau, and the world in general, had largely forgotten his brief moment of glory in that odd little war. For although he was now well respected in his new life, the lawyer was still an exile from his previous one: he missed the proud, aristocratic and strict military world that had formed him, the old "Planet Army" as he now referred to it. A planet that, between the 1930 military coup and the last, failed, *carapintada*[1] uprising in 1990, had made Argentina its natural satellite.

The satellite was now in orbit around other places that weren't much better.

What was clear was that after the restoration of democracy in 1984, and the clashes and settling of old scores by a rancorous and chaotic civilian world, military power had crumbled.

The Armed Forces, hated for years of genocide and mismanagement, topped off by a war declared without sense and lost without honour, began to lose under democratic rule, one by one, all of their old legal and economic caste privileges, until finally turning into pariahs themselves. Socially and politically, they became like the scrap metal that now served as their equipment: tanks immobilized for the lack of spare parts, planes so decrepit they fell out of the sky and rusty ships with no fuel to propel them.

In the thirty years since the war, Argentina – a country much given to crazy experiments, Martiniau often thought –

---

1 Literally, the "painted faces". Military right-wing mutineers who rose repeatedly against Argentina's democratic governments between 1987 and 1990

had gone from a state of chronic militarism to one of unilateral disarmament, in a world where smaller and crueler wars abounded, and while its neighbours were spending fortunes on arming themselves to the teeth. This situation, on top of his old unhealed wounds and unremitting pains, had finally disrupted Martiniau's sleep patterns. He was now as insomniac as a bat.

Resigning from the army back in 1982 had been for Martiniau a brutal act of separation and self-flagellation, akin to choosing to be an orphan. But in the light of both the country's and the Army's subsequent fate, it now seemed more like disembarking from the Titanic a minute before it set sail.

Although no spring chicken, Martiniau knew that he might be dull and grey-haired, he was also a lucky man. That didn't mean, however, a happy one. "You have a great soul, Felix, but there's a hole in it somewhere. And you've never been able to tell me what it is, in all our eight years together," was Alejandra's sad diagnosis when they separated, by mutual agreement and, for once, without quarrelling.

He is about to arrive at Las Heras when the penny finally drops, and he identifies the man who has just saved him from spending a frozen night in the middle of the steppe.

'Sonrisal, you son of a fucking whore,' he mutters.

He jams on the brakes: the car stops, momentarily enveloped in blue smoke from the burnt tyres. Martiniau remains in silence for a few seconds, very grave, clasping the steering wheel, looking at the horizon with unseeing eyes, thinking.

He glances at the glove box, wherein lies the *FM*, with a bullet in the chamber and thirteen more in the magazine.

Then he does a three point turn in the vacant road and heads back the way he came, his foot to the floor. And meanwhile, the memories come flooding back.

III

The memories come back like photographs: powerful images, full of colour and detail, sometimes static, with neither movement nor order and other times without sound.

One is of the corral, after the surrender. Five thousand captured and disarmed Argentines have been shut up inside enormous sheep pens, which the British have reinforced with barbed wire.

It's snowing heavily. They are close to the landing strip at Puerto Argentino, which in the meantime has become Port Stanley once more and proudly flies the British flag. The prisoners are awaiting the ship that will take them back home.

Martiniau is almost completely deaf, even when they shout at him. But he's stubborn and, as he reckons this state of affairs might last a long time, he's already beginning to lip read a little, based on observation, trial and error.

They spend all their days out of doors. Sometimes it rains, sometimes it's freezing and he's already got back some of his hearing, although what there is of it is accompanied by a dreadful humming in his left ear. He doesn't just believe, he knows – and quite rightly - that the latter phenomenon will indeed be permanent.

The degree of filthiness, grime and malnourishment evinced by this troop of conscripts is indescribable. But in spite of this and the cold and the snow, the soldiers don't complain, because the British are feeding them much better than their own chiefs - when they were still their chiefs, that is. Paradoxically, the British do this at no cost to themselves, thanks to the thousands and thousands of Argentine ration packs that are piled up to the rafters in storerooms and hangars, and were never distributed.

The high- and middle-ranking Argentine officers, who are well fed, clothed and sheltered, and on surrendering, negotiated the right to keep their pistols to save them from being murdered by their own troops, have already made their own sacrosanct separate quarters, in the corner of the corral best protected from the wind and the rain. They are far away from the other corner where hundreds of miserable conscripts are afflicted by violent diarrhoea, after drinking water taken from coliform-infested streams and puddles.

Martiniau however, his arm in a sling, numb with cold as ever, his face a mass of scabs, almost totally covered with bandages, his clothing disfigured by tears and scorches, maintains his place among the plebs, alongside his few remaining men. He smokes, taciturn, despite the clowning and buggering about of Palacios and Sarmiento, who, just for a change, are making poor Corporal Lattanzio's life a misery.

These three are all that's left of a section numbering 46 that saw battle on 27 May at Darwin, where only a dozen managed to escape, by the skin of their teeth.

More of his charges were killed on the last night of the war, on the west face of Tumbledown. And with the first light of dawn, just hours before the ceasefire, still more died on the north face of Sapper, where they ran into the final storm of naval artillery fire that left hardly a man standing. The lieutenant missed out on this British parting shot, however, because he happened to be, for the second time, unconscious.

So, between the missing, the blown-up and the deserters (who are now beginning to turn up alive in the corrals, and report to him, ashamedly), only three remain from Martiniau's section, which fought on till the end: Corporal Lattanzio, alias Lata, the butt of so many jokes, and his two eternal tormentors, Private Palacios (alias *el Negro*; a train driver, poet, musician and guitarist) and Private Sarmiento, (alias *Sonrisal*, an electrician in a textile factory, twice as broad as tall, a cheerful orang-utan who could carry an *FAP* in his arms as if it were a feather).

Now, safe and sound, and overjoyed about being banged up and smelling like shit but still alive, and with a guaranteed sixty-odd more years of raising hell ahead of him, Negro Palacios, a smiling skeleton with impeccable white teeth, is saying to Lata, who's green-faced and struggling with his guts:

> '*A mí no me matan penas*
> *mientras tenga el cuero sano;*
> *venga el sol en el verano*
> *y la escarcha en el invierno:*
> *Si este mundo es un infierno,*
> *¿Por qué afligirse el cristiano?*'[2]

'Your mother's a whore, Negro, you useless fucker,' answers Lata, doubled over with the spasms.

---

2 Sorrow won't kill me, while I'm in one piece;
come sun in summer, and frost in winter,
If this world is hell,
What reason for a Christian to worry?

'*Cabo... Pero no pa' rebenque,*[3]' declares El Negro, who's well up on his *gauchesque* authors. And, as always, everyone laughs and he takes another bollocking with a smile, as if it were a prize.

Wonderful Negro, the lawyer Martiniau mutters to himself almost thirty years later, as he crosses the empty steppe like a lightning bolt on the heels of the other king of the shagabout, Private Sonrisal.

Sonrisal, now he was quieter but altogether more dangerous. Rather than tell jokes, he played practical jokes, and pretty cruel ones, like the time he left the mail orderly's motorbike hanging fifteen feet off the ground, tied to the top of a telephone pole, because he was always late with the letters, or forgot to deliver them.

And even if they threatened to stake him to the ground, Sonrisal always laughed. He was completely unafraid of his superiors and shrugged off every punishment by laughing, hence his nickname. Martiniau had recognised him now because of his arms. And because of those enormous hands like crane buckets or "like two bunches of dicks", as *el Negro* had once described them. In those hands, things that were broken seemed to fix themselves.

El Sonrisal hadn't changed in that respect, at least. He had in others.

The lawyer smiles cynically to himself. He won't need to ask Sonrisal why he's became so unfriendly.

---

3 "Good Corporal, but not good enough to make a horse-whip!" "Cabo" means "Corporal", but also the handle of a horse-whip, or "rebenque". Negro Palacios is at the same time making an oblique reference to *Don Segundo Sombra*, by Ricardo Guiraldes (1926), the most important gauchesque novel of the twentieth century, and saying that Corporal Lattanzio has not got much authority.

Then a second image comes to him, from about three weeks before the surrender, much before everything that happened in the corrals.

They are in a trench, soaking wet and shivering, with water up to their knees. It is 29 May, and it's dawn in Darwin. Gauzy fog drifts slowly over the flatlands and, after considerable rain, snow has fallen.

The British paratroopers, with balls of steel, last night managed to snake their way up through the minefields in the teeth of the withering fire sustained by Sub-Lieutenant Gómez Centurión (now there's a tough lad for you) and his section, and the gringos managed to take up positions on top of the damned hill, the key to the Goose Green isthmus. Now, already up there in the breaking dawn, they've just set up their heavy machine gun and they're throwing everything they've got.

Martiniau is trying to direct the distant 105 howitzer artillery counter-fire by radio, to dislodge the British from their newly-won balcony, but Sonrisal and Lata are making such a racket next to him with their FAPs that they drown out the distant metallic voice of the Argentine battery officer, who's calmly asking for better coordinates. Obediently, Sonrisal stops firing. He and Lata use the time to change the gun barrel, while Martiniau relays the exact position of the enemy machine gun nest. They watch the projectiles sailing high over their heads in a slow-falling parabola towards the British stronghold. One scores a direct hit. They can clearly see three bodies flying through the air, one of them enormous, like a gorilla. How strange, thinks Martiniau; for obvious reasons, the Paras are usually muscular types, but rather on the short side.

They start firing again and the gringos, undaunted, set up another gun. They've got the high ground, and they want revenge. Orange and white tracer bullets fly all around, flying from and towards the top of the hill, someone has just shouted, or is shouting, "Rocket!" when an anti-tank missile lands just three metres away and everything goes blank. Martiniau's first bout of oblivion.

In the following photo, Martiniau is being carried on Private Sonrisal's shoulders, bent double at the waist, his legs dangling in front of the soldier's vast chest, and his head hanging down his gigantic back. He's just been awoken by the cold, and the first thing he sees are the heels of Sonrisal's boots sinking five centimetres into the peat, with a kind of liquid squelching effect, as the man moves forward, weighed down, trying not to topple over. Each duly thought-out step leaves behind a footprint that fills immediately with cold, brown water. Sonrisal's damaged boots are stained with blood that is leaking from somewhere or other. It's actually coming from Martiniau's face, although he doesn't realise this.

'Are we running away?' he asks nobody in particular, head down.

"We're off to Puerto Argentino, Lieutenant. Seems that they've surrendered in Ganso Verde, we haven't heard shooting for over two hours,' the boots answer.

They surrendered, thinks Martiniau. And we didn't. He swoons again, happy.

Next photo: a muddy crossroads at the pass between the Rivadavia Mountains. Halfway to Puerto Argentino, just forty kilometres to go now. Hills, valleys, rocks, silvery pastures of tussocks that sway fitfully in the wind. Occasional flurries of swirling light rain, peat like slushy soup that sucks at your boots. And nothing else. Around 500 sheep, cautious or impassive, graze, shit and watch them go past from a distance.

Martiniau can walk again, but only with help, by leaning on Negro Palacios, who is tall, roughly the same height, and who looks after his lieutenant with a mother's dedication. Now they've left him sitting on a rock, smoking the only remaining cigarette, which they insisted he should take, to his embarrassment.

Meanwhile, Sonrisal and Negro Palacios, inseparable, with their hands and faces a mass of burns and cuts, are laughing as they give a 180-degree turn to the gringo roadside signposts, those arrows that say: "Goose Green", "Fitzroy", "Darwin" and "Moody Brook" and indicate the distance in miles.

As if this schoolboy prank would confuse the advancing British who are following on their heels, the silly sods. The lieutenant laughs to himself, but says nothing. Firstly, because he still finds it difficult to talk but, moreover, the foolhardy combativeness that his lads show makes him feel ever so slightly proud.

Then the *chop-chop-chop* sound of a faraway helicopter is heard – it just so happens to be English - and everyone throws themselves headlong into the mud or between the rocks.

Except for Martiniau, who carries on smoking, sitting on his boulder. The Gazelle comes in cautiously and Martiniau stays there, unflappable, letting himself be seen by the gringos who are two hundred yards away. They've got their side machine gun trained on him, but they can't make up their minds whether to shoot or not. Martiniau looks at them while he smokes. Maybe it's because he's got blue eyes (or one, at least) or maybe it's because the Johnnies get bored and don't understand, that they look at each other and shrug their shoulders and the helicopter goes floating away.

The *chop-chop-chop* can no longer be heard. Bit by bit, the troops start to get back on their feet. They all look incredulously at Martiniau.

The next photo, from the beginning of June, in Puerto Argentino: a field hospital, and a lieutenant-colonel from Intelligence is asking him questions totally devoid of same, while a military doctor takes hold of Martiniau's face and, aided by a sergeant medic, picks out the shards of stone and metal from his cheekbone and jaw.

In spite of the Lidocaine, Martiniau screams unashamedly, which seems to deeply annoy the doctor, who expects greater heroism.

Outside, the chill of the late afternoon awaits him, along with Negro Palacios who, on seeing his face all bandaged up like a mummy, pretends to strum an imaginary guitar, and serenades him:

> *'Amigazo, pa' sufrir*
> *han nacido los varones.*
> *Ésas son las ocasiones*
> *De mostrarse un hombre juerte,*
> *Hasta que venga la muerte*
> *Y lo agarre a coscorrones'.*[4]

---

4 "We men were born to suffer, my friend.
Such are the times
For a man to show his mettle,
Until death and its grip
Doth everything settle."

Almost 30 years later, Doctor Martiniau, with several very noticeable scars on his face, is driving along crying with laughter as he remembers how he thrashed that amiable idiot with beatings and squat thrusts. Over there, a good laugh was scarcer than food or shelter: an ounce of laughter was worth its weight in gold. And El Negro brought tons and tons of laughter along with him.

The next photo, Stanley House, the old Falklands town hall, a solid, squat stone building set in a village-cum-capital made entirely of wood and corrugated iron. The waiting room next to the office of General Ménendez, the islands' military governor. San Martin[5], wrapped in a flag, looks down undaunted from the wall just like in every other Argentine military bureau. Above the portrait of San Martin, there's an almost life-sized crucifix.

Martiniau has been given combat gear that is new but, above all, dry and even ironed so that he looks presentable. The feeling of the silky cotton on his skin gives him intense physical pleasure, and he catches himself smiling several times. It is the first time in two months that he isn't shivering.

But why would General Menéndez want to see him, an obscure lieutenant? On account of his double-barrelled surname, which is anything but obscure? Most probably. Beyond their differences in rank, both he and the General have something in common: very important parents. Barrack room politics, at the end of the day.

The following image, a week after that meeting. Martiniau is already muddy, soaking wet, happy and shivering once

5 General San Martin: an Argentine soldier whose campaigns decided the independence of Argentina, Peru and Chile, the iconic figure in Argentine history. He died in poverty, exiled in France, because his respect for civilians made him decide not to ever bear arms against his own countrymen, when The Anarchy Wars followed independence.

more, which is only fitting. He's been deployed on the west side of Mount Tumbledown, alongside the leftovers from other exhausted army units, and a few infantry marines from the BIM 5[6] who have yet to have their first taste of war and are waiting expectantly like a bride on her wedding night. He's under naval authority now, represented here by a corvette lieutenant, a certain Vázquez; an expert, tough, faultless character, who treats Martiniau – who's already got a reputation – with deference and a touch of jealousy.

Tumbledown is only a low mountainous area, but the plentiful rocks offer ample cover to well-dug-in and camouflaged fox holes. Unlike at Darwin, the BIM have plenty of ammunition: mortars, rocket launchers, 12.7mm heavy machine-guns, MAGs, you want it, they've got it. The hill itself is surrounded by greenish, peaty lowlands. If the Brits want to capture it, they'll have to come splashing through the mud, treading on landmines till their heart's content and under fire from the high ground.

Well that's evened things out a bit, at last. If it weren't raining so much, it would be heavenly.

Sonrisal's hairy hands have just fixed the aforesaid Vázquez's MAG, which jammed firing its first burst, and El Negro, who has already nicknamed Vásquez "Popeye", sometimes makes him laugh with his gags, or else gets on his tits by playing Beatles or Queen songs.

'Sing some *chacarera*[7], you useless fucker, not enemy music,' the naval officer lectures him. *El Negro* Palacios nods his assent, tunes his guitar – nobody knows where the hell he keeps it - and answers with a *chacarera* version of Yesterday,

---

6 *BIM-5*: The 5th. Marine Infantry Battalion
7 Popular Argentine folk music.

to which the officer doesn't really know how to respond, until he finally laughs and bollocks him. El Negro, Clown-in-Chief of the Armed Forces of Argentina, collects bollockings from his superiors as if they were medals. And Martiniau himself has to hide the pride he feels at Negro's effrontery.

The professional respect with which the Navy marines treat them enables those two turncoats, *el Negro* and Sonrisal, to sate their backlog of hunger, thanks to the stupendous navy rations that Vázquez dishes them out regularly, much better than the shit that the army eats - when it eats, that is. But they're good lads, they share everything with the other soldiers, and with the corporal and the lieutenant too, who don't really like to ask, but are in no position – skinniness *oblige* – to stand on ceremony.

The following image: the same place, early morning on 14 June, half past one in the morning. A blackness like Indian ink, and confusion reigns. Shouts, streams of tracer bullets curving through the darkness, explosions, and flashes and yet more shouting. Here come the Scots, crudely illuminated by yellow flares, running impetuously up the valley, completely unprotected, their movements made jerky by the stroboscopic lighting. They advance howling and firing through a red smoke barrage, along a battle front two hundred metres wide. Behind and above them, the flares reveal an armada of helicopters hanging in the night. The Brits are coming!

And although the Scots Guards drop like flies, they are unstoppable. Instead of seeking cover, they charge ahead as if the bullets were papier-mache, finally manage to scale the hill and then run zigzagging among the fox holes. They throw white phosphorous grenades into the holes and trenches and the desperate cries of the Argentine lads are heard, before they're burnt alive right down to the bone.

And as the gringos have broken through the defences and fighting is taking place around a 360-degree ring, with the attackers both behind and around you, the shells are coming from all possible angles and friendly fire is as fatal as the enemy's. And in the trenches, beneath the short bursts of aerial tracer fire, there's no time left to reload and matters are being settled with bayonets and rifle butts. That's how Martiniau saves his own life, putting three slugs into the face of some Scot who'd come to carve him up like a Sunday roast.

Just then dozens of 81mm and 105mm shells begin raining down on and around the defensive positions, causing general mayhem. Anyone who's outside of a fox hole is bound to be British and therefore either dead or about to die. The enemy helicopters retreat to get away from that deluge of steel. It seems that some pitiless bastard from the Navy, it must have been Vázquez, ordered the artillery stationed behind the hill to bombard its own positions. Martiniau shouts an explanation to the astounded Sonrisal, during a brief interlude of silence.

The interlude doesn't last. More shells fall, Martiniau fires and fires and he's just, he thinks, bagged another Scots Guard when a mortar, probably friendly, blows up the neighbouring fox hole, where a group of young soldiers from Córdoba were spraying lead enthusiastically.

Martiniau doesn't know where he is for a while. He's totally deaf and covered in blood and human mincemeat, which he doesn't even notice. Fifteen or twenty more mortars fall around him in the following five seconds. This barrage scares the gringos stiff and they start running back down the hill, but the world around them has turned into a volcano, and the Argentines shoot them down like rabbits.

Martiniau, fully conscious once more, is firing his FAL at anything that moves, his upper body out of the trench, swearing and blaspheming, heedless of the shrapnel flying around and of his own self. Infected by his courage, his troops also go mad. The ground trembles when something suddenly lands and explodes behind them – either an enemy or a friendly shell - and men fall all around him in the fox hole, doubled over. Oh my God! he supposes he hears, because everyone screams the same when you kill them, and the lieutenant still doesn't know that he is, and will continue to be, deaf.

That's why, as if nothing at all had happened, Martiniau calls for some covering fire, for fuck's sake, and leaves the tiny fox hole, his FM in his right hand, to retrieve two of his own wounded men who've ended up outside, both shot to pieces, one with an arm missing and another with his guts hanging out. A brave young soldier who follows him out to help immediately falls over backwards, his face turned into a gaping hole.

Shouting he knows not what, completely beside himself, Martiniau lashes out with his pistol at the enormous ginger-haired Action Men that are leaping down the slopes towards him like goats, with their faces painted like demons, now starkly illuminated by a twinkling green flare. But he can't get more than ten paces towards his wounded men, he's got enemies in front, to the side and behind, and although the Johnnies are on the run and in a hurry, they shoot at him on sight, and he's getting lead from all sides.

He forgets the damn wounded and takes cover among some rocks. When he hears, or believes he hears, English-speaking voices through the deep cotton wool of his deafness, he throws a grenade downhill in that direction, expecting to hear an explosion followed by screams and groans. But he's still deaf and he's not going to hear a damn thing, so he throws another and another, before something smacks him on the head.

Blackout again. Second bout of oblivion.

More images follow. They would be better forgotten, but he's never managed to erase them.

The next photo: those damned freezing sheep pens are now far behind them. They're aboard the Norland, a British ferry-cum-troop ship that will take them back to Montevideo. There, another ship, this time belonging to the Argentine Navy, will take them on home.

It's no longer cold. Indeed, it is stiflingly hot.

The Johnnies have separated him from his section. The lieutenant doesn't know if they are on the same ship, nor does he look for them or even enquire about them. He doesn't want to see them, ever again. He's got death on his soul.

He's shut up inside a minuscule cabin with a private bathroom, alongside two other officers, a major and a captain, who spend their time moaning about the dreadful British food, how badly the Brits cook and always have done, fucking gringos, that's why the Germans didn't invade them in 1941 - out of sheer disgust. Martiniau infers from their conversation that neither of them has seen combat.

Martiniau doesn't speak to them; he spends all day sleeping. The other men are sometimes offended by his silence – in which they detect disdain – and other times they feel sorry for him and, thinking that he can't hear anything, say "cranial traumatism, reduced hearing, that what the medics say,". Or, "combat fatigue". Or, "he saw all the toughest fighting". But most frequently they mention his father, an advisor to Galtieri, with reverence. They imagine the lieutenant, with his surname and his wealth (and, in passing, his bollocks) laden down with medals, with good postings, missions overseas, appointments, the directorship of some great state enterprise, a glittering career, full of business opportunities.

The lieutenant is regaining a little of his hearing, which only confirms that the buzzing in his left ear will never leave him in peace.

But that's enough remembering for the moment.

Now, in his Ford Focus, he ascends to the high plateaus to the west, close by the mountain ranges, which although still unseen can already be felt.

Close to Perito Moreno, the endless straight line of the road is cut by an abrupt canyon. Deep in the bottom a river flows, unusual in this desert solitude, surrounded by succulent pastures, a green patch amidst all the grey.

Coming out of the hairpin bend that leads down to the canyon, Martiniau sees, from up above, the panorama he's seen so many times before when he's stopped at that vantage point, where he almost always stops. To take in the view.

A black-chested buzzard eagle soars tranquilly on high, up on the thermal currents. The deep valley is down below, where there's a house or a school and even a few trees. The road bridge straddles the stream of water that flows among rocks and reeds and glistens in the sunlight. A single, solitary cow is loose upon the verdant pasture. And, just passing over the bridge is the old yellow Chevrolet lorry, driven by ex-infantryman Private Pedro Sarmiento, alias Sonrisal, Class of '62, who's just beginning to climb very slowly up the opposite side of the oasis and head for the desert once more.

Instead of chasing after him, however, the lawyer brakes.

And he gets out of the car, as he always does when he gets here, in spite of the wind that makes it hard to open the door. He closes the door behind him and remains watching, from on high, arms akimbo, his hair and his tie stirred by the wind's glacial violence.

And he watches Sonrisal get further away, heading upwards, in his rheumatic lorry.

And he says things to Sonrisal. He says them only in his thoughts, for Christ's sake, because how the hell is Sonrisal going to hear anything if he's over three hundred metres away and the wind is coming from the opposite direction, the west, and shouting is in vain? And, moreover, even if Sonrisal did hear him, how the fuck is he meant to believe him, if Martiniau can't believe himself, even when he's telling the truth? He tells the truth with his thoughts.

And the truth is, Martiniau explains to Sonrisal, that he can never repay his debt to him, nor to Negro Palacios, because when that lump of shrapnel knocked him out, the lads came out with no protection from that storm of steel, dragged him back to the fox hole, gave him first aid, and saved him from dying in the two subsequent attacks on that same morning of 14 June on Tumbledown, both repelled by the same, simple method: allowing yourself to be massacred by your own artillery, until the ammunition ran out.

Later, when they were in the sheep pen, *el Negro* Palacios told Martiniau, half shouting to his face to make himself understood, that one minute before ordering the withdrawal, Corvette Lieutenant Vázquez, even fired his last 60mm mortar shell vertically into the air, without a clue where it would fall. Then, when the defence of the west side of Tumbledown finally caved in to the third attack, Sonrisal, Negro Palacios and Lata carried their unconscious lieutenant between them on their shoulders. No fucking way were they going to leave him there to die or be captured.

They humped him along like a bundle, taking turns, snaking their way between the minefields, terrified of losing a foot to one of those little round anti-personnel mines, the size of a bar of fucking soap. And they wouldn't let him go when the frigates unleashed their final artillery barrage from the sea upon the retreating Argentines. And they only agreed to separate from him after the surrender, at midday, through gritted teeth, when a British medical officer approached, politely asked through sign language if he could inspect the gravely-wounded man, and took charge of Martiniau.

That's why, twenty-odd years later, the lieutenant is explaining to Private Sonrisal, albeit in his mind, that with his record of having fought like a terrier at Darwin and escaping without surrendering through the British encirclement, it would have been impossible for General Menéndez to dispatch the remains of Martiniau's section to Tumbledown, alongside the nutcases from BIM-5.

Or out of the frying pan into the fire, rather.

No, Ménendez would never have done that if he, Lieutenant Martiniau had remained silent and accepted promotion and a gong, with a little, shall we say, barrack-room political sense. A medal that would have pleased his father, General Martiniau, and consequently, General Galtieri as well.

It was a case of playing the game, as the British would say. Play the Game, just like the Queen song that Palacios used to murder day and night with his dreadful English.

But when your head is full of shrapnel and with so many dead men weighing down on your soul, you sometimes forget what the real world is like. That's why, when Generals Jofré and Parada, Ménendez's right-hand men, asked what did he, Lieutenant Martiniau, think of the fact that a few British paratroopers had triumphed against overwhelming numbers at Darwin, Martiniau, instead of having recourse to the usual official lament regarding much-superior British equipment and the lack of combativeness evinced by the Argentine conscripts, couldn't keep his trap shut.

And, in front of those three warriors who hadn't smelt gunpowder since the war began, he said out loud the things that one should never say.

For example, that what he was most ashamed of was that a young soldier had died at Darwin from a heart attack three weeks before the British even arrived, due to the hunger, cold and suffering he'd undergone there. And he was also ashamed that he'd had to evacuate five more due to malnourishment, almost in a coma, a week before. After they'd already spent two months in the muddy trenches, open to the elements, without winter clothing or adequate food. And because no hot, or even cold, food ever reached the fox holes either. And that every sheep and bustard in the zone had disappeared, tired of being hunted down by the starving soldiery.'

And when the gringos had arrived, and the party had begun, it was a disgrace that not a single officer above the rank of first lieutenant was seen in the firing line at Darwin, because they'd seen plenty of British officers, who risked their skins when the bullets were flying, and died like men. And that British superiority wasn't a question of numbers or equipment; but of leadership.

And with Puerto Argentino surrounded and given the nature of the British naval offensive, which combines to perfection naval gunnery, aerial support, artillery, helicopters, tanks and the use of portable anti-trench missiles wielded by expertly-trained troops, he, Lieutenant Martiniau saw the surrender of the Falklands capital as inevitable. The alternative, my dear generals, is a massacre of Argentine boy soldiers.

But according to the extremely strict current military code, Martiniau continued, before the astonished eyes of the three generals, surrender was impossible unless two thirds of the effective forces were lost, or all the ammunition expended.

And therefore, out of respect for the military code and, at the same time to avoid a massacre of conscripted troops, and the inevitable lingering hatred that would engender in civil society, what he, Lieutenant Martiniau proposed, was to notify the British by radio that the thousands of Argentine soldiers who didn't wish to fight would be given up as surrendered prisoners. The British would be notified six hours before, not consulted. There go the lads: you deal with them.

There was a moment's silence. Ménendez looked at Jofre, who looked in turn at Parada.

And to ensure that nothing bad happened to the lads because they were unarmed, continued Lieutenant Martiniau,

181

the aforesaid soldiers would cross no-man's land between the battle lines under the white flag, but well mixed in with the nearly two thousand kelpers resident in the town, who would be evacuated compulsorily, but also for their own good.

Such a unilateral gesture, Martiniau explained school-teacherishly, would create a tremendous logistical problem for the British, who would have no idea of how to feed and shelter a human flock of that size.

He put the case like a brilliant lawyer before three judges. Without noticing, or caring, however, that the judges might feel they were being accused.

Meanwhile, continued the future lawyer Martiniau, the remaining professional NCOs and the middle and high-ranking officers of the Army and other forces, as well as the few conscripts who wanted to remain voluntarily with their chiefs, would entrench themselves in Puerto Argentino and prepare for the final battle, street by street and house by house.

To the death.

Rallied around the flag.

When he'd finished, Martiniau fell silent and waited.

Parada, Jofré and Menéndez were dumbfounded, un-surprisingly. They sat speechless. Us Martiniaus don't talk very much as a rule but, by God, when we're assailed by a flight of eloquence...The four of us were alone, the august generals and I, with no other witnesses apart from San Martín, who was long ago reduced to being just a classroom poster, unfortunately.

In order to break the silence, and to finish draining the putrefaction from his soul, Martiniau, who saw the three chiefs through only one eye – because the other was covered by a bandage - added that he thought his proposal was the only way for Argentine society to avoid losing its respect for the Armed Forces for ever. With all the dangers that that might entail for South America as a whole, where, at the end of the day, my dear generals, no matter what they did, the communist menace never abated.

Unbelievably, it seems that Martiniau expected to be listened to. Circumspect and rather cold, he would never have allowed himself such an outburst for the sake of mere catharsis. He really believed they would listen to him. He was hoping to make a difference.

Jofré bit his lips. Parada, livid, threw a searching glance at Ménendez, who was looking elsewhere. When the silence had become altogether intolerable once more, Ménendez cleared his throat, stood up without looking at Martiniau, and, with his gaze still downwards, dryly told him to go outside and await further orders.

That's where I screwed up your life up, Sonrisal, says the lawyer Martiniau to the Chevrolet lorry that is slowly ascending the gradient on the other side. Your life, *el Negro*'s, Lata's, and mine too. You like practical jokes so much; well, what about the one I played on you?

He looks around. How could anyone be watching? The Santa Cruz desert is the ideal place to talk to oneself. And he is talking out loud, all alone.

I screwed up all of our lives, he adds, after meditating for a while. Because those three generals sent us all to our doom, so that I, who'd obviously lost the plot or thought myself immune from reprisals because I was a Martiniau, could die heroically and stop being a pain in the ass. And so that I wouldn't get the time, or the opportunity, to repeat such patriotic bullshit in front of, say, a journalist.

Martiniau dries his eyes with a handkerchief, and breathes in the fine, sharp, healing air, that smells of nothing, only of air, or perhaps of distance and of ice, air that comes tumbling down from the faraway and unseen Andes. And he adds: but I never imagined, dear Private Sonrisal, that when those bastard fellow-officers of mine surrendered, they would accept the British demand to use you, the conscripts, for mine-clearing duties.

And he adds:

Nor could I ever imagine that, because I was so fucked up or deaf, or obedient or resigned or just a complete tosser, I don't know, that I wouldn't have opposed this.

And he adds:

I would simply never have imagined that before. And I can't forgive myself now.

I reckon I'm never going to forgive myself, he says a bit later, with a sob. The ex-combatant's little lorry continues to climb the incline, indifferent to the second flight of eloquence in Martiniau's life. It's nearly at the top now.

And then the final photo falls into place before Martiniau's eyes: the image that for so many years tormented him every night, just like the buzzing in his left ear pestered him during the daytime. It's his final memory of the days shut up inside the sheep pens.

It's the image of Negro Palacios, burned, sprawled on the ground without clothing, lacking arms, a leg missing, an eye missing, without ears or nose or bollocks, twisting in agony among the snow and the rocks.

In this almost still image, however, there are moving elements.

For example, Corporal Lattanzio, is now trying to get up after also being knocked flat by the anti-tank mine that Palacios was carrying. Another moving element is Private Sonrisal, frozen with horror but still intact, with a similar mine, a large grey disc the size of a soup plate, in his arms, about twenty metres away, trying hard not to trip up and fall over himself.

And the third element, the most mobile of all, is the British sergeant, with a maroon beret and a blond horseshoe-shaped moustache, an athletic paratrooper who was acting as foreman in charge of the transfer and loading operation.

And the sergeant, a practical type, comes rapidly but unhurriedly across with his Sterling machine gun to Palacios, a bundle that groans and cries and mumbles and hiccups and looks at him, pleadingly, with his one remaining eye, opened far too wide.

And the gringo pins Negro Palacios to the ground with a long burst from his machine gun.

Martiniau has fallen silent, watching the empty road, where the lorry disappeared from view quite a while ago. He feels the cold and looks, perplexedly, at his watch. He notices the sun has started to go down.

Hours have gone by.

Chapter Six

Invincible, *Las Pelotas...*

14 July 1982. The journalist Gustavo Enríquez hung up the telephone and looked at his wife in rapt admiration.

'Hell, yes! The New York Times is going to buy! On the condition that...'

As he told Isabel all about it, he started to dance a waltz around the bed, an exceedingly limited space, given that space is the very commodity that cheap hotels in the Big Apple skimp on. He took her in his bear-like arms, trying to make her spin around.

'On the condition that you...what?' she cut him short. Their feet got tangled up, they stumbled and the man's back bumped hard against the wall, but stopped them from falling. Now they were still, a little agitated, breathing with their faces close together and looking into each other's eyes. He thought all of a sudden that his wife, now nearing forty, was even more beautiful than at thirty. He smiled.

She didn't.

At that moment someone knocked on the door and Isabel disengaged herself from his embrace and went to open it. The two kids, seven and nine years old respectively, were there, with their enormous blue eyes (taking after their mother) and both strikingly good-looking in her same long, skinny way. Both were a little frightened.

'We heard a big bump. Is everything alright?' asked Lucas, the eldest.

The walls were thin, with no acoustic insulation. The YMCA's Sloane House, a clumsy hotel-cum-anthill-cum-skyscraper from around the 1920s was no great shakes on the privacy front, although that didn't seem to bother the cockroaches. It didn't bother Gustavo Enriquez today, either: he bestowed an enormous smile on his family.

'Alright? It's more than alright! We're in heaven!'

And to the tune of *Cheek to Cheek*, the Ella Fitzgerald version that he'd listened to so many times during long car journeys, he started to croon, trying not to sing totally out of tune, whilst performing a Danny Kaye-style tap dance. Not an easy task for a big man in such a small space.

'Money, we'll make money,
heaps of money that'll make us filthy rich,
when The Times displays the pictures you've seen,
that show how well we fucked the bloody Brits!'

He came up with these kinds of improvisations all the time, like rabbits out of a hat, and the kids loved it. And he could do it equally well in Spanish or English, a language he'd managed to make them understand by playing them Sinatra,

187

the Beatles and Handel day and night. But Isabel threw her husband one of her glacial glances, the children's laughter became first doubtful before drying up completely, and she told them they must never ever repeat the swear word their father had let slip, and to go back to their room, to the TV, their books, to their Simon[1], and other good things like that.

The children's' barely-concealed joy showed that they would spend the rest of the afternoon saying the word "fuck" over and over to each other, just for a laugh. As they were closing the door behind them, trying to keep a straight face, this certainty made Isabel even more furious. Just before the door closed, Lucas winked at his old man.

She pretended not to notice and turned to Enrique with her arms crossed.

'So, the kids will miss two weeks of school and probably have to repeat the year, their father teaches them to talk like urchins and, on top of that, we're going to be rich. Wonderful, isn't it?' she said, calmly.

He avoided her gaze. No arguing today. Keep to the subject at hand.

'Rich…I don't know how rich. A little bit rich. But that we're well set, definitely. As soon as I hand over the photos that back up the article, and the experts examine them and say (and he began singing again, this time to the tune of the Ode to Joy from Beethoven's Ninth):

'These are very honest, perfect, untinkered with piiiiic-tures,
    these are…'

---

1 Simon was a very popular (and primitive) electronic toy at the beginning of the 1980s.

Gustavo Enríquez was full of enough joy to melt or at least thaw out his wife, which more or less summed up their marriage. Other men might have been more socially acceptable, but none other could have resuscitated the curious and daring girl that she had probably once been, before the nuns had hammered her mind flat into the submissive, resentful and joyless format of a good catholic, Argentine, upper-class girl. That was why her inner little girl chose Gustavo, albeit with great difficulty. And with the predictable opposition of her family, a deplorable, insufferable and snooty clan of prim conservatives fallen on hard times, who had pinned their hopes of a comeback to posh Buenos Aires society on marrying Isabel off to Someone Minted.

The as yet un-minted Gustavo began leading her again to the tune of a waltz and singing her the Beethoven thing, but she resisted although not so strongly. It was like trying to get a corpse to dance. Alright, she wouldn't dance? Well, then, she'd have to listen. He immediately became conciliatory. He was good at that, too.

'Look, party-pooper: what I've got here is front page material. It'll be published by the Times. After which we'll be able to stay in New York while I make my way as a freelance journalist. Or, Plan B, we go back to Buenos Aires and I get a good job at *La República*, *La Nación* or even on the telly. This isn't a pipe dream. This is the best opportunity we've ever had, and you know it.'

She appeared somewhat confused.

'Our best opportunity, or another one of your schemes, Gustavo? So you can get us into yet more debt, and suddenly head off to Brazil, and hire that plane or other crazy stuff?

Then you come back home one night and get us into even more debt, and drag us out of the house like cattle and make the kids miss the school year and bring us to…' she regarded the miserable hotel room with desperation, '…this place? And all because you think you've struck gold, and we've all got to be here to see your moment of triumph?'

'Our moment of triumph,' he said, quietly.

'That's right. Look at our triumph,' she looked around again. 'Haven't we been through this so many times before? Well, haven't we?'

Her eyes were sodden. Self possessed as she was, this was the closest she ever let herself get to crying.

He responded with a deep, joyous laugh, confident she'd change her mind instantly. Then he got serious. He hugged her in silence and she put up less resistance. He had a way of hugging her that…Isabel couldn't find the right word for it. He was the one who supplied the right words in that family.

He looked her straight in the eye.

'Now listen to me, gorgeous. I risked everything finding that damned aircraft carrier – I risked my life, in fact. And I didn't do it for my career or even for you, milady Isabel, although I love you to bits. I did it for those two boys in the next room. And believe me, it hurts me too, all this messing around; the expense, ruining their school year, owing money to practically everyone. And I also hate this flea pit. But, as you admitted a few weeks ago when you saw the pictures, this time it really is serious. In my line, that's the sort of material that makes you famous.'

She didn't answer. She was on the point of sobbing.

'Alright, Isabel. Forget New York. Forget it completely. Bye-bye. It's gone. You hate New York, then I do as well. Too many cockroaches. We'll go back to Buenos Aires. You know I've got some good offers besides this. We can pay back what we owe down to the last penny and even help your family out, now that the Military are in free-fall and their civilian collaborators are losing their perks and positions.

She looked at him with fury, before calming down and regarding him, meditatively.

'Alright, Gustavo. Convince me. Try again,' she said quietly.

'That's just what I will do, as always. Look, with this story I'm dealing with a national need, something that's impossible to quantify. Don't you understand? A question of pride. You feel this need yourself. And I'm not talking about military pride; I'm talking about the people's pride. The pride of all of us, the stupid Argentines in the street. The ones who were ruined and humiliated when those idiots first sparked off that war and then lost it. When the Invincible thing's published, established and proved, then we'll all feel just a bit better in Argentina. And that's that. Which is why I reckon this story'll get me a weekly column in the International section of *La República*. Rosenblum himself promised me that, on the proviso I got it published here first.'

'Oh, yeah? She answered, enraged. 'And didn't it ever occur to you, Mr. Clever Clogs Journalist, that it's very odd that Rosenblum, who's always hated you, passes up the chance of getting the scoop on this for *La República*, ahead of the entire national and international press?'

'Babe, as Shakespeare said: "Uneasy lies the head that wears a crown". And Rosenblum's head isn't lying easy. In the first place, no-one believes him anymore. The old man and the newspaper chiefs made too many shady deals with the Military. They provided the names of people who later disappeared. Now there are lots of young pups on the paper just dying to bite his wrinkly old ass. As soon as democracy is reinstated (and that won't be long) they'll have his guts for garters, you'll see. He hates everyone of late. And it's true that he doesn't exactly trust in me. He hates the mavericks like me because he can't control them, but he hates his own ass-lickers even more, because he knows full well they're conspiring against him. He's a paranoid and a psychopath and that's exactly why he's been Number One for so long. As far as he's concerned, me and my story might be just a booby trap set up by any one of his countless enemies. So he acts like a king, and gets someone else to taste the food to make sure it's not poisoned. To minimize the risk even more, the bastard uses an emperor, instead of a lackey, as food taster. That's how clever he is. So he gives me this bloke McCallum's card and, well, you know the rest. He calls him long-distance direct, without secretaries or intermediaries, just like that, hello McCallum, Rosenblum here. He presses the hands-free button and they hold a teleconference right in front of me. Rosenblum puts the business to him: Enríquez – that's me! – takes the story to the Times first, and if the Times thinks it's good, they go worldwide with it. When the British react and deny it, we at *La República* publish the rest of the evidence we've got up our sleeves and we bury Maggie Thatcher under layers and layers of proof of how close she was to losing the war, and of how she won it by the breadth of one her grey fanny hairs (at this point, Isabel winced). And this bloke McCallum wavers, obviously surprised, and says: "alright Rosenblum, it's a deal. Let me get things ready on this side. Get Enríquez to me in two days with the photos, negatives and everything. And get him to phone this number, or he'll never get past my secretary." And Rosenblum says "OK" and hangs up and looks at me in that funny way of his and winks and says: "You're getting the first plane to New York tomorrow." Then the stingy bastard adds: "At your own expense, of course." But you know how things go, Babe (and here Gustavo began singing again in an almost acceptable imitation of a slightly over-the-hill Sinatra):

"If I can make it here, I'll make it anywhere!
It's up to you, New York, New Yoooork!"

She said nothing; she merely regarded him with a neutral expression that showed no anger, which showed absolutely nothing. She was a tough nut to crack, alright. And he'd always loved her for it. She always made out that she was unconquerable. "The Invincible!" he thought but, to keep the peace, he kept the joke to himself.

'Isabel, Isabel. Why did I have to fall in love with such a terribly serious girl? I sometimes think you'd be better off with some fat rich bloke who'd treat you badly. Then you could have an affair with me, or with someone like me. That's what a lot of your old convent school friends do, isn't it?'

She winced again. Her eyes filled with tears.

'Look, my girl, now we can really put the boys through school in Argentina. My God, it could be, it will be…a British school. What do you reckon? Wouldn't that be…symbolic?'

193

She looked at him, open-mouthed.

'That's right, think about it, Isabel. A very distinguished school. Very, very British. A hangover from the old Empire. Let's say the Saint Andrew's Scots? What about that? Now what's the matter, Isabel? Why are you crying?'

II

30 May 1982.

On a dull, wet midday in Patagonia, young Ensign Gerardo Isaac, the squadron's most junior member, looked at his watch. It was 11.45. As the minutes passed in no particular hurry, he and five other more experienced Argentine pilots revved the turbines of their fighter-bombers, which gave off their usual stink of half-burnt JP1 fuel.

The engines were already warm enough to begin the long and difficult take-off from BAM Rio Grande[2], on the north-west shore of Tierra del Fuego, but the idiot in the control tower was taking a lifetime to give them the go-ahead. Would this mission also be aborted for technical reasons? Or because someone changed his mind again? Shit!

The planes, trembling but restrained, loaded to the limit with fuel and ammunition, were beasts of two very different orders. Waiting for the green light could be seen two large, magnificent blue *Super Étendards* (or SUEs), of French manufacture. Immediately behind these were four small American A4C Skyhawks (the so-called Charlies, one of which was Isaac's), with their grimy earthen-coloured camouflage. They looked, respectively, like aristocracy and its poor relations.

---

2 *BAM (Base Aérea Militar)* The Rio Grande Military Air Base.

The Charlies belonged to the Argentine Air Force and the Sues to the CANA[3]. Although Argentina was losing the war, (perhaps because of it) this would be the first combined attack of both air arms together. They had, up until then, conducted incoherent and autistic parallel campaigns. The Navy's fault, of course, with its ridiculous sense of superiority.

The *SUE*s were proud new systems, equipped with Matra low-radiation radar capable of sniffing out and acquiring enemy targets forty miles away, without themselves being seen, the lucky sods. Beneath the ample wing of one of them, piloted by Navy Lieutenant Luis Collavino, with whom he had shaken hands just minutes before (a total stranger to him, like everything naval), Isaac could see the last ace up Argentina's sleeve: a low-flying *Aérospatiale* AM-39 Exocet missile, of the "fire & forget" type, painted orange

The four predecessors of this supersonic ship-sinking steel beast, fired that same month, had caused tremendous damage to the British Task Force, and simultaneously given a tremendous fillip to French arms exports. One of the first ones used had sunk the destroyer HMS Sheffield on 4 May, exacting vengeance for the loss of 323 Argentine lives aboard the cruiser ARA Belgrano a few days before, and multiplying by five the missile's asking price, set by the manufacturer *Aérospatiale*, from one day to the next. The only clear winners in the war so far? The Frogs.

As he awaited the order for chocks away, Isaac looked at his watch again, kept the revs up and tried to forget that in this particular adventure he was only a dispensable backup system. An intelligent flying robot, that big French cock,

---

3 *Comando de Aviación Naval* (*CANA*). Argentine Naval Aviation Command

would do almost all the work. The sign of things to come, if he survived this war? It didn't seem that likely he would.

On 25 May, or five days before that rainy midday, two more of the Navy's aforementioned flying beasts appeared from the north and unexpectedly pierced the defensive perimeter of a British convoy steaming on its way to rendezvous with the landing fleet. As usual, one of the missiles fell foul of electronic countermeasures and the anti-aircraft rockets that disperse trails of "chaff", aluminium strips that confuse radars by appearing to be targets. That Exocet fell into the sea. But the other, after charging into an intangible patch of chaff to no good purpose and flying parallel to HMS Hermes, reset itself to acquire a new target and cleverly chose the juiciest one on offer. It went for, set fire to, gutted and sank with all its cargo something almost as big and important as an aircraft carrier: the STUFT Atlantic Conveyor, a merchant container ship. This meant that the already-disembarked British had to fight the entire campaign in brutal weather and terrain with hardly any tents or heavy helicopters.

The Exocet, however, had really been aimed at HMS Hermes: apart from its symbolic value, damaging an aircraft carrier would have greatly incapacitated a Task Force that only had two available, HMS Hermes and HMS Invincible. The British were well aware of this, so much so that towards the end of May, while the French were still rubbing their hands gloating over their marketing success, their furious NATO allies were busy twisting their arms to obtain the codes and specifications needed to fool the Exocets.

The Exocets however, probably because they're French, have complex personalities and don't always agree to be fooled. They even showed themselves more discerning than the pilots, who insisted on fighting against destroyers and frigates, instead of attacking the fat, and rewarding, transport vessels.

As a pilot, Isaac came from a simpler and older world. At the age of 23, he loved the unsophisticated 1950s machine that trembled around him. And he loved it for its ability to bring him safely back home.

Five days before, as the Atlantic Conveyor was going up like a tinder box on the high seas, Isaac took part in a second mission in a different place. He and three other pilots managed to gatecrash San Carlos Water by surprise, at 550 knots, the bay replete with ships. There, they divided into pairs and attacked, respectively, an amphibious landing craft and a small frigate, whilst both vessels chucked fireworks at them like it was Guy Fawkes Night. Five seconds later, half of the attacking force had been shot down and Isaac's own plane, riddled with bullet holes and shrapnel, began to rapidly bleed JP1. Well, may as well drop the bombs and then die as God ordains, he thought.

He dropped them accurately on the frigate's waterline, then escaped skipping and zigzagging, following the contours of the hills, to avoid possible anti-aircraft missiles. After several hair-raising and terrifying low-flying acrobatics, he turned sharply to starboard, flew like an arrow over East Falkland and headed towards the sea, with his heart in his mouth and his hands trembling.

As he gained altitude and left the islands behind, the round-faced, lightly-built and youthful-looking pilot began to get a grip of himself. He stared intently at his instruments, made a few worried mental calculations and thereby gained an accurate idea of God's plans for him: 29 minutes, give or take a minute, of fuel left before the engines cut out. Then he would have to eject and fall into the enormous, mountainous, freezing and desolate Argentine Sea, 100 miles away from the continent. Well, God's will seemed rather pitiless. The total number of Argentine flyers rescued from those waters so far: zero.

But God changed his plans. In the following 25 minutes, somehow or other he and another battered survivor, Lieutenant Paredi, were carefully shepherded by their air controllers. Until, miraculously, they saw the glint of an Argentine KC-130 tanker plane at 11 o' clock, a "Chancha"[4], which was slowly orbiting halfway between the continent and the islands.

Isaac made contact with the tow boom when only two minutes-worth of fuel remained in his tanks. Thereafter, the two Skyhawks hobbled slowly towards undisputed Argentine soil hanging from the tanker's nipples, sucking, burning and bleeding JP1 at a constant rate: like their pilots, the planes had refused to die.

It was this very robustness, and their low maintenance cost, that had made the Skyhawks popular amongst Argentine airmen. The Air Force acquired the first lot of second-hand Type B units in 1966 from the United States, and they were so well liked that in 1974 they ordered 25 more, of the C type (called P by the USAF), more or less the same article, but with superior weapons, turbines and range.

Before the war, Argentina had received only seventeen Charlies like Isaac's, in "sold as is" condition. Meaning, in plain English, "with all sorts of defective instruments, a bro-

---

4 Literally, a sow. Thus nicknamed due to their tubby appearance.

ken-down radar thrown in for good measure, or no radar at all". As blind as bats, they would have been obsolete for fighting in Korea, let alone Vietnam. And on top of that, although these Charlies could take you to hell and back, they wouldn't do much for your reputation, given that they even lacked a damned camera on the wing to film what you'd machine-gunned or bombed in the realms of Satan.

Further prospects for the Charlie business that year looked even worse. In addition to those one-thousand mile "delivery" missions over the Argentine Sea, there were Harrier patrols carrying those pitiless American Sidewinder missiles, and gringo destroyers with their Sea Darts lying in ambush among the islands, just waiting to trash you the moment you started that desperate ascent to save fuel, so you could get back home.

Adding it all up, Isaac accepted with a shrug of the shoulders that he wouldn't get to the ripe old age of 24 or 25. With two hair-breadth's escapes in only two missions, the odds were already against him: something would one day kill him. Today's long haul, probably.

Three days after the 25 May attack, an Intelligence officer informed Isaac and Paredi of the mission's estimated "score": Captain García, shot down and missing, presumed dead and Lieutenant Lucero also shot down but plucked from the sea by the British with God knows how many broken bones. And, in revenge, that thin Type 21 frigate, the HMS Avenger and that other, tubbier ship, apparently the HMS Fearless, each perforated with a 1000 lb Mark 17 bomb (Made in England!), neither of which exploded.

It was always the same story. Equipped with hard fuses and programmed to explode with enough delay to allow the pilot time to escape, the inertia of these enormous bombs made them crash right down into the guts of the British ships, or sent them sailing straight through from one gunwhale to the other and into the sea, without their noticing that a ship *had* been in the way.

Those damned navy pilots, also flying in Skyhawks (albeit of the aircraft carrier variety), certainly did know how to trash a ship at the first attempt. But the toffee-nosed navy bastards kept the secret to themselves, and the Air Force wouldn't give them the satisfaction of asking how it was done.

The plane that growled beneath the seat of Isaac's trousers carried an imitation of the naval combination: a cluster of three Spanish-made 500lb parachute retarded bombs, with a twelve-second time delay contact fuse. The cluster was attached to the pylon under the fuselage, almost touching the airstrip, and five tons of kerosene hung from the underwing pylons, in two ungainly external tanks. Carrying such bulk, the little Charlie looked, and was, about as easy to fly as an articulated lorry.

It's already 12:48 and they still haven't departed. And the weather is getting worse. The war is lost, but still rages furiously. The improbable success of today's mission will not now change its course. Was it worth dying for that, just to regain a little national pride or, to be frank, just not to lose it altogether? That's not a question that a fighter pilot ever asks himself.

Some, however, were now asking it. The previous week, the decimated ranks of the strike pilots at the three active coastal air bases had rebelled against the idiotic way their superior officers, bravely manning their desks, sent them off to die, and all for nothing. They objected to making only isolated and reactive attacks, they asked why the British were allowed to always take the initiative; they wanted to know why the Navy didn't coordinate a generalised strike alongside the Air Force, and asked what was happening in that respect. Today's mission was perhaps a tardy and ineffective first step in the right direction.

The young pilots' rebellion had been silently suppressed by the brigade commanders. Although they wouldn't be court martialing anybody, they did expect the gentlemen pilots to get on with their work in the usual way and to die patriotically, in order to cover up their chiefs' ineptitude and even cover them with some sort of glory.

Given the Argentine Military's propensity to believe its own propaganda, the Air Force had taken heed of the delinquents in the Navy and, above all, of the cretins in the Army. The latter in particular were convinced that Argentina had become US President Ronald Reagan's greatest geo-political asset in the hemisphere, thanks to the little group of Argentine officers who were helping out the Contras in Nicaragua. It was inevitable that after Argentina had invaded the Falklands, the USA, full of gratitude, would gallantly intercede with the British to prevent the Empire from striking back, and would even twist the trident-wielding arm of the blonde Miss Britannia and force her to negotiate.

"You gentlemen must accept," said the Chiefs of Staff to the pilots at the beginning of the war, "that a move such as constructing an advance base for strike aircraft in the islands themselves would be considered too negative for the imminent negotiations. Our current aim, gentlemen, is to achieve joint administration of the Falklands by Argentina, the United Kingdom and the UN. Forget about exclusive Argentine sovereignty for the moment. We do not wish to antagonise the British any further. We just want to bring them to the negotiating table but, this time, it'll be their turn to have their trousers around their ankles. We are realists, gentlemen."

Well, the bloody unrealistic British seemed rather annoyed anyway, despite the fact that Argentina, with 100 fighters, strike and bomber aircraft on land and eight more on an aircraft carrier at sea, had graciously conceded air supremacy over the islands to a precarious sea-borne aerial strike force, made up of two small aircraft carriers and about twenty Harriers.

Very irritable people, these British. It was already 11.52. Drizzle, drizzle, more drizzle and wind, the inevitable wind, shaking the aircraft, loaded down as it was. The mission could be aborted at any moment. But what a time to think of his parents, while the other half of his mind was occupied running through the pre-flight checklist for the third time! Why now? Why that lump in his throat?

The target that unknowingly awaited Isaac's bombs at the end of the trajectory was so incredibly distant that not even all the fuel he carried, extra tanks included, would take him a third of the way. To get there, he would need two more high-precision rendezvous with the Chanchas *en route*.

These had already ostentatiously departed an hour before, taking different courses in order to fool the FACH[5] radar at Punta Arenas. The Chileans pretended to be neutral

5 *FACH: Fuerza Aérea Chilena.* The Chilean Air Force.

but really spent their time spying for the British, due to their own protracted border disputes with Argentina. The bastards. When the Argentines surrendered in the islands, they would probably launch an attack to grab another chunk of Patagonia. Well, Isaac wouldn't be alive to fight in any future wars... Damn, it's 11.54 already!

Suddenly the light indicated take-off. The brakes released, the screeching aircraft began to move slowly forwards, clumsily, bobbing and rolling beneath the rain and wind until they picked up speed and thrust. The beautiful SUEs left the rest behind, spitting blue dragon flames out of their tails due to their afterburners - another little detail that the Charlies lacked.

Now they were all precariously in the air and flying in close formation over the sea, practically blinded by the drizzle, but without gaining altitude, trying rather to keep their heads down below the Chilean radar's radiation lobes. They almost immediately left the island of Tierra del Fuego behind them. Flying persistently close to the sea, they set off on a 120-degree bearing that would take them over the desolate waters far to the south of the Falklands, to meet up there with the tankers and, hopefully, evade detection by the British alarm systems.

The British Harriers and missile-firing frigates would, it was hoped, be fully occupied in bombing the fuck out of the Argentine Army's chaotic retreat. All their attention would be placed on covering their own troops, as they bulldozed all remaining pockets of Argentine resistance on land.

Treeless rocks, forgotten and probably useless as they were, lost down there in the Atlantic, the Falklands still represented for Isaac and for any other Argentine, irrespective of political persuasion, the only part of national soil ever taken away by force - a bitter pill to swallow. Argentina, peaceful in its foreign policy, but never defeated in war, had patiently put up with this infamy ever since 1833. Put simply, the mission of such an unimportant chap like young Isaac was not to ensure the exclusive or even shared possession of the islands – something that was already clearly impossible – but merely to wash away a little bit of that shame for the coming century. Nothing more and nothing less.

His fears assuaged, Isaac flew with his mind concentrated only on his instruments and what awaited him. The target was now the HMS Invincible.

Invincible my left foot, as the gringos said.

Or *las pelotas*, as we say in Argentina.[6]

An attack that flew in the face of accepted wisdom

'How did the operation start?' I ask Lieutenant Isaac a few months later. He's very agile, like almost all pilots. His round face is still that of a young lad but his eyes, compared with pre-war photographs, are now of an older man. He doesn't seem to be weighed down by the decorations and prestige that he's now receiving. He keeps a low profile.

After the defeat the Argentine press developed a tremendous mistrust regarding the war communiqués released by the Military: almost all of them, like the one reporting the sinking of the Canberra, turned out to be false. The pilots simply refused to talk with the previously-gagged press, which was now in rebellion against the government.

And this pilot in particular doesn't like me, or what I represent, at all. He only agreed to receive me following strict or-

---

6 Literally: bollocks!

ders: I have my contacts in the Armed Forces and the military chiefs know what I can do for them: save them some prestige in their hour of need.

'Well, then, who gave the information?' I insist.

'Well, anyway,' he shrugged his shoulders. He doesn't know, or makes out that he doesn't. 'Nobody can point a finger at the Russians,' he adds, reading my mind.

He seems quite good at this mind-reading business. 'There was never any contact with the Russians,' he insists. 'The CANA air controllers and the electronic warfare people knew what they were about. As they observed the return route taken by the Harrier patrols, the navy concluded that the Invincible was sailing in circles about 200 miles to the east of Puerto Argentino, the islands' capital.'

'And it seemed to be unprotected on the south flank. The gringos probably thought the ship was too far east to be reached by our planes, all of which were operating from the continent, so far away from that point out to sea.'

'Then why the hell didn't the Air Force put a Skyhawk base in Puerto Argentino, for starters?' I ask Isaac, the lad with the eyes that are older and probably wiser than they were months ago. He shrugs his shoulders.

'Too complicated.'

'Do you mean in political terms?' I insist.

'No, I mean in technical terms,' he answers rapidly. Well, well, well, he was ready for that one.

'Oh, come on!' I answer. 'Is it so complicated to lengthen an airstrip by a thousand metres?'

He shrugs his shoulders again. 'You have no idea of the complexity and quantity of operative equipment that an air strike base needs. It's not just a question of bulldozing and throwing down tarmac. It's a logistic nightmare'.

'So how come the Air Force did exactly that in San Julian, on the continent? I respond.

'Exactly what?' asks Isaac, looking straight at me, seriously. When he does this, I feel like a British frigate.

'Lieutenant, you know the answer. The Air Force transformed a shithole of a Patagonian aerodrome, designed for Pipers and Cessnas, into an operative base for Mirage Vs at Puerto San Julian. And it took them a month.'

He looks at me thoughtfully, but doesn't answer. He has his orders and I decide not to press the point. If I do, he'll stop the interview, which was hard enough to get in the first place. He has just looked at his wristwatch again. He thinks that'll make me feel uncomfortable. He's right.

I can hear another timepiece, a clock on the wall, going tick-tock in the dark and silent apartment. He regards me in silence. I decide to resist and look straight at him.

He clears his throat, a sign that the interview will continue.

'So what happened after you took off?' I change tack.

'We fly and fly for ages. The Royal Navy had done its homework and deployed frigates as a radar screen, but far to the west of the aircraft carrier. That way they cut off the shortest approach routes, which could only come from the continent and even so were still too long for us. That way, they probably thought they were safe. We fucked them good and proper. We designed an even trickier route, going right down to the south and then to the east. We cut across the Invincible's longitude coordinates about 100 miles to the east, then we turned north-east and caught the Invincible on a final run on bearing 340, coming "out of the blue", as the gringos say, from behind them, from the south-east, from the most desolate seas on the planet. Not bad, eh?'

I look at him in astonished silence. He likes that.

'Can you give me more details?'

'Yes, up to a point. It was the Navy who came up with the idea; I give them credit for that. But no way could their SUEs get there and they needed the Air Force to give them a hand with some tankers, at least three of them. "Three *Chanchas* is all we ask for" is what the Naval liaison officer apparently said. And we replied: "That's all we've got. We can't afford to lose any of them."'

I can just picture that meeting, I think to myself. Teach the Navy some manners, right?

'So, after some bargaining we supplied the *Chanchas,* with certain conditions. "Only if we can come along as well. You can fire the missile, that's fine, but we follow the smoke trail in with four fighter-bombers and we blow up the aircraft carrier like in the old days, with gravity bombs. How does that sound?" So they shook hands and it was agreed.'

'But how did things really happen after that? How did the mission go? Did it go as expected?

Young Gerardo Isaac looks at his watch again. The point of no-return went by minutes ago. Too late to abort the mission now.

Two hours pass without incident, the six planes are flying at ten thousand feet, just slightly above the distinct blanket of cumulus clouds that covers the sea, above which the sun shines furiously, for the first time in five weeks. The radios are totally silent.

Then, hand signals are exchanged from cockpit to cockpit: two identical glints are seen at 12.00, the tankers, there they are, that's good, just in time. Ugly fucking Chanchas, we love 'em so much. In strict silence the strike aircraft reduce their speed to that of a Hercules, which is really slow. Extending their flaps in order not to stall, they start to fill their tanks, one after the other. They take it in turns during 120 miles, meaning 30 tense minutes.

Then there are more hand signals, which mean: "that's your lot, mate!" from the cockpits of the two Hercules. And the fighters, with their fuel tanks now full, accelerate once more to cruise economy speed, turn in unison onto bearing 340 and begin a slow, blind descent through some bad weather until they are almost at sea level, where no radar will be looking for them or could distinguish them from the strong reflections given off by the waves.

An hour and fifty more minutes like this, thought Isaac, quite relaxed. He is absorbed in the Byzantine routine of checking and re-checking the systems that keep such a complex aircraft in the air, and its pilot too busy to understand that he's just summed up his life expectancy.

The same calm probably reigned in each cockpit as the six planes roared towards their goal, flying through sudden squalls and leaping over immense waves. Their windscreens were already opaque from the salt deposits found in the moisture that floats just above the surface of a choppy sea – that's how low they were flying. The arrogant SUEs in the middle and the humble Charlies grouped into pairs flanking them, a pair on each side.

More sign language: First Lieutenant Vázquez ordered his pairing, First Lieutenant Castillo, to switch to the other flank, the port side of the formation, according to the original plan. Castillo obeyed and interchanged positions with Isaac. This left Isaac, Ureta's pairing, on the starboard side of the line of attack. Both were eventually saved by this changeover, although neither was aware of it at the time.

They continued flying.

Now, in the final 40 miles, the SUEs began to "pop up" to 300 feet and down again, in order to locate the target and programme the steel beast. Sure enough, some echoes appeared in the expected area, one of them very big. The final run began, and with the throttle fully opened, things happened pretty quickly.

At 14.24, one Exocet was fired by the SUEs, which fell freely for several metres and, just when it seemed about to drop into the ocean, suddenly woke up, spat out blue flames, accelerated very quickly and left the planes well behind. Gone.

Then one of the SUE pilots broke radio silence and said "Twenty miles, right in front!" the damned idiot, before both planes made a sudden turn westwards and were lost from view. Fuck, shit, bollocks. That idiot's given the game away. Typical bloody navy, just like them.

Now they know they've been heard, the four Charlie pilots can imagine the pandemonium that's probably broken out at Task Force air control. How could the gringos fail to pick up that radio signal? They must now be desperately seeking us all over their screens. Or maybe not?

Oh, my God. Still a hundred eternal seconds between us and the target. Knowing that they've now probably acquired us and are even now firing at us with their super-fucking-sonic Sea Darts, that you don't see and don't even know they've hit you.

The Exocet's blue flame seemed to twinkle at times, now almost out of visual range.

The black, squat hulk of an aircraft carrier seen from the stern appears suddenly on the horizon, obscured by squalls. Look at that! On its own, as well, thank God, can't see any frigates. Then a white lightening bolt briefly lights up the aircraft carrier and its sharp outlines are momentarily dulled, probably by smoke. Impact! Gotcha! The beast has hit the Invincible. *Viva la patria*! Suck on that, you fucking pirates! Check the time: it's 14.27. We're still going in!

The four Charlies, divided into pairs, converge at full speed on the Invincible's wake, at an agonisingly slow 590 knots. Knowing that the entire Task Force is now just dying to kill them. There are just seven nautical miles remaining to be covered when…wham! Vázquez, the squadron leader, disappears in an orange flash. Where the hell did that come from? Those damned invisible frigates, somewhere off to port and over the horizon. Now we know they've got us on our radars. We're fucked.

Now there are just two nautical miles separating them from the aircraft carrier, apparently disabled and dead in the water, even incapable of maintaining defensive anti-aircraft fire when …wham again! And Castillo, the survivor on the port flank, disappears in another flash. Isaac has a slow-motion view of aluminium panels that rip apart due to the eruption of orange flames and, as the explosion takes place at barely a dozen metres away, the turbulence hits him like a poleaxe, and his only thought in the world is to regain some sort of control and nail the target dead on before the third Sea Dart gets him as well.

He and Ureta are attacking the aircraft carrier from the stern, flying about ten metres beneath the level of the deck. Ureta, now slightly in front and to the port of Isaac, is trying to fire the machine-gun. But both barrels of his Charlie's useless fucking 30mm guns jam at the second burst, and he howls in frustration. The smoke that erupts port and starboard from the aircraft carrier's gigantic silhouette reminds the silent Isaac of enormous nineteenth-century moustaches, with the waxed ends pointing upwards.

Ureta, in front, strikes first. His final run is a diagonal that cuts a twenty-degree angle across the centre of the Invincible, from stern to port. Flying well below deck level, Ureta suddenly turns the nose of his Charlie a few degrees upwards, pointing towards the monstrous island, which is divided into blocks by two great funnels and a conical, robust mast: the very structure that houses the Invincible central command. And he drops three 500lb. bombs from a horizontal distance of 800 feet.

The bombs maintain the plane's velocity and direction, opening out slightly as they fly and they perforate the vertical surfaces like any other anti-tank ammunition would, bong, bong, bong! Ureta has now leaped over the second funnel, just missing it, and holding back the now-lightened Charlie's instantaneous tendency to float upwards, he plunges once more to sea level, skids to the side and zigzags like a startled snake to avoid the artillery or anti-aircraft fire from the forecastle. But there are no missiles or flak. The aircraft carrier seems to be in an electronic coma: she still doesn't know what she's been hit with.

Isaac sees all this as time flows by very, very slowly, like lava or melted rubber, subdivided into fractions of eternal seconds. The only important thing in his life is right there in front of his plane's nose: he's got the worst case of target fixation, as he pursues the ship at a gallop, machine-gunning the stern until his magazines empty and go clack! He catches a glimpse of the stern, colourless, a straight wall of steel, full of holes, that jumps towards him like a charging cliff face, and seems about to crush him.

He'll bomb the boat in enfilade, as they say in the navy, which means that the shot enters through the stern and runs through the ships entrails along her axis, maximising the damage. Much worse than a lateral impact.

And then, when his Charlie seems about to crash into the steel wall, he drops his bombs, yanks the joystick backwards and towards the left, then pushes it forwards whilst pushing hard on the left pedal to make the plane flatten out. Then follows a series of wave-hugging acrobatics and then, bye-bye! He's off!

Where the hell is the Invincible? Isaac puts the plane into a skid and looks over his shoulder. But it's the wrong question. Hell is *inside* the Invincible. The aircraft carrier, already small in the distance, cannot be seen or recognised at all. There's only a gigantic cloud, a shapeless pile of black smoke. But Isaac can't hang about to confirm. Anti-aircraft missiles usually stop the regular A4 pilot from ejecting, given that the plane's brightest infra red spot is just nine feet behind him. He heads off on a bearing of 230, towards the south-east, fleeing from the invisible frigates.

Then, while the longest minutes since the invention of time slip slowly by and his small rear view mirror shows no furious glint of pursuing missiles, Isaac realises that he's far to the south, out of the range of the Sea Dart. He lets out a huge sigh of relief.

Now he's completely alone in the middle of the immense, stormy Atlantic. He holds the same course, his heart thumping like a steam hammer. Then he starts to wonder where Ureta has got to. Shot down, too?

Vázquez and Castillo, the entire squadron port flank, the closest to the line of frigates hidden over the horizon, then woosh! and they vanished. Now Isaac feels guilty. Castillo got the rocket that was meant for him, for Isaac. And he feels very small and very much alone, in that toy airplane. With those giant, tragic black clouds up above and the dark, desolate Atlantic below.

Fuel situation? All's well. He hasn't been holed, for once. How did he manage that? The British were experts at turning his plane into a colander. Incredibly, the Invincible didn't defend herself at all. Funny, to fly home in an undamaged aircraft...

The miracle of still being alive begins to dawn on Isaac. As he regains self awareness, he notices that he is sweating and dripping like a turkey in the oven, and that his face is burning. So he tries to turn down the rheostat that heats the oxygen feeding into his mask, but his left arm, with the hand still hysterically clutching the fuel lever, is rigid and paralysed. He tries over and over to regain use of his fingers, to open them one at a time. No dice. So his fucking hand won't open now? Well, he'll just have to roast in peace, then.

But he's still not out of it. At a good 100 nautical miles from the burning aircraft carrier, hurtling towards the south-east at low altitude, he keeps an eye out on the skies around him, automatically, trying to pick out possible enemies. There, at two o' clock, a little dot. Damn, fuck my luck. A Harrier this far south?

Shit, why did he go and shoot off all the ammo? There's no point trying to hide, the air controllers are probably already telling the gringo pilot he's got an Argy on his tail. Well, he could at least give the bastard a fright before dying with a smile on his lips. He gets into line, approaching very, very slowly, from six o' clock and from below. But no, it's not a Harrier! It's Ureta, who dips his wings in a terrified gesture of recognition. Don't shoot, you crazy bastard! So Ureta's alive, thanks be to God.

That means that I'm also going to live.

They fly side by side, and give the thumbs up signal. That's right, we trashed it, there was no way of missing, it was like bombing a shack. No photo, unfortunately. They don't exchange words, they must continue still in radio silence. But they wouldn't feel much like talking anyway. The mood is sombre, because of Castillo and Vázquez.

Their fuel is quickly running out, so they reduce speed and climb to a more economical cruising altitude. Ureta takes charge and plots a course that will take them to the third refuelling station. It's a complex calculation, very difficult with no computer aboard.

When the Hercules finally appears, in the distance, Isaac, completely exhausted, looks at his watch. As he does so he notices that he's mysteriously regained the use of his left arm and hand, and of the wrist he wears his watch on. Three hours and 47 very long minutes have gone by since they took off.

And several months and several medals later, Gerardo Isaac's wristwatch is still ticking rather well in this elegant apartment, with the dark wooden panelling that gives it an almost English air. As he waits for this bothersome journalist to hurry up and get lost. And to leave him alone so he can dine with his parents in peace.

At peace.

III

'Yes Sirree, Bob! Now that's what I call real purty writing, but I'll be damned if that's good journalism, son. Very showy, very cool, and lord knows what else. And full of opinions, too. You put a lot of your ideas in the other guy's head, while he's waiting to take off. And criticising the way the war's being run? That's just supposition, bo, more'n just plain facts. And you know that ain't professional. You just cain't do things like that, bo. But with a bit of editing, now, it'll just get good enough to publish,' said Mr. Brinks, after reading the manuscript from end to end.

And just who was this Mr. Brinks, for starters? Gustavo Enríquez had been negotiating by telephone with a certain George McCallum, chief editor, who hadn't once mentioned Brinks. One of McCallum's ass-lickers, no doubt.

An interview with some stand-in wasn't a good start.

This Brinks had obviously been chosen at the last moment and didn't have a clue about the matter at hand. McCallum, Gustavo decided, must be busy putting out one of those spontaneous wildfires that happen so often in newspapers: the main headline planned for the next day's front page has just "gone down", has to be shelved and something worth reading put in its place. Or those idiots in the publicity department have just sold the very three columns where you planned to put the day's best article, to a shampoo manufacturer.

Brinks had read and reread everything very carefully, as if the material were completely new to him. And that had taken him ten minutes, during which time Enríquez's heart had beat slightly faster.

'Well, tell me what needs cutting.'

'No need of that, bo. We'll take care of it.

Enríquez was furious. He was about to say: "my ass, you will" but he refrained. This damn southerner, probably a Texan, hadn't even given him a card or made clear what his position was within the New York Times hierarchy. And the interview was taking place not in Brinks's probably cramped and untidy office, but rather in a large, anonymous conference room, devoid of elegance and reeking of stale tobacco, one probably used by the editorial boards of all the different sections. At the moment, though, it was empty except for the two of them, and for two paper cups filled with execrable American "regular coffee".

'You got the photos, son?' asked Brinks, who seemed to be reading the last page for the third time.

Son? Who the fuck gave you the right, Mr. John fucking Wayne, to call me "son"? Enríquez didn't say, but he did throw the envelope down in front of Brinks, instead of passing it to him. Brinks didn't seem to place much importance on good manners, though. He was the living archetype of the ugly American. Enormous, balding, untidy. A Republican from head to toes. A dago-hating Anglo-Saxon, for sure. And probably baffled that Enríquez's blond, Caucasian appearance didn't tie in with his heavy Hispanic accent.

This time Brinks flicked through the photos very quickly. Twice he stopped and grunted "yes, sirree!" and "well, looky here!" when he saw the holes gaping on the deck like open jaws, the soot and scrap metal strewn around and the repair gangs working and looking at the camera in alarmed stupor. Where the hell did that fucking plane come from?

'This is a good one, bo. You can even see some bits of Harrier and helicopter down there in the hold. Only shame is there's no British flag floating over that heap of junk. Jesus, bo. This'll get you the Pulitzer. You got any more?'

Enríquez suppressed an immense feeling of pride, shook his head and congratulated himself inside. He wasn't going to, of course, not unless they asked him, but what he was really itching to tell Brinks, was how he, with the limited knowledge of yacht navigation he'd acquired in his youth, had plotted the possible sailing directions of the Invincible, under repair on the high seas, far away from cameras, where she could be reconstructed and thereafter returned to port looking spruce and presentable, as if nothing had happened.

And Enríquez had been right. Four hundred miles out to sea, off the Brazilian coast, in a spot far removed from commercial shipping lanes and relatively free from tropical storms, was where she had to be. Guided by this mad hunch, he'd invested his own money on a trip from Buenos Aires to Fortaleza, in the north of Brazil. Once there, he hired a twin-engine Cessna probably used by drug-traffickers, again at his own expense and thereby categorically condemned his family to bankruptcy.

This time, however, he struck gold at the first time of asking. There she was, hidden in the middle of the ocean, still stained dark with grease and soot and disembowelled: the Invincible. Towed by some sort of ship repair vessel, and flanked by an even bigger tug, all in navy grey, and no visible flags flying anywhere.

Enríquez had bribed the pilot into flying very low; all pilots hate doing this but drug-traffickers are used to it. And the gringos were taken by surprise once more and didn't fire a single bullet or missile at them, while Enríquez took thirty six photos in a thirty-second run with his motorised Nikon. And then they departed.

'*Qué merda foi isso?*'[7] barked the pilot, escaping at full speed and suspecting he'd been duped and that his own life had been, and continued to be, under threat. It took another pile of dollars to calm him down.

The man Brinks seemed to be sunk in deep reflection. Then he suddenly looked Enríquez full in the eyes and said:

'Good show, old chap!'

He suddenly didn't sound like a Texan anymore, more like an old Oxonian, in fact. He even looked different. The hunched posture had gone. And there before Enríquez's incredulous eyes, Brinks fed the typescript, the full twelve pages, then the photos as well, into a machine which the Argentine took some time to identify as a document shredder. He'd heard of them, but never seen one.

He was frozen to the spot. Enríquez didn't utter a word while the most important piece of journalistic research of his life was being destroyed.

---

7 In Portuguese: What the hell was that?

When the job was over, the enormous Brinks spoke to him in his new clipped, pompous English accent.

'That's right; you're on the right track. Military Intelligence. The SIS, or MI-6, as some people call us. Or perhaps I should say: "Bond, James Bond" to add a touch of light relief to this, for you at least, rather sad situation.'

Enríquez still could neither talk nor move.

'We identified the plane and found the pilot almost as soon as he landed, but the man, of course, had no flight log or receipts. In any case, you'd given him a false name and that was all we could get out of him, along with your identikit image. So we combed the area over and over again, but after two days it became clear that you'd expertly given us the slip. When months went by without anyone publishing the photos, we could only surmise that the Argentine Military wasn't behind this. It must be a civilian, probably a journalist trying to put together a complete package, with photos to back up an article. And we imagined that the Argentine Military made it difficult for you to interview the pilots who knocked the hell out of our poor ship. All things considered, that was good news because it excluded the bigger Argentine newspapers, which've got their own short cuts through military barriers. On the contrary, the situation seemed to suggest you were a very daring freelance reporter, but without much influence. Knowing the profession well, as I used to be in it myself, my hunch was that you'd be waiting for the first anniversary of the Argentine surrender to publish. So, we set up a few traps and alarms here and there, put the thing on ice and waited for you to trip one of them. I had another hunch that also came up trumps: that you'd agree to be sent to one of the big papers in the United States or even Britain. For a small-potatoes Argentine journalist, the temptation to become some sort of international figure in next to no time must have been very great. And it seems I was right, my good man, because here you jolly well are. Welcome, by the way. I see the physical description the pilot gave us is pretty close, although the identikit was useless. They usually are.'

Enríquez smelt danger. Although he'd boxed and learned karate as a youth, he wasn't sure that he could knock this man Brinks out quickly. He felt like doing it, though. And escaping.

'What are you going to do with me?' he asked, seemingly very calm.

'Nothing, I think.'

'I can re-write the story. I know it off by heart. And I've got the negatives.'

'Untrue. I've got them. Here they are, in fact. Like to see?'

Brinks extracted a familiar-looking envelope from his briefcase, opened it and showed Enríquez the negatives before also shredding them in the machine.

'Your wife gave them to us. She wants a divorce, immediately and with no fuss. Along with American citizenship, and a well-paid job. She's a tough nut to crack. Very able negotiator, your wife.'

Enríquez wanted to cry, but he was still frozen.

'And what happens to the boys?'

'Ah, yes, the boys...She takes them with her. Furthermore, I can tell you they're at this very minute in a plane flying somewhere over this vast country, under false names, and you'll never see them again. Unless...'

'Unless what?'

Brinks seemed somewhat uncomfortable as Enríquez held back the tears. He tried to avoid his eyes.

'Unless, well, look here: these are also very good photos. Have a little look at these…'

Faced with the image of his wife shagging a stranger, but in an utterly familiar bedroom (his own), his jaw dropped. It was as if he'd been punched in the stomach.

For a long while, neither spoke. Finally, Enríquez regained the capacity to think.

'So the slut thinks she's going to take my kids away, does she? Not if you give me those photos.'

'That's the point, old bean. That's exactly the point. We'll give you the photos and all the intelligence: names, dates, everything. And your family's new whereabouts. You'll have to go through a lengthy legal process in your own country. Get a restitution order from a judge there, take it to the American embassy and trust in the American legal system, which is pretty fair compared with the one you've got in Argentina. And that way, you may perhaps, over time, get your kids back.'

'But only if I remain silent.'

'Silent, but still alive.'

Enríquez took another while to digest the last comment.

'Why are you also betraying my wife, Brinks?'

'I could answer that by saying "Rome does not pay traitors", but that'd be a dreadful lie. In my case, I must admit that I don't particularly like your wife. She's very bad news. She even tried to threaten us. She doesn't particularly hate you, however, if that's any consolation. She only wants you out of her life - and out of the kids' lives, of course. But she still respects you somewhat, because she said that if we dared to liquidate you, she'd go public. So, why shouldn't we just liquidate her as well - we had to ask ourselves - and the children, too, while we're about it?'

Enríquez's heart stopped beating.

'Well, because that was too complicated. We don't like killing children, on the whole, although the matter was very passionately discussed at the office, believe you me. Finally, we decided not to touch a hair of their heads and to keep you alive, but very quiet.'

'Quiet for a while, Brinks. Just for a while,' said Enríquez under his breath.

'Of course. The time it takes you to get your children back. On that score, you might do well to call your wife's mental stability into question – it's pretty feeble. I should know – I've got a doctorate in Psychiatry. But you'll only get them back if you're lucky and if you keep your trap shut. We get along very well with the Americans and know how to get around their legal system, provided they go along with things.'

'I understand.'

'Good, I'm glad. There are some other things you should consider. The Argentine legal system works at a snail's pace. Add on the consular delays and the appeals your wife will lodge in an American court, and years will have gone by before the custody of your children is settled one way or the other. So, if you end up telling your story in ten years or so, who'll give a damn?'

'I don't understand.'

'The scourge of Thatcher and her cronies (and you can add the admirals and generals involved in this conflict) will be retired by then and growing roses in their country houses. There'll be a new government, a different political agenda and probably a more exciting little war in some other corner of the planet. And everyone in Britain will have forgotten again where the ruddy Falkland Islands are, and they won't care two hoots what did or didn't happen to the HMS Invincible. Within a few years we'll probably have sold or scrapped her anyway. And remember, you have no photos to back up your story.'

Enríquez laughed dryly.

'Don't you hate your job sometimes, Brinks?'

Brinks sighed.

'Brinks isn't my real name, actually, but… at the end of the day, it's a job. Even so, my heart's in the right place. It was nice old Uncle Brinks's idea to photograph your wife and her rich lover. From where I stand, he's just a common crook and a wee bit mature for her, as he's twenty years older, but her family seem to like him, if you'd like to know. Furthermore, it was good old Uncle Brinks who had the good sense to introduce them in the first place, and thereby avoid killing anybody, including your kids. Which means, old chap, that the official story stays official. The HMS Invincible was never attacked. The Argentine pilots got the wrong ship, the HMS Avenger, which everyone knows is identical to an aircraft carrier, except it has no flight deck and displaces nine times less tonnage. But your poor compatriots were so stupid that they missed. Even the Exocet fired by the *Étendard*s was knocked out by gunfire from the Avenger, which is like stopping a .45 bullet with a .22. And it fell into the sea, etc, etc, etc. My dear chum, I'll grant you that one must be a total idiot to believe such a load of old codswallop, but we're rather good at peddling codswallop and, up till now, our public hasn't asked any difficult questions and are still singing "Rule, Britannia!" Please, keep these photographs of your wife and her geriatric lover. Well...' Brinks looked at his watch with a gesture similar to Isaac's. 'I regret to say that I must be off.'

Enríquez took the envelope with a trembling hand, realising that he'd one day have to open it again. And again and again. Brinks avoided looking at him, before closing the door very carefully.

Chapter Seven

Chess on the Uganda

At last, the Intelligence officer left to be replaced by the chief medical officer, one of those doctors so thoroughly "doctorly" that the mere sight of them makes you feel better. The Intelligence officer, in contrast, gave me the willies, like all his sort do. Since I woke up, dumbfounded, aboard the Uganda, this was the fifth time he'd tried to get information out of me. Campbell, that was his name, the damned snooper. And although he acted bored, he suspected me.

He always came in with the same list of 40 or 50 questions, that never varied, and I answered them with evasions, contradictions, extreme and improvised emotional reactions or sudden losses of memory: I unashamedly tied him up in knots. Inured to frustration, officious and bored, Campbell always left as empty-handed as he'd come, but ever more suspicious. I was secure in the knowledge that at least they wouldn't torture me on the ship: there were too many doctors aboard, and the doctors were too English.

Obviously, if the truth were discovered, all the gringos, including the sawbones, perhaps primarily them and especially the three nurses, would have had me shot in the back of the head and thrown overboard into the Atlantic. Bye-bye, Argy, and no regrets.

But torture me? Definitely not cricket!

I imagined what Lieutenant Peralta would have done in Campbell's shoes. That bastard Peralta would have had me staked out naked on deck for two days and two nights, until I was on the brink of death from hypothermia. And that just for starters. During those nights on the Uganda, I frequently dreamed about Peralta, that he came back to stake me out once more beneath the rain.

Thirty years have passed, and Peralta still comes back. From the dead.

He still livens up my occasional nightmares.

The doctor was fifty-ish, blond, enormous, clumsy and broad in the beam. He had a not-very British surname: Mathiasen. He couldn't care less whether I was Argentine, or about the circumstances of my capture. I remember little about it myself: when the British started throwing mortars at us I was already nearly unconscious, with an Argentine bullet – courtesy of the aforementioned Lieutenant Peralta – in the leg and shortly afterwards, it seems, I caught some British shrapnel in the knee.

Of the bullet I remember the astonishing pain, when the wound got cold; of the shrapnel that hit me after, I remember nothing. They told me about it, in English, on the hospital ship, hours after they'd dug it out of my tibia. I didn't feel it go in and I didn't feel it come out.

Peralta's shot went through the thigh and if it'd been a .45 bullet instead of a 9mm, or if it had gone a few millimetres to the left, it would have severed my femoral artery: you bleed to death in a minute. That short distance meant the wound was just an anecdote, already healing. The shrapnel, however, still makes me limp, so long after. Anyway, for Mathiasen, I was just a knee, and knees have no nationality.

The doctor gently lifted the bandages with a pair of tweezers and surveyed my wound, without touching it, with a slight smile, admiring it or perhaps in admiration of himself. He must have been the one who operated on me.

There was love between this man and my knee: he even smelt it, he knelt down – with difficulty, he was as big as a bear, like I said – not to admire his handiwork but to check that the tube they used to drain the blood hadn't got blocked. He got up with an effort, checked the plasma and physiological serum drip flow rate, reread the clinical data at the foot of the bed, scribbled a bit more, spoke to me in abominable Spanish and I, as always, smiled in appreciation and refrained from answering him in English.

I was willing to play the fool and not utter half a word of the language of Billy Shakespeare until I disembarked in Montevideo, to return from there to Buenos Aires and face up to the rest of my life, which loomed long, painful and, above all, lame.

Mathiasen made some of those sudden throat-clearing noises that Her Majesty's subjects make when they're about to speak. He opened a folder and showed me some X-rays. I took them carefully from his hands and contemplated my knee as I'd never seen it before: from the inside and full of screws.

'I think that you'll be fine. Your knee, *tu rodilla*, will, how do you say keep working? *Seguir funcionando?* There'll probably be some consequences, *secuelas*; stiffness, a slight limp, *rigidez, cojera*?'

I swallowed. I looked him in the eyes.

'But doctor, will I ever be able to walk again?'

'Yes, most certainly! I mean, *sí,*' Mathiasen smiled with genuine happiness. 'But,' he frowned, 'it's probable, *muy probable*, that in a few years you'll need a steel implant. *Rodilla de metal*, do you understand?'

'Yes, my father had one of those.' I refrained from telling him that my father was in prison and that we didn't miss him. Neither him nor his knee.

'Really? What a coincidence! *Yo también*. Me, too!"

He lifted the trouser leg of the bottle green two-piece suit that doctors wear nowadays, instead of those white tunics they used to don when I was a boy and, in effect, his left knee displayed a sizeable, almost proud scar, which contrasted starkly with a very white leg, streaked by a few premature varicose veins.

'Osteoarthritis, unfortunately. You've got a shrapnel wound and *yo por viejo*, because I'm am old man. They do titanium replacements nowadays, *en lugar de acero*, but even in England, with the National Health Service and everything, they're very expensive, *muy caro,* you know',' he added. And he covered his knee rather proprietarily, and blushed.

I was just 19 and now I knew that in Argentina, as well as a mother and two younger siblings that I couldn't support, there was a titanium knee waiting that I wouldn't be able to afford. I tried to smile.

'I'd better start saving, then.'

He looked at me slightly worriedly, murmured "excuse me" and opened my eyes to check the colour of the whites, obviously to see if my hematocrit levels were very low. An old-school military doctor, always closer to the muck and bullets than to the laboratories. One of those who smells a wound to see if it's infected, like my grandfather used to.

'And? Are my red corpuscles down, doctor?'

'Not really. *Un poco, nomás.* You're a very tough lad. Anyway, *ya sabe*, we've given you blood transfusions, *cinco bolsas de sangre*, while you were unconscious.'

'So now I've got four pints of British blood.'

He laughed. He looked twenty years younger when he laughed.

'So you know something about *medicina*, or at least about doctors.'

'*En mi familia*, all doctors. If you no doctor,' and I thought of my father, '*te echan*, out.'

'Poor you!' he laughed. 'See you later, young man.'

He went away, with the same limp that I would one day have, looking first at the bloke on one side and then the one on the other, but those poor sods were all seriously messed up and they didn't talk.

As always, the slow rolling of the ship induced a feeling of drowsiness in me in the mornings. The days went flying past, meaning I spent all day sleeping. The Uganda rolled agreeably; it was a comfortable and maternal cradle despite the tumultuous waves that must have been heaving out there, in the wintry Atlantic. And this wasn't really a military ship, but in fact a transatlantic liner hurriedly reconverted into a Red Cross floating hospital. It was, and continues to be, the best trauma unit I've ever seen. And I've seen quite a few. A real treat.

Jackie, a buxom, likeable nurse, used to come round, depending on the rota. I would have dragged her into bed at the first opportunity if I'd felt like it at all. But if you've lost four pints of blood and a good deal of your shin, you don't really feel like it.

Jackie - thirty years old, and wearing a wedding ring – used to extract my blood, change my urine-collecting bag (embarrassingly, I had one of those damn tubes they stick down the end of your cock), take my temperature and blood pressure, put stickers with bar codes on the flasks containing my bodily fluids, write things down in a notebook, and graciously take her leave before going off to the other beds where, as I said before, there were British, who were amputees and burns victims, or both things at once. They were mostly in a coma, very heavily sedated or barely awake.

After a while, Jackie would disappear into the office and you could hear the printer scribbling out all the results on one of those continuous forms they used in those days. Computers! They've got everything, I used to think. A quarter of an hour later, punctually, a black nurse would come by, Stewart, who would attach the printed data sheet to the foot of my bed before continuing, patient by patient, through the length of the ward, which must once have been the first-class dining room or the dance hall. What an organisation! I thought once more.

I deduced from our proximity to the upper decks that this had been the first class area in less-bloodthirsty times:

the hypnotic roll of the Uganda up there was very long and soothing, and furthermore from above the ceiling could be clearly heard the racket of the helicopters bringing in one fucked-up bloke after another, most of my own making in all probability. The heliport must have been just a few metres above my face.

I'd counted about fifty beds in my ward, mostly occupied by mummies who needed the Furacin-gauze dressings on their hands and faces changed constantly. The burns appeared in all their unsightliness when the doctors and nurses cautiously peeled away the bandages from those parts. When they saw the destroyed tissue, they painted it with antiseptics before looking at each other with an air that seemed to say "well, what do we do next?" The bodies, however, seemed quite intact: people had copped the full blast of the flames from the explosion on the Galahad on the parts not covered by the Antarctic clothing. So, whenever someone came in with bullet wounds, I knew he was of somebody else's manufacture.

But the mummies, they were all mine.

Gringos are a breed apart. The ones who were conscious, even the amputees, swapped jokes from bed to bed, or chatted up the three nurses. Who the fuck thought of sending us off to fight against people like that? I asked myself, as I watched them laugh as if they weren't suffering pain or torturing themselves inside wondering what would happen to them and their lives once they got back to Britain.

I said that I slept a lot so as not to see or think too much, but I also pretended to doze sometimes to avoid problems. Because it once happened that some bloke Howard Whatshisname, I can never remember his surname, the one in the bed opposite me, when he found out I was a "fucking Argy" desperately shouted insults at me for the longest half-hour of my life and one of the last ones of his. Until my favourite nurse, Jackie, appeared, and knocked him out with a syringe-full of something or other. For all I cared, it could have been cyanide.

And if there was any left over, she could have injected me with it, too.

That lad, Howard, knew that he was dying. He wasn't insulting me, he was insulting death itself. He'd literally got even his bollocks burnt off. His hands looked like two bunches of black puddings. His face, so swollen, looked like a panda's, only all black. And he couldn't see anything, because the swelling had reduced his eyes to two slits. Jackie told me that in Southampton, it seems, there was a girl waiting to marry him. Marry him. That was a laugh.

Events took over that saved the girl from having to make dreadful decisions, which would have turned her into a heroine or a villain. That very night, hours after giving me such a hard time and being sedated, the girl's fiancée got septicaemia and entered into shock. The monitor alarm went off, and the doctors came running in with the defibrillator just like in a TV series and when he didn't respond to the third electric jolt, they took him hell for leather to intensive care. From whence he never returned.

I wondered what would happen to the girl from Southampton.

Next day, there was a different mummy in that bed, but one with slightly better prospects.

Jackie gave me the gen on the girl a bit later, in even more rudimentary Spanish than Doctor Mathiasen's. And I swear it brought the tears to my eyes. The nurse looked at me curiously, she didn't say anything, she just carefully puffed up my pillow before continuing on her rounds. From that moment on we became friends, in that tacit but intense way that English people have of showing their love for you, taking care of you without anyone noticing, and omitting all important or personal matters from the conversation.

From where I lay, I could see four duly-roasted Gurkhas and also another Argentine, about twenty metres away, un-cooked. All you could see were his eyes. We didn't exchange a word, not even when they wrapped my leg in a steel bar and Velcro brace that made me look like Robocop, and let me walk over to his bed on my Lofstrand crutches. I greeted him and said: "Hola, varón!" He looked at me, he just looked and that was that. I supposed that my compatriot was too depressed to speak. Until Jackie told me that he'd copped a 7.62mm bullet in the mouth. Well, that would test the elo-quence of a Demosthenes.

I still remember Jackie's efforts to get this boy, who was fed by nasogastric tube, to swallow some baby food. In that instant, I reckon I would have offered to marry her.

The day I awoke on the Uganda was 10 June, which means it was the second day after the attack on the Gala-had. Which means I spent two whole days virtually out of this world. Until the 13 June, the almost continuous racket of the helicopters could be heard aboard ship, bringing in new Welsh mummies and a number of Nepalese. During those first few days, the monitor alarms were going off constantly and the doctors and nurses, bleary-eyed and groggy, would go running from one bed to the next with the defibrillator, or taking someone in shock off to intensive care. I don't know how, but they somehow managed to bring most of them back.

Apart from Demosthenes the Uncooked, not only was I the only Argentine on the ward, but also the one principally and secretly responsible for what was going on there. What bothered me the most, however, weren't the ones who kicked it, luckily, in intensive care, but the others, the ones condemned to live. The ones who came back to their beds, to join the ranks of the monsters for evermore. And to spend the rest of their lives with tortoise skin-like faces, seeing the terrified look in their wives' eyes, and longing to touch them with hook-like paws.

And I, the one who'd fucked them all up, was getting away with just a permanent limp. It wasn't fair.

Well, I wasn't going to be the one to tell them.

II

What follows next is the story of how they found out.

My first few days on the Uganda always followed the same routine. Jackie would bring me a big breakfast that I, now catheter-less and as happy as a man who's just regained control of his dick can be, used to bolt down like a gaunt, hungry gannet.

The way I devoured my food pleased Jackie, and made me rather tired, but there was never much time for a post-prandial nap, because punctually, just as my eyes were beginning to close, by coincidence, that asshole Campbell would appear, with his same old fifty questions, to see if I contradicted myself with any of them. When I felt particularly like making his day, I used to contradict myself on all of them, all fifty. He was, however, unflappable.

Then the good doctor Mathiasen would arrive. He'd be pleased at my progress, he'd check that my recently-stitched wound, which only the day before still had a drainage tube coming out of it, was healing correctly, and order the duty nurse to prepare some X-ray or other to have a look how things were going down there, then he'd say goodbye as if apologising for the brevity of his visit and continue on his rounds.

In the afternoon, as I was waking up, Jackie would come back. She'd spent nearly three absolutely shattering weeks doing shifts of four hours on and four hours off but now, after my compatriots' surrender and with things a bit calmer, it seemed they were letting her get more sleep. But she confessed she was having trouble sleeping. And not for lack of sleeping pills. It was more due to an overload of horror and impotence. She trembled a little when she admitted that, then she blushed and tried not to look me in the eye.

I wasn't surprised. That's the effect I have on women, including English women: they talk too much to me. Is it because I inspire confidence? Or because I make them laugh? I would have liked to have held her in my arms until she went to sleep, poor Jackie. I was good at that when I was young, at helping insomniac women get to sleep.

A week and a half later, I was already walking for two or three hours a day on my Lofstrand crutches and with my leg full of iron, Robocop-style. In order to avoid putting up with me prowling the ward like a caged lion, Mathiasen let me out a bit. They'd given me some warm pyjamas, felt slippers and a padded dressing gown. The British, whether they were doctors, nurses, or guards, didn't even seem to notice my Argentine presence in the corridors, even though I have pretty typical mixed-race looks. My acquaintances and I - Jackie, Mathiasen, Stewart and other nurses and doctors - would greet each other with a wink, or with a succinct "hello". They were always tired, always hurrying to and fro.

My freedom of movement had well-defined limits. They let me go to the bathroom and even pass through an area that in times of peace must have been the duty-free shop. Finally, after the surrender, they let me go on my own to the bar where I would amuse myself drinking a ginger ale at the expense, and to the health of, Her Majesty (sic) or watching the the latest video tapes from England with programmes and news on the TV, which was always switched on, albeit with the sound turned down low. The news was days old, of course, but still news to me, and I was rather proud of being the only Argentine – I suspected that there must be many more aboard – to enjoy these privileges.

According to the BBC, we were at anchor in front of Puerto Argentino (well, now it seemed that it was Port Stanley once more) to take on board more British wounded. And some more of my lot, who would probably be disembarked in Montevideo.

That's what the TV said.

I watched this stale but probably valid piece of news over and over, as well as a lot of English football – which was very good – and then general British news, about as interesting as watching paint dry, interrupted now and then by small items showing scenes of jubilation, with special forces already back in Britain in their Hercules or Galaxy aircraft. But there was already a lot of coverage of the Israeli occupation of Lebanon, where a bewildering array of opponents were at it hammer and tongs.

Local politics, Lebanon, Israel and football.

Our little local, southern war was already drifting from the planet's short memory. The expressions on the British faces all around me, absorbed in their drinks or on the screen, betrayed exactly the same thought that assailed me: "And what about us? Don't we exist any more?" they asked themselves. But they were British, so they didn't say a word.

I was watching Manchester United against some other club, I can't remember if it was Tottenham or Arsenal, and United were hammering them, when Jackie came into the room, with those dark patches under her eyes, she smiled almost without seeing me, leaned on the bar – I was watching her from the side, furtively – and she knocked back, as if it were nothing, one, two, three double shots of Glenfiddich, without water or ice.

How lovely she was and how screwed up she must have been. She'd just finished her shift and she was so over-exhausted that she had to slaughter herself with whisky before she could even sleep three of her now guaranteed eight-hour rest period. Some other kid had probably just died on her. Jackie was like that.

Just then, something happened.

As nearly all the BBC's war correspondents were already back in Britain, the short excerpts that the broadcaster mechanically inserted between the really important news were by now mere rehashes, recordings from the previous week, already archive material. In the bar, nobody now paid them any notice.

What I mean is that, by that time, our defeat was already very old news to me. Mathiasen had broken it to me delicately, almost in passing, as if attaching less importance to it, the day he took some screws out of my legs. And he achieved it. The thing I was most concerned about that day were the fucking screws, rather than our defeat.

But then came the TV picture, which the rest of the planet must have already been sick of seeing, but that was new to me: the one of the blue-and-white flag being taken down in Governor Rex Hunt's garden and replaced once more with the Union Jack. That twenty-second recording caught me by surprise. And it made me limp hurriedly to the bar toilet and throw everything up, everything, what I'd eaten and what I'd gone without, the savagery I'd endured and inflicted on others. So many deaths for this. All that stuff with Peralta, just for this. Tano Comte, for this.

I was as sick as a dog.

When I came out of the toilet, I was trembling and probably rather green-faced. Jackie had left her drink unfinished on the bar: she was waiting for me, arms akimbo.

'You need some fresh air, laddie,' she said, in English and I, like an idiot, agreed.

She took me out on deck. That was after exchanging a few words with the marine on guard duty, some gingernut armed with a Sterling machine gun, who didn't seem that happy to let me through the inner door to the exterior. He shrugged his shoulders, however, when she pulled rank on him. The girl knew how to politely bully people, if that was what was called for. She was worth marrying alright, like I said.

Cold, wind, seagulls. Port Stanley, which before the war had been very pretty and unspoilt when approached from the sea, was unspeakably untidy, dirty and teeming with troops. Streets full of rubbish, dozens of warships of all classes and sizes in the inlet, cranes that lifted lorries into the ships' cargo holds, enormous queues of prisoners on the quays, launches and helicopters coming and going.

Jackie took off her bonnet, shaking out her leonine mane. The two of us were alone, leaning on a rail about a yard away from each other – a very chaste and English distance – her hair blowing in the frozen wind, watching the tremendous spectacle of a war in its closing stages. The only thing that wasn't being folded, loaded and embarked for the return journey were the islands themselves.

It was like they were taking down a stage set.

Jackie turned to me and regarded me with the most beautiful pair of grey-green eyes in the southern hemisphere. Slightly drunken eyes, too.

'You must be freezing, dearie. Let's get in.'

'I'd rather stay out a bit, if you don't mind.'

She hesitated for a moment.

'Be my guest.'

'Well, I am already. Sort of.'

We were laughing for quite a while, like two fools. I think we took advantage of the laughter to cry a little, too. I suppose that each of us had more than enough things to cry about.

239

After a while she dried her eyes and became very serious, too serious, and sombre. She stopped looking at me. She made me go back inside and before leaving she ordered me, almost with hate in her voice, to go back to my ward and my bed.

What had got into her? Couldn't she hold her drink? As I left the bar I stopped at the door for a second and looked at her from the corner of my eye. She was back at the bar and she was just downing her fourth dram of Glenfiddich, a double. She seemed to want to drink herself stupid. She had her back to me, but I could clearly see her face in the mirror and our eyes met there, for a second.

With just one look, the woman told me that I'd been found out.

III

That night I was very restless until they put me to sleep with something different, because rather than fall asleep, I fainted. A black sleep, with no Peralta or stakings or mummies, but still full of things blacker than blackness itself. I woke up very late and exhausted, as if I'd been working physically hard the day before. I felt dizzy and nauseous; I suddenly couldn't stand the ship's rolling movement, which I'd found so comforting before. Stewart brought me my breakfast, but I couldn't even finish the orange juice.

When I'd drunk half a glassful, I threw everything up, and it was pure gastric juice. They had to change the sheets.

Jackie didn't appear, ever again.

We were heading north, I noticed. I can't explain my sense of direction, but I always know where I am and which way we're headed, even in an enclosed space – it's always been like that. The dull rumble of the floor told me that we were going at full steam. Doing a few mental calculations and supposing that the Uganda must be capable of doing 30 knots, I estimated that we were two days sailing away from Montevideo.

I was tense, waiting for something to happen. That asshole Campbell didn't appear. The morning was becoming unbearable, when a couple of marines with 9mm pistols in their belts came into the ward, spoke to Stewart, came over to my bed and told me to put on my dressing gown, get my crutches and follow them. The hair stood up on my neck, thighs and arms, but I kept my best poker face.

We walked through corridors that I'd previously been denied access to, and then took a lift down to another deck. The ship was like a city. Other passageways led us to a door, which on opening revealed Mathiasen, except that he had different clothes, a different rank, a different name, I would almost say a different face, a different way of carrying himself and obviously a different profession. He was no longer dressed as a doctor, but as an army officer. And he wasn't a captain, but a brigadier. And his name wasn't Mathiasen but Brinks and just one look at his eyes was enough to tell me that this character was from Intelligence and that I was well and truly screwed.

Jackie, you and your fucking whore of a mother, I thought. That snitching British bitch.

Mathiasen, or rather Brinks, gestured for me to sit down and dismissed the marines with a gesture. When he spoke, it was in a very acceptable Rio de la Plata Spanish, spoken by the kind of Englishman who'd been living for a long time in Buenos Aires, Montevideo, Rosario or around there. A damned spy. There must have been dozen of them in our country.

'To put your mind at rest, I'm not going to have you killed or tortured, young man. Yesterday we made you talk more than enough when you were asleep, and that was something you seemed very worried about. What we were looking for, the fundamental information, we've now already obtained: it was you who gave the Argentine Air Force the positions of the Galahad and the Tristam.

'Sodium Pentothal?'

'A small dose, young man. Very small,' he looked apologetic. 'I know that you're not feeling very well at the moment but don't worry. In a few hours the nausea will have worn off. What I want now is the story, the whole story and in the right sequence, as far as possible. For the record.'

'And what makes you think that I'm going to tell you?'

'If you don't tell me, I have ways of letting the Argentine Army have certain information, that I imagine you'd rather remained a secret.'

'Are you referring to anything in particular, Brigadier Brinks?'

Brinks suddenly became very cold. It was just a minor transformation, but it was spectacular. It terrified me. I hid my fear. I think.

'You, a supposedly simple soldier, killed your supposedly superior officer, Lieutenant Roberto Peralta, the officer in charge of your advanced observation group. I don't know if this...shall we say, execution, was carried out by yourself and another man named Comte before or after you signalled details of the Bluff Cove landings by radio. I am also unaware of the reasons that prompted you to get rid of the officer. I could even say that I don't really care. But your superiors probably will care about those things. And it's my job to be aware of absolutely everything, do you understand?'

I looked at him with a serene expression. Brinks sighed, opened an envelope and took out some photos, recently obtained in some sort of field morgue. Lumps of bodies that were recognisable, but recognisable only with difficulty. Oh, my God, there was Comte. Sliced up like a side of beef. A mortar shell must have exploded right on top of him.

I was seized by a sudden painful retching, but luckily vomited very little. Brinks, considerately, passed me a cloth so I could clean myself up and stopped me when, out of sheer embarrassment, I was about to clean the floor. He called in the two pistol-packing marines from outside. They swabbed the floor and cleared up the mess.

'Our forensic boys did a good job, although it was hard,' he continued. 'The injury that killed Lieutenant Peralta was this one, on the throat. And it was inflicted by a bayonet from an Argentine *FAL* rifle.'

'Your troops have the same bayonets.'

Brinks paid not the slightest attention to this. He put the photos in an envelope and the envelope in a drawer.

'Your fingerprints, young man, show up quite clearly on the handle of the bayonet that killed Lieutenant Peralta. Peralta's blood is there too, on the blade and the handle, and liberally sprinkled on the clothing you were wearing. It's A positive, a rather rare blood group. And very different from yours, which is O Rhesus negative.'

'No comment, as your politicians say.'

'The inevitable conclusion?' continued Brinks. 'Peralta was murdered by the pair of you, or at least by you. And that must have happened before we could locate the source of the radio signal that betrayed the Galahad and the Tristam, and give the order to open mortar fire on it. With results that you were able to see for yourself. Incredibly enough, despite the state he was in, Comte survived for several hours. He must have been a very strong man.

My heart shrivelled inside me. I didn't want to ask which particular part of Comte had survived for several hours. At the end of the day, I hadn't been able to save him. I failed you, Cordobés.[1]

'There seems to be something you're unsure about,' said Brinks after a silence that had perhaps been uncomfortable for him but not for me, as I was feeling so perplexed and distracted.

'There is something I don't understand, Brigadier Brinks. There've already been hundreds of deaths on both sides, and more people will die in the coming months, because we've left the damned islands full of mines and booby traps. But you go and play at being Sherlock Holmes in the midst of all this killing. That's all very well in a 1950s film or a book, but in this war…Could you explain to me what the fucking point is?'

Brinks looked at me rather apologetically.

'Professionalism, my dear boy. Professionalism. When something goes wrong, we want to know where we fouled up. The Galahad incident was the biggest single slaughter of

[1] One who hails from Córdoba, Argentina.

British troops since WWII. Obviously, there are investigations underway: one is official, and the other is this one. And this one includes you.'

'Well, investigate all you like. If I believed that by speaking I could resuscitate a single one of the lads I killed, if I thought for a moment they'd at least die with dignity, then don't doubt for a minute, Brigadier Brinks, that you'd have a job to make me shut up. Believe me, I wouldn't stop talking.'

Brinks looked at me as if I were mad, but he did believe me. However, he also had a job to do.

'Two days before, the islanders informed us that an Argentine recce party had infiltrated the area close to the Bluff Cove landing site. Our lads in the SBS were spread out over the zone, searching under every bush and in every gully. Our Signals Corps was on the alert, ready to pick up the slightest signal from your group, fix its position, scramble its radio and wipe it out.

'Didn't they do exactly that?'

'Yes, but too late. We made every mistake in the book. For two days, our special forces looked for you in vain. We should've accepted the islanders' suggestion and used their sheep dogs. That was the first error. We did manage to pick up the signal, but due to the infernal frequency shifts your equipment was making, it was at least a full minute after you'd started to transmit. Our second mistake. Your team was using very advanced equipment with a very fast and complicated frequency shift pattern. Our computers couldn't decipher the algorithm. Then, when we'd finally pinned it down, we took at least another minute before giving the order to open fire on the area.'

'Why was that?' I asked, with curiosity.

'Because there was an SBS patrol looking for you less than 300 metres away and we gave them time to get away. We didn't want to kill them with another episode of friendly fire, or "blue on blue" as we say. We've had more than our fair share of that in this little war, believe me. And maybe that was our biggest mistake. To save ten men, we sacrificed we still don't know how many dozens more.'

Now Brinks really was furious, but his fury was directed against himself.

'I don't agree, Brigadier,' I said, trying to make things easier for him. 'I think your side made an even bigger mistake.'

Brinks eyed me with curiosity.

'Although you knew you'd been rumbled, you didn't cancel the landing. You didn't even send the Harriers to protect it. I reckon you didn't take us seriously enough.'

Brinks thought about this for a few seconds.

'You're right. It's rather a relief to know that at least you and I think the same way. But I must say that it wasn't my mistake: I tried everything in my power to…well, some heads are going to roll after this, heads higher up than mine, I promise you. As if that were any damn consolation. Perhaps you'd like some tea?'

An enemy brigadier from Military Intelligence was making confessions, slagging off his superior officers and offering me tea - little me, an insignificant conscript and enemy soldier. And there's me saying yes, thank you, and nodding my head. There was an extraordinarily unreal air about it. Something was very wrong. These people really are masters of subterfuge.

'Was it Jackie who grassed on me?'

Please let him say no, I thought. Although I also thought that if he did say no, I wouldn't have believed him.

'No. Well, yes. She not one of ours, I mean she's not in Intelligence. Our girls are real bitches. Jackie is just a nursing NCO, that's all.'

I said nothing. He looked at me, attentively.

'Adorable, isn't she? I wouldn't blame you at all if, given the circumstances, you'd fallen just a bit in love with her. But, at heart, Jackie is a British servicewoman, every bit as steadfast as Admiral Woodward or I. We explained our suspicions to the girl, asked her to let you have the run of the ship when you started walking again, told her to treat you almost lovingly and to keep an eye on you. Obviously, when she saw you spend hours in front of the TV, seemingly understanding what was being said, and finally, when she made you speak English, out suspicions were confirmed.'

'What suspicions, exactly?'

Brinks looked at me very carefully.

'That in spite of your youthful appearance and honesty, you are a well-trained Argentine Intelligence officer. The only one amongst you who warrants my respect, at least. You caused us 150 casualties in under two minutes.'

I was astonished. Then I laughed for a long while. Brinks remained impassive.

'Now I understand why you're treating me like an equal and giving me tea, Brigadier. You've mistaken me for one in your own trade. But you're wasting your hospitality on a simple conscript. I'll be turning twenty in two weeks time - if you let me, of course.'

247

Brinks remained thoughtful and filled up my teacup once more, perhaps to hide his confusion, or to pretend that's what he was doing. God knows why the hell these people like drinking tea so much. I drank mine to be polite and hoped that there wouldn't be a third cup.

'So, you'd like to turn twenty...'

'If it's not too much to ask.'

'I think we can probably arrange it. Why do you speak English so well?'

'It's a long story.'

'It's part of my job to listen to long stories, although not necessarily to believe them.'

'My great-grandmother was an Indian slave in Tierra del Fuego, my great-grandfather was an adventurous gold digger from Buenos Aires who died very young trying to free her, and my grandfather was a labourer on a ranch in Patagonia. He was adopted by a doctor from the Buenos Aires aristocracy called Charlie Thompson, the latest in a long line of doctors called Thompson, which was founded after the British invasions of Buenos Aires in 1806. Shall I continue? My family's story is like a South American soap opera.'

'I love South American soap operas. And I see that you know rather a lot about medicine.'

'Well, those are things I learned from my grandfather, when I used to accompany him on his rounds in the car. I have an Italian surname, I feel completely Argentine and I haven't got, and I've never had, the slightest urge to become a doctor. I was obliged to learn English from a very young age at the Southern District British School, a sort of St. Andrew's for lower-middle class people. That was all my mother's money could run to.

'I warn you that I have people in Buenos Aires who can check if your story stands up or not before we get to Montevideo. And that's just two days away.'

'And if my story doesn't stand up, am I in for a fall? Over the rail, for instance?'

'Let's go back to the beginning, young man. Why did you kill Peralta?'

I thought for two or three seconds.

'Because he was a coward. And a right bastard. But above all because he was a coward. That's right, mainly because he was a coward.'

'Can you elaborate on that?'

'I was with the observers from the GA3 artillery unit on Sapper Hill. When our first 155mm Sofma gun arrived, we had to shoot long range either by guesswork or with a little Rasit radar. We also had to put up with the aforesaid Lieutenant Roberto Peralta as our commanding officer.'

'You did a good job, then. When there was fighting in the hills around Port Stanley, those 155mms killed loads of people. And at the end of May, they put a stop to our nocturnal naval bombardments. It was hell: the bombs fell just 50 yards from the ships. They even hit a frigate. And you were firing with a single gun from eleven miles away! Up until now, I'd always admired Lieutenant Peralta.

'I didn't. For two whole months Peralta ate while his soldiers went hungry. Peralta slept in a dry bunker we dug for him on the top of the hill, while we slept out in the rain with no bivouacs, in shallow, flooded holes in the peat, or beneath improvised roofs made of overhanging metal sheets. Peralta used the hot water from the field catering tent for washing

249

in, while we were going down with diarrhoea, from drinking river water with turds in it. Peralta raided the ration boxes that turned up now and then, which were already ridiculously small. Did you see them?'

He shook his head.

'They were like that, more or less,' I showed him with my hands. 'They were just 25 by 25 by 10 cms and mostly full of air. They were nearly empty, except for two miserable cans, one of lentil stew and the other with some Swift meatballs. There was a sheet of paper and an envelope, (but no pencil), two sweets, two broken Express biscuits and a tin of solid alcohol fuel, but no matches to light the fuel with. All completely useless. A typical contract negotiated with some army supplier, no doubt. Fuck-ups that have happened since the days of *Martin Fierro*.'[2]

'And that's what you ate?'

'No, Peralta kept all the meatballs and shared out the lentils between his two NCOs. One of my mates, Ayestarán, was staked to the ground in the open for two whole days by Peralta, because he'd gone down the mountain to a kelper's farmhouse and slaughtered a sheep. And he was in such a bad way afterwards, Ayestarán, that they had to evacuate him to Puerto Argentino with pneumonia. He'd already turned blue. He didn't last the journey because Peralta refused to call a helicopter, and they had to carry him down. When they told us by radio that Ayestarán had arrived dead at Puerto Argentino, Peralta's comment was: "Well, that's one black bastard less."'

'Is that why you killed him?'

---

2 The fictional *gaucho* character from the 1870s eponymous epic poem by Jóse Hernández.

'Yes. And because I'm also a "black bastard" myself. And for many other things. I was with Ayestarán when he stole the food. Moreover, as I've already told you, I'm pretty dark-skinned myself, meaning that I was just another black bastard in Peralta's eyes. That's why he had me staked out alongside him, alongside Ayestarán. For two days and two nights.'

'Last night you were talking about something like that in your sleep. Now I understand.'

'The thing is that I never get ill and I only rarely get angry. Some of us black bastards never get ill or angry.'

'And how did you get from Sapper Hill over to the Bluff Cove area? That's days away over almost impossible terrain.'

I laughed.

'That was Peralta's bad fucking luck. Double bad luck. Your frigates finally silenced our guns on Sapper Hill and killed or wounded almost the entire battery, soldiers, NCOs, everyone. A direct hit on the munitions dump. As we were in those badly-protected trenches, you can imagine the carnage. Then, when Peralta and I started the withdrawal back towards Puerto Argentino, Peralta, much to his chagrin, gets a direct radio order from General Menéndez himself to take up a forward observation position in the Bluff Cove area. I swear that he went white; he made them repeat the order three times, as if he hadn't heard it properly. And I realised his intention was to shout that he couldn't hear anything and smash the radio against a rock. But then he saw my face and knew I'd report him if he did that. I'm certain that was the moment he started thinking about how he could kill me, but I had my FAL in my hands, so…he had to think again.'

'And what happened next?'

'He was in a foul temper, as you can imagine. I forgot about him and started picking up bits of my companions, collecting their dog-tags, if they still had them, putting everything in a trench and waiting for the ambulances to come. He just sat there smoking, not speaking, and he didn't lift a finger to help. At one point he was about to order me to get his dinner ready, but he saw the expression on my face again and changed his mind.'

Brinks offered me a Dunhill, which I refused. He lit one, slowly.

'We waited all day for the radio ham to arrive. He was one of those civilian volunteers who'd offered themselves to the Air Force as observers. They used to send them to the most isolated spots, where we didn't have any radars, to pinpoint the positions of frigates or give air-raid warnings. They worked in groups of two or three, usually a civilian and a pair of NCOs. They lived a very risky, and shitty, existence. Out in the open, dying from hunger and hiding away from the helicopters and your special force patrols.'

'Is that what Comte told you?'

'Yes, that's what he told me. They'd also killed his entire platoon. And then, as if nothing had happened, he volunteered again and came walking all the way up from Puerto Argentino, along the muddy track that starts where Ross Road ends, with no-one to give him a lift in a jeep. He was a brave beast, *tano*[3] and *cordobés*, built like a brick shithouse, about two metres tall. And, like I said, he turned up late in the afternoon, all on his own, on foot, carrying just a few ragged clothes and a very powerful and modern-looking radio.

3 Tano: of Italian origin.

Me and Comte got on great guns right from the start. As the only survivor from Peralta's platoon, I had to provide armed protection for the two of them. At that stage of the game, Peralta always thought twice before giving me an order and would have killed me ten times over if I'd taken my eyes off him for more than a second. Because I'm one of those black bastards who looks out of the corner of his eye and pretends to be doing something else, but lets you know he's looking. However, a man's got to sleep sometimes. So if it hadn't been for that brave crazy fool Comte, Peralta would have probably taken his chance whilst I was asleep. Really, I could only afford the luxury of sleep whenever Tano stayed up on guard. You should've seen him, old Tano...'

Brinks filled up my teacup again before I could stop him.

'Ever since Ayestarán's death, Peralta had it in for me. I've often noticed before how people are frightened of us, the ones who never lose our tempers. If I didn't even get angry when I had to pick up the pieces of eight of my companions, chopped up like cattle, with someone's arm here, someone's head there, God knows whose foot over there...then I'll never get angry.'

I drank my tea all at once. It was scalding hot.

'So, we walked and walked for two whole nights until we were a certain distance from Bluff Cove, and absolutely done in with fatigue and covered in mud. There we were, the three of us with nothing but our souls, in the rain and the snow, on high ground, with good visibility and therefore completely in the open. But that also meant it was probably under close surveillance. We bivouacked in a water-filled hole, a depression next to the river...we dug it out to make it a bit bigger and we kept it covered with camouflage nets and branches night and day. Inside that rat hole we had the stink of our own piss and shit in our nostrils, as we didn't shit outside so as not to give our position away. At night we would sometimes hear the voices of people searching for us. Peralta was in a bad way, he got very bad diarrhoea, but he just couldn't deal with it like I could. He'd turned yellow, was running a fever and whenever he managed to sleep he had nightmares, which he couldn't stand either. Hepatitis A, obviously.'

'How did you know that?'

'His shit was white, he pissed the colour of Coca Cola, his complexion was yellow and he was confused.'

'Forgive me, young man, I'd quite forgotten your medical background.'

'The fact he had hepatitis cheered me up no end. But I told no one my diagnosis. That would have given Peralta the medical justification for aborting the mission and going back to Puerto Argentino. Moreover, with my way of watching him without looking at him, of just being there, silent, I managed to unsettle him, keep him from resting and weaken him still further. And I waited.

'Pray continue.'

'We detected the arrival of the ships in the bay on 6 June. Can you believe that, on 8 June, Peralta was still repeatedly refusing to use the radio to communicate the news? When we insisted, he went berserk, screaming that with so much rain and snow it was useless: our air force was destroyed and furthermore they could do nothing in such dreadful weather anyway. But he didn't stop there. He insulted us, called us insubordinate idiots, he called me a black bastard and Comte a bastard civilian. Comte, either because he was a civilian, or because he was almost two metres tall, wasn't used to be called a bastard anything.

'Then what happened?'

'Almost from the word go, Comte and I understood each other just by exchanging glances. Peralta, who was no fool, also knew the score. It was inevitable he'd end up trying to murder us to eradicate all traces of his cowardice and get back to Puerto Argentino alive, or give himself up to the British right there and then. That's what Comte and I said to each other, just with our eyes. We didn't say a word. It's incredible how many things you can say just with sign language. Especially with someone from Córdoba.'

'So, why didn't you just kill him?'

'I believe that Comte was too good a person, and because for me it was too soon. I wanted to make Peralta suffer before I dealt with him. Also, even though he was young and strong, the hepatitis was making him weaker and weaker. Why take a risk?'

'But you did take a risk in the end.'

'No, things just happened by themselves. On 8 June, the weather started to change and it cleared up a bit. You probably remember. At least, it cleared up in Bluff Cove.

'Yes, and that's what worried me. But Woodward wasn't at all bothered. "They're already finished and the weather is still terrible," he told me.'

'What a coincidence - that's the same thing that Peralta told us. So very quietly, and without asking the lieutenant's permission, who was deep in one of his feverish, nightmarish slumbers, Comte and I took the radio equipment out of the cave and extended the antenna, which is one of those tall things, bigger than a ship's mast. We switched it on and started to transmit according to the code book. We knew it was suicide, but we didn't expect what happened next.'

'And what did happen?'

'Peralta woke up and came out of the cave, furiously, with his pistol in his hand, and ordered us to turn off the radio. We refused. There was a very brief argument. Peralta was completely beside himself, he called us insubordinate black bastards again and he put the pistol to the head of the nearest and most dangerous of the two, Comte, who could have smashed his head like an egg just by squeezing with one hand.

Brinks listened in silence.

'Peralta was about to shoot, but I leapt on top of him. I knocked him over, pushed his jaw upwards to stretch out his throat and sank the bayonet under his Adam's apple, turning it slowly around, looking into his eyes while I turned and twisted it. What terror he felt, the poor bastard, when he realised he was going to die, and how long I was going to take about it. His eyes were popping out from pain and terror. But he still hadn't let go of the pistol, my mistake, and in his death throes he fired off the bullet into my thigh, which I swear I hardly felt at all. I was too busy trying to sever his windpipe that I didn't have time for distractions. I was possessed by the very devil. Even when that thing had stopped trembling and kicking it was hard for me to stop. Just imagine that: I didn't have hepatitis, but I'd had the shits for a week and a half, hadn't eaten properly for two months and, to cap it all, I now had a bullet in me.

'Did Comte help you?'

'Poor Tano, he did what he could. During the struggle he froze, not knowing what to do. Thereafter he didn't really know what to say to me for a while, but as I didn't speak either and looked on the point of fainting, he gave me a couple of pretty hard slaps to bring me around, bandaged up my leg as best he could and we set out to try sending another transmission. And at last, on the second attempt, they confirmed they'd received us.'

'We also picked that up.'

'So, we gave the over and out signal. Mission completed. Tano and I hugged each other: we'd just signed our own death warrants: that much was clear, but we couldn't give a fuck about it. We laughed like two school kids who've just played a joke on the school warden. We still didn't know what to do with Peralta's body, which could have given our position away, stretched out there on the ground. You know what it's like – some people are a nuisance even after they're dead. We were just packing up our equipment to get back into our cave again, thinking that just maybe, with a bit of luck, inside the cave, we might just survive, who knows? But that's when your mortars started raining down on us and after that I can't remember a thing.

'You'd never killed anyone before?'

I laughed bitterly.

'No. I started just with Peralta, but a bit later I progressed to I don't know how many Gurkhas and Welsh Guards. Funny how things turned out, isn't it? Pretty soon I went wholesale.'

Brinks pondered for a while.

'If you're lying, I must admit that you're an excellent liar.

257

And if you're not lying, you're also an excellent liar.'

'I see you like logical paradoxes, Brigadier Brinks.'

'You are, because of the way you handled an impossible situation. Whichever way, you're still a very interesting character.'

'And what do you do with interesting characters?'

'We lock them up.'

'And afterwards?'

He shrugged his shoulders.

'Sometimes we kill them, with a bullet in the brain, sometimes we let them go, and sometimes we even offer them a job.'

'I'm not asking for a bullet in the brain, but don't bother offering me a job, Brigadier. I'm allergic to work. And I'm sure the Queen doesn't pay very much, or on time.'

He looked at me as if making a decision.

'For the moment, you're going to stay in a cell. Don't worry, it'll be quite small, but comfortable. More for your own protection than anything else, because if news of what you did got around on the ship…Jackie received very strict orders to keep her mouth shut, and she seems to have followed them by drinking herself half to death. I'll also make sure you receive medical supervision, because you're still weak. I believe that with the information you've given me, in the next 24 hours, I can have a pretty reliable report concerning your life and identity delivered to my office. At least, enough to tell whether you were lying to me or not.'

'And if I have been lying?'

'Then I congratulate you. I consider you to be a born spy. Goodbye, young man.'

Incredibly enough, he shook my hand. It's well known that the English are a little bit mad. Their common sense is affected by professionalism and hobbies.

The two pistol-packing marines took me elsewhere.

I never saw Brinks again.

I lost all track of time, because they'd taken away my wristwatch (which they never gave me back) and I was shut up inside a tiny little cabin, probably a mechanic's, without a porthole to let in even a single ray of sunlight. A doctor whom I'd never seen before visited me twice, but we hardly spoke to each other. The rest of the time I spent smoking or sleeping.

I had another nightmare. Peralta, again.

Later, I woke up in a sweat, and heard those screeches and shifts in velocity that the engine makes when a ship enters port. Then silence. The vibration of the floor, which was very strong down there, stopped and I suddenly began to hear the cries of seagulls and the thud of the ship against those large tyres they hang on the quays to protect the stonework. I wasn't in a hurry to get out, but I did feel curious. I'd never seen Montevideo before.

Hours later, I went limping down a ramp to the quayside, alongside dozens of my assortedly-wounded compatriots, some on crutches, some in plaster, others with bandaged eyes who were led by the hand, others on stretchers. A miserable troop of wretches, beneath the shining grey sky of a winter's day on the Rio de la Plata.

Beneath us, cordoned off by two circles of impassive Uruguayan policemen, the appalling, vociferous officers and NCOs of the Argentine Army were waiting to shout abuse at us. All those Peraltas and would-be Peraltas. We were crammed, with pushes, blows from rifle butts and vituperations, into the waiting buses, while they shouted that we, the soldiers, had lost the war, because we were a bunch of pimps, faggots and chickens.

I paid no attention. They were already as dead as Peralta, they just hadn't realised it yet. They'd soon start to.

Sitting by the window overlooking the docks, I made myself comfortable, despite the crutches and the limp that Her Majesty had awarded me. I scanned the top decks of the Uganda, hoping to glimpse Jackie's rotund silhouette, at the same point by the rail where we went for some fresh air that time.

But there was nobody there.

Chapter Eight

That Hole in the Soul, II

Buenos Aires, 11 June.

Dear Doctor Estévez:

Please forgive me, dear Helena, for writing, which I do with the utmost reservation. I stopped being your patient six years ago and if I bother you now it's for three reasons: First, you once very quickly helped me overcome the saddest moment of my life, after separating from Félix, and you might have to do so again. The second is that they've tried to kill Félix twice, and the second time they almost succeeded. The third is that the person who saved Félix from the first attempt is another Falklands War veteran. I've just seen him, he's in a lot of trouble and perhaps you could help him. If he lets you, that is.

I'll take the last point first, as it's the most urgent at the moment. The gentleman says his name is Gabriel Cittadini.

He's a man of about forty, of middling height, almost totally white hair, green eyes and very indigenous features. He limps slightly, I suppose from an old war wound. I met him face to face yesterday for the first time and in rather strange circumstances. I already knew about him: if it weren't for his warning, Félix would already be dead. Since yesterday I've been looking for him in all the veteran data bases, and can you believe that in some I'm treated like family, but in others they shut the door in my face? They're at permanent loggerheads with each other.

But you're a national symbol, and nobody is going to deny you access to information.

As a lawyer, I've been trained to set things out in the correct order, and I'll try to do just that in this email, although my head doesn't feel particularly orderly at the moment. Please, Helena, I beg you to find a slot in your agenda and give me a session as soon as possible. I'm not planning on going back into therapy, but the mere act of writing to you obliges me to think clearly. I always wanted to be like you, tall, beautiful, dark, clear-headed and eloquent. Instead of which, I'm short, red-haired and rather repetitive, not to mention incoherent when I'm trying to construct sentences in such a state of anguish.

So if I may again use you as a role model, as I used to do somewhat consciously when I was doing therapy, I'll do my best to explain everything in order. I'll be linear and chronological.

I heard that Félix's situation was getting worse from his colleague and partner down there in Comodoro Rivadavia, Roberto Jáuregui, the lawyer. He already phoned me a month and a half ago to tell me that things had taken a turn for the worse.

This was also confirmed by another of Félix's personal friends. At the moment, this man is his main – or only – protector, and he has also been threatened. He's the owner and the chief editor of a small but influential local newspaper, the *Patagonia Argentina*. The journalist, it goes without saying, is Gustavo Enríquez and years ago – when Félix and I were still married – my ex-husband won an international court case on his behalf, concerning the custody and residence of his children, who were in the United States at that time. After Félix and I separated, Enríquez and I have exchanged emails at Christmas, but not much more than that.

It seems that Félix's problem started three months ago, with the latest wave of strikes in the oil fields at Chubut Sur and Santa Cruz Norte. Almost all of Argentina's crude oil comes from there these days. I understand the subject of oil interests you as much as it does me, i.e. not at all, but the owner of the most productive local wells is *la Brit*. And with the recent international increase in oil prices and wage stagnation in Argentina, the company is nowadays plagued by strikes. There are getting ever worse and more violent, much more than is reported by the media in Buenos Aires, which I imagine to be well remunerated by *la Brit*'s local partners – consists, as always, but now increasingly, in selling silence rather than information.'

As you can well imagine, my ex-Falklands hero has not been short of the kind of work that he's so good at: defending dismissed strikers, something that he – as an aristocrat with no working-class sympathies at all – does to a large extent to make things difficult for the British. For him – and this is something you are certainly aware of, Helena – the war is not over. It just continued somewhere else and in different ways. And he became a lawyer only to carry on the war as a civilian rather than a soldier. It was you, in fact, who helped me to understand Félix's madness and my need to break with such a crazy relationship. I wanted to get away from his war.

But it seems that I can't. Our marriage is like a recurrent illness: it always comes back. Three times in fifteen years. And a number of times we've separated since I began therapy with you.

I swear that today, with Félix in intensive care, it's a tremendous effort to explain things in the order they happened. Come on, Alejandra! Get on with it!

Three weeks ago, Félix received a visit from this Cittadini, who described himself as a recently-dismissed administrative worker from the Cerro Dragón oil fields. His job description didn't fit in with his attire: it's unusual to see Armani suits and Gucci ties in the oil fields and, the truth be told, in all Patagonia. This dandy added, almost in passing, that he was a veteran. As usually happens amongst ex-combatants with business to conduct, Félix and he spoke for a long time of things from long ago and far away, before getting down to brass tacks.

And they went into great detail. According to Jáuregui, who witnessed the conversation, Cittadini knew about and admired my ex-husband's deeds, despite the fact they've never been publicised outside of very specialist, almost academic, circles. Even most veterans themselves know very little about them.

Cittadini, for his part, said that he'd fought in the islands as a conscript. He admitted, with a blush, according
to Jáuregui, that he'd performed some rather useful services
as a forward observer in a place called Bluff Cave or Cove,
I didn't rightly understand the name or what he did there,
and neither did Jáuregui. Félix, however, knew immediately
what he was talking about, because from that moment on his
behaviour towards Cittadini lost all reserve. "They looked like
long-lost cousins," Jáuregui told me.

At that point in the conversation, Cittadini suddenly
grew serious, changed the subject and told Félix that (sic)
they were going to try and kill him, Félix, in three weeks time.
He gave details: it would be on the Santa Cruz provincial
Highway 43, near Las Heras, an oil-producing zone.

The man was very accurate and clear. There was no
way he could have known that Félix would be driving at such
a time and on such a day in that area, but he did know, only
too well. He even indicated the GPS coordinates on his mobile phone. It was at a point where a minor road crosses
Highway 43, in a very lonely place.

Félix was alarmed. Jáuregui got out a provincial road
map and spread it out on the table.

When asked how he knew all of this, Cittadini chose not
to answer, but he did add more tactical information. He identified the vehicles to be used in the coming assault (a van and
a car, with their description and respective number plates,
which turned out to be completely accurate) and he revealed
the real names of the four hitmen who'd been contracted,
along with their present whereabouts.

It was all very alarming. Three of these characters were
already known to Jàuregui and my ex-husband. They are

(or were) people from the local Comodoro Rivadavia under-world, with links to prostitution and cocaine pushing in the petroleum-producing zones. All ex-jailbirds.

What is even more surprising is the following: when the astonished Félix insisted that Cittadini reveal the source of the information, the latter became very uncomfortable. After a rather theatrical pause he said that he had orchestrated the contracts and details of the operation himself.

Can you imagine the sense of puzzlement and confusion, Helena?

Cittadini then went on to say – and now he seemed more frightened than confused – that with this betrayal he was risking his life. There would be a price on his head from that moment on – in pounds sterling rather than euros, he added with his typical Buenos Aires humour. He had to vanish from Argentina permanently or somebody would do it for him, he added.

Obviously, he was asking Félix and his partner for money.

Jáuregui didn't believe a word. Félix, an enlightened idiot who's famous for his hunches, did believe him, unreservedly, and so as not to waste time, went straight to the matter at hand and asked how much. Cittadini fired off a figure in dollars that you and I would both consider astronomical. Do you know what I mean, Helena? Much more than a small provincial legal firm, or the regional branch of a trade union at loggerheads with its national leadership, could afford.

But Félix's work has meant that he's owed rather unmentionable favours by a whole series of dodgy characters. A list starting in the underworld, passing through the trade unions and reaching as far as the police and provincial government. I'm talking about characters that move mountains of black money. Felix guessed that three of those "grateful clients" could produce the necessary dollars between them. Payable to someone else's name, not Cittadini's. And in another province, of course, Cittadini rapidly clarified. Alright, but only if there proved to be any substance behind the allegations, my ex-husband specified. And they shook hands.

Well, there was some substance behind it all.

But I'm getting ahead of events. After Cittadini had left, the next thing my ex-husband and his partner Jáuregui did was to arrange a meeting with the aforesaid journalist, Gustavo Enríquez, to, in Jáuregui's words, "prepare an umbrella of local press support, for when the shit hit the fan".

Before continuing with the story, I'll say a few words about the Patagonia Argentina, Enríquez's newspaper. It started just a few years ago as a simple website, updated on a daily basis. Now it's got a press run of 10,000 copies, at least twice that number read it online, and they're proud of the fact that they don't receive a peso's worth of publicity from either the Government or the oil companies. This enables it to be the only regional medium that denounces the extravagant and illegal concessions handed out to the oil drillers by provincial governments, puts the strikes on the front page, and exposes the government in other incidents of corruption.

Apart from its excessive regionalism it's a good newspaper and even well written, without those atrocious spelling and syntactical errors so prevalent in the Buenos Aires press. They have a couple of really competent journalists, people who could easily play in the media "premier league" in the Federal Capital.

Forgive me for dwelling on the subject. According to Félix, owning this newspaper places Gustavo Enríquez in some rather tricky situations. These range from cyber attacks on the newspaper's servers, or even robbery of part of the press run before it hits the kiosks. These frequently occur after discreet "working lunches" with emissaries from the governor or some mayor or corporate chairman, who invariably offer to pay for publicity for local government or for State sub-contractors, but also say that their boss "would like to express his concern that the Patagonia Argentina seems to promote industrial strife and to discourage foreign investment in the province." It's not uncommon for a cyber attack or some broken windows at the newspaper's offices to be preceded by an anonymous phone call.

Beyond the defiant, juvenile and rather moving attitude of these two grey-haired fifty-year olds in a country which will never see another *Cordobazo*[1], Gustavo Enríquez considers himself to be my ex-husband's Sancho Panza, the one charged with imposing some common sense amid all the madness. He follows him wherever he goes and for whatever purpose, since Félix got him back the custody of his two kids, taken away by his ex-wife, it seems, in 1982.

These family "happy endings", you know better than I do, are not usually either happy or final. Two adolescents who speak Spanish with difficulty, brought here under duress, who don't really know their father, hate living in a Patagonian town and who want to get straight back to the United States as soon as they are old enough. Poor Enríquez, after fighting so hard for his kids...

---

1 A civil uprising in Córdoba, in May 1969, that ended General Onganía's explicit plans to stay as Argentina's president for twenty years.

That's the man that Félix looked to for protection: En-ríquez. A man who already faces enough danger of his own, even if he wasn't a friend of that walking target, my ex-husband.

Gustavo Enríquez refuses to say a word about what was discussed in that meeting at the newspaper's offices, as well as in subsequent meetings with undesirable people in bars and places of ill repute. They must have been authentic councils of war of all the local "families". I'm glad I know nothing about them.

I can, however, tell you what happened in the days that followed. The four men who were supposedly going to whack Félix disappeared from Comodoro Rivadavia. One was found dead five days later, with a bullet in the forehead, near a *cigüeña*.[2] That's what they call the mobile units used for secondary pumping in old oil wells in Patagonia. That was in an oil field not far from Caleta Olivia, a town in Santa Cruz. Nobody in Chubut seems to have mourned the deceased. He'd killed at least one person and was a known rapist. Of the other three, nothing more was heard.

The Santa Cruz police force decided not to delve too deeply and to put everything down to turf wars among drug traffickers. The Patagonia Argentina, however, gave full coverage to the matter and connected the case to the conflicts in the oil-producing region. The article didn't give full details, but insinuated that the newspaper was holding a few aces up its sleeve. That was very clever, but it didn't work. There were too many enemies, they were too powerful and too unknown.

I'm not criticising Félix. What else could he do? The only reason he's still alive is because of his audaciousness. His

2 Literally, a stork.

message was: "Do you want to kill me? Be my guest, but there's a price to pay."

It's disgusting, Helena, but that's the world that Félix lives in today, the man who –idiot that I am – I just can't seem to let go.

You'll understand how lucky I am that I don't live in the same sewer, that I got away in time. As a criminal lawyer in Buenos Aires I see aberrant situations every day, but always from the outside. Work is one thing and my life is something else.

Two weeks ago, when the enemy seemed cowed and things seemed to be calming down, a bomb exploded in Félix's car. Someone managed to avoid the news being broadcast in the Buenos Aires media: perhaps this e-mail is the first you've heard of it.

Félix lost a leg and has dreadful burns and cuts on the other. Add that to all the other injuries his body suffered back in 1982: reduced vision in one eye, shrapnel splinters they could never remove from his thorax and face…it's as if they were killing him in instalments.

He'll live, but he's still in intensive care. This time the Patagonia Argentina played all its trump cards and for two days doubled its circulation. It accused the oil companies and named names. On the third day, the newspaper's offices were torched.

The Buenos Aires press finally had no alternative but to take an interest in the story. Whenever someone makes an attempt on a journalist's life or a newspaper is physically attacked, the few remaining independent newspapers and radio stations get up in arms and the multimedia giants can no longer sell their silence...or, at least, they sell it at a higher price.

Here's an interesting fact; they're already trying to contain the information leaks. According to the big newspapers in the capital, the fire at the Patagonia Argentina is not related to the attempt on Félix's life. It's not that they don't link the two events. They deny one of them. The attempted murder never happened.

That's how they control our lives.

When they blew up Félix's car, Jáuregui was miraculously saved. He'd been delayed on the office telephone as my ex-husband was starting the car. Two hours later, even though I hadn't seen or even talked to Félix for two years, his partner called me from the hospital waiting room and told me the news. Who else was he going to call, if Félix and his ghastly family haven't spoken since 1982? And I take the first flight to Comodoro Rivadavia, which is still in shock. And from where I have just returned, a physical and emotional wreck.

Helena, even if Félix does get over this, I'm under no illusions about the future. It's obvious on which side the provincial government is playing, and the national government just looks the other way (they insist this is not a federal matter). Even if the campaign against Félix were only a locally-inspired affair (and I have my doubts about that), I can't dismiss the idea that he'll one day be discovered at dawn lying next to a *cigüeña* himself. Even though he's always armed and knows how to fight dirty. This crazy Don Quixote of mine isn't tilting at windmills, but at real giants. And evil ones, at that.

Which brings me back to my request. I need to find Gabriel Cittadini and you might perhaps find him quicker than I

271

can. Cittadini, God knows why, betrayed the ones who contracted him, and there's now a price on his head. To be perfectly honest, I couldn't give a damn about his life. Excuse me. But, really, that's the way I feel. I do, however, want to find him before his ex-employers, and make him talk and sing and tell me who contracted him. And to publish it.

The Patagonia Argentina tripled its number of followers on Internet after the fire, despite suffering another cyber attack yesterday that crashed their server for seven hours. To publish the names of those behind the attempted murder of Félix, come what may, is the only thing that can stop them from coming back to finish the job. Perhaps it's also the only way that Cittadini himself can save his own life, although that appears not to bother him too much. I'll come back to that later.

Enríquez, who now uses an old mimeograph to print his paper, just like we did with our old left-wing rags back in the 1970s, is backing me up. Helena, with your undoubted free data base access, we can get to the end of the thread very quickly. There were no more than 12,000 Argentines deployed in the Falklands, nearly 800 died in combat, nearly 500 committed suicide in the thirty years that followed. And a few emigrated.

Espionage isn't really my field. But as a criminal lawyer I do know gangsters quite well and I intuitively know that Cittadini contracted some gangsters without being himself one at all. And I'm talking about fourth division mafia. And I suspect that he did it on purpose, to sabotage the entire operation, to make it ridiculously patent. My instinct tells me that Cittadini is an Argentine probably mixed up in some shady business, who probably had some sort of trouble with the police and had to become a grass against his will. But I also think he's a master of deception, and that he's played a massive trick on his bosses. And I think his real bosses were neither our clumsy bureaucratic trade unionists, nor our entrepreneurs terrified of bad publicity: no. My instinct tells me that these are people much more lethal, methodical and silent, and are based in London.

So, by a simple process of elimination we have to seek among those who emigrated to England and then came back home. These are records I can find much easier with your help, Helena, and they'll narrow down the search area considerably.

The third pertinent fact is the limp: the Argentine soldiers who came back from the islands with serious leg injuries. Their records must be in the archives of the Central Military Hospital, which admitted all those who disembarked in Montevideo. By cross-referencing these two groups, the ones who've been in England with those who have a limp, there must be a point of intersection. That's where we'll find our man.

Then, we'll have to do exactly what the enemy would do, but before the enemy does it: find his current hideout. Maybe some family member is hiding him, maybe an old friend. Maybe another veteran.

This is not some stupid Bond, James Bond novel. I find myself in a world I know nothing about and with no protection at all. And as frightened as you can imagine.

Finding Cittadini alive and making him talk, provoking an international incident, that causes our Chancellery and the British Foreign Office to become embroiled in diplomatic wrangling… I can see no other way of guaranteeing Félix's survival.

Do I seem absolutely mad to you? Do you think I'm going to get myself killed without achieving a thing? That's what the little bit of sense left in my head keeps telling me. It tells me I'm gambling beyond my means in a casino where they kill you. But the thing is that, apart from Enríquez, everyone is deserting Félix. His partner Jáuregui told me that he's getting out right now, that he wasn't cut out to be a martyr, that he's got children to bring up, etc.

I'm not criticising him. How many times did I myself retreat from the burning circus that is Félix's life? It's just that I could never keep to that decision.

I've just sent a registered telegram to the private clinic in Comodoro, where Félix regains consciousness from time to time. Apart from Enríquez, sometimes, nobody goes to visit him. The doctors want to ship him off as soon as possible to a public hospital because they're frightened of another attack. If they so much as move him a metre from the intensive care unit, I tell them in my telegram, I'll be accusing them of dereliction of duty and I don't know how many other things. Whether or not they believe me, and are frightened, is anybody's guess.

When we were married, Félix made me read a lot about the British secret services and their ingenuity for setting up scams of the "smoke and mirrors" variety. They repeatedly deceived the Germans during WWII, the Malayan Communists and the nationalist government of Iran in the post-war period and us, during the entire Falklands war. They are the masters of mind control, and of making their opponents kill themselves. Félix used to contrast the elegant and lethal magic of the British spies with the brutality of the Argentine "experts", so well versed in the art of kidnapping and torturing students, workers, housewives and other dangerous beings. And killing them.

Helena, as I put the finishing touches to this e-mail, I realise that I might not get to send it now, but just save it as a draft for a few days. I may even delete it, and never send it. Because just for having visited Félix in hospital, having met Enríquez the journalist, having sent that telegram to the clinic and for being a well-known lawyer here in the capital, for all these reasons, I imagine that my e-mails must be read by a lot of people. I feel as exposed as a hamster in a cage.

Whatever I do, writing this has helped to clear things up for me, as it did six years ago, when I used to speak with you personally, during the course of therapy that lasted for some time.

Helena, it's good talking to you, even in your absence.'

Tomorrow, I'll carry on with what is probably a letter to myself.

Buenos Aires, 12 June

Dear Helena Estévez (or Dear Alejandra Leibovich?):

I was right to postpone sending this e-mail until today.

I spent all morning mulling over the past week. I stayed in Comodoro for several days (a city that I hate), sitting on the staircase that leads to the intensive care unit on the first floor, waiting for the two daily medical reports – at eight in the morning and five in the afternoon – and the fifteen minute visiting period, from twelve o' clock onwards. And, of course, there was no bench or a chair to sit on. The clinic is very good at making you know you're not wanted there. My body, especially my lumbar and cervical vertebrae, are not up to this kind of thing anymore.

Writing this story has made me realise once more that I've never loved any man like I love Félix, and that it would be difficult to live something so intense ever again. "Now tell me something I didn't know, Alejandra." I can almost see you smiling while saying that to me. With that smile of yours that men probably adore.

But the thing with Félix is over. I have loved men, and will love them again. Perhaps a little less, and men perhaps a little less terrible. Much less terrible, I hope. I'm still an attractive woman, very attractive for some, a bit too complicated, perhaps too intense and unpredictable. But, all in all, I recognise that Félix was too much even for me. The man's a refugee from a Greek tragedy. He's made on a different scale. Not on mine.

What is certain is that re-reading what I wrote yesterday, and with fear in my heart, I'm going to take the same decision I took years ago. I'm leaving.

Wracked with guilt, I'm leaving him alone with his demons. I already did it once, twice, three times, I can do it again. I hope this time it's for ever.

I realise that, at the age of 53, I can face up to this constant intimate betrayal and, despite everything, still enjoy the challenges and conquests that lie before me. My economic position is secure and allows me to dedicate more and more time to the two things I most value: travel, on the one hand and giving free legal advice as a volunteer on the other – yes, I know, it's rather ironic, you don't need to say anything – to some of the NGOs that exist for Falklands veterans, that handful of small brotherhoods that, typical of Argentines, cordially exchange letters with British veterans, but refuse to talk to each other. This is where you and I got to know each other and I became your patient and you drew me out of my guilt and darkness.

It's very clear to me today why I continue to defend those grey-haired gentlemen, who at the age of seventeen left so many pieces of their bodies and souls behind in that forgotten little war. With so many other crushed, broken and forgotten people in Argentina I chose them because, as Félix always said, they risked everything for their country, yet in their country nobody looks after them.

But that's not true. That's not entirely true. I chose them for Félix. But that's not true, either. I chose them for me, to atone for not having been able to help Félix. And that's also untrue. I don't know why I do it. But I don't care; I do it, that's all.

My children have grown up, graduated and are now independent. They live with their respective partners and worry unnecessarily about their mother's loneliness. I don't, because it's only a relative loneliness and I know with some satisfaction (women can be so wicked) that after our separation, Félix had many other women but he also could not, or didn't want to, remain with any of them. He didn't manage to replace me, either.

Sometimes life can be so cruel that two people who can't stand each other fall in love. Worse still, they can't stand each other for the very same reasons that they love each other.

While on the subject, and just for the sake of gossip, I always wondered why you came back to Buenos Aires after having lived for so long in Montevideo, where you had such a successful practice. And why you left your old speciality (childhood traumas) in order to offer your service free of charge to those neglected phantoms of the Falklands war. In "psychoanalyzed" Buenos Aires circles certain urban legends have arisen, the truth of which I'm unsure of, but I'd love to find out. I imagine, Helena, that by volunteering you are somehow healing your own previous life story. Perhaps in the same way as I am.

To alleviate someone else's horror, which is what we both do in our own ways but with the same group of people, is in my case now something very real and sordid. A few months ago, during one of my typical sleepless summer nights, Eduardo E. called me on the phone, desperate. Thirty years ago Eduardo was an adolescent and he worked an anti-aircraft battery close to Moody Brook. I don't know where that is and I don't really care. Nowadays, Eduardo is a radiologist technician, and coordinator at a centre for war veterans. He's a solid and well-respected character.

"Pedro M. has committed suicide," Eduardo blurted out as soon as I lifted the receiver. Pedro M...I knew almost immediately who he meant. A man with no friends who was seen at the centre only infrequently, well-decorated for his bravery on the battlefield, an NCO who for some tremendous act of valour became an instant legend, only to be quickly forgotten.

"And what can I do?" I asked Eduardo.

'Come and chase the TV cameras away," he answered.

And so, at two o' clock on a Sunday morning, there I was acting as a scare-cameraman, doing my best to frighten away the sinister paparazzi from the Argentine popular press.

Behind the door I'm trying to block is Pedro M., who was once so brave. After coming back to Argentina, in spite of his medals and doing as best he could trying to complete some kind of technical studies, he never managed to get a decent or steady job. Employers here systematically reject Falklands veterans.

Then it was the same old story: constant nightmares, abject poverty, he becomes an alcoholic, the second and the third wife also leave, he even loses the right to see his kids. 21 years after the war, the new government, President Kirchner's, finally remembers him, and others like him, a little bit. They get him a job as a corporal in the police force, but it was small consolation and it came a quarter of a century too late. It couldn't change anything.

He lived out his last years in this room in a little pension on Mansilla Street, where he's just committed suicide. He's behind me, behind that door, hanging from a beam. This happened in summer, like I said. Given that he never got any visitors, he was found by the neighbours and only because he'd started to stink. From where I'm standing and in spite of the door, I can smell him as if he were right next to me.

So my mission this night, as spokesperson for the *Centro Porteño de Veteranos*[3], consists in telling the outside

3 Falklands Veterans Centre of Buenos Aires

broadcast TV crews (with all the severity I could muster) that they're only authorised to tell the story, interview neighbours, and film the door of the boarding house or of the room itself, etc. But that the first one who tries to get past the door, in order to obtain gruesome pictures of a national hero's fly-ridden body, is going straight to jail. And if the channel broadcasts it, it'll end up paying a fortune for moral damages and losses.

Obviously, my authority, my profession, my sex and my slight stature cuts no ice with the camera crews. Nor do they impress the policemen, who've just arrived and are mounting a reluctant guard in front of the door whilst, inside, the forensic boys are taking photos. They are restrained rather more by the aforesaid Eduardo's musculature (he became a body-builder to get over his depressions and panic attacks) and the surly faces of the two or three dishevelled and dog-tired veterans whom Eduardo has managed to round up this morning, calling them on their mobiles and dragging them away from their families and their beds. An *Armada Branca-leone*[4] whose body language, the details in one man's bearing that other men unfailingly pick up on, exudes such burnt-out rage it would inspire caution in all but a complete idiot. One of our lot, the smallest, darkest and most anonymous one, has eyes that, if you look at them properly, are rather scary. I wonder who he is, and what his story is.

Just then, the cameramen from two channels try to force an entrance. They push me, I fall in a heap, and at that point the policemen, who are like painted dummies, look at each other and ask themselves whether they should come out of their catatonic trance or not. Then Eduardo and the rest of the gang join the fray and, three minutes later, we all have

---

4 A rag, tag and bobtail army of very strange characters. A film by Monicelli (1966).

to join forces, the police included, to stop the little dark one, who's already kicked a camera to pieces, from doing exactly the same to the cameraman. "Why didn't you come and film him when he had to sell his blood so he could feed his kids, you son of a bitch?" the bloke is shouting.

Here we have Alejandra Leibovich, the lawyer, at the age of 53, playing Antigona.

And we also have – I'm sure it's him, from his description – Gabriel Cittadini, the veteran.

The man I no longer have to search for.

So, why am I telling you this story? As far as Félix is concerned, the decision has been made. I'm making it as I write and I'm writing so that I can make it, for the third time, the final one. Because it's so difficult for me. Félix changed my life for good and for bad, he took me to his planet, up to a point (I even took out citizenship there), but I must leave him again, with his never-ending war and his ancient mythologies and his unutterable guilt. It's all too much for me.

I could never persuade him, and probably never will, to live with me in the here and now, rather than carry on with his stupid, absurd fight against the world and the history of the world, a fight that just gets more absurd and ever lonelier.

I don't think I'll trouble you for that appointment to clear my head up after all, Doctor Estévez. You never let me down, even *in absentia*. It's already more than clear. Nor do I need your help to meet Gabriel Cittadini face to face again, the man with whom I shared a battle and to whom I owe the fact that Félix is still more or less alive. I no longer care about him; I don't want to know who was behind the murder attempts. Cittadini is a poor devil and will probably have to live clandestinely for a long time. Maybe they'll find him, maybe they'll kill him, or maybe he'll escape. Jáuregui told me he'd already collected almost all the money he asked for. Well, let him manage his own soul as best he can, as I'll manage mine.

I'll tell Eduardo M. not to call me any more at night. Better still, never to call me again. Even though I won't be able to look him in the eye when I tell him. Even though I won't be able to stand his bewilderment. I won't go back to Comodoro to see Félix start rehabilitation with a titanium leg. And watch him struggle – I know him so well – for months and months in the gym, until he can walk almost normally and even, never giving up, self-disciplined like no-one else in this world, gets back to driving a car again, despite his impaired vision.

I won't be there to see how, probably accompanied by his faithful shield-bearer Gustavo Enríquez, he turns up one day at his office - this time with no Jáuregui and no secretary – and picks up a few folders and besmirches his fingers with dust while flicking through the pages and then sneezes, because he's becomes quite allergic to dust. And then begins to call this person or the other on the phone and tries to pick up his profession of sane lawyer and mad patriot where he left off, as if nothing had happened. As if nothing more could happen to him.

I will never again spend an entire week of my life without sleeping, watching him through a glass window, unconscious, his body full of tubes and catheters, asking myself questions that have no answers. I love him. You know how much.

I'll always love him, but as I told him the first time I left, he's got a hole in his soul. And I never found out what it was. And I could never close it, and never will.

Chapter Nine

The Girl from Southampton

It was a nasty, rainy night in London. A rather small man was hurriedly crossing the square in front of Saint Bartholomew's Hospital. He stopped suddenly when the big man emerged from the circle of almond trees, headed him off and stood right in front of him.

Both men were still for a few seconds, face to face, ten yards apart, observing each other, completely alone. Recent urban renewal has meant that Barts and its surroundings have been pedestrianised and are now rather attractive, but at that time of night and in that foul weather, not another soul was to be seen there.

The man thus intercepted, his face covered by the collar flaps of his macintosh, knew that his bad knee wouldn't allow him to escape. He had a flick knife in his pocket, although it wouldn't give him much of a chance against the giant in front of him who, although now still, he'd already seen moving like a cat. But as far as everything else went, at that particular point in time, life didn't matter to him and he was therefore not afraid. So, he waited – he was very good at waiting – and said nothing.

'I'm not from the police,' the big man introduced himself at last, uncomfortably.

That was an unnecessary explanation. He didn't behave like a policeman. Although he had to raise his voice slightly to make himself heard over the sounds of the storm, he had a middle-class London accent, educated but not pompous. Neither a professor, nor a hooligan. What the fuck was he, then?

The man in the mac remained silent, with his hands in his pockets, waiting either for further explanations or for a fight to finally kick off. He was left-handed and the fingers of his left hand surreptitiously touched and then closed around his knife, his thumb on the button.

'Majors didn't send me, either, Gabriel. I think it would be best if you left that knife alone. I've no wish to have my throat cut and I've already killed too many Argentines. But you're in trouble and I can help you.'

The man called Gabriel remained impassive, asking himself how come this gorilla knew his real name. Or Majors' name. Or about the knife. He thought his only chance was to make a feint for the stomach but then stab him in the neck and run, run for his life. That is, if his leg would let him. Anyway, the big man would be choking and flailing around on the floor...

'I know you don't believe a word I say, and that you're wondering how you can kill me. If I'd wanted to kill you, I could have done it from behind, by surprise and very easily.

I've been very well trained for that. I would've done it, and I wouldn't be here talking to you and risking you doing something stupid. Worse still, I wouldn't be getting soaking wet. In my state, I can't afford to get the flu, believe me.

Gabriel's impassiveness gradually turned into curiosity. It was a very odd situation. He decided to carry on listening. Furthermore, he had no choice.

'All I'm asking for is half an hour of your time. I know your wife's in a deep coma and I don't suppose you feel like talking to me, or to anybody in particular. However, I also know that by order of your probation officer, the police will be at the hospital in half an hour. Furthermore, I foresee that if you don't come with me now, in 45 minutes' time a policeman called Rutherford will arrest you at Euston Station. And everything that happens after that gets very messy.'

The shorter man remained silent but doubtfully took his hands out of his pockets, as if to show them. So, this orang-utan not only knew his name, but also his wife's condition and even his plan of escape. He knew, or said he knew, about the police dragnet. One part of his mind was still occupied in thinking of ways he could kill the person speaking to him, but the other needed to process, and hear more of, this surprising information. Both parts of his mind coincided in the thought that it was a long time – 30 years – since he'd last killed an Englishman and he wasn't going to start again now. So he spoke:

'I agree that we shouldn't stand out in the rain, Mister...?'

'Wolfe.'

'Wolfe. Of course. And I'm Princess Diana.'

'Big Bad Wolfe to his friends, Princess.'

'Are we friends already?' The man in the mackintosh smiled.

The big man's body detected the implied threat. That shitty little dwarf looked quite a handful.

'I suggest The Caduceum,' he answered, pretending he hadn't understood. 'It's only a hundred yards away. Nobody's ever heard of it, it's not in any guide books, there's no music, only doctors and nurses and families of the patients at Barts go there, and the beer's alright. It's the last place the cops will look for you. It's too near the hospital.'

The little man shrugged his shoulders in a sign of acceptance.

The pub was a clone of thousands upon thousands of similar places that regulate life in Britain: an interior done out with dark wooden panelling, a bar decorated with strips of bronze, clients who prefer to drink standing up and chat quietly and the obligatory two or three blokes throwing a few darts in the background. On one wall was a flat TV screen, on which Tottenham could be seen thrashing Manchester United for once. A notice pinned over the bar politely asked the dear customers to refrain from using their mobile phones inside, and the dear customers obliged. The only odd thing were the relatively few business-suited men and trouser-suited women taking advantage of the happy hour, contrasting sharply with the abundance of those in burgundy, pale green or sky-blue medical clothing. Everyone was drinking as if Armageddon were a mere two hours away.

Just people from Barts, trying hard not to take death home with them.

The reddish, malty, luke-warm beer, smelling slightly of walnuts and toasted bread that was put down in front of them was also not dissimilar in any way from the stuff being drunk that night by the swimming pool-full in any other part of the drenched British Isles. Having lived there for so long, the Argentine had become accustomed to such brews, without ever becoming a fanatic.

Without his mackintosh it was easier to see that he was dark, angular, with hardly any grey hair, in spite of being around fifty. He might have passed for a light-skinned Pakistani if it weren't for the restless, slightly oblique and rather feline green eyes which, in general, nobody noticed. The giant, a kind of prematurely grey-haired Tarzan - even his skin was ashen - of indefinable age, should have attracted many more stares. But, the Argentine noticed, he had some mysterious way of avoiding them.

'So, who the hell are you and what in blazes do you want?' asked Gabriel, calmly, after downing his pint, without looking him in the eyes, gangster style.

'To talk to you about your wife,' answered the big man, straightforwardly, looking right at him. 'At this very moment she's dying and her mind is already starting to enter into mine. It started to happen a few hours ago.'

A lunatic, who ought to be locked up, of course. One more. Why did he always have to find nutcases waiting for him on every corner? He'd attracted them by the dozen all his life, like the Pied Piper of Hamelin attracted rats, but without wanting or trying to. The Argentine weighed up his increasingly narrowing options again. Break one of the whisky glasses hanging upside down over the bar, cut the giant's jugular and make with the legs? It wasn't impossible, but it was far too dramatic. And why bother? They'd catch him before he was three blocks away. He sighed.

'I see that you're still thinking about killing me, Gabriel, although not quite so enthusiastically. Maybe another beer will help you change your mind. And perhaps you'd like to know how it is I know so much about you and your wife, the girl from Southampton.'

Southampton and your fucking whore of a mother. If you mention my wife or Southampton once more I'll definitely kill you, you bastard, thought Gabriel. His beer went down the wrong way and he started to cough. A couple of doctors standing near them turned to contemplate him with professional curiosity, discarded him as clinically uninteresting and went on with their own conversation. While his breathing got back to normal, Gabriel ordered two more pints. Then he looked the big man in the face for the first time.

'Alright, then. Talk, for fuck's sake.'

'What should I talk about first Gabriel? Your plan of escape? Forget it. It won't work. A while ago the police got a court order allowing them to search your wife's flat, and they've taken away your Italian passport. Getting out of the UK by air, sea or train is going to be very tricky.'

Just then the big man made a painful grimace and went pale and sweaty. The Argentine regarded him with curiosity. The giant closed his eyes, waited for a moment before slowly expelling his breath, as if someone had been extracting one of his teeth with forceps, and it had finally come out. Immediately afterwards he opened his eyes.

Now he was even greyer, there were tears in his eyes and his forehead was wet.

'Oh, God, forgive me. I can't get used to it. It's her, your wife. She just went in completely. Here,' he said, pointing to his head with a trembling finger.

'Do you mean that she's…?'

The big man nodded. He seemed queasy.

Gabriel felt like they were tearing out his heart. The bastard son of a bitch, he had no right to make fun of …

The other man closed his fists and his eyes and continued in a strained voice.

'Her heart stopped a few minutes ago. They were trying to bring her round, but she didn't respond. Total shut down. They're now disconnecting her from the life-support systems. Please, yes, a couple of malt whiskies. Don't worry, it'll pass. That's the one, barman, my friend here likes Talisker.'

And how the fuck did he know about the Talisker? The Argentine, who had been struggling not to either cry or explode, made an even more heroic effort to force down that savage, dark, very strong whisky, with its reek of burnt peat.

He was furious. They were stealing the most painful moment of his life. It had been transformed in an instant into something absurd. All he wanted to do was retreat to a hole somewhere and howl. But no, instead he was drinking with some inexplicably well-informed imbecile who, on top of it, seemed convinced that he was a clairvoyant or a medium.

Gabriel sank deeper and deeper into the sense of unreality. He hated that sensation. Unreality, a companion to extreme pain, suspends reason, which meant that he was beginning to believe every fucking word the madman was saying. But, to make things worse, now that Gabriel was ready to believe him, Wolfe seemed to have run out of words and was rather on the point of shutting up, with an exhausted air.

A few minutes went past, and Manchester United unexpectedly regained the initiative with a lightning strike of a goal against Tottenham, as if to restore the natural order of things. The darts players broke off from their game for a few seconds and made some dry comments. In spite of the rain, the screen showed a half-full and enthusiastic stadium, but the pub landlord had his own ideas about acceptable noise levels in his establishment and, in the same way he prohibited the use of mobile phones, he only allowed football matches to be shown with the sound turned off. Good for him.

'Did she suffer much?' asked the Argentine at last.

The big man simply passed him a paper napkin so he could dry his eyes, and shook his head.

'Not at all. She didn't suffer at all. There was a little pain, but I absorbed almost all of it. And you gave her some unexpected joy at the end. You made her laugh. That was her last memory.'

'And now?'

'Now? Nothing. She's within me. But she's dead.'

The Argentine couldn't stop himself from sobbing. He needed to regain his incredulity or else lose it altogether. He thought about a second whisky, but refrained.

'I don't understand what you're saying. I don't understand anything. I don't believe you.'

'I don't understand much either, Gabriel, but I've no alternative but to believe myself. Imagine an mp3 that you were listening to for a while and then the song finishes. You save that melody to the hard disc of your computer. In reality, the song continues to exist, but it's saved, compressed. It's there, except that no one's playing it and no one listens to it.'

'Is that what being dead is like?'

'Something like that.'

'Well, death seems rather ridiculous, then. You just turn into a saved file.'

'I don't know. The saved song, in some way, continues to exist. But it's a code, it's not being run. I listen to the lives of the people that dwell in me and as I do so, I run the code. Although there are exceptions – like yourself – most of my… let's call them inhabitants, have died. But I can live those lives whenever I want to. I think about this person or that one and their existences are relived within me, complete, every moment, every perception experienced throughout an entire existence, everything returns. It's not a metaphor. They really do live again. They're doing it right now, as we speak. It's just that those living again don't know they've been revived by me. I perceive them, but they don't perceive me or each other. I am their world. Or their worlds, the world of each one of them.'

'You must have a very polyphonic head, Wolfe,' Gabriel sneered.

The other man agreed, ignoring the sneer. After a while he continued: 'Polyphony's a good definition. But – guessing what your next question will be – I'm unsure whether these files will be lost or will continue to exist in someone else's mind after my own death. And that won't be long, as you've probably guessed from my unhealthy colour. The doctors have given me a maximum of a year left to live. That's right, just like your wife.'

'I'm sorry about that,' answered Gabriel, sincerely.

The other man nodded.

A long while passed in which neither man said a word.

'Even so, I still don't understand a thing,' the Argentine picked up where he'd left off.

'I don't understand it all, either. It just happens. And has done for thirty years.'

'I'm not in the mood to listen to such utter nonsense, and even less so today, right now. I feel like smashing a chair over your head, know what I mean?' said the smaller man, suddenly furious, itching for a fight.

The giant didn't respond. He shrugged his shoulders. After a while, he said: 'It won't make you feel any better.'

'So, you're some sort of hard disc that stores mp3 recordings of dead wives?' the little man continued defiantly.

'I'm more like a part of a network of souls. I must be something like just another server within a network of souls. I think.'

'Fantastic. Facebook. Souls.'

'Yes, generally the souls of soldiers who fought in the Falklands, but also, over time, the lives that were connected to them have also been added to those souls: their wives, girlfriends, children. That's how I discovered your wife, when you met her. I've had you in my head for a long time. I first detected you on 8 June 1982, at the height of that shambles, when all this started. Afterwards we were in the same ward, on the Uganda. Our beds were quite close to each other. It's just that I was catatonic, I mean that I was lost amid all these things, these beings, these people...'

Gabriel said nothing. Mumbo jumbo, he thought. Just mumbo jumbo.

'I don't know how many people I have inside my head. You won't believe how anyone can live like that, so inhabited.

It's something that started to happen to me during the explosion of the Galahad, at Bluff cove. There was an Argentine Air Force bomb that blew up at my very feet and…it's a long story. But the fact of the matter is that you are directly responsible and that has marked my life. As you well know.'

Gabriel remained completely silent. So, the bloke was a spy after all. From the police or the army? Now he really was fucked. Now he really did desperately need another whisky. But, once more, he refrained from ordering one.

'And it marked your life so much that you ended up leaving your own country for the enemy's country, mine. And after many adventures - what a coincidence! what a paradox! - you end up getting married to the ex-fiancée of the same Welsh Guard called Howard who died in front of you, in the bed opposite you. And he died howling and blaspheming because of the terrible burns he suffered in the air raid, which happened because of you, so many years ago…my God, how time flies. Do you want me to go on with the story, or now are you starting to believe me?'

Gabriel didn't answer. He picked up another paper napkin to dry his eyes.

'That lad, Howard. She could never forget him.'

'Women don't forget, Gabriel.'

'Did she ever find out? That he died because of me?'

'No, but it doesn't matter. Women know everything, always.'

'Ah, finally.'

'Finally, what?'

'You finally said something sensible.'

Wolfe laughed a little.

'Don't count on me being sensible and don't bother asking if I'm mad or not. Of course I am, according to any psychiatric definition. Furthermore, I've been admitted to psychiatric hospital three times.'

'That makes me feel a lot better. You've no idea how much.'

'It doesn't make the psychiatrists feel better. The problem is that I don't fit into their statistics. They never knew what the fuck to do with me. Cases of multiple personality are not that frequent, but they exist, they do exist, and the doctors always love finding one so they can write an article about it. If I let them, they could organize entire congresses about my case. Because what no psychiatrist, or neurologist, or Anglican priest or Australian witch doctor or Peruvian *ayahuasca*-using shaman has ever been able to explain is why, for thirty years, instead of four or five incompatible or mutually-exclusive personalities inside my brain, the type that take it in turns to take centre stage, let's say the classic scenario, there seem to be nearly a thousand human beings all living simultaneously in me, now including your wife. And although they don't communicate with each other – they are saved, unmodifiable, read-only files, like I told you – I've got the records and the computer and I can read them all, open them in parallel and run hundreds of them at the same time. Which means that what I know about you, I know from more than one source. And the main source is you, yourself. Other sources are, let's say, saved files. And I'm not just talking about your wife. Do you remember a volunteer from Córdoba called Comte?'

'Comte, of course. So, poor old Comte is also inside of you, is he? But he was even bigger than you. Give my regards to Tano, Wolfe. Did they ever give you electro-shock treatment?'

'Of course they did. Twice. And I lose count of all the conventional and atypical antipsychotics they made me take. They don't change anything. And you can't offend me, because you already know I'm telling the truth. I can give you dozens of examples of proof. For example, shall we talk about another read-only file, another file that you saved (what a word!) yourself, Lieutenant Peralta?'

The little man shook his head vigorously. Then he finally gave in to temptation and ordered his second malt whisky and another one for Wolfe, who made a gesture of appreciation. He drank in silence, waiting. That settled it, then. A damned spy. The SIS, probably.

But why was a British Government spy after him, a petty criminal, and thirty years after the events at Bluff Cove? And furthermore, why did they send some idiot who pretended to suffer this extreme, almost gross, form of madness? And, finally, wasn't it a bit late to get revenge for what happened to that ship?

'Forget what you're thinking, Gabriel. I'm not what you think. And no, don't worry, I'm not reading your mind. It's just that I know you so well. I can also see you the way your wife used to see you. Didn't she used to frequently read your mind?'

'All women do that,' answered Gabriel. But then he faltered. 'Am I speaking with my wife, then?

The question was a perfectly serious one. The big man laughed, uncomfortably, and thought for a while about the absurdity of it all.

'In a way, yes. But in another way, no.'

'That's not a very good answer.'

'It's an impossible question. You're speaking to me, not to her.'

'Oh, really?'

'What I mean is that she can't see you, or hear you. I'll tell you again that her last memory is that you made her laugh. But that's the end of her story. Her file is saved and it can't be changed further, new information cannot be added. It can only be re-run indefinitely, as it was, without changes. I'm in there with her, her entire life is accessible to me, I can run it, to use a dreadful computer programming term, but not change it: she can't see you, touch you or hear you anymore, Gabriel. Because she no longer sees, touches or hears. She's dead. As a medium, you'll have noticed, I'm a disaster. I haven't got someone knocking on the table, or a message to give you from beyond.'

Gabriel's eyes filled with tears for the second time. The barman, who was professionally ignoring the conversation, was accustomed to seeing some rather un-British attitudes, like crying in public: they were excusable due to the pub's proximity to a hospital. He looked expertly to one side and, in solidarity with the efforts the Pakistani gentleman seemed to be making to get a grip on himself, he poured him another dram of Talisker, and left it within reach, as if by coincidence. In the rather medicinal code book of The Caduceum, that meant "this one's on the house".

'Now that you're beginning to believe me, Gabriel, you're now asking yourself how I became a multiple being,' the big man continued. 'But the truth is that I don't really know and it's not really that important. Wouldn't you prefer to know how to get away from the police and get out of Britain?'

Gabriel saw the new glass of whisky and without asking where it came from, downed it in one go. It tasted like tar.

'Make it two this time, and it's my round,' said the giant, signalling to the barman. Then he turned his gaze back on the Argentine: 'But I reckon that this should be your last one, Gabriel. Whisky will merely enhance your feelings of being in a film, and this is no film. As one of your fellow-countrymen once wrote, unreality is a feature of atrocity. That means it's better to cling to the idea that everything that's happening to you at this very moment is completely real. Because it is.'

'Well, it doesn't seem that way at all.'

'No, not even to me and I should be used to these things by now.'

Gabriel wondered what he meant by "these things". The only thing he wanted was to be alone and to cry. But he'd lost the ability to cry, years before.

The big man had small, grey, sad and rather strange eyes. They were looking at him but at the same time seemed to be reading his mind.

'I'm afraid it's too early for tears. You'll have the rest of your life for that, if that's what you want. During the coming hours you'll need to be on your toes, Gabriel. Take this business card. Call the number I'm writing on it. You'll have the pleasure of getting an old acquaintance of yours out of bed.'

'An old acquaintance of mine. I see.'

'That's right. And of mine, too. I know you think I'm a spy, but I'm not. I can guarantee you, however, that the man you're about to get out of bed certainly was a spy, and one of the best. He already knows me due to other, shall we say, recommendations of mine; interesting people who needed help and who I forwarded to him. He's had me investigated and he knows that I suffer from the mother of all deliriums, but he's no fool and he knows that I'm no fool either.'

'I'm understanding less and less.'

'You met him aboard the Uganda. The man is sleeping at the moment – something he finds harder and harder to do –and he wiped you out of his active memory years ago. Believe me, you're going to take him by surprise and worse still, full of Clonazepam, which isn't very good for the memory. But remember he will. The fact is that you'll give him a fright.'

'Well, this is starting to be an amusing evening.'

'The bloke's retired, but he's still got connexions in all the right places. When he's shaken off his lethargy and his fear, because he's a man who's lived and still lives with fear and he knows how to use it in his favour, his mind will instantly come together and he'll know what to do in your case. And he'll know, no doubt, because he's very clear thinking. He's not a bad bloke. Although I warn you that he's done some dreadful things. Like me. Well, like you, too.'

The big man finished his drink and left some banknotes on the bar. Then he pulled out a mobile phone.

'You can phone him from here.'

'Not according to that sign, you can't. And in this country, the barmen rule,' said Gabriel, quite rightly.

'You're right. What I meant to say was to call him from this phone, but from outside the pub door, of course. You've already broken too many laws in this country to, on top of it all, disobey a barman.'

'And why should I use your mobile?'

'To avoid using your own. You'd better give me that one, so I can use it in two or three hours time in some place far off place like Hendon, so the police detect it there. That'll throw them of the scent completely. They'll be running around in circles all night. I love doing that. And while I'm there, I'll go and visit the aircraft museum again, when it's open in the morning. Isn't it fantastic?'

'It's a good museum. But they could do with a Pucará.'

'That's true.'

Gabriel Cittadini laughed as well. Then he blinked, as if awakening, and handed his mobile phone over to the grey giant. He now felt entirely alert and connected. No sense of unreality. Some great entertainment was about to begin.

'Hanging over there behind that column, next to your Mackintosh, you'll find a dark overcoat, a rain hat, and some fake glasses, with very heavy frames, in the inside pocket. I brought all that for you and I think it'll make you pretty unrecognisable.

'In fact, it'll make you look like an alien. In ten minutes time, get up and put all that on as if it were yours. Leave your mack here, hanging on the peg, with your ID, your driving licence and your knife.'

'My knife, too?' Gabriel was indignant.

'It'll confuse the police even more. They know how much that knife means to you. They'll probably play with the hypothesis that you went walking over to the Thames and threw yourself in. But they'll do that tomorrow, in the morning, when the barman tells them about your lost mackintosh, ID and knife, after looking high and low for you in Hendon and other places. He'll confirm that you were here after your wife had died, and that you had too much to drink in the company of a stranger. And that you seemed very upset.'

Gabriel Cittadini listened attentively. Well, at least this was a game where there were enemies and you were sportingly obliged to beat them. His head had suddenly become clear and operative.

There's no better anaesthetic than danger, nor greater relief than one's enemies. Giving the police the run around again seemed the best antidote to the impending combination of widowhood, solitude and old age. It was a great way of getting through the worst moment in your life. Although he knew that much later, during the following months and years, there would be more than enough time to look at himself in the mirror in the mornings, experience some black thoughts during rare moments of enjoyment, feel her absence, always, even in the company of other women who he would probably learn, with an effort, to love. And the never-ending Sunday afternoons.

Maybe the Thames wasn't such a bad idea after all.

'Stop thinking such rubbish. In fifteen minutes I'll be waiting on my motorbike in front of the Museum of London. It's an old BMW,' Wolfe added, bringing him back to the here and now.

'Good choice for a big lad. Boxer engine, low centre of gravity.'

'I thought you'd say that. You have a very logical mind. I like that. I've got a spare helmet, too.'

'Excellent. Then my logical mind will be protected by fibre glass.'

'It's got a visor. No-one will see your face. Now, when you make the phone call, tell your contact that in exactly an hour you'll be in the telephone booth on the corner of Albany Road and Bagshot Street.'

Gabriel scratched his forehead, one of those rare moments when he expressed anything gesture-wise. And what he expressed was perplexity.

'I don't know where Bagshot Street is, but Albany Road? Isn't that a bit far from here, or a bit near, depending how you look at it?'

'I hit on the place because it's near your contact's house. It'll take him a good while and a lot of coffee before he's sufficiently awake to dare to drive at night. I wouldn't want the man who's orchestrated so many car accidents to now have one. But there is that risk.'

Gabriel asked why, with just a glance.

'He's got a bit of macular degeneration. What can you say? It's his age. But in spite of his fear, he won't be able to contain his curiosity, which is infinite. He won't alert the police – blokes like him are hardly aware the police even exist – but he will make a few phone calls. To old colleagues, and probably to the poor devil on duty now at Vauxhall Cross, in the South American section.'

'I get you. Anything else?'

'When you meet this man, he'll be alone but armed, wearing a microphone and very much on the alert. So make sure you present yourself calmly, as if you'd seen him only the other day. Keep your hands visible at all times and don't do anything to scare him. However, try to be as mysterious as possible and delay mentioning my name for as as long as possible. It's important he feels he's dealing with a colleague. He had that rapport with you once before, when you were just a kid. As soon as the two of you've met and come to an agreement, then my responsibility for you is at an end.'

Responsibility? Gabriel chewed that over for a while. The sensation of unreality became stronger once more. Then it suddenly dissipated.

'Now I know who you're talking about.'

'Yes, of course you do. Call him what you want, because when it comes to names, Brinks has had quite a few. Your problem will be explaining how you managed to reach him.'

'And when I tell him the truth, what will happen?'

Wolfe chuckled to himself.

'Which truth? The second time I was admitted to psychiatric hospital was because of him. He's believed, at one time or another, that I work for the Russians, the Israelis, the North Koreans or the Armenian mafia. But I've already sent him two new talents. So, you can tell it whichever way you want, he won't believe you, but he'll find a use for you, you'll see.'

'Would you believe this meeting, if it were a story?' joked Gabriel.

'No, and I don't believe it right at this moment, or not entirely at least. The thing is that most of my attention is on the other side and in another time. That almost always happens to me. I warned you that my head is a pretty weird place. You get used to feeling odd things.'

'If you're mad.'

'Yes, if you're mad. That's very true.'

There was a silence. Then Gabriel loosened up a little.

'I was fed up with Argentina and with living in poverty. I came here a long time ago. And within my chosen field of business I could say that things didn't go at all badly, although I've tripped up a few times lately. And, of course, three years ago I met her, and so I tried to straighten out. But when I found out she was the very girl who was waiting for that roasted Welsh lad... Anyway, I was already too much in love with her at that stage of the ball game. I've always lied a little bit to women, but...'

'Yes, I imagine that you would have preferred to have told her the truth. But anyway, you can no longer tell her anything, ever again. File saved as read-only, like I said. And, at the end of the day, your love affair with her does have a certain historical, ethical and even legal backing.'

'You don't say.'

'Something remains of Viking culture in these islands. When you killed a married Viking, you were responsible for marrying his wife and looking after her, as compensation. Well, you did your duty. And she, I suppose, fulfilled her destiny.

Gabriel smiled. She would have laughed a lot at that reflection.

'So you fought down there, Wolfe? I mean...'

'Yes. The reality is that I am still there, in the Falklands, at Bluff Cove, to be exact, where you sparked off that catastrophe with your damned radio message. Really, you're an absolute cunt. If we'd collared you and your mate Comte two minutes earlier...'

'I don't understand what you mean. What's all that about still being there?'

'It doesn't matter. It's a complicated story. You'll never believe it. How can I explain to you that right at this moment, as I speak to you, whilst that damned ship is burning up majestically in front of me and your dead wife's ex fiancée is being roasted inside, that I am an uninterested mussel stuck to a rock in Bluff Cove, a hundred yards away? It's the mussel that doesn't believe very much of what is happening now in this bar. And what difference does it make, anyway, if I'm mad?'

'Please don't ever let me forget this, ever. It's the first time I've ever spoken to a mussel.'

There was a silence.

'How many of your lot did I kill, in the end?'

'A lot more than Her Majesty would ever admit to. But that's not important, either.'

'It is to me, Because, if there's anything more absurd than having killed so many of you, it's having to change sides now. Because Her Majesty will probably set me to work spying on my own country.'

'That's within the bounds of reason. But it might not necessarily be like that. Brinks is unpredictable and imaginative. And the alternative, right now, is being made prisoner. And you know the local customs: this time the judges will come down hard on you. Right, I'm off. I'll see you in half an hour in front of the museum.'

The big man left some money on the bar, put on an enormous jacket, the sort a retired bouncer might wear, and walked out through the door with the demeanour of a bear and the gait of a tiger. No one, however, even looked at him. How did he do that?

Gabriel Cittadini checked his mobile phone, thanked the barman, added some of his own money to settle the bill, went to the clothes peg, put on the black raincoat – which didn't suit him – and left.

He caught his reflection in a glass door panel. With those heavy-rimmed glasses and rain hat, his face was pretty outlandish. It didn't really look much like his face. Now it was an old man's face. But he wasn't an old man. Recently widowed, yes, but not an old man. Or at least, if he was an old man, he was a different one, he wasn't that one. He took refuge under an awning and dialled the number scrawled on the card. It rang for a long time.

'Who the hell is calling at this time of night?' asked a worn out, but vaguely familiar, voice.

'Brinks?'

'Wrong number, you idiot.'

'If you want, I can call you Doctor Mathiasen.'

There was silence and astonishment at the end of the line. Gabriel felt immensely satisfied. The old man's unease could be perceived even through the earpiece. Well, you phoney fucking doctor, have some of your own medicine back.

'More than thirty years ago you told me that people like you sometimes offered people like me a job.'

Gabriel heard more disconcerted silence and imagined Brinks trying desperately to put two and two together. He remembered his wife, the girl from Southampton, and her final burst of laughter. File saved, read-only.

He smiled bitterly. Buckets of rain fell, as if it had always rained, as if it would never stop.

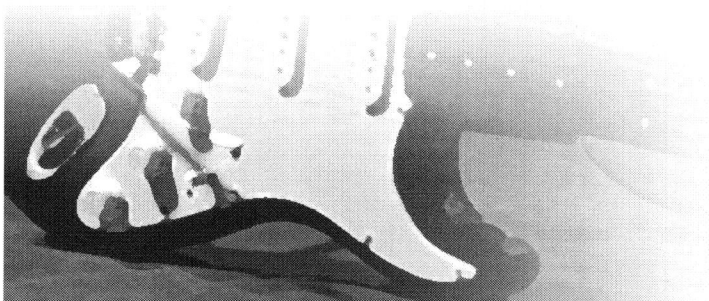

Chapter Ten

Epilogues

I

Ladies and Gentlemen, colleagues,

Into this rocky ground we commend the body of someone who died defending it, Lieutenant Félix Martiniau. Now he's no longer with us, I am free once more to cite his military rank, which he renounced after the Falklands War due to drastic differences about army leadership. It was in those islands that Martiniau showed for the first time that he was an exceptional being. He came back laden with medals which he returned, and afflicted with wounds which he couldn't.

Wounds to his body and to his soul; untreatable pains that wouldn't let him sleep for nearly thirty years. We often used to joke about the dark patches under his eyes, or how he used to nod off during our meetings...

But it was here on the mainland that Martiniau had his second, and more prolonged, moment of glory. In a country that has surrendered its sovereignty and even gives away, alongside its future, the depleted petroleum reserves it lacks for its own use, Martiniau, the lawyer, was a thorn in the side of a State that prostitutes itself, and a constant source of irritation for the multinationals that live off it, like parasites.

To be a Savonarola amidst such depravation is not only poorly paid: you often pay highly for it yourself. Whether defending workers, or denouncing those who sell their country, Félix lived austerely. More than money, he gained many cowardly enemies and a few utterly loyal friends, the same few that now surround his grave in disbelief and inwardly curse themselves for not having been able to defend him till the end.

I specifically include his ex-wife Alejandra Leibovich in the group of unrelenting loyals who were never able to save him from his destiny. I believe Félix loved her until the end of his days. Alejandra's plane was delayed at Buenos Aires and is probably landing at this very moment. I also include several of the country's war veterans associations, who have sent so many painful and heartfelt messages of condolence that it would be impossible to read them all. Those men will never accept Martiniau's death. Neither shall we. To Martiniau, death was prohibited.

I also include this soldier among those who tried to enforce the aforesaid prohibition…could you tell us your name, please? Well, no matter, you don't need to. Although you prefer to remain anonymous, I know you by your nickname, sir. Félix mentioned it many times in private, ever since you found each other again and began to re-establish a friendship. This man, ladies and gentlemen, nicknamed "Sonrisal", is one of the last survivors of Félix's platoon. He fought bravely under his command, twice helped to save his life and now, when he heard the news, crossed half Patagonia in his lorry just to be here.

I also include a couple of British ex-combatant associations with whom Félix frequently exchanged correspondence. They telephoned me – excuse me if my voice is rather shaky – I said, they telephoned asking me to give public expression to their admiration for our friend, their enemy, their friend.

After surviving terrible wounds at the battles of Goose Green and Tumbledown, Félix could only treat as a joke the multiple death threats he received from so many little gangsters or powerful traitors, elements so common in our fledgling democracy. We all thought he'd continue to recover from the bombing last year, in which he lost his right leg, a matter that is still pending investigation. But his health had been undermined by age and injuries and he was, I believe, tired and alone. For once, he could not recover.

All who today surround his coffin – and it hurts me to see none of his family here – owe him an everlasting personal favour. Félix helped me, for example, to regain, albeit briefly, the status and dignity of a father. And to him we all owe the belief that a republic wherein reside men such as Félix Martiniau, Lieutenant Martiniau, soldier and Argentine to the core, can only be strong, just, peaceful and difficult to affront.

It lies with us, who are so few, but who loved him so well, the duty to ensure his deeds are not forgotten and that his work is continued. Félix, old friend, may you finally get some sleep. Nobody I know ever quite deserved it so much.'

■■■■■■■■■■ II ■■■■■■■■■■

Ladies and Gentlemen,

Today we say goodbye to a great friend and an old servant of this country, Peter Doyle, OBE and DSC, unknown perhaps to the public, but almost a legend within our little community, in which he was known by such *noms de guerre* as Brinks, Mathiasen and others.

Doyle enjoyed a long career with us. As a young man, almost a youth, he employed coolness, a talent for languages and acting skills on a par with those of Peter Sellers, when he operated behind enemy lines in occupied Paris, posing as a Belgian businessman. His contribution to the organisation of the French Resistance between 1942 and 1944 has yet to be duly studied and evaluated.

So many years have passed since he retired. In the role of unofficial academic SIS historian that life seems to have placed me in, however, I can categorically confirm that the anonymity surrounding the figure of Doyle no longer corresponds to motives of state security. It is due only to his own modesty.

Born and educated in Inverness, Scotland, Doyle played a part in almost all of the post-war conflicts in which our land, sea and air forces participated: the Suez Crisis, the defeat of the Communist guerrilla in Malaysia, the "Troubles" in Ulster and, finally, the brief but unpleasant war in the South Atlantic, after which Peter retired.

I am proud to have been his friend. I could mention several things about him that set him a category apart – and that in a service in which extraordinary characters abound. He never boasted of his deeds, but he sometimes used to tell me that the most important contribution he'd made to this country had been by the wars he'd helped to avoid, rather than those he'd helped to win.

His retirement in 1983, rather premature, according to his peers, was due – and this can and must today be clearly stated – to his continuous differences with our Foreign Office, especially during the two Margaret Thatcher administrations, over our country's policy towards Argentina, a country that might have been an important ally of the Crown but which - and here I quote the words used by Peter Doyle himself to justify his decision to retire - "due to our mistreatment for the last century and a half, we have literally pushed into hostility against Great Britain, and we continue to do so."

In the following years, now almost blind, Peter Doyle continued to be an essential and always-willing consultant, as well as a controversial and bitter critic of the Intelligence community. One day, when the actions he undertook can be more widely diffused, I have no doubt that someone more qualified than I will take up the task of writing his biography, and that it will serve as an inspiration for some enthusiastic youngsters to follow in his footsteps.

Sir Jeremy Clark, OBE, DFC.

━━━━━━━━━━━━━━━━━ III ━━━━━━━━━━━━━━━━━

God and Jimi Hendrix Await Him

Liverpool has still not recovered from the after effects of the Wallis Brothers' concert, during the course of which this city (and I might add Great Britain as a whole and the rest of the world) entered into a kind of unforeseen trance while the backing band were performing.

The band was the, until yesterday, unknown Welsh group called The Rascals, made up of old amateurs who, judging from what happened on Saturday night, might have become the greatest musical revelation since the Fab Four themselves, but seem destined not to, because their leader is at this very moment fighting for his life in hospital.

The story is as follows: during a rather boring and predictable performance of 1960s cover versions, the group's lead guitarist, the almost 60-year-old Thomas Lucas Wolfe, and his bassist James Jones suddenly broke into a tremendous riff, a whole new form of music that will probably change the history of rock and roll, a polyphonic improvisation of phrasings and counterpoint that words cannot describe nor do they need to, as readers of these lines will have already listened to the music on their computers, their hair standing on end.

Those were five minutes of inhuman magic that, in the last 48 hours, have gone around the world several times over thanks to YouTube. Those five minutes literally made the old rectangular stadium of Anfield Road explode like a volcano. When the bizarre performance was over, and everyone, in a stadium crammed to the rafters, cried and hugged each other without understanding why – and I include myself amongst those who were crying – the band left the stage unnoticed amid the commotion.

It was noticeable that the rest of the concert, including the headline band's recital, carried on rather mundanely in a stadium that grew slowly emptier. I asked various twenty-year-olds why they were leaving before the event had finished. The main answer I got was that "we've already heard all you can hear."

Today, the British music scene continues in uproar. The latest news concerning the health of Thomas Lucas Wolfe, the man whose future legend seems to consist in the fact that he could have been a legend, is not promising. The latest medical bulletin, here at Southport, states that Wolfe was admitted with a non-Hodgkin's lymphoma that, incredibly, had never been treated, infectious complications, general decompensation and practically in coma. Not much is known about Wolfe's previous existence: reports from Scotland Yard and the MOD suggest that he had many different jobs and served in at least two wars (Northern Ireland and the Falklands) as an NCO in the Parachute Regiment.

James Jones, barman, another Falklands veteran, the bassist who, alongside Wolfe, played the most significant five minutes in the history of rock since the 1960s, and now The Rascals' reluctant spokesman, declared that not only was he saddened by the imminent loss of the leader of the band, but also for "all the people who depended on him". We suppose that this is a cryptic allusion to the band itself, as Wolfe seems to have had no immediate family.

Jones added that he doesn't think Wolfe will pull through, quote "having already played his part" unquote. We have not been able to obtain statements from the rest of the band, or even discover their whereabouts.

Cynthia Crawford, Southport, BBC.

Daniel E. Arias, 25th May 2009.

Daniel E. Arias, was born in 1953 in Buenos Aires, and underwent one of those English primary school educations where they still talked about the Empire well into the late 1960s, when it was clearly the USA (through the Argentine military) that was calling the shots in Argentina. His secondary education was undertaken in the *Colegio Nacional de Buenos Aires*, a place of academic excellence and a cauldron of future scientists, artists and political militants, where the long list of students and ex-alumni murdered or disappeared between 1969 and 1983 bears testimony to a certain aversion to empires in general, and to some generals as well.

To make ends meet while getting his degree in Literature at the *University of Buenos Aires,* Arias became a Jack-of-all-trades, selling clothes, squaring accounts, driving lorries, but mostly, he taught English. When he graduated and realised that he wasn't going to get rich as a Literature Professor, in 1985 he tried his luck at becoming a science writer for the newspapers. In this capacity, he published in most of the big Argentine press, became a name (sort of) for a couple of decades and took a number of prizes. In his free time, he tried at least twice to be an acceptable husband, also a dad to two beloved kids, and wrote books.

Daniel Arias has written *Argentina mirada y pensada* (Lunwerg-Planeta, Barcelona, 2008), a coffee table book with good pictures, *Eternidad maldita* (Alfaguara, Serie Roja, Buenos Aires, 2009), a novel and *Aquella guerrita olvidada (Guid Publicaciones, 2011).* Thus, you are perusing Arias' first novel translated into English.

There is more stuff in the pipeline: *Todos mis padres*, a Patagonian saga, will also be published by Guid Publicaciones on dates yet to be announced. And then there is this short story collection, to be sold also as audio-text. And a science-fiction novel in progress, and...

We'll keep you posted.

315

26574636R00180

Printed in Great Britain
by Amazon